Karen grew up in a small country town in north-eastern Victoria, Australia. She spent her childhood riding horses through beautiful scenery of eucalypts, lakes, and snow-capped mountains and her love of landscape deeply affects her writing. She worked in a range of educational settings and holds a Ph.D and M.Ed (Hons) in the areas of fantasy. She is particularly interested in the power of the hero's inner journey which she explores through Deep Fantasy. Karen has travelled extensively overseas but enjoys nothing more than camping in the Australian Outback. She lives in Melbourne and now writes full-time. You can find out more about Karen and her books on her website.

Connect with K.S. Nikakis

Amazon:	https://www.amazon.com/author/ksnikakis
Twitter:	https://twitter.com/KSNikakis
Facebook:	www.facebook.com/ksnikakis
Goodreads:	www.goodreads.com
Website:	www.ksnikakis.com
Email:	author@ksnikakis.com

WORKS BY K S NIKAKIS

Non Fiction

Journey: Seeking the Sacred, Spirit
and Soul in the Australian Wilderness

Fantasy Novel Series

Angel Caste series:
Angel Blood
Angel Breath
Angel Bone
Angel Bound
Angel Blessed
Angel Caste – Complete 5 Book Series

The Kira Chronicles trilogy (remnant hard copies only):
The Whisper of Leaves
The Song of the Silvercades
The Cry of the Marwing

The Kira Chronicles series:
The Whisper of Leaves
The Silence of Stone
The Secrets of Stars
The Thunder of Hoofs
The Crying of Birds
The Music of Home
The Kira Chronicles – Complete 6 Book Series

Fantasy Novels

The Emerald Serpent
Heart Hunter
The Third Moon
Messenger

I Heard the Wolf Call My Name
Finalist - Best YA Novel Aurealis Awards, 2019

Fantasy Short Stories

The Gift
The Tale of Prince Anura
Dragon Sprite
Glass-Heart
Short-Listed – Best YA Short Story, Aurealis Awards, 2019

Heart Hunter

K.S. NIKAKIS

Publisher: SOV Media
Melbourne, Australia.

Cover by AS Nikakis: http://asnikakis.com
Veniamin Kraskov/Bigstock
Subbotina Anna/Bigstock

National Library of Australia
Cataloguing-in-Publication entry:
Nikakis, Karen Simpson
Heart Hunter
ISBN 978-0-6482652-0-7

For Rachel, Tim, Angus and Hazel

Heart Hunter

What lives dies,
what's given, is taken back.
She the Moon knows
and the bone that abandons flesh,
that birth means death,
Talabraith.

1

Fleet sped down the slope, the scinton closing fast. The void beckoned, cold as a knife-blade, and her brain screamed to relinquish her kill or relinquish her life, but she refused. She hurled herself into the empty streambed and fled down its length while the scinton bounded along the bank, so close she could feel its hot breath on her neck.

Twenty lengths to safety, fifteen, ten; she wasn't going to make it! She snatched the knife from her belt, slashed the cord that bound the chet carcass to her shoulders, and flung the still-warm corpse to the scinton. The scinton stopped, satisfied with its prize, but Fleet raced on, her blood-soaked shirt chill against her skin. She passed the cleft that would have saved her *and* her kill but ran on until she reached the edge of the Redlands. Her chest heaved but she tasted the air for the scent of threat then clambered out into the safety of the trees.

Only then did she curse, angered by the loss of the chet and the effort it had cost to hunt it, *and* by the loss of meat for those in Berian-tur. Snowmelt's delay meant the streambeds were empty of water and fish, and when hunters returned empty-handed too, the Sceadu hungered.

Fleet was tempted to resume her hunt, despite the scinton, but she had already been gone from the girls' Turrel too long. She snorted. The Aunts seemed to think her some newly earth-named Little Sister rather than a woman on the verge of air-naming, and if she didn't return soon, would take their concerns to Ket and the last thing Fleet wanted was her elderly hunter guide upset.

Fleet tossed back her long, loose hair and set off east, flaring her nostrils to better taste the air as she strode along. The ice-gnarled trees and patchy snow of the Whitelands' edge soon gave way to the straighter boles of fyr and ashin and the Redlands' leaf litter, rich with rot. The air under the trees was warmer too and full of crystaleyes, their calls as pure as the snow she left behind.

Fleet glanced behind her often and not just to check for threats. Ashali's sprawling ice-locked slopes drew her. Snowhawks wove their courtship dances above the mountain's brilliant peak and she stopped to watch, thrilled by their beauty. Cock-bird flew with cock-bird and not even Ket knew why they ignored the brown hen-birds, although they mustn't ignore them *all* the time or else there would be no more snowhawks!

Dusk purpled the trees and Fleet's hunter-senses sharpened. Berian foraged at night and despite snowcome's icy grip, might still be abroad. She went on until the night was filled with the rustle of cone-mice in the detritus, then found a protected rise and wrapped herself in her shelter-sheet, laid her weapons ready, and slept.

Fleet was grateful weariness granted her a dreamless sleep, for a faceless man had lately plagued her dreams and sometimes now she woke in fright. But she told no one of them: such dreams belonged to Siahs not to hunters.

Fleet was on her way again before dawn, her footfalls soft on the frost-rimmed litter, her breath pluming the air. She was never happier than when she journeyed. The chill might nip at her face but it made the shard-spiders' webs glitter with ice. She touched one gently as she passed and smiled as its owner scuttled over to investigate.

Her hunter's gaze took in a murrow burrow and the stale detritus scattered at its mouth. The murrow still slept, snug within the earth, waiting as the Sceadu did for the return of snow-melt's warmth.

Fleet's hunt had taken her deep into berian territory and now, on her return journey, she searched out their paths and took care not to cross them. Berian had once roamed these lands alone and were owed respect.

Fleet saw and smelled no berian though, and her thoughts drifted to her coming air-naming. She looked forward to being away from the endless chatter of the girls' Turrel *and* from the Aunts' eternal vigilance, but most of all she looked forward to marrying Ashin. She smiled as she considered his gold-streaked hair; his slim hips . . . then something moved on the edge of her vision and her attention jerked back to the trees.

Too late! She was hurled to the ground, the impact snapping her head back onto stone. There was a sharp burst of pain and the day disintegrated into blackness.

Fleet's first awareness was of a throbbing head, followed by the smell of burning lart, but she kept her eyes closed as she struggled to make sense of what had happened. There was a man's familiar scent too and, confused, she opened her eyes. It *was* Tor, one of the Sceadu's finest hunters. She had long admired his skills but too often they highlighted her own lack and she struggled to sit up.

The pain in her head doubled to a nauseating thud and then, humiliatingly, she vomited. Tor steadied her until she spat the sourness from her mouth then offered her his waterskin but Fleet's head had cleared enough for her to remember what had happened, and she pushed the waterskin away.

'You attacked me!' she exclaimed.

'I *tested* you,' corrected Tor, 'and found you as unaware as a Little Sister. But I'm sorry your head landed on stone.' Fleet glared at him while her fingers explored the tender, sticky spot on the back of her skull. The light's ripeness told her she had been unconscious for some time. 'What happened to the chet you killed?' he asked.

'What makes you think an *unaware* Little Sister killed anything?'

'Your shirt's blood-stained across the shoulders,' said Tor. 'Come across a berian, did you, pleased to have saved itself the trouble of hunting?' Fleet's face fired at the closeness of his guess but she refused to confirm it. 'You went to the Whitelands?' he continued.

'You do.'

'I didn't go there before I was air-named. It's too dangerous.'

'You surprise me,' said Fleet. 'I didn't think *anything* threatened the mighty hunter Tor.'

Tor's lips thinned and he stamped out the fire. 'A *good* hunter isn't ruled by arrogance *or* ignorance, Fleet.'

'Don't you dare—' she began, and scrambled to her feet, but the sudden movement was a mistake. The trees tilted sideways and only Tor's quick grab of her arm stopped her falling.

'Someone needs to *dare* tell you these things,' he said, thrusting his face close. 'The Sceadu can't afford to lose hunters.'

They were the same height, for Fleet was tall, and though Tor's self-assured face was aggravatingly familiar, she had never looked into his eyes. They were darker than Ashin's but not black like hers, more like the streambed-pools left behind after snowmelt. His male scent added to her dizziness and then he drew back and her head cleared a little. But he didn't release her arm and when she bent to retrieve her pack, he relieved her of it smoothly and slung it over his own shoulder.

Fleet was annoyed by his smug acquisition of authority but more annoyed to realise what he said was true. She *hadn't* been attending and if he *had* been a berian, she would be dead. The risk remained while they journeyed through berian forage too and she flared her nostrils to better taste the air.

'That's an improvement,' he said, his keen eyes on her face.

4

'Why are you here?' she demanded 'Did the Aunts send you chasing after me?'

'No one sent me *chasing* after you, Fleet. I came across one of your agemates concerned about how long you had been gone and decided to reconnoiter.'

'Who? Firn?' she asked, naming her agemate and fellow hunter.

'Ashin. He gathered sweetbloom and darklip. Spark's sickened again and he seemed in a hurry to return to her.'

Tor's gaze sharpened on her face but Fleet scarcely noticed, her thoughts on the rub Ashin had concocted last snowcome. It had eased the pain in Ket's hips and allowed the old hunter to sleep again. Other Sceadu elders used it too. Ashin had always been interested in healing so it was no surprise he was out gathering *or* that the frail Spark was ill again.

'Ashin is sure to be air-named a healer,' she murmured. 'Then after I'm air-named a hunter, we will—' she flushed, not having intended to voice her thoughts.

'A healer and a hunter,' said Tor. 'Not a union that suggests harmony, not like a hunter paired with a hunter.'

Fleet snorted as she considered the hunters in her ageset. 'You're not suggesting I marry Shale or Firn?' she said. Shale spent more time trying to out-run his ageset than seeking beasts and while Firn was a good friend, he would never be more than that.

'You're right, I'm *not* suggesting it,' said Tor with such vehemence that Fleet glanced at him in surprise. The movement woke her dizziness again and they were forced to stop. 'I'm sorry I made you hit your head,' he repeated.

'You almost sound like you mean it,' said Fleet, made irritable by pain.

'Given the hardness of your skull, I'm sure there's no lasting damage,' he retorted. 'But we'll travel faster tomorrow if we set camp early tonight. We're near the Zair streambed in any case.'

The Zair marked the western edge of berian forage and should be safe enough given that most berian were still in their dens. Tor steadied her down the Zair's bank and when they reached a small clearing, extricated her shelter-sheet from her pack, flipped it open, and lowered her onto it. Fleet hated feeling helpless, in front of Tor of all people, but felt too ill to protest.

Tor helped her on with her jacket and she hugged herself as she watched him gather windfall. He never neglected to scan or taste the air and while his pack remained near her, he kept his arrows and bow with him.

It was odd to see Tor without his agemates. Tor, Snowhawk and Serest had been inseparable since their air-namings but now Fleet recalled Firn saying that Serest had shifted her belongings into Snowhawk's tur. It seemed the chestnut-haired beauty had chosen the blue-eyed hunter over the dark-eyed one. *Poor Tor will be all alone now*, Firn had quipped.

Tor deposited his load of windfall at the fire site, struck spark into glice leaves, and huffed into them. The flare of new flame illuminated the lines of earth- and air-name patterning on his face and Fleet's gaze moved over the rest of him. He wore his dark hair to his shoulders, which were as well-muscled as his haunches, bulging as he crouched. His powerful build was very different to Firn's slightness and her own ranginess and yet Tor was fast, as hunters must be.

'What were you earth-named?' she asked curiously.

'Swift.'

It suited him but earth-names were usually well-chosen. Ashin was earth-named after the tall, narrow, white-barked trees; Firn for the restless west wind that rolled down Ashali's slopes; and Spark, with her strange glittery eyes, for the fire struck from stone.

Fleet was pleased with her own earth-name and wondered what air-name Siah would pluck from the void for her. Whatever it was, it would be of speed and skill. Fleet was a hunter and it must be a hunter's name.

'Do you think my earth-name apt?' asked Tor, interrupting her thoughts. It was a simple enough question but he managed to give it an ironic twist, as if he humored her that her opinion mattered, when they both knew it didn't.

'You're swift,' she said with a shrug.

'And my air-name?'

'A stone that stands alone; appropriate for a hunter,' she said, wishing she had held her tongue.

'It's true hunters journey alone which is why they need to take care,' he said pointedly, 'but there's no reason why they should live alone, is there Fleet?'

Tor's gaze was piercing and Fleet dropped her eyes to the fire. 'No,' she said, thinking of Ashin again. 'No reason at all.'

Snowhawk lay with his lover in a bower that was invisible to all but the most skilled of hunters. Only at times like these did he feel truly at peace, when the sweet languor of lovemaking still clothed his skin and his lover's heart beat next to his. But all too soon the fear of discovery would creep back and with it all his cares.

Every man who gave his heart fretted over losing it and over the loss of his beloved by some illness or mischance, but Snowhawk also feared losing his hunter bond with Tor.

They had travelled the hunter's path together since being Little Brothers under the Uncles' care and, as air-named hunters, had stared into the void reflected in the eyes of the dying beast. Knowing the fragility of what divided the sunlit world from the void's darkness bound them in a way that went beyond Berian-tur's small happenings. It was an understanding shared by hunters and Siahs, and one that made Snowhawk's time with his lover all the more precious.

He rolled over and cradled his lover's face between his hands. Sunlight spangled their bower and crystaleyes chimed in the leaf-roof. 'I love you,' he whispered, staring into eyes as blue as his own. 'I love you, I love you, I love you!' Then he laughed aloud with the sheer joy of it and gave himself up to the pleasure of his new-found love all over again.

2

Fleet woke the next morning to a deserted campsite. Mist hung low in the trees but the fire burned high which meant Tor had tended it before going off, most likely to relieve himself. Fleet needed to relieve herself too but waited, mortified by the possibility of blundering into Tor in the murk.

She felt almost recovered, which was a relief, but the air was clammy and she shuffled closer to the flames. Tor had piled the fire with lart branches and she inhaled their spicy smoke. The air held other scents too and she teased them out. Fyr and ashin were there of course, and the ubiquitous scent of cone-mice, *and* the faint scent of a whisper-owl.

The odours of the Redlands were as familiar to her as her own fragrance but then another scent intruded and she tensed. The trees remained quiet but her hand fastened on the end of a sturdy branch protruding from the fire. Still there was silence and her grip tightened and then relaxed as she recognised Tor's scent.

He crunched back over the frosty grass, scowling as he deposited a double handful of white-nuts on the ground. Sleep hadn't improved his mood, concluded Fleet.

'I might have been a berian and you didn't even turn, let alone set an arrow,' he said.

'I took your scent.'

'You could have been mistaken.'

'I don't mistake scent,' she said and, scrambling up, stomped away into the mist.

Tor watched the swing of her blue-black hair disappear into the murk, and then snapped the white-nuts from their shells and tossed them into the pan. He wondered whether Fleet's sense of smell was as good as she claimed, and if so, whether he smelled pleasant to her. Probably not after the previous night, he conceded.

He had intended to give her a fright to make her more wary and had been appalled to hear the clunk of her head hit stone. Her carelessness had been out of character. She was usually hunter-attuned, even in full flight, and his first glimpse of her racing through the Redlands had stayed with him. She had the speed of a young aperion and a grace that was all her own.

Fleet had been distracted yesterday and what she muttered in her sleep added to Tor's concerns. Ketwing had once called her side-blind and given the Sceadu's need of hunters, it didn't bode well.

The chime of crystaleyes joined the white-nuts' sizzle and Fleet reappeared and settled beside him, her growling stomach adding to the cacophony.

'Hungry?' he asked, and she nodded, her gaze on the pan as he tossed in errem disks. 'You talk in your sleep,' he said.

Unexpectedly Fleet smiled, bringing her whole face alight. 'My ageset complains about my sleep-chatter all the time,' she said cheerfully.

Fleet had muttered *Ashin* in her sleep but Tor wagered *Fleet* wasn't the name her handsome agemate sleep-spoke. 'You've been friends with Ashin, Firn and Spark a long time,' he said, as he stirred the food.

'Since earth-naming,' confirmed Fleet, still intent on the pan.

'And soon you will all be air-named, free of the Turrels, and going your separate ways.'

'Air-naming won't make any difference,' said Fleet, glancing up.

'On the contrary, it will make all the difference in the world,' said Tor and offered her the pan. She thanked him and used an errem disk to scoop up a generous portion of nuts. 'With the air-name comes your life task and permission to choose a wife or husband. Many paths open up and not all lead in the same direction.'

Her face was hidden by a curtain of blue-black hair and Tor thought of Serest whose hair he had never seen unbraided. Perhaps she only loosed it at night for *Snowhawk*. 'Your path will be that of a hunter,' he continued, struggling to keep his voice even, 'which means you'll spend most of your time in the Whitelands. If Ashin becomes a healer, he'll forage in the Redlands, and even if Firn joins you in hunting and Spark shares the healer path with Ashin, four becomes two and two.'

Fleet's eyes flashed in annoyance. 'And in your case, three became two and one, didn't it?'

'Three doesn't split as cleanly as four,' conceded Tor, rueing how few things stayed private in Berian-tur, 'and it can be hard to remain friends when the break comes. I think I've managed it with Serest and Snowhawk but I wonder if you'll manage it with *your* agemates.'

'After we marry, I see no reason why Ashin and I won't stay friends with Spark and Firn.'

'And if Ashin and Spark marry?' Fleet wouldn't welcome such a question but her answer was important. A distracted hunter was vulnerable and the Sceadu couldn't afford to lose even a single hunter, not when snowcome showed no signs of ending.

'I don't see how any of this is your concern.'

'No, you don't, do you?' said Tor, annoyed Fleet hadn't answered his question. He didn't pursue it. He was a hunter, and hunters knew the importance of patience; he could afford to wait.

Fleet watched in bemusement as Tor cleaned the pan and thrust it back into his pack. He had barely spoken to her on their previous encounters and certainly not of matters so personal. He had simply nodded as he had passed her in the Redlands, an aperion or scinton slung across his shoulders, his mocking gaze on the scrawny murrow or chet she bore.

Tor and Snowhawk had already roamed the Whitelands while she and Spark had giggled over the tales they concocted to escape the girls' Turrel. They were often ill and had convinced the Aunts the must search for special herbs. Ashin and Firn had come up with excuses to escape the boys' Turrel too.

Once away, the four of them had explored derelict chet lairs or searched out murrow burrows, or in she and Firn's case, pretended to be great hunters. Ashin and Spark had played along but as Fleet's bouts of illness grew fewer, she had ranged further with Firn to practise real hunter skills.

Spark and Ashin had searched for healing herbs but as Spark remained frail, they hadn't strayed far. Fleet and Firn recounted their exploits on their return and, as they trekked back to the Turrels, Fleet walked behind with Ashin to share her special achievements.

As Fleet grew stronger, she and Spark organised their escapes separately and when Ket chose Fleet for hunter training, the breach widened. There was no longer a need for an excuse to leave the girls' Turrel, not when the mighty hunter Ketwing requested it. Even if Spark had been hunter-inclined, illness robbed her of the strength to follow where Fleet roamed with Ket. But Ashin ensured Spark hadn't been left lonely; his kind-heartedness just one of the things Fleet loved him for.

Ket's bones might have been twisted into odd shapes by snowcome's cold but she could still take scents from the wind; tell the number of murrow in a burrow from the scrapings outside; identify a whisper-owl's prey from its scats; and find where blackfish spawned and fed.

Ket took Fleet into the deep, shadowed places of the Redlands; to where the streambeds frayed and broke and came back together again; to places hidden by countless snowmelts of fallen ashin and fyr; and up to the very edges of the Whitelands, where sunlight fought with ice to wrest the water free.

Sometimes Ket kept her crooked legs close to the fire and sent Fleet out alone. Once she sent Fleet to the Ruthvin streambed for lave-flower, a pretty dye-plant, but one useless to hunters. The Ruthvin's sides were as steep as cliffs and far more treacherous and it was dusk before Fleet spied lave-flower in the Ruthvin's bed.

She was in a hurry to return to Ket and launched herself over the edge, intending to ride a layer of loose stone to the bottom, but she triggered a serest that rolled her over and over to leave her bruised and bleeding at the bottom.

Fleet had limped back to the campsite expecting praise but Ket had simply said that there were many paths to follow apart from the one in front. Fleet had been too annoyed to question her guide's meaning, but she had soon forgotten the incident as they chanted around the fire that night, the air full of fire-sparks and the colder light of the stars above.

Tor resumed the previous day's interrogation as they walked. Firstly he demanded to know how many times she had been to the Whitelands, then how far she had ventured into them, and what she had hunted there. Fleet's resentment of his badgering grew, fed by a fear he would tell the Aunts of her forays. Being confined to the Turrel would just about cap off being robbed of her kill, knocked unconscious, and grilled about her romantic intentions.

'Are you going to tell the Aunts where I've been?' she asked finally.

'You are all but air-named, Fleet. The Aunts won't have time to take you to task when they must soon deal with a new ageset. It would be better if you accompanied me the next time I hunt the Whitelands and learn how to hunt there in safety.'

Fleet's heart leapt at the prospect of being instructed by a hunter of Tor's skill but before she could speak, he caught her arm and gestured for quiet. A she-berian was just visible through the lart. She foraged with her cub and Fleet grinned as the cub nosed at some talith, pricked its snout, and jumped back.

'They're from their den early,' she whispered, as the berian moved away upslope.

'No, snowmelt's late again,' said Tor. 'You saw how the splay-spruce and grapple dominated the snowline?' Fleet nodded. 'When my father was my number of snowmelts, that whole area was thick with ashin and fyr, and in *his* father's time, snowmelt revealed a track over Ashali.

'Snowmelt's faltered, Fleet, and the Sceadu need hunters whose blood beats in rhythm with Talabraith.' Fleet stared at him astonishment; it was the sort of thing Ket would have said. 'Ketwing trained me too,' he confirmed.

'I didn't know,' she breathed.

'Ketwing said I would be the last, for even then the cold had eaten her bones, but then you emerged from the gaggle of

Little Sisters and Ketwing saw how fast you were, and how strong, and how *side-blind*.'

'Side-blind?'

'Her word, not mine,' said Tor with a smile. 'It means you see only what lies ahead, not what's important to either side.'

'I don't . . .' began Fleet indignantly.

Tor raised his hand. 'Whatever Ketwing's meaning, she didn't drag her bones from the Great Turrel's warmth for your feats *or* failings alone, but because she saw you were in tune with Talabraith. Not just here,' he said, touching his head, 'but here, where it counts,' he said, and tapped his jacket over his heart. 'There will be food enough for the Sceadu, despite the failure of snowmelt, if Talabraith is served.'

Siah lay in the dimness of the Great Turrel's Seeing-Place, having left behind the failing husk of her body and slipped into the dreamways of trance. It was easy now, not like the early snowmelts of her art when each trance-journey was a nightmare of paralysing fear she wouldn't find her way home.

She had been Flame then, and so terrified of her dreams, she had tried not to sleep. Her exhaustion had grown so that, in the end, the dream realm had snatched her away during waking as well. Then the Aunts had taken her to the old Siah who, with her dishevelled hair and silvery eyes, had been as terrifying as the dreams.

Yet despite her blindness, the old Siah had seen and known all. 'Welcome, Flame,' she had whispered. 'I have been waiting for you.'

Siah smiled in gratitude, even in trance, for the knowledge, comfort and love the older woman had gifted. Now as she too approached the end of her time in the sunlit world, she hastened along the dreamways on the same quest as her predecessor—to find her replacement. Siah had glimpsed two figures on earlier trance-journeys, one of whom would become the next Siah, but the trance had yet to reveal which.

As the young Flame, Siah had endured the terror of trance-visitations alone but such power in the hands of a frightened Little Sister was perilous, not only to the Little Sister, but to the Sceadu who the new Siah must guide. So Siah was anxious to identify the next Siah as quickly as possible, as were the Circle of elders.

Yet the task was far from simple. Siahs often manifested in the void as hunters, for they hunted snatches of the future, but the presence of hunters didn't necessarily mean the next Siah *was* a hunter, for the dream-world spoke a different tongue to that of the waking-world.

Now as Siah travelled the dreamways, she glimpsed the hunters again but as she strove to separate the Sceadu's next spirit guide from her companion, a wind struck her so sere, it all but robbed her of sight.

Siah hadn't known such terror since she was Flame and with desperate strength, threw herself out of the void. She woke shuddering on the floor and it was a long time before she could crawl closer to the brazier, where Ketwing found her and where they remained.

Ketwing had coaxed broth down her agemate's throat but when Siah's eyes closed again, she set the bowl aside. Ketwing didn't know whether Siah entered sleep or the place of vision but she knew her agemate slipped away and the understanding filled her with grief.

They had played together as Little Sisters and, as Flame and Wind, had grown to womanhood in the girls' Turrel. Then Flame had become Siah, mistress of the trance and seeker along the darkways of dream, and Wind had become Ketwing, hunter of the frigid Whitelands and the kinder, leaf-sheltered Redlands. Their friendship had endured but Ketwing knew the void was about to reclaim its own.

It was the way of the void to give and take back, in the same way as the hunter's arrow found the scinton's throat and sometimes the scinton's jaws the hunter's. Ketwing's sorrow was exacerbated by dread, for the Sceadu's next spirit guide had yet to be named. Snowmelt faltered, and if the line of Siahs faltered too, Berian-tur would be no more.

Siah's eyes flickered open and Ketwing leaned forward as her friend struggled to speak. 'I know what it is . . . you fear,

Ketwing,' whispered Siah, 'and you are right to. Snowmelt stumbles . . . the ice closes in.'

Ketwing smoothed the hair from her agemate's brow. 'You must rest,' she said.

'We both know I must . . . journey,' replied Siah, her voice so hoarse that Ketwing bent close to hear her. 'There are two . . . stay with me, agemate. I may not return . . . to meet . . . the Circle.'

Siah's eyes closed before Ketwing could protest, and her head rocked from side to side. Foam flecked her lips and it was a long time before her eyes slitted open and, when they did, Ketwing gasped. They held the same light as the mortally wounded beast.

She swiftly brought her ear close to Siah's mouth and in Siah's last breath, was the name Ketwing needed. Ketwing closed her eyes in gratitude and offered up thanks, and then she gathered her agemate's lifeless body into her arms and wept.

3

Fleet and Tor reached Stoney-rise at dusk; the view from the small hill making it one of Fleet's favorite places. She could see where the forest's canopy enclosed the perfect circle of the Great Turrel's roof and where the foliage creased as gullies and streambeds cut across the forest floor.

She could see the roof of the girls' Turrel too, but the trees hid the boys' Turrel. Fleet turned towards it anyway, imagining what Ashin and his ageset were doing. It was too late to find out. The Aunts and Uncles insisted that protocols be observed, even by those close to air-naming, and that meant no mingling after dark.

'Ashali farewells the sun,' said Tor behind her, and Fleet dragged her attention back to the mountain.

Ashali's massive flanks spread north and south to form a vast icy wall, and it seemed incomprehensible there had once been a path over it. She wondered whether it was merely one of Tor's boasts but then forgot about Tor as the snow burned red and gold. It seemed as if the very mountain were on fire but all too soon, the usual blue reclaimed Ashali's slopes as the sun gifted its warmth to Ashali's western face, and Fleet shivered.

'Time to go,' said Tor briskly and set off down the wooded slope. His quick pace suited Fleet who was keen to track down Ashin for a visit. 'Are you intending to go to the girls' Turrel tonight or to Talith's tur?' he asked as they went.

Fleet was surprised Tor knew her mother's name though not by the question. Those who were close to air-naming were permitted to await Siah's summons at their parents' turs but Brin and Talith were long dead and Fleet hadn't been to their tur for many snowmelts. She remembered how peaceful it was *unlike* the chatter of the girls' Turrel.

Yet the idea of being alone made her uneasy. 'I'll go to the girls' Turrel,' she said.

The answer seemed to please Tor and his parting words, as he turned in the direction of his own tur, pleased Fleet. *If hunters have killed, we will hunt again in five days, and if not, in two.* Fleet grinned as she continued on alone. In just two days' time, she could be hunting the Whitelands in the company of one of the Sceadu's finest hunters!

Five days was the usual rest day between hunts but when the stewpots held only a broth of white-nuts, rin-tuber and the shreds of last snowmelt's fish, hunters were forced out sooner. Even Tor's order to make sure she was *properly* prepared this time, failed to dint Fleet's excitement.

Shard-spider webs glinted and a chet's eyes shone as it bounded up a fyr, and she broke into a jog then threw her head back and laughed. She was a hunter on the verge of womanhood and marriage, and Berian-tur had never been more beautiful.

The girls' Turrel was unusually quiet, even given the night's lateness, and when Fleet stepped inside she saw why. All of the Aunts were absent, except Glimmer and all of her ageset too, except Song. Fleet dropped her pack to the floor and rolled her shoulders as she considered the dozing Aunt and the snoring Song.

As agesets neared the end of their time in the Turrel, it was common for Aunts to reassure themselves their charges knew exactly how to fashion the things they would need for their new lives in their turs. Some dye plants were more potent at night and Fleet guessed the Aunts had herded their charges off on a final *supervised* visit.

Fleet was glad to have missed the excursion; honing her hunting skills was far more important. She filled a bowl from the stewpot and settled on her sleep-mat, eating slowly, despite her hunger, and holding the broth in her mouth as long as possible before swallowing. She licked the bowl clean and then lay down on her side, her head too tender to lie on her back. She wanted to think of her future with Ashin, but the demands of the hunt, coupled with food and warmth, made the pull of sleep too strong.

But Fleet had only been in the dream realm a short time before the faceless man intruded and she jolted awake. He was still there! He loomed over her and Fleet reached for her knife and then realised it was Glimmer.

The Aunt seemed oblivious to Fleet's fright and simply launched into a rambling account of a call to the Great Turrel interspersed with news of Song's latest misadventure and questions about Fleet's recent whereabouts.

Fleet still had no idea why her ageset had gone to the Great Turrel even after the Aunt had fallen silent, but a good idea why Glimmer had acquired her name. *Fog* would have suited her better, concluded Fleet irritably but regardless, she was keen to join her ageset, because if they had been summoned, the boys' Turrel would have been summoned too.

She interrupted Glimmer to gain her consent, then swiftly gathered her weapons and set off through the frigid air. Dawn silvered the ashins and fyrs and as her breath formed moist clouds, she broke into a jog to warm herself. She couldn't wait to tell Ashin about Tor's invitation to hunt with him *and* about her latest hunts and she was startled to realise it was close to a moon since she had spoken to him.

She had returned from hunting to spend several freezing nights skulking around the boy's Turrel only to learn from Shale that Ashin had gone gathering, and then she had hunted again and had returned to discover she had missed him again.

The Aunts had filled her days with visits to the clay pits and the gathering of fibre plants and she had hunted a third time, the hunt taking longer than planned and ending with being knocked unconscious by Tor of all people.

The ashin leaves rattled, stiff with frost, but Fleet was warm now and ran with the easy lope of a hunter. The golden eyes of a whisper-owl peered down as she wove between lart and fyr but as she neared the Great Turrel, she heard chanting and slewed to a stop. Chanters farewelled the old *earth-named* self at naming ceremonies, and welcomed the new *air-named* self but they also escorted the spirit back to the void and the sheer volume of chanting told Fleet that the chanters marked a death.

The pyre would have already released the spirit from its physical shell, Fleet reassured herself, but her feet refused to move. Once, when she and Firn were very young, they had gone to the burning-place of Tarchen-tur in a game of dare, and it had been the most terrifying experience of Fleet's life.

But it hadn't been the charred bones that had sent her screaming into the trees; it had been the dark fingers that had reached for her from the void. Firn had laughed at her fright but Fleet had never spoken of what she had seen or of the moons of disturbing dreams that followed.

Knowing Ashin was ahead was the only reason she went on and she reached the curved walls of the Great Turrel as the sun's first rays washed them a watery gold. She propped her bow, quiver and knife near the door and went in. Weapons weren't permitted in the Great Turrel, for they brought death, and death had no place where the elders and the newborn, and those who cared for them both, were housed.

Yet at the far end of the Turrel, where the walls curled in upon themselves, death *did* dwell, *and* life, and all else the void gifted and took back. This was the Seeing-Place, the place of Siahs.

Fleet stopped just inside the door, overwhelmed by the sheer volume of chanting. It was amplified by the enclosed space and shocking after so many days of solitary hunting. The smoke of burning neri bark added to her distress and she blinked savagely to clear her eyes as she slotted in amongst her ageset.

Leaf smiled wanly and Fleet smiled back but her attention was on the young men opposite. She spied Firn, who cocked an eyebrow at her, then Chet with Bright and Rush, but there was no sign of Ashin. Spark was absent too and Fleet's heart missed as she wondered whether it was *Spark* who had died. But the chanting marked a more important death than an agemate's.

It was hard to see beyond the Sceadu in front and Fleet drew herself up to her full height and peered over their heads. The Circle gathered further up the Turrel but there was no one at their centre and Fleet's heart jolted. Siah was missing! She spun back to Leaf, but Leaf had closed her eyes, either out of weariness or respect.

The Sceadu in front swayed like trees in the wind then parted as a group of elders made their way back to the stewpots. Ket was amongst them, her eyes red with weeping. Ket and Siah were agemates and panic threatened as Fleet became certain that Siah *had* died. No Siah returned to the void without leaving a Siah in her place, she reminded herself, and who that Siah was, was the Circle's concern, not hers.

As the day wore on, Fleet grew increasingly frustrated at Ashin's absence *and* increasingly weary. She'd had little rest since hunting and even less to eat, and she finally edged away from her agemates and slipped back through the crowd to the stewpots. The broth was scarcely more than water but she grabbed a bowl and gulped it down and then a part spicy, part bitter odour intruded, and she grinned, having no need to turn to know it was Firn.

'Did you kill?' he asked, filling a bowl.

It should have been an easy question to answer but Fleet was caught between denying her skill in taking the chet and revealing her stupidity in losing it. 'The hunt was unsuccessful,' she muttered.

'I haven't killed either,' he grumbled, 'and I'm sick of being stuck here *and* of this broth.'

'Siah's dead?'

Firn nodded but before Fleet could question him further, she sensed someone tall beside her and whirled. Her delight was short-lived. The scent wasn't Ashin's but Tor's and unlike Fleet, he'd had time to bathe and change his clothes. Tor's muscularity made him even more imposing in the crowded space and Firn looked like a newly earth-named Little Brother in comparison.

Tor greeted her courteously but his message was brief: as there had been no more kills, Fleet was to rest this day and be ready to leave at dawn.

'You're hunting together?' interrupted Firn.

'Yes,' said Fleet excitedly. 'Tor's taking me into the Whitelands.'

'Then he can take me too,' said Firn.

'I'll not be burdening myself with a second beginner hunter,' said Tor. 'I suggest you hunt the Redlands, Firn.' Then, with a brief nod to Fleet, he moved off.

'*Beginner* hunter,' muttered Firn as he glowered after him. 'You have to wonder why the *mighty* Tor's prepared to *burden* himself with any hunter at all.' He kinked an eyebrow at her and Fleet shrugged.

'Don't let your imagination run away with you, Firn. Tor's just reached the ripe old age when his protective Uncle tendencies have kicked in.'

Firn scowled, making the bend in his nose more pronounced. It and his broken front teeth were the result of a berian strike suffered as a Little Brother. 'It's more likely Serest going off with Snowhawk has made him look elsewhere for a wife,' he said. 'And what better wife for a hunter than another hunter?'

Fleet swallowed her broth in gulp. 'That berian strike must have damaged your brain,' she spluttered.

'Maybe,' said Firn, 'but it didn't damage my eyesight. Mind you, by the morrow Serest might have gone back to Tor *or* be with someone else. She's like a snowflake in a swirl-wind.'

'How do you know that?' asked Fleet in astonishment.

'Everyone knows it, except you perhaps and the *mighty* Tor. That's the trouble with you hunters. Aware of everything in the White- and Redlands, and blind to everything in the Turrels.'

'*You're* a hunter too,' pointed out Fleet.

'Only a *beginner* one.'

'Tor called me that as well,' she said, not liking to see her agemate upset.

'Ah, but he's taking *you* with him. Your *beginner* hunting skills obviously have charms mine lack although Tor's interest in hunters marrying hunters might have some merit. Perhaps you should marry me,' he said with a wink.

'I'm to marry Ashin, wherever he is,' said Fleet distractedly. She had many preparations to make before Tor would take her with him and the news Firn suddenly offered up, that Ashin gathered deep in the Redlands and wouldn't be back for two or three days, didn't help.

'Tell Ashin where I've gone then, will you, and that I'll

speak with him on my return,' she said.

But for once, Firn was reluctant to pass on Fleet's message. 'I think you should delay this hunt until Ashin returns. You've barely seen him recently. You need to speak with him *before* you go, Fleet. You've been absent a lot lately and if you're to hunt the Whitelands with Tor, you'll be gone at least another six days.'

Fleet shook her head. 'Tor won't delay the hunt, Firn, and I have to ready my pack. Just tell Ashin where I've gone,' she said, and hurried away.

4

Fleet's excitement at hunting with Tor lasted less than a day. Even before they set out, he checked the contents of her pack *as if she were a Little Sister* and ordered her to carry spare socks and boots. Then he took the lead, *as if she didn't know her way through the Redlands*.

It was close to midday when a fierce wind woke. It sent stinging showers of twigs that made Tor's mood even worse. He reprimanded her for not scanning sufficiently, then for failing to notice a derelict berian path and not detouring around it.

Fleet held her tongue, not wanting to give him reason to send her back, but her good intentions evaporated like water on firestones when Tor wasted valuable hunting time by insisting they set camp soon after dusk.

'It's perilous to journey through berian forage in darkness so close to snowmelt,' he replied in response to her objections.

'I can smell when berian are near. There's no risk.'

'No flow of scent is true in winds like these,' he countered. 'And the noise makes it impossible to hear their approach. Only a fool would continue. We stay here until dawn.' Fleet tossed her pack on the ground in disgust but Tor didn't remove his. 'The wind will die before half-night and the air chill,' he said. 'We'll need a good fire site and plenty of windfall to see us through the night.'

Fleet refused to give Tor an excuse to call her lazy as well as a *fool*, and laboured long and hard to collect a large pile of wood and then, just as Tor had predicted, the wind dropped and the cold intensified.

He lit the fire, heated water, and added a gob of sweet-sap. 'I forgot to thank you for gathering the windfall,' he said, as he handed her a steaming mug.

23

'I suppose a *fool* is good for something.'

Tor eyed her from the other side of the fire. 'You really do find it hard to take instruction, don't you?' he said. 'I'm surprised Ketwing persevered with you.'

'You shouldn't be,' retorted Fleet. 'No doubt teaching you gave her the patience she needed to teach me.' Tor burst out laughing and after a moment, Fleet grinned too. 'I'm used to hunting alone,' she admitted.

'So am I,' said Tor, as he sipped his sweetened water. 'But I wonder whether working with another hunter, at least some of the time, might be more effective.'

'It's the Sceadu way to hunt alone.'

'Perhaps our ways will have to change just as the rhythm of snowmelt and snowcome have changed.' He stared up at the stars for a moment. 'It's the worst possible time to lose a Siah,' he murmured, almost to himself.

Fleet was used to Ashin and Firn's faces and she stared at this less familiar male face curiously. Tor's eyes were wider set than Ashin's, his brows more arched, his lips thinner and now hard with worry. Fleet's stomach tightened in response. She knew the ways of chet and aperion; of murrow and white-hare; but the failure of snowmelt was beyond her. It was Siah's task to mend such things, not hers, she consoled herself.

'Nothing stays the same, Fleet,' said Tor. 'Once these lands belonged to the berian alone, their paths trod so often they creased the very bones of the earth. Then we came from the west, but we can't return that way, even if we wanted to; the ice prevents it. The void is taking back what it once gave but will gift again. All we can do is wait and keep the dance of Talabraith.'

The new day was gentle, as if to make up for the previous day's gales, and the days that followed were mild too. The fine weather cheered Fleet and she pushed aside worries about snowmelt's delay. The continued upslope and then brilliant patches of snow heralded the Whiteland's edge. Fleet hastened forward as Ashali's mighty sweep became visible through the gnarled lattice of branches.

'Stop!' ordered Tor, with such authority Fleet obeyed without thinking.

'Surely we aren't going to set camp now,' she said, all but dancing with impatience. 'Midday's scarcely passed.'

'Are you so poor a hunter that you rush headlong into the unknown?'

'The air tells of no berian, scinton or chet,' said Fleet. 'Even *you* should be able to smell how free of threat it is.'

Tor eyed her sardonically. 'It's true I can't smell serests, bone-breaking crevices hidden beneath the snow, or scinton lairs too deep for scent to escape, so perhaps you can tell me whether any of these dangers exist.'

'I can't smell them either,' she admitted.

'Even Ketwing couldn't and she was the best hunter of her ageset. A good hunter knows their own lack, Fleet.'

'Another lesson from the Uncle,' she sneered.

'And the last unless you behave like a hunter! I'd take you back to the Aunts right now except it would mean more days of hunger in the Turrels.' He slipped off his pack and dropped it at her feet. 'Wait here,' he said, and strode off through the trees.

Tor was a fellow hunter, not some Aunt who *must be obeyed*, and Fleet only delayed to set an arrow before she followed. The sprawl of grapple and splay-spruce reminded her this area had once been Redlands and then, as she cleared the trees, Ashali's vast slopes scoured even that thought from her mind.

A dull rumble sounded and she flinched, and then an icy plume rose from beyond Ashali's massive shoulder. The warming earth weakened the snow's grip sending serests thundering down Ashali's slopes, annihilating all in their paths. The Sceadu welcomed serests, despite their dangers, for they heralded more kindly weather. Thankfully, this one was on Ashali's northern slopes.

Scent intruded and her bow came up but it was only Tor returning from his reconnoiter. His reaction mirrored hers but whereas he lowered his bow, Fleet didn't and he continued towards her until the barb all but grazed his chest.

'Perhaps this is why Sceadu hunters hunt alone,' he said, as he brushed past.

Fleet un-nocked the arrow and followed him back to his pack. She felt shamed by her behavior, which she scarcely understood, but Tor seemed perfectly at ease as he retrieved chunks of mur from his pack, and handed her some.

They ate in silence and then he heaved his pack back on. 'Scinton spoor goes west,' he said. 'Did you take its scent when you disobeyed my orders and followed?'

Fleet shook her head. The word *disobeyed* rankled but she was more annoyed she had been too distracted by the serest to taste the air.

'If we track far into the Whitelands, we will need to sleep in snow caves,' continued Tor. 'Are you willing?'

'Yes,' said Fleet eagerly, her head already full of her triumphant return to the Great Turrel bearing the scinton.

'Come then,' he said, and strode off.

Fleet hadn't ventured far from the snowline on her previous expeditions and she now discovered how treacherous Ashali's exposed slopes were. In places the snow barely covered her boots and then without warning, she was plunged in up to her knees. Tor ordered her to follow in his prints but she fell twice before she took his advice, then her breathing steadied and she was able to take in the information he tossed over his shoulder.

He described how the snow held the tracks of beasts or let them go; of how a scinton made its lair and hid its kittens while it hunted; of how the pattern of a gyar and snowhawk's flight pinpointed the leavings of a scinton's kill.

Fleet was excited by what she learned and by the scinton's scent on the air. It was faint but suddenly strengthened as they toiled up a spur. 'It's near,' she whispered, setting an arrow, but Tor's attention was on the sun's slide behind Ashali's crest.

'Time to make camp,' he announced.

'But the scinton's close,' hissed Fleet. 'We can—'

'You don't track after dusk in the Whitelands; you build snow caves. There's a good site higher on the spur,' he added, and crunched away upslope. Fleet swore, too incensed to care whether Tor heard her, but he kept going and she was forced to follow.

Tor stopped where the slope tapered to a narrow plateau and extricated a small shovel from his pack. 'You'll need yours too,' he said. 'The first stage of building a snow cave is making a big pile of snow. Start digging.'

Fleet dug. The mound grew and as dusk darkened to night, their sweat was pungent in the air. 'The advantage of being all but frozen to death is that the snow stays hard,' said Tor, his teeth flashing in a smile. 'While I build the entrance tunnel, push arrows into the mound, three quarters of the way in, all the way round.'

Fleet did as he asked but it seemed ridiculous and she suspected he would later laugh over her gullibility with his age-mates. Now she had stopped digging the cold returned in full force and she reclaimed her jacket and thrust her hands deep into its pockets.

The silence of the Whitelands pressed down on her too. It was like a living, breathing thing and she was glad when Tor beckoned. 'We must hollow out the mound now,' he said. 'When you feel the arrow barbs, don't remove any more snow. That way the roof will stay nice and strong and not fall in.'

Fleet nodded, relieved Tor hadn't played a humiliating trick on her after all.

They gouged out the snow and when Tor was satisfied, he broke through the snow between the mound and the tunnel and they crawled inside. It was cramped and Fleet muttered apologies each time she bumped Tor, which was often. He seemed not to notice, intent on constructing a sleeping platform. As he worked, he explained how the tunnel's slope allowed the colder air to slide away and how the platform elevated sleepers to the warmest air.

He asked her to go outside and remove all but the top arrow, which she did, before she crawled back inside. It was already noticeably warmer and she squatted on her haunches while Tor finished the platform. Then he grasped the barbed end of the remaining arrow, worked it back and forth to enlarge the hole, and pulled it through.

'You *must* leave a hole for air,' he said, in the tone he reserved for important information. Fleet nodded, tired and hungry, but elated by her new knowledge. 'Time to eat,' he said cheerfully, and shuffled backwards out of the tunnel.

Tor made a hollow in the snow outside, pulled lart cones from his pack, and tipped a small container of white-nut oil over them. Then he struck flints and flames caught, filling the frigid air with resinous fumes.

Fleet perched on her pack beside the fire, warming her hands as Tor prepared a meal. His actions were quick and methodical, as if he had prepared many such meals, which he had, realised Fleet, feeling young and ignorant. He filled a pan with snow and tossed in chunks of mur, rin-tuber and herbs, the aroma making Fleet's stomach grumble.

'The snow gives you a keen hunger, which is why you need to carry more food,' said Tor, as he toasted errem disks on an arrow barb. 'There's something about the Whitelands,' he murmured, as he looked up at the stars. 'Their vastness and emptiness . . .'

Fleet nodded as she followed his gaze. It was as if everything familiar had been stripped away. She the Moon was as slender as a scinton's claw and Fleet recalled her times under She the Moon's light with Ket, and the chants Ket had taught her.

'*She the Moon, She the Moon, I ask of you: give me the eyes of the gyar and the silence of snow, the breath of wind that does not blow. Give me the beast, Willing in death, and—*'

'*To you I pledge Talabraith*,' finished Tor. 'Ketwing taught me that chant as well.' He guided the steaming contents of the pan into two mugs and passed her one. 'My training with her seems a long time ago now. I was young and thought I knew everything.'

'Nothing's changed then,' said Fleet. Tor's jaw tightened and Fleet instantly regretted the jibe. She gripped the mug, barely aware of its hotness, as she searched for a way to make amends.

'A lot has changed,' said Tor. 'Then I was thirteen snow-melts, now I'm twenty-three. Then I thought I would marry Serest, now she's to marry Snowhawk. Then I thought all was well with the world and now I know it isn't. You're like I was then, Fleet. You think you will marry Ashin and the failure of snowmelt will right itself.'

Fleet swallowed her stew in a single gulp, scalding her throat. 'You never cease to amaze me,' she choked. 'What makes you think you know more about my life than I do? Have you hidden nearby while I've been with Ashin? Listened to us, spied on us?'

'None of these things, Fleet. But I'm a hunter, as you are. We both know the first flutterings of the hatchling and the last steps of the old as they lurch towards the void and, in between, we know the courtship dance of renewal: the ketwings' fine strut; the aperions' twined necks; the berians' slow circle. I've seen how Ashin and Spark walk together, Fleet. They *will* marry. You need to look elsewhere for a husband.'

Fleet wanted to run, to use the exhaustion of muscle and bone to scour away Tor's words but there was nowhere to run *to*, and she locked her arms around her knees and stared at the flames.

'I haven't said these things to hurt you,' he said more gently, as he cleaned the pan.

'You surprise me.'

The fire spat as Tor extinguished it and the sudden absence of heat added to the chill between them. 'If you need to relieve yourself best do it now,' he said, business-like again. 'Once we're in the cave, I'll seal the door and you'll have to stay put till morning.'

His steps rasped away and Fleet grimaced as she recalled Firn's claim that Tor sought her as a wife. Tor's want to interfere in her life was driven by nothing more than conceit! She fumed as she stared skywards but She the Moon had drawn away to leave the heavens to a jagged scatter of stars, while behind her, Ashali crouched like a monstrous scinton.

Relieving herself hurriedly, she crawled up the tunnel into the cave. It was pitch black inside and she heard Tor's pack scrape across the entrance. His shelter-sheet covered the entire platform too.

'I have my own shelter-sheet,' she said, groping with numb fingers in her pack.

'We share,' said Tor brusquely, taking up position uncomfortably close. 'You said you were willing.'

'But I thought—'

'We sleep like agemates do, back to back, for warmth. It's usual in snow caves. Change your boots and socks before you lie down. You won't sleep well with wet feet.' Fleet did as she was bid, but remained sitting, mortified at the situation she found herself in, and Tor's voice finally echoed from the darkness. 'If I were going to force myself on you, I would have done it by now.'

'I didn't think . . . I don't believe . . .'

'Then lie down,' he said. 'I'm tired and cold.'

Fleet lay down but Tor suddenly leaned over her and she fumbled for her knife. He didn't seem to notice; just pulled the sheet into position before he turned his back. His breathing sank to an even rhythm but Fleet remained rigid and increasingly cold.

She and Spark had curled up with Ashin and Firn countless times, but this was different. Tor had a sureness about him that marked him as a man, whereas Ashin . . . she cut the thought short. Ashin was just as strong and skilled as Tor, she asserted, but as a healer, not a hunter.

Tor was almost a stranger to her and a bossy one at that, and she resolved to keep her distance, but as the cold intensified, she shuffled across until her back touched his and, as his delicious warmth seeped into her, she slept too.

5

Those in the Great Turrel also slept except for Ketwing who was too upset, and Must, who chose to keep her company. They sat near the cooking fire, keeping their voices low and Ketwing occasionally wiping her eyes, her grief for the old Siah still fresh.

She was glad of Must's company and of his calmness. Even as a Little Brother, he had been tranquil and had been earthnamed *Pool,* then he became the patterner whose steady hand imprinted the lines of earth-name, air-name and marriage on each new generation of Sceadu; lines that showed what each Sceadu *must* be and do *if* Berian-tur were to endure.

Now as the earth turned back toward the light, Ketwing spoke of what troubled her most—the shocking speed of the new Siah's air-naming, marriage and visioning.

'You speak as a hunter,' said Must, when Ketwing's torrent of speech had ended. 'Hunters prefer a slow unfolding.' Ketwing shook her head. 'A Siah was taken and a Siah given,' Must reminded her. 'We have much to be thankful for.'

Ketwing pushed her crooked fingers through her hair as she recalled the awful meeting with the new Siah. 'This Siah's visions fill me with fear,' she whispered, '*if* she is the Siah given.'

Must's eyebrows rose. 'Do you doubt what you told the Circle?'

'Her name was in Siah's dying breath but Siah was so ill. Perhaps she mistook what the void showed.'

'Your hearts were close, Ketwing. Do you believe that, in the end, her spirit-sight failed her?' Ketwing said nothing and Must touched her gently on the knee. 'She-who-is-now Siah suffered illness in her growing and has been gifted potent dreams. The void has long signalled its messengers thus.'

'What you say is true and yet dread clothes me like a cape.'

'It clothes *all* the Circle,' acknowledged Must. 'Siah's vision of hunter deaths is dark indeed.'

'Tor, Fleet and Firn remain beyond Berian-tur,' said Ketwing. 'How can I hope we have acknowledged the rightful Siah when to do so, is to hope for the death of one or all of them?'

Must made no reply and Ketwing wondered whether her feelings simply stemmed from resentment of the young woman who had replaced her dead friend. The notion was abhorrent but she forced herself to examine it, as hunters forced themselves to examine failed hunts, and concluded her antagonism flowed from the new Siah's rawness.

The *new* Siah had still been in the girls' Turrel when the old Siah had died and now she was air-named, married *and* visioning. She'd had no time to be just a woman, or just a Siah, or just a wife. It was akin to a hunter learning to kill a scinton while trying to master a bow and arrow and practise a hunter's run.

'Where does Fleet hunt?' asked Must abruptly.

'In the Whitelands with Tor,' said Ketwing, hoping the odd chance of them being together helped their chances of survival. Tor was strong, skilled and careful, whereas Fleet was fast, reckless and blind to all but her quarry and yet, in their adherence to Talabraith, Tor and Fleet were one. The void should have no reason to be displeased with either of them.

'And Firn?' pursued Must.

'In the Redlands.'

'Six days at most then,' said Must.

Ketwing nodded grimly. In the next six days, the Sceadu would have to chant the spirits of their dead hunters back to the void or accept they had appointed the wrong spirit guide to keep them safe in the dark times ahead.

Fleet was high in the Whitelands when she stopped, flared her nostrils, and scanned. Ashali's peak glittered like a huge frosty gem, beautiful against the cloudless sky, and yet her skin flicked. Tor seemed to feel nothing as he trekked ahead down the slope of a small valley and yet Fleet was so anxious all conversation had died some time ago.

He stopped for her to catch up and his irritation was plain. 'What are you sulking about now?' he demanded.

'I'm not sulking.'

'Well, there's something—' His gaze slid to her belt and Fleet realised she had gripped her knife. 'What frightens you?' he asked more gently.

'I don't like it here.'

'Why?'

Fleet was surprised he took her feelings seriously and stared self-consciously up at Ashali. 'I can feel a storm coming,' she said.

He followed her gaze. 'There's no evidence of it.' Fleet didn't expect storm clouds to sprout from Ashali's crown either but the air felt tight, and she could think of no better way to describe it.

Tor took a swig from his waterskin and wiped his mouth. 'When I first came here, I felt like an ice-mouse must before a whisper-owl takes it,' he said. 'The openness of the snow makes you feel exposed, as if a layer of skin's been stripped away.'

Fleet was grateful for Tor's candor and wondered whether the menace she sensed simply flowed from the absence of a leaf-roof.

'The scinton's not far ahead,' he went on, 'but if it's not Willing before dusk, we'll turn back and seek chet in the Redlands.'

Fleet nodded but was dismayed by how relieved she felt at the prospect of leaving the Whitelands behind. She had longed to hunt there but now all she wanted was to flee back to the shelter of the trees.

They went on but hadn't gone far before thunder boomed and Fleet whirled in astonishment. She half expected to see storm clouds boil above Ashali's peak after all but instead saw an enormous wall of snow rushing down the valley towards them.

'Back!' screamed Tor, and they began a mad scramble up the slope.

Serests flowed like rivers and if they could get far enough

up the valley's side, the serest would pass behind them. Fleet's breath tore in and out as she clawed her way up but the thunder grew to a roar and snow pelted, hard as stones. And then the air turned white and she was hurled into the torrent.

The serest's boom echoed around the Sceadu valleys and the aperion Firn had tracked bounded away. He barely noticed, astounded by the explosion of noise. The serest must have been enormous and his anxious thoughts went to Tor and Fleet, high in the Whitelands. Then the trees behind him splintered as a massive he-berian blundered through. It had been maddened by the noise, realised Firn in terror.

In the Great Turrel, Little Sisters screamed and clung to their carers, and those who knew of Siah's visioning bowed their heads, grieving for the dead but comforted by Siah's true reading of the void.

Ketwing's head remained unbowed. Grunting with pain, she forced her crooked legs outside and stared up at Ashali's peak, as if by sheer force of will, she could discover Fleet's fate, but Ashali's blank face told her nothing.

Must finished his patterning of Syra's cheeks, set aside his blade, and repeated the instructions he had uttered countless times before. She was to rest, soothe her throbbing face with the mixture he'd prepared, and calm her fears by sipping the tincture he'd set ready.

Syra nodded but Must delayed his departure, despite knowing the Circle waited in the hall outside. He must be sure Syra had understood and remained safe. She was vulnerable at this moment while her earth-named self drifted towards the void and her air-named self had yet to be bestowed. So it was that earth- and air-naming ceremonies were conducted in the Seeing-Place, whose curved walls closed in upon themselves to keep the void confined.

When Must was confident Syra was well enough to leave, he made his way through the chanting Sceadu to the far end of the Turrel where the Circle gathered. He went slowly, weary from the air-naming ceremonies of the past days. The new Siah looked weary too, as if she drank too greedily from the spirit-stream.

Must took up his usual position next to Ketwing and, as the Circle came into line, the chanting quickened and they advanced solemnly back up the hall and into the Seeing-Place. Syra rose from the pallet and Must saw her face had reddened along the line he'd positioned below the old line of earth-naming.

Must still felt satisfaction at his precision, despite the hundreds of lines he had imprinted as patterner. Siahs might travel the dreamways to retrieve the void's precious wishes but it was he, Must the patterner, with his black ink and blade, who wrote them on the Sceadu's faces for all to see.

Syra knelt and bowed her head before Siah, and the naming ceremony began, but Siah's voice was just an echo to Ketwing, whose thoughts roamed the Whitelands and Redlands in search of Fleet, Tor and Firn. There had been times she had longed for her namesake's ability to fly, but the void had never granted her wings and had long ago reclaimed her human quickness. Now she feared it had reclaimed the young Sceadu hunter she loved too.

Five days had passed since the serest had rocked Berian-tur and while Fleet and Tor might not have had time to return, Firn's absence was ominous. Siah had rejected the Circle's proposal to mount a search, which suggested the void's intentions had come to pass but unlike Siah, to whom the void gifted certainty, Ketwing found the waiting unbearable.

That is the problem with hunters, Must had chided her. *They are patient while tracking the Willing beast and impatient in every other situation.* Ketwing had grudgingly agreed but it did nothing to lessen her frustration.

The naming ceremony ended and Ketwing followed the Circle back into the hall but didn't linger there, continuing through the chanters and into the frosty air outside. Her preference had long been for the openness of sky and stars and, although her twisted limbs no longer carried her deep into the Redlands, they could still take her to the stone seat in the clearing nearby.

The small space captured the sunlight's precious warmth and she closed her eyes as the pain receded, but her peace was short-lived. Twigs broke under foot as someone joined her and she wedged her eyes open. It was Siah's husband Scead. He looked as grim as Ketwing felt and it was little wonder; two of the missing hunters were his agemates.

'There will be no naming ceremonies tomorrow,' he said. 'Siah must rest and I must replenish my healing stocks. I'll gather westward and search for signs of them.'

Ketwing nodded gratefully. 'Berian might be abroad,' she said. 'Take care.'

'There's no danger there for me,' he replied, his face lighting in a smile that turned his eyes to sunshine. 'Fore-knowledge is an advantage of being married to a Siah.'

And an advantage of being a Siah was to choose the handsomest man from your ageset for a husband, thought Ketwing.

She shifted slightly and winced and Scead's smile disappeared. 'When I return, I'll make some more of that rub for your hips. It *does* help?' he asked anxiously.

'It does indeed,' said Ketwing, and smiled for the first time in days.

6

The serest hurled Fleet over and over, pounding and smashing her, and when all seemed lost, flung her out the side and crashed on down the valley without her. Fleet lay gasping on her belly. Her pack, arrows and bow had been ripped from her and blood from her forehead formed a brilliant pool on the snow.

Then, as the awful silence intruded, she realised she was alone. She blinked the blood from her eyes and stared panic-stricken at the rucked snow below. 'Tor!' she screamed, but there was no answer. She struggled upright and staggered down the slope. Tor could be anywhere; buried beneath her feet or swept halfway to the Redlands.

Give up! A voice in her head demanded; *you have no food and no shelter. Get off the mountain!* Fleet shook her head in savage rebuttal, spraying bright droplets over the snow. Tor had been close behind her; he *had* to be near.

She ranged up and down in a frantic search for scent. *Too late, too late*, badgered the voice in her head but then she smelled something, dropped to her knees and dug. Her frozen hands turned to lumps of wood but she didn't stop. Tor's jacket emerged from the white and she redoubled her efforts, gripped it and heaved. But it wasn't his jacket; it was his pack. Sobbing with disappointment, Fleet resumed her search but his scent grew ever fainter and then disappeared.

He will have suffocated by now, the voice in her head insisted. Ketwing would have taught him how to shape an air pocket, retorted Fleet fiercely. His scent came to her again and, again she dug until she had uncovered a square of black. It *was* his jacket this time but Fleet feared it had been torn from him.

Then she found his hand and dug like a mad woman to gouge his face clear. His eyes were closed and his entombed chest made it impossible to tell whether he breathed.

Weariness descended like a blow and Fleet extricated the rest of his body, opened his jacket, and laid her ear against his chest. She heard nothing at first and then blessedly, she heard a heartbeat and tears tracked down her bloodied face. Tor might still be too hurt to live and even if uninjured, the Redlands' safety was a two-day trek away.

She trudged back to retrieve Tor's pack, scanning as she went, saw a level area of snow nearby and set to work with his shovel. Despite a terrible fear Tor would die *or was already dead*, she took great care with her building of the cave. She packed the snow down hard, using arrows to ensure the roof was thick enough, and stifled a burst of hysterical laughter at the thought of surviving a serest only to be suffocated by a collapsed snow cave.

Stars glinted like ice-shards by the time she finished but getting Tor's unconscious body onto the sleeping platform was all but impossible. In the end, she looped his pack straps around his chest, braced her feet against the edge of the platform, and heaved. The corner of the platform collapsed but Tor was on it and the shelter-sheet under him.

Fleet hauled his pack across the entranceway, gulped down water from his waterskin, and crawled up beside him. She tucked the shelter-sheet over them both and lay with her back hard against his but found herself straining for his every sound. He seemed no warmer and she touched his cheek. It was icy and she struggled to quell her panic.

Ashin had told her how healers had once used body heat to save a Little Brother who had wandered away during snowcome and Fleet hauled Tor over to face her, undid his jacket and her own, and pulled him into her arms. She had never slept with an agemate like this, let alone a man, but the reassuring thud of his heart and his resinous, peppery scent comforted her.

She held Tor to warm him but he warmed her too and her eyelids drooped. As she began to drift, she wondered whether she would wake holding a corpse, but in the end, she was too tired to care.

Tor still slept when Fleet woke but the snow cave's filtered light made it hard to tell if his colour were normal. She peered at him closely and then his eyes flickered open, and Fleet jumped back and pulled her jacket closed.

'You've got blood all over your face,' he croaked, then coughed to clear his throat. His gaze searched their surroundings and he frowned. 'The last thing I remember is the serest hitting me and yet I'm in a snow cave. How can that be?'

'Give me a moment,' she muttered, needing some space. She shuffled out of the tunnel and cranked herself upright. Every battered muscle ached and she took a deep breath. Fear for Tor and holding him close had changed him from a distant, arrogant hunter into something else, and Fleet didn't feel ready to deal with whatever that *something else* was.

The snow offered no answers and she crawled back into the cave. Tor was rummaging through his pack and she decided that he *did* look pale. 'Are you in pain?' she asked.

'I hurt everywhere, like you do, no doubt,' he said shortly. 'And that gash on your forehead needs to be washed.'

He reached for his waterskin but Fleet stayed his hand. 'We'll need the water to drink,' she said. 'I've lost my pack.'

'Tell me what happened.'

'I was fortunate,' she said slowly, reluctant to relive the horror. 'The serest tossed me out the side but it buried you. I dug you out.'

'With your hands, by the look of them,' said Tor. 'Why not use the shovel?'

'Because I'm a fool, I suppose,' said Fleet, stung by the implied criticism.

'So,' said Tor, 'correct me if I've got any of this wrong. You were hit by the serest, gashed your head, found me somehow, dug me out, built a snow cave, got me into it and managed to warm me. I don't call these things the actions of a fool, Fleet. I call them the actions of someone brave and strong and selfless.' Fleet's cheeks warmed and to make matters worse, Tor brought his fingers under her chin so she must look at him. 'Thank you,' he said solemnly.

'You would have done the same for me,' she mumbled, her

heart all over the place.

'I would have *tried* to find you, that's true, but I don't have your sense of smell.' He paused. 'I've sometimes wondered what my scent is like to you.'

'Like lart cones,' said Fleet eagerly, glad of the change of subject. 'Everyone has their own scent. Spark is more like fyr, Firn a bitter version of cone-flower, while Ashin . . .' She smiled. 'He's as sweet as syra-flowers.' Tor's expression had cooled, much to Fleet's relief, and she hoped his sense of obligation faded just as fast.

'We need to get back to the Redlands,' he said.

'There might be a Willing beast here,' said Fleet, hating the thought of returning to Berian-tur empty-handed yet again.

'Hunting's no longer a priority.'

'I could still—' began Fleet.

'You can't hunt with just a knife and that's all you've got left,' said Tor, and that ended the argument.

Fleet morosely considered the labour of replacing her lost weapons as they made their way east. Hunters spent many days selecting wood for shafts and searching out feathers, and countless more fashioning them into bows and arrows, and adding the barbs the metal-smiths wrought. To make matters worse, a weaponless hunter couldn't contribute to the Great Turrel's stewpots.

Tor's heavy limp added to her worries. It slowed them and it was soon clear they must spend another night in the Whitelands. The sun slipped behind Ashali's peak, shrouding the slopes with a chill blue, but when Fleet found a snow cave site, Tor took charge of the shovel.

'You've done enough damage to your hands already,' he said as he started to dig.

'But you're injured,' she objected.

'We're *both* injured,' he countered, and when she continued to protest, stopped and turned to her. 'Let me do this for you, Fleet,' he said quietly.

Fleet nodded but felt worse than useless as she watched

him work and when the snow cave was finished, he even prepared stew for her. She perched beside him on his pack, having to hold her mug with her fingertips to avoid burning her raw palms.

'Ask Ashin to salve them for you when we get back,' he said, '*and* your forehead, as you won't let *me* touch it.' Fleet was taken aback by the affront Tor seemed to feel and by his dismissal of her explanation that they needed to save water.

'Cleaning a wound isn't wasting water,' he retorted, 'and in any case, we have enough water until we reach the springs at the snowline. If that *were* the reason for your refusal, I'll clean the gash now.' Fleet nodded, not wanting to make matters worse, but Tor's nearness woke the horror of her search for him after the serest and she started to shake.

'I'm sorry I'm hurting you, but the wound is deep,' he said. 'I'm not surprised you lost so much blood.'

'It doesn't h . . . hurt,' said Fleet.

'Time to get out of the cold then.' Fleet followed him into the snow cave but her shuddering grew worse and Tor spread his shelter-sheet and helped her up beside him. 'You don't feel that cold,' he said, puzzled.

Fleet made no reply, appalled to feel sobs rise in her throat. She was glad the darkness hid her but Tor's fingers skimmed her hair and brushed her wet cheeks. 'I'm sorry I hurt you,' he repeated.

'You . . . didn't . . .' she choked.

He lay down and brought his arms around her, enclosing her in his warmth while she wept. Fleet had no idea why she cried or why she couldn't stop. Tor said nothing, just stroked her hair back from her forehead, his tenderness reminiscent of another time potent with misery when Talith had died and Ket had held her.

'That was stupid,' she said, when she was able.

'That was shock. Alright now?'

'Yes.'

'Sleep, then,' he said, and turned his back.

Fleet was surprised at how bereft she felt at his withdrawal and, as the night deepened, shuffled across until her back touched his. 'Normal snow cave behaviour,' she told herself, and slipped into sleep.

7

It was evening before they reached the Redlands and Fleet was grateful to be back under the trees, despite the perils of newly woken berian. She knew what challenged, angered or frightened them for, like all living things, berian were predictable even in their flashes of ferocious unpredictability. But the Whitelands weren't predictable, for the Whitelands didn't live. Tor seemed to have no liking for them either, despite hunting there, and Fleet pondered the anomaly as she shared Tor's shelter-sheet that night.

The leaf litter was soft but she felt every one of her bruised muscles and it might have been pain that filled her dreams with rivers that tossed her over and over like a serest. The horror of near suffocation jerked her awake and as she gulped down the lart-scented air in an attempt to calm, another odour intruded.

Tor still slept but his bow and quiver were nearby and she reached for them, slid from the shelter-sheet, and crept away into the trees. Foliage scattered cool droplets over her skin as she slipped through the undergrowth and then the aperion came into sight. It was male, about three snowmelts, and well-fleshed.

Fleet was close enough to shoot it but not close enough to be sure of a kill, and a wounded aperion could cover long distances quickly, only to die in a stand of garron or rocky streambed, the gift wasted and Talabraith breached.

The aperion grazed on talith blooms, its velvety lips drawn back to avoid the thorns, but as she moved closer, it raised its head and looked at her. Its clear eyes revealed a depth beyond the world that held them both, hunter and hunted, things of flesh and bone, and Fleet released the arrow. She felt the shock of it hit, as if she herself had been shot, had been Willing, was falling backwards into the slow spiral of the void.

Then the aperion crashed sideways and Tor was suddenly beside her, his face split in a wide grin. 'Well hunted,' he said, 'especially since you used strange weapons.'

'It was Willing,' said Fleet thickly.

'It's about time something was,' he said and limped forward. They pulled the aperion clear of the thatch and set to work with their knives, working in silence so as not disturb its lope towards the void by reminding it of the world it had left behind. They placed its head in the thatch for the small creatures that burrowed there; its entrails amongst the tree roots for the white-fox; and wedged its heart and other organs in the branches for berian or birds.

Then they carried the carcass back to the fire. The hide would be tanned; the sinews used in bows, sewing and securing; the flesh roasted, smoked or boiled; and all else find its way into the stewpots, the gift honoured and Talabraith served.

Fleet and Tor took turns carrying the heavier aperion and lighter pack, not just because they were both battered from the serest, but because the beast had been rendered Willing by Tor's weapons and Fleet's skill. Tor's good mood lasted the rest of the day and as they sat by the fire that night, his stew carried the tang of the jar-spur he had taken the trouble to search for.

Fleet was eager to share the news of her success with Ashin but frustratingly, Tor's limp and their burdens meant spending a second night in the Redlands. At least this time her sleep was empty of dreams and, when she woke the next morning, her aches had faded.

They were on their way again before dawn, Fleet happy despite the potential of the close-growing fyrs to hide berian. Fleet smelled none but her excitement at seeing Ashin again was marred by a strange and troublingly familiar scent. She flared her nostrils but its source remained elusive.

'Fearing another storm?' asked Tor, when they had walked for a time in silence.

'Yes, but there are no serests here.'

'Fortunately,' said Tor and glanced sideways at her. 'You're the best judge of what you feel, Fleet, although judging the *truth* of feelings comes with age.'

'So your judgements are always accurate?' asked Fleet, keen for a distraction.

'Mostly, although I've also been utterly wrong.' He paused. 'Doubtless there were many in Berian-tur who knew Serest would choose Snowhawk but it didn't occur to me until she shifted to his tur.' Fleet remained silent, hoping to avert another diatribe about Ashin and Spark.

'Still smell a storm coming?' he asked eventually. Fleet nodded. 'Stay close then.

Snowmelt's delay means berian leave their dens to find the streambeds empty of water and fish. It must be annoying after an entire snowcome on an empty belly.'

Tor spoke lightly but the risk of berian strike was real and Fleet thought longingly of her lost bow and quiver. Talabraith prohibited berian being harmed, unless they attacked, but it would have reassured Fleet to have her weapons. Then a screech in the leaf-roof made her jump.

'Just a juvenile snowhawk,' said Tor. 'They don't usually hunt east of the snowline; it must be scavenging.'

Fleet stumbled to a stop. The moment Tor said it, she knew the strange scent was a combination of rotting flesh and …

Tor stopped too. 'You're pale, Fleet. Are you ill?' The snowhawk screeched again and there was a flash of white as it landed and hopped forward. Fleet started forward too but Tor caught her arm. 'You take the aperion,' he said, and before she could object, slid it onto her shoulders. Then he reclaimed his pack and set an arrow. 'If we have to surrender the aperion and run, we will.'

Fleet's gaze was fixed on the snowhawk. It struggled with something too heavy to lift and Tor gave her a shake. 'If I tell you to drop the aperion and run, do it!' he ordered.

Fleet nodded and as they crept forward, the snowhawk relinquished its prize and flapped a few lengths away. It was a chunk of putrefying meat, longer than it was wide, and then Fleet realised it was an arm, torn off below the shoulder and missing the hand. Fleet slumped to her knees, dropping the aperion, and then Tor's warm hand closed over hers, stilling it as it wiped at her mouth.

He pressed his waterskin to her lips but nothing could wash away the taste. 'It's Firn,' she whispered.

'It might not be—'

'It's Firn!' she shrieked.

'Quiet!' hissed Tor, but too late. Foliage broke as something moved swiftly towards them and as the snowhawk took flight, Tor raised her and eased her slowly backwards. She struggled against him and he cursed, then saw what Fleet had sensed. It was no berian that approached but a man and, as he cleared the trees, Fleet wrenched herself from Tor's grip and threw herself sobbing into his arms.

Tor noted the new lines of air-name and marriage on the face of he-who-had-been Ashin without surprise. It was clear from the way he held Fleet he had affection for her but not enough to resist the charms of his other agemate. In that, he was like Serest.

Fleet's sobs quieted but she didn't raise her head and Tor resolved to get what was to come over with as soon as possible. 'I greet you . . .' he began, using the usual term of courtesy, but forced to leave it incomplete.

'Scead,' supplied he-who-had-been Ashin. 'I greet you, Tor,' he reciprocated.

Scead was the air-name the void gifted a Siah's husband, for if the Siah haunted the void's amorphous mists, then her husband must be as substantial as the Sceadu's flesh and blood.

Tor had guessed Ashin would marry Spark but not that Spark would become Siah, although it made sense. She-who-had-been Spark was often ill and malaise was a predictor of those who travelled the void.

The previous Siah had lived to a ripe old age but many Siahs died young and Tor didn't know whether health was the price the void extracted for its secrets. Whatever the case, it was hard to imagine a worse sequence of events for Fleet, who had lost one agemate to berian strike and two to each other.

Had the Great Turrel been closer, Tor would have left Scead to explain himself to Fleet in private, but berian might be nearby, at least one of which had discovered the sweetness of human flesh. Nor did he believe Scead could prevent Fleet, in her anger and upset, from putting herself at risk.

Even as the thought crossed his mind, Fleet raised her head and froze. 'Who?' she whispered hoarsely, eyes fixed on Scead's face.

'Siah,' said Scead, and when Fleet showed no comprehension, added, 'she-who-was Spark.'

'You traded *our* love for Spark? For *power*?' gasped Fleet.

Scead glanced at Tor uncomfortably. 'You are injured, Fleet. I'll salve that gash and then we need to get you back to the Great Turrel.'

He went to brush her hair from the wound but she knocked his hand away. 'I'm not going anywhere with you!'

'We stay together,' said Tor quickly. 'Berian that have attacked once, are likely to again. Take the aperion, Fleet. Scead and I will bring Firn for proper ceremony.' Fleet seemed not to hear him; her fists were clenched and she panted as if she'd run. 'Take the aperion, Fleet,' he repeated. 'The Sceadu *hunger* and the longer we delay, the greater the risk the beast's *gift* will be *wasted*. And we must take *your* agemate back.'

Fleet started, as if waking from a dream, and heaved the aperion back over her shoulder but Tor waited until he was confident she wouldn't flee before he set off with Scead into the trees.

'I found a part of Firn's shoulder back the way I came,' said Scead softly, as they trawled the undergrowth. 'He had a distinctive scar from when he was attacked as a Little Brother. I found no other trace of him though.' Tor retrieved the arm, wrapped it in his spare shirt and placed it gently in his pack.

'Siah foretold the loss of hunters,' whispered Scead, as they made their way back. 'And terrible though Firn's death is, I am thankful you and Fleet survived.'

'We were caught in a serest,' said Tor. 'I live only because Fleet dug me out.'

'Fleet won't abandon anything or anyone,' murmured Scead. 'It's both her greatest strength and her greatest flaw.'

The small party went on until they reached where Scead had found another part of Firn's remains and he detoured to collect them. Tor waited with Fleet in silence. The gash was vivid against her pale face and she hugged herself as if in pain. He could think of no words of comfort and his thoughts turned to Firn. The rest of his body might have been consumed or dragged to a den. They would probably never know.

As they continued, Tor watched Scead as much as he watched Fleet. Scead glanced at Fleet often and it was clear how troubled he was. Having lost one agemate in Firn, Tor guessed he feared losing a second in Fleet, as well he might. Fleet's fury was palpable and, when they stopped to eat, she turned her back.

As they trudged on, Fleet felt as though she had been caught in a second serest that not only battered her but smashed everything familiar to pieces. Firn was dead while Ashin . . . She could scarcely bear to think of him. All she wanted was to crawl away somewhere quiet and stay there until the world had righted itself.

She finally stumbled to a stop and slid the aperion to the ground. 'I'm going to the girls' Turrel,' she muttered.

'It's best you come to the Great Turrel,' said Scead. 'Most of your ageset are already air-named or await Siah's summons at their parents' turs. There's a new ageset at the girls' Turrel now. Come to the Great Turrel, Fleet,' he repeated.

'I'm not going to the Great Turrel!'

'The beast gifted itself to you,' interrupted Tor. 'It's your duty to present it to Siah. You *have to* go there, Fleet.'

Fleet turned on him furiously. 'Don't tell me what I *have to* do!'

Delivering the gift to Siah meant kneeling before *Spark* and she would *never* do that. Tor's weapons had taken the beast anyway and that made its gift equally his. The understanding freed her and before Tor could react, she sprang away and fled through the trees.

Grief and anger pushed her on long after Tor's shouts had faded into the distance and she only became aware of her surroundings again when the ground steepened and Talith's tur emerged from the darkness. Fleet staggered to a stop and sleeved the sweat from her eyes. She hadn't been here since Talith's death but the tur held happy as well as sad memories and she struggled up the slope and pushed the door open.

It was pitch black inside and scarcely warmer than outside. Fleet groped along the shelf for flints and felt her way back to the fire circle. It had been left piled high with lart cones, now tinder-dry with age, and they burst into flames as soon as she struck spark. The heat was intense but brief and despite knowing she must gather more or freeze later, she remained crouched by the fire.

Thinking of Firn was agony but at least she could think of Scead now and the more she considered him, the more she saw how his sweet nature had betrayed him. Scead had comforted Siah in her bouts of sickness, and Siah had grown used to having him at her disposal. It was understandable then, that when she-who-had-been Spark became Siah, she had wanted him with her *permanently*.

The Sceadu called such ill-considered unions *snow-come-snowmelts*, after the short bursts of unseasonably warm weather that falsely heralded snowmelt, and they had a remedy for them too. A marriage could be broken within its first season, without shame and without prejudicing any further union, but after that, the marriage was as set as Ashali's ice.

The cones collapsed into a crush of ash and as the cold seeped back, Fleet cranked her aching muscles up, and went back out into the icy air. Tinsel-flies swirled like stars but she took no pleasure in them. She felt jarred, as if she had fallen out of step with Talabraith, and then her skin flashed warning and she dropped into a crouch.

Berian didn't come north of the Ige streambed, but they might, if they were hungry enough. Her hand tightened on her knife and then the darkness moved.

8

It was late when Scead returned to the Great Turrel, the elders and young already asleep around the fires. He picked his way through their motionless bodies and then felt his way along the curved walls into the Seeing-Place, so weary he could barely move.

He had told Ketwing of Firn's death and of Fleet and Tor's survival, mixed a salve for Fleet's forehead Tor had promised to deliver, and prepared Firn's remains for the pyre. Lastly, he had gone to the wash-tur and scrubbed himself down.

He had wept for his lost agemate then, his grief worsened by worry Fleet was lost to him too. The void's demands couldn't be denied but he was sorry he had dismissed Firn's claims that Fleet's feelings for him went beyond friendship. Scead had seen her so rarely recently, the claims had seemed ridiculous, then again, he knew how swiftly happiness in another's company could flash to a wanting so intense even marriage failed to sate it.

The brazier's crimson glow showed that Siah slept and he was glad. A Siah's duties were onerous but his wife's visions of death were particularly hard, and the horror was yet to end. He undressed quietly and slipped under the cover. He wanted Siah in his arms but she needed sleep, and he distracted himself by considering the herbs snowmelt would soon deliver to him.

'Scead?'

Siah's voice was husky and his carefully constructed calm disintegrated. 'Sleep, Siah,' he managed to say, but her hair brushed his face as she leaned over him.

'I can sleep any time.'

'You need—' he began, but her lips came to his, hot as her breath.

'I need . . . you. Would you refuse me, husband?'

'Never,' he said, but his throat tightened with a fear that was never far away. There was a price for the void's secrets and Siah burned with a fire that consumed her strength. If only he could find herbs that would . . . But then she slid on top of him, her scent as heady as talith blooms under a snowmelt sun, and he forgot everything but her.

Scead woke. The night was quiet but Siah trembled and he drew away so as not to inflict greater hurt. All he could do was offer a restorative when she returned from the void but it wasn't enough.

Her shaking gave way to an uneasy sleep and dawn was close before she confirmed the dream-vision had reinforced the earlier ones. 'I must meet with the Circle,' she said shakily. 'They must be prepared.'

'And Fleet?'

'Fleet needs time to grieve for Firn *and* for you. I want to give her that time, Scead but the void grows strident.' She shuddered. 'You need to speak with her.'

'She's angry. She won't accept our union.'

'Anger is good,' said Siah unexpectedly. 'It will give her strength to survive what she must do, and she *must* survive.'

Scead nodded but in his heart, he knew that even someone as strong as Fleet couldn't survive what was to come.

Tor was less than halfway to Talith's tur with the salve when voices brought him to a stop. The night was freezing and he wondered why anyone would be from their fires. The speakers came his way and he decided to stay put. Word of Firn's death had spread and the Sceadu might even attack berian or what they *mistook* for berian, if they were frightened enough.

His injured leg throbbed as his muscles cooled and he had just resolved to go on when figures appeared upslope. She the Moon's faint light was enough to illuminate Snowhawk's white-blonde hair but Tor didn't recognise his young companion.

They had stopped and Snowhawk said something too low for Tor to hear, then the boy laughed and Tor was surprised to see Snowhawk give him a quick hug. Snowhawk must have become an Uncle and Tor wondered at Serest's feelings. Being an Uncle demanded much time.

Tor had only seen Snowhawk once since Serest had chosen him and was keen that this meeting be less awkward, but he had closed most of the distance between them before Snowhawk even noticed him.

'I greet you, Snowhawk,' said Tor, nonplussed by his age-mate's carelessness. 'And I greet you . . .?'

'Mist,' supplied Snowhawk smoothly. 'I greet you, Tor. I have been teaching Mist how to track using a whisper-owl's scats. He's considering the life of a hunter.'

More likely the life of a song-smith or dyer, thought Tor, taking in Mist's slender frame.

'Given what you've endured, Tor, I expected you to be sleeping,' continued Snowhawk.

'I have an errand to complete first.'

'Come to my tur afterwards to eat and rest,' said Snowhawk.

That meant seeing Serest and Tor knew he wasn't ready. 'Perhaps in a few days,' he said, nodded and strode away. His stomach churned and he needed time for it to settle, but as he neared Talith's tur, he sensed movement a second time. It seemed half the Sceadu roamed the trees this night!

It was Fleet and he was relieved to see her practice hunter caution, unlike Snowhawk.

She sheathed her knife and straightened. 'Come to gloat, have you?' she demanded.

'Ketwing sends food and Scead a salve for that gash,' he said evenly. 'I thought we might spend one last night together in Talith's tur or is it Fleet's tur now?'

'I'm no longer part of the girls' Turrel.'

'If you're collecting windfall, best get it done and out of this cold.'

Fleet nodded and when they could carry no more wood they made their way back up to the tur. Tor glanced at Fleet as he rebuilt the fire. 'Don't interpret it as gloating if I tell you I'm sorry about Scead,' he said.

'He's made a mistake, that's all,' said Fleet. 'He was always tender-hearted and he's let his sympathy for Siah cloud his judgement. He'll realise it soon enough and break the marriage.'

Tor knew better than to argue, especially when Fleet's feelings were so raw. In the end, she would have to accept Scead's loss and until then, it was vital she remained safe. He portioned the food and they ate in silence, and then he retrieved the salve. 'I need to salve that gash,' he said, and when she made no objection, he unstoppered the pot. Being near her again reminded him of waking in her arms in the snow cave, an intimacy Snowhawk enjoyed *every* night with Serest.

She closed her eyes as he salved the wound and for the first time he really looked at her. Her cheekbones were sharp and her face angular but her mouth was surprisingly sensuous and on an impulse, he brought his lips to hers. The urge to kiss her more deeply was surprisingly strong but she jerked away, eyes a flash in the firelight.

'Why did you do that?' she demanded.

'I don't really know,' he said, nonplussed by the power of the kiss.

'I'm going to marry Scead.'

Her whole body had tensed against him and he changed tack. 'Do you think there are hunting skills I can still teach you?' Her face displayed a moment's confusion then she nodded. 'In that case, it's best for the Sceadu that I do. It's also safer, Fleet. I would have died had I been alone when the serest struck and Firn was alone when he was killed.'

Fleet's mouth trembled at the mention of her dead agemate but she nodded again and Tor exhaled. Taking Fleet on hunt would keep her safe but it would give him time to test his feelings for her too. It would be akin to courting with the advantage of excluding other suitors, but thoughts of courting reminded him of its strictures. Ketwing and Scead had been keen Fleet not be alone this night but it was frowned upon to share turs before marriage.

'It's improper I stay,' he said and gathered his things.

'We shared a snow cave, what difference does it make?'

He paused. 'Do you want me to stay?' he asked, hoping Fleet felt *something* for him.

'Berian forage at night and as you keep reminding me, the Sceadu can't afford to lose another hunter.'

Fleet didn't want to find chunks of him scattered through the trees like Firn and, while it was hardly an expression of affection, it would do for now.

9

etwing waited a day after Siah's meeting with the Circle before she set out for Talith's tur, a delay she agreed to at Must's insistence. He had warned that anger would serve neither Fleet nor the Sceadu and had entreated her to let her temper cool, and it had, into a core of resentment, tempered by a frost of despair.

If Siah's dream had come to her many times, with each visitation more insistent than the last, then it was a dream of great power that couldn't be denied. Such a dream had once sent the Sceadu east on a journey over Ashali and into the kindly valleys of Berian-tur. Great good had come from that dream, for the Sceadu had left a place of desolation for one bright with fish-filled streams, but Siah's dream wasn't a dream of life; it was a dream of death.

Anger surged again as Ketwing mulled over the meeting. Even Must had raised his voice in the end but to no avail. The Circle could advise and debate but it was Siah who read the void's weft and warp to keep the Sceadu safe.

Ketwing picked her way down into the Fine streambed, still empty of everything but last snowmelt's detritus and, as she struggled up the other side, grimly considered how she had once taken such crossings in a single bound.

The sight of early greyberries cheered her and she gathered them as she walked, enjoying their tart squirt of juice until Talith's tur emerged from the trees. Fleet's tur now, for the time she had left.

Ketwing's skin told her the tur was empty but she pushed the door open anyway. The table held a handful of white-nuts and covers were piled high on the single chair. There was no waterpot, bowls, plates or mugs and her lips thinned. It was as if Fleet sensed she would never live there but then Ketwing dismissed the troubling notion. Fleet simply acted as she always had, oblivious to everything except the hunt.

Ketwing decided to wait despite knowing her return to the Great Turrel would be in darkness. Scead had visited more than once without seeing his agemate and Ketwing wanted to reassure herself Fleet was well.

She grunted as she lowered herself onto the doorstep, propped her weapons by the door, and thought of the happy times here with Talith. Fleet's mother had been amongst the most beautiful of her ageset and had chosen the handsome Brin as a husband. Air-named after the slithery bird of the garron forests, Brin's nature had been obvious to everyone *except* Talith and, for all Fleet's hunter acuity, she shared her mother's blindness.

There was a flick of movement in the lart and Ketwing hauled herself upright as Fleet made her way up the slope. In the haze of the setting sun, it seemed as if she gazed upon Talith, but then Fleet raised her head and the illusion vanished. Fleet's honed features were Brin's, as were her height and black eyes, but her grace was all her own.

Her face lit in a smile but she greeted Ketwing formally and led the way inside, tossing the sleep covers in the corner so that Ketwing could sit. Then she rebuilt the fire, set white-nuts on to roast, and settled at Ketwing's feet as she had so many times before.

Only the crack of flames broke the silence and Ketwing slid her hunting weapons from her shoulder. 'I've brought you a new bow and quiver,' she said.

Fleet looked at her in surprise. 'But they're yours.'

'I haven't used them for many snowmelts and it will save you the trouble of making new ones. It would make me happy for you to have them,' she added, as Fleet hesitated. Fleet nodded and laid them carefully at her side.

'Gifting my weapons isn't the only reason I came, Fleet,' said Ketwing and moistened her lips. 'I bring message from Siah.' Fleet's face hardened and Ketwing leaned forward. 'Spark is Siah now,' she said urgently. 'What's gone before, friendships or feuds, are as ash in the wind.'

'What does she want?'

'The dream has spoken. You are to come at dawn.'

Fleet looked away. A stranger might think her merely angry but Ketwing saw fear in her face too. She yearned to warn Fleet of what was to come but only a Siah could voice the void's demands.

'Being air-named is more difficult than being earth-named,' she said instead. 'But it's the Sceadu way, Fleet, and you are Sceadu; remember that.'

Tor's thoughts were also on Fleet as he wandered about his tur. He hadn't seen her since he'd salved her face *and* kissed her, but if hunters didn't find a Willing beast soon, he would need to take her on hunt. Not *need*, he corrected, for he could hunt alone; it was more a case of *want*.

He grimaced. Soon he would be loitering around Fleet's tur like he had loitered around Serest's, although Serest had welcomed his presence *and* Snowhawk's, as it turned out. He managed to still the surge of ill will. It was Serest's nature to want attention and even as youngsters, she had sought out Moss or Ember when he and Snowhawk hunted. He doubted she would be happy sharing Snowhawk with Mist for the same reason.

Fleet couldn't be more different. Hunting required long periods alone but Tor had seen Fleet solitary enough to know she was content in her own company. Even Scead had failed to hold her in Berian-tur and Tor wondered if her solitariness were the cause for her delayed air-naming. Even the dull-witted she-who-had-been Song now answered to the air-name of Mirian, after the sluggish streams of the Drylands.

A knock interrupted his thoughts and, despite knowing it was unlikely, his heart leapt at the possibility it was Fleet. It wasn't, it was Serest, and he gasped. Her face was bare of the marriage line.

'I've made a terrible mistake,' she said, and collapsed sobbing into his arms.

Tor woke with Serest's silken hair loose against his chest and stroked it gently as he wondered if he had been wrong to take her in love. But in truth, it had been *she* who had taken him. One moment she had been weeping in his arms and the next her salty mouth had fastened on his and her hands roved up and down under his shirt. She had been quick and unhesitating and, in the moments before desire had swamped reason, he'd wondered whether Snowhawk had taught her such skills.

Even as he considered the possibility, she stretched sleepily, arching her back so that her breasts pressed against him. 'We need to talk,' he said, somehow managing to pull away, but Serest's fingers slid down over his belly.

'Later,' she murmured.

'Later,' he agreed, and surrendered to the delicious throb of his body.

It was nearer midday when he rose and tossed the last of the dried fish into a pan with nut oil and jar-spur. Aromas filled the tur and his rumbling stomach reminded him of Fleet's in the Whitelands. His courting of her hadn't survived the night and nor, he feared, had his hunter bond with Snowhawk.

'You look troubled,' said Serest. She had propped on her elbow, careless that the cover had slipped below her breasts.

'I was thinking of Snowhawk,' he said, unable to tear his gaze from her.

'I'm disappointed you weren't thinking of me.'

'I'm thinking of you now,' he said, and wondered how many times it was possible to make love in single day.

Serest smiled, dressed and settled beside him. 'That smells inviting,' she said. 'You always were a fine cook.'

'But not fine enough to tempt you to my tur.'

The words were blunter than he'd intended, but Serest seemed unconcerned. 'Now that I have been tempted, I'm sorry it took so long,' she said.

Tor divided the pan's contents between two platters and handed her one. 'Why *have* you come?' he asked as they ate.

'Snowhawk was a mistake, but we haven't married so

there's no harm done.' Tor doubted it, given the pain Serest's rejection had inflicted on *him*, but Serest dismissed his concerns over Snowhawk's feelings. 'He doesn't want a wife,' she said. 'He has a lover.'

'A lover? I don't think—'

'Pairing outside marriage is more common than people think. I've heard you're keeping company with a hunter from the Turrel's last ageset, a tall girl named Flight.'

'Fleet,' corrected Tor, again rueing Berian-tur's gossips. 'But it's hardly the same thing. Fleet hasn't lived in my tur or been on the verge of marrying me.' He paused. 'Neither have you.'

'I'm considering both now,' said Serest softly. A few moons ago her words would have filled Tor with joy but doubts gnawed. 'Don't you want me either?' she asked, as he hesitated.

'I've always wanted you,' he admitted. 'It just concerns me that until yesterday, you wanted Snowhawk.'

'Snowhawk's handsome, to be sure. All the women admire him *and* many of the men,' she added dryly. 'And he's been a good friend to me, *to us*, in all the snowmelts of the Turrels and since. I just mistook his kindness for something else, that's all.'

'So, you've come back to a *less* handsome man,' said Tor.

'I've come back to a man who has also been a friend and who might want me as his wife. He's certainly a man I want as a husband.'

Tor wanted to avoid the acrimony he had witnessed between Fleet, Siah and Scead and wondered if he should insist Serest think through what she *really* wanted, rather than running to him in response to what might be an imagined slight. But Serest was named after the snow that surged down Ashali's slopes and waiting wasn't in her nature.

She leaned over and brought her mouth to his and, as her intimate scent enveloped him, Tor could see no reason to wait either.

10

Fleet was rigid, the pallet at her back preventing retreat and Must's patterning-blade insisting on stillness. How she had yearned for this day. To be air-named a woman; to know her life task as a hunter; to marry Ashin. Fleet's fists clenched and Must hissed for her to be still.

He refilled the blade with dye and the jabs of pain continued, falling into the same rhythm as the chanting in the hall outside. Dreams drew her into their glittering embrace and she was aware of nothing more until the chill touch of water roused her. Must had finished his work, she numbly realised, and rinsed the blood from her face.

He put the cloth aside and she managed to sit and then, unexpectedly, he gripped her hands. 'Fleet . . .' he began but stopped, then turned and hurried away.

Fleet's hand went to the empty knife sheath at her belt and then she half shook her head in confusion. The Seeing-Place was in the very heart of Berian-tur and Berian-tur was safe. The chanting quickened, as did her heart, and she slipped off the pallet and braced herself as the solemn faces of the Circle appeared around the curved wall.

Nima the gatherer came first, partnered by Turan the wood-worker, then Sai the keeper of songs with Prin the weaver, Talin the healer with Win the metal-smith and finally Ket, accompanied by Must. Only Ket's eyes met hers and they were filled with pity.

Fleet's confusion grew but she dropped to her knees as she must and waited. The Circle waited too as Siah and her husband advanced into the Seeing-Place. Fleet knew the void had gifted her agemates new selves but nothing prepared her for the sight of them together.

Scead was as she remembered but Siah was scarcely recognisable. Her honed face made her eyes appear huge and power flickered like flame over her translucent skin, but what held Fleet's gaze was her arm linked possessively through Scead's.

They came to a stop in front of her and Siah stepped forward and raised her arms in a sweeping gesture of embrace. Fleet kept her attention on Scead. It helped her endure Siah's presence but she also wanted to remind him he'd made a mistake in choosing Siah over her.

'The tarn has given you, the water taken you, the earth named you,' intoned Siah solemnly, using the phrases Fleet remembered from her earth-naming ceremony. It was a long time ago now, when friendships had been true.

'Now at the time of coming woman, now at the time of coming Sceadu, the void has spoken,' continued Siah, and paused. The Circle stirred like the Redlands in wind but Fleet kept her attention on Scead.

'The void sends a teller of tales to weave new ways of doing for the Sceadu. We give back to the void she who was Fleet and we receive from the void, she who is Chant.'

The name smashed into Fleet's consciousness like a stone through ice. She was to be a messenger, *not* a hunter, *not* of the wild, open places! Fury ignited and she leapt to her feet. 'You are mistaken!'

'The dream tells truly.'

'*You* are mistaken!'

There was utter silence and then Ket's voice boomed. 'Kneel, Fleet!'

Fleet whirled. 'Ket, I—'

'Would you insult those who let you grow?' her hunter guide demanded. 'Would you insult the Sceadu? You *will* kneel!'

Blood roared in Fleet's ears and she stumbled back to her knees.

'It seemed strange to me that one so skilled in hunting should be given such a name,' acknowledged Siah, 'and so I searched the void many times and it has spoken many times, and always it is the same, Chant.'

Fleet kept her head down, desperate to be gone from this

place of betrayal, but Siah's next words weren't the words of ending. 'I have spoken with the Circle, Chant, not because I doubt what the void sends, but because the dreams speak of more than naming. Snowcome consumes snowmelt and the ice withholds its water. Unless the streams flow, the Sceadu cannot live, no matter the skill of the hunter.'

The Circle murmured agreement but all Fleet's attention was focussed on not fleeing.

'The dreams speak of a great tarn many days to the west,' continued Siah. 'At this place lies something that will unlock the snowcome ice. It is there you must go, Chant.'

Siah's words penetrated Fleet's panicked brain and her head jerked up. 'There's no way over the mountains.' Her voice held no anger; even the smallest Little Sister knew that.

'I have seen you there on the edge of that great tarn,' said Siah with such conviction that for a moment Fleet believed the vision to be true, but then she glanced back to Scead.

'There's no way over the mountains,' she spat. 'You send me to my death!'

The Circle gasped at the insult but Siah's eyes flashed to fire. '*Do not* speak to *me* of what I do or do not do!' she thundered. 'I have seen where the crowns of alien forests pierce the sky and where berian travel in the dark places under the earth, and I tell you, Chant, that you *will* go to that place in the west, and that you *will* return. I have seen it and it *will* be so!'

There was utter silence and as the fire in Siah's eyes sank to a smoulder, she brought her arms down in a gesture of finality and spoke the words of ending. 'The void has taken and the void given back. The Sceadu give welcome.'

Ketwing sat on the seat in the clearing, so still that starwings squabbled over a black-moth carcass at her feet. Logic told her regret was as useless as wishing the snowcome ice away but still she brooded over the naming ceremony. She had never seen such an ill-fitting air-name bestowed nor so perilous a life task assigned. Everyone knew Ashali was impassable and yet that was the path Siah had set for Chant and Ketwing the hunter had been party to its madness.

She winced as she recalled how Chant had sought her aid and how she had denied it and yet she had acted as she must. To have allowed Chant to break the naming ceremony would have been to leave her in a place more desolate than the Whitelands, neither of the girls' Turrel nor truly a woman, and never to be a full member of the Sceadu community.

Ketwing sighed as she searched her memory for something that might help. When she had been in the girls' Turrel, the Aunts had spoken of a time when the Sceadu had roamed far beyond the Redlands; when fish had swum in the streams even in the deepest part of snowcome; and when strangers had come over Ashali.

Ketwing stiffened. If strangers *had* breached Ashali, there must have been paths, and they would still be there, in the Sceadu chants and songs, if not discernible in the mountains.

She hauled herself upright, oblivious to the starwings' scatter. She would seek out Sai and her knowing of the oldest songs and together they would search for what the songs told. Chant might have to find a way over Ashali alone, but she need not do it without aid, not while Ketwing the hunter had strength left in her bones.

Fleet used every shred of her strength and speed to take her as far as possible from Siah's falseness and the Circle's complicity and, as dusk turned to night, she still lay where she had flung herself. Her only witnesses were murrow early from their burrows and white-hares late to theirs, but as dew settled on her clothes, her hunter self harried her with demands for shelter.

Anger propelled her upright and she set off swiftly downslope. A chet sharpened its claws on a fyr but Fleet passed unnoticed, delighting in the hunter skills Siah sought to rob her of. She was so quiet that she was all but on Snowhawk and his companion before she saw them.

They scrambled up, hastily adjusting their clothes and Fleet blinked as she realised Snowhawk's trysting partner wasn't Serest. Chinks of She the Moon's light revealed Snowhawk's grim expression and, as his lover shrank against him, the flight of the snowhawks came back to her, cock-bird with cock-bird.

'I greet you, Snowhawk,' she said, belatedly remembering her manners.

'I greet you Fl . . .' he began and peered at her face. 'What are you air-named?'

'Chant,' she mumbled, finding it hard to utter the name. 'But Siah saw falsely and would have me something I am not.'

'I know what it is to live like that,' said Snowhawk, 'but I haven't been misnamed.'

'No,' said Fleet uncomfortably.

'Will you tell of what you've seen?' he asked directly.

Fleet knew little of Snowhawk beyond him being one of Berian-tur's best hunters *and* that he had stolen the woman Tor loved. She hadn't really considered Tor's feelings before, even when he had spoken of them openly, but Siah's theft of Scead gave her a deeper understanding.

'You should tell Serest you don't love her,' she said, wanting Tor to have the happiness denied her.

'It's hard to tell someone who loves you that you can't return their love.'

Snowhawk's words struck an uneasy chord and Fleet moved restlessly. 'I won't speak of tonight,' she said and, cutting short Snowhawk's thanks, hurried away. The day had been long and she yearned for sleep, but when she finally reached Talith's tur, someone waited for her.

Scead watched Chant's approach, struck afresh by the differences between his agemates. Chant was like sunlight glancing off ice while Siah was akin to the gentle rains of snowmelt, or not so gentle, he amended proudly, as he recalled her battles with the Circle. Of course, the Circle hadn't questioned her ability to travel the dreamways, just her understanding of them.

She is very young in her art, Must had said. Scead smiled mirthlessly. Siah had known of her path since a Little Sister; she wasn't young in *anything*.

He carried an aperion hide that Siah gifted to Chant. *The*

task that lies before Chant is extraordinarily perilous, his wife had said. *She must leave knowing your love and friendship awaits her return. Chant must know this*, she had emphasised.

'And *your* love and friendship,' Scead had reminded her.

Siah had smiled sadly. *Chant will never believe that.*

Chant's face had softened and Scead took a deep breath. 'I greet you, Chant,' he said.

'My name is Fleet,' she retorted, all softness vanishing.

'You don't need me to explain the nature of air-naming,' he said gently. 'Even Little Sisters are well versed in it. The void has taken back she-who-was Fleet and gifted us she-who-is Chant. To refuse the gift of the new self is to live between earth-name and air-name, as insubstantial as the Redlands' mist. I wouldn't wish that on anyone, least of all you, agemate.'

'No, you'd rather I died in the Whitelands!'

'The dream-vision says you will return.'

'*Siah* says I will return. No one knows what the dream sends or indeed, whether such a dream exists.'

Scead had been prepared for Chant's antagonism but the depth of the insult rocked him. Siah endured the agony of the void to keep the Sceadu safe and to suggest that any Siah would lie, that *his* wife would lie . . .

Only Siah's warnings stopped him from striding away but it was hard to keep the anger from his voice. 'I know you're distressed by your naming *and* by your task, Chant, so I forgive your words,' he gritted, and proffered the hide. 'Siah gifts you this to make your tur more comfortable for your return.'

Chant ignored the gesture and stepped closer, her eyes catching She the Moon's light. 'I know you better than Siah will *ever* know you, Scead, better even than you know yourself. Before the next snowmelt, you will understand what true love is and break this marriage.'

Despite his best efforts, Scead's temper flared. 'Do you think me so faithless I would marry on a whim? Don't confuse me with your father, Chant, *or* with your Little Sister notions of love.'

'Those are Siah's words, not yours! She whispers in your ear to—'

'Enough!' he roared. The silence brittled and he placed the aperion hide on the ground and stepped back. 'If I don't see you again before you depart, I wish you a safe journey and will wait, as all the Sceadu will, with love in our hearts for your return.'

Fleet still glared into the darkness long after Scead had disappeared into the night. He was too tender-hearted to see what was obvious to everyone in Berian-tur and Siah didn't fool anyone either. The Circle's unease had been clear during the ceremony but they had bowed to Siah, as they must, and Siah had taken what she wanted, Scead, in this case, and set her rival a lethal task.

Fleet snatched up the hide and strode the rest of the way up to the tur. It was freezing inside and she tossed the hide on the sleep covers in the corner and rebuilt the fire. But even the flames failed to cheer her and she found herself longing for the noisy camaraderie of the girls' Turrel.

Yet those days had gone. Some of her ageset had even married but Fleet couldn't marry, even if Scead admitted his mistake, because Siah had made Fleet's adulthood dependent on an impossible task. Clever, cunning Siah!

Fleet threw another armful of cones on the fire. She wanted a blaze that would shout her defiance to all of Berian-tur, but her desolation remained and she wearily dragged a cover from the pile and dislodged the pelt. It rolled down and came to rest at her feet and she flicked it open.

It glistened in the firelight but Fleet took no pleasure in it. Scead said she could use the hide to make her tur more comfortable but Scead and Siah were already comfortable *in each other's arms*! With a howl of fury, Fleet flung the hide from her and then time seemed to slow. She watched it arc through the air and descend, as gently as snowflake, *onto the fire*!

Fleet gasped and darted forward, but the flames were already high and their scorch held her at bay, and then they roared higher still, found the hide's fat, and devoured it.

11

Tor slammed the door shut behind him and stood, hands on hips, staring down at the lart. The firestone had been cold to the ground which meant the fire hadn't been lit for days and his jaw clenched as he wondered whether Fleet lay injured somewhere. He should have sought her out sooner but Snow-hawk had killed. He grimaced. That wasn't the reason he had kept away, he conceded. The last weeks with Serest had been the happiest of his life and he had been loath to tell Fleet he no longer desired her company.

He set off down the slope, kicking lart cones from his path and hadn't gone far when crystaleyes warned of someone or *something's* approach. He waited with an arrow set but it was Ketwing who appeared and he hastened forward to save her fur-ther travel. Knowing Ketwing had endured great pain to reach Fleet's tur, added to his worries.

He helped her settle on a fallen lart and briefly outlined his fears for Fleet' safety but astonishingly, Ketwing didn't share them. 'She-who-was Fleet is now Chant and her life task is to cross Ashali to a great tarn in the west. As her tur is deserted, it's likely she has already set out.'

'*Cross* Ashali?' repeated Tor, wondering if he had misheard.

'Her air-naming was a moon-third ago,' continued Ketwing calmly. 'I've spent the time since with Sai and other keepers of songs and chants, in search of tales of how Ashali was crossed in more recent times and might be crossed again. There must be a way over, despite the snow, or else the void wouldn't have demanded Chant go that way to return water to our streambeds.'

'But . . . even if it *were* possible to cross Ashali, it's not possible to change the seasons,' said Tor.

'Siah disagrees.'

Tor took several agitated steps away and swung back. 'And Fl—Chant agreed to this task?'

'No and would have broken the naming ceremony had I not prevented it.'

'I should have come earlier,' muttered Tor. 'She saved my life and now I've failed to save hers.'

'We both know nothing can be done once the void gifts Siah a dream *and* the consequences of refusing the new self *or* task. I hoped to aid Chant, not turn her aside from what she must do, but my search took too long.' Ketwing's ancient face crumpled for a moment before she managed to steady. 'And yet Chant made no farewells,' she murmured. 'Are you sure she's not on hunt?'

'It's been too long,' said Tor. 'And why make farewells when you go to your death?'

'Because it is the right and proper thing to do,' said Ketwing, her dark eyes fixed on his. 'Our lives are woven about by the void, Tor, and the Siahs given to guide our understanding of its warp and weft. The young sometimes doubt the veracity of Siahs but the old have learned to trust.'

'I would have gone with her on this journey,' said Tor, but as his thoughts turned to Serest, he wondered if it were true.

'And I might have found the songs to guide her,' said Ketwing, 'but Chant waited for neither of us, perhaps as the void intended.'

'Or her impetuousness dictated,' said Tor, pacing again.

'Whatever the case, I will rest here a while before starting back. I don't ask that you to wait with me.'

Tor took his leave, knowing that despite Ketwing's deference to the void, she needed time to grieve for the young hunter she had guided. He needed time as well to find sense in what had happened. Meanwhile, he had another visit to make, this time to Snowhawk's tur, and he feared it would bring him just as little joy.

Fleet was high in the Whitelands when she heard the sound she feared most. She was too weary to run; all she could do was crouch and cover her head with her arms. The snow vibrated under her feet but the spur's height kept her safe, and the serest thundered down the valley behind. Still, she was so shaken it took her a long time to drag her attention back to the beast she hunted.

It bore no scent and left no print but she had kept pace with it for many days. She had almost lost it in the Redlands' shadows but it had grown strong again in the Whitelands' bright light and, as time had passed, Fleet had fooled herself into believing it *could* be hunted and that, at hunt's end, she *could* turn back to Berian-tur's safety.

But now her heart whispered of the foolishness of such beliefs. She was like a slain chet or scinton that jerked and twitched in a bizarre parody of life. Panic threatened and she forced her attention back to the beast. She had journeyed this far only because she'd kept her fear trapped like water under tarn ice. To let the thaw of truth come even now, would mean to be truly lost.

The sun climbed the sky even as Fleet climbed the mountain and as the shadow-beast shrank to a puddle under her feet, she finally raised her eyes. Ashali soared above her: huge, white and terrible. There was no way over. She was engulfed in a wave of despair and was so weary, all she wanted was to lie down and die.

Surely it made no difference whether she paid her debt to Talabraith here or further on? But Ket's stern voice intruded: *a hunter does not turn aside; a hunter goes on until the end.*

Fleet trudged on and as darkness fell, a small wind woke. It whispered across the slope and spoke of nothing that grew or yearned or feared. It lifted the snow into spiralling columns and sent them this way and that. Fleet followed them with eager eyes for to think of them was not to think of death.

Some snowy columns were large and fully formed while others barely took shape before the wind tossed them back into the night. Occasionally flurries were born near each other and then their dance took on the intensity of the hunt, until the wind tore them apart, to leave Fleet alone again.

She was going to her death alone. It was rare for Sceadu to die thus; the old gathered their agemates around them and the young were held close. Why was she doing this? Why had she left the warmth of the Redlands for this frigid wasteland? Not for the flawed Siah, not even for the Sceadu, but for Talabraith.

From the moment the fire had devoured the hide, wasting the Willing beast's gift, her path had been set. Now *she* must make gift, must herself be Willing, but she wasn't Willing; her heart held only the bitterest resentment.

Something moved on the slope ahead and Fleet stopped, dashed the snow from her eyes and strained into the gloom. Within the darkness was a deeper darkness. Fleet gasped. It was a massive she-berian! Had the void sent *her* to take Fleet into death?

The berian turned and for a moment outside time, each regarded the other, and then the berian moved off and, desperate not to be alone, Fleet struggled after it. The wind moaned and the snow eddied and whirled, so thick it seemed the berian walked upon air and Fleet did too. Earth and sky became one and the ice a deadly embrace.

A seductive languor invaded her body and she swayed, staggered and pitched forward. The impact jolted Fleet back into awareness and she struggled to her knees and stared about. The berian was gone. Fleet clawed her way upright and staggered on. One step, two steps and then the snow collapsed in upon itself and, with a terrified scream, she plunged into oblivion.

Tel flung himself from his bed and was out in the corral's cool air before he realised the snarl of bears had come from *within* his dream. He took a steadying breath, grateful that Islan still slept, *and* the rest of the Stead, judging from the quiet of the neighbouring corrals. The last thing he wanted were witnesses to his bizarre behaviour. Then the door behind him creaked and he tensed. It seemed Islan didn't sleep after all.

'What troubles you, Tel?'

'Go back to bed,' he said, keeping his face to the mountains. 'I'm going to stretch my legs.'

'Are you going to the ford? Can I come too?'

'No and no,' he snapped and as the silence stretched, softened his voice. 'In a few days perhaps,' he said, and strode off. The stars faded around Ashali's peak as he set off along the eastern path but he didn't go far before he turned up a steep, stony track all but lost amongst the silverwort.

Early honeyapple blossoms were visible through the trees and the orchards would soon be abuzz with the honey-makers and, if the weather stayed favourable, fruit would set, swell and sweeten.

The tangled silverwort confirmed no one had used the track since his last foray; the Sunnen content to stay near their own corrals and gardens, *except* for the males of *his* line. Tel grimaced as considered his grandfather and father's restless urges *and* his own and swore as briars snagged his jacket. If the dream hadn't robbed him of his wits, he would have brought his knife to hack a way through.

Ashali's snowy peak had blushed pink by the time the track delivered him to the top of the small hill and he stared over the honeycomb of corrals that enclosed each family's stays, and the patchwork of gardens and orchards that clothed the valley's sides. But mist lingered in soft grey streamers and hid the stonestreams, the very things he had come to see.

Tel had devised them to provide for his own gardens but they had ensured plenty for the gardens of others in the Stead too and earned praise from the Council. It had made Merala proud of him and inspired admiration in Islan but it had also attracted less welcome attention.

He scowled as he considered the recent visit of Sal's wife Galena. She had sought advice on the marriage of her daughter Nasala. While it was usual for Sunnen to marry within the Stead, there were suitable matches amongst their kin the Meduin and the Okianos. Tel was one of the few Sunnen to have visited the Okianos, who dwelt in the flat valleys near the sea, and he had described the provisioning needed for journeys to them, and to the closer Meduin.

Galena had listened intently and thanked him afterwards but Tel had found the interview unsettling and had spoken of it later to Tanalan and Merala. Tanalan had scoffed at the idea Galena sought a husband for Nasala amongst the Okianos. *The candidate is much closer to home*, she had smirked. Merala had hissed at her daughter's impudence but Tel had an uncomfortable feeling his sister had been right.

Tel took a quick round of the hill. He wasn't ready to marry *yet*, if indeed he ever would be; a mother, brother and two sisters more than enough to care for. Not that he disliked being head of corral, or his life in the Sunnen Stead, it was just that . . .

He came to a stop and sighed. Lately he had come to fear he would still be standing on this hill as an old man, having spent his entire life repeating a single season of living. A desire had grown in him to go east, deep into the snow, but he couldn't; no one could. In past seasons, bears had come from the mountains, crossed the Sunwash and invaded the Stead. They had smashed the gardens, trampled the berrem, and torn down the fruiting trees.

The Council had come to him for advice and again he hadn't failed them. Tel's grandfather had been a wanderer in strange lands and had seen things beyond the imaginings of most Sunnen. He had spoken of them to his son Barin, and Barin in turn, to his son Tel. The traps Tel devised were of metal: heavy, toothed and chained, and had been set above the Sunwash along the bear trails, and in the dark, tangled growth to either side. Even Tel, who had helped lay them, had no clear memory of where they were. To go east was to invite injury and death.

Tel strode back down the track, venting his frustration on the silverwort. If Barin hadn't paid a second *unnecessary* visit to the Okianos *and* died there when Tel was twelve, Tel wouldn't have had to take responsibility for the corral *and* come to the attention of women like Galena.

He mulled over his duties as he went and then his mood suddenly lightened. As head of corral, he was *obliged* to pay his respects to his kin and while he had visited the Meduin several times, he had only exchanged greetings with Turai and her Okianos husband once, after his father's death.

The journey to the Okianos Stead was difficult but had one major advantage: it would remove him from the appraising eyes of women like Galena for many, many days.

12

*F*leet plummeted through the darkness, glanced off an ice-slicked wall, and plunged into an enormous mound of snow. The impact flung plumes of it into the air and then the mound rolled her down its side onto the cavern floor.

Fleet lay gasping on her back while above her, snow swirled in from the crevice to rebuild the mound her fall had disrupted. It was this mountain within a mountain that had saved her, but Fleet didn't know whether to be grateful. Landing on stone would have repaid her debt to Talabraith quickly and cleanly, but now a slower, more painful death probably awaited her. And yet, despite everything, hope flared.

Her shoulder throbbed from her clash with the wall but she was otherwise unhurt and she could taste the scent of berian in the air! They were older than the Sceadu and their knowing wise; if berian had come this way, there must be a way out. But it wasn't back through the crevice in the roof, it was too high, and before she could start any search, she needed to eat and rest.

She retrieved some dried sherenberries and her waterskin from her pack with her right hand, her shoulder making her hunting hand too painful to use and settled against the wall to eat. The sweet berries and fragrant water reminded her of the sunlit world she had left behind, bringing comfort and, when she had finished, she pulled her jacket close, curled up on the stone and slept.

Tor was close to Snowhawk's tur when Scead emerged from the fyrs carrying a bulging herbal sling. Scead greeted Tor courteously, despite clearly being in a hurry.

'You've made a good harvest considering how chill it still is,' said Tor politely.

Scead nodded. 'But coolbright and whitewand aren't sufficient to reduce fever. For that I need sourslip and sourslip needs snowmelt.'

'Siah is unwell again?'

Scead's lips bent in a smile that failed to reach his eyes. 'Few understand the price of entering the void's dreamscapes.'

'There are pockets south of the Fine streamed that catch enough sun for grey- and sherenberries to ripen, even now. You might try there.'

'I will,' said Scead, brightening. 'Thank you, Tor,' he added, and hurried away.

Scead's anxiety added to Tor's tension as he neared Snowhawk's tur. Smoke told him Snowhawk was within and he propped his hunting weapons near the door. Tor had felt no ill will towards Snowhawk when Serest had been with him, but he was unsure if the reverse were true and, if they came to blows, he didn't want weapons involved.

But Snowhawk seemed genuinely pleased to see him and Tor's tension eased as they settled by the fire. The tur smelled of dye and Snowhawk's fingers were stained purple. 'I had forgotten how messy dyeing is,' said Snowhawk, as he gave the dye pot a stir, 'but Serest complained about the dullness of the bed-cover and I'm inclined to agree.'

Tor looked at his agemate sharply wondering if Snowhawk sent him a message by mentioning Serest and the bed in the same sentence. Tor had never known Snowhawk to practice deceit but doubt niggled. 'You know Serest is with me?' he said bluntly.

'Well I know she isn't here.'

'We are lovers and will marry.' Tor braced but Snowhawk simply looked thoughtful. The window's light intensified the blue of his eyes and bleached his blond hair almost white, reminding Tor of Serest's description of him as *handsome*.

'Do you have faith in the veracity of Siahs?' asked Snowhawk unexpectedly.

'Yes . . . of course.'

Snowhawk smiled. 'You don't sound like you do.'

'When a hunter can be air-named Chant . . .'

'I agree Chant's an odd name for a hunter, but she's young and it might still prove apt. As for we three . . .' Snowhawk paused to stir the dye. 'In their rush down the mountains, serests turn everything awry and yet without them, Berian-tur would be as barren as the Drylands. And while a tor is strong enough to endure snowcome's winds, its fate is to stand alone.'

Snowhawk smiled again as if to ease his words but Tor's heart pounded. 'And the snowhawk?' he challenged.

'Ah well,' said Snowhawk, intent on the dye. 'The cock-bird's plumage is much admired and yet it can be so lost that it seeks its own kind as a mate.'

'So, you see Serest as someone who hurts others and me as doomed to be alone?'

'I was simply musing on our names and that names can mean more than one thing. Hunting isn't confined to seeking beasts, Tor. Chanters hunt words to tell of what has gone and what is yet to come, just as Siahs hunt the void.' Tor made no response and Snowhawk set the dye pot aside and cleaned his hands. 'If Serest is with you, Tor, and that makes you both happy, then I am happy too.'

'You don't mind?'

'I love Serest and I love you, agemate. How could I possibly mind? The only thing that matters is that our love for each other endures, isn't it?' Snowhawk's tone was bantering but Tor was surprised to see fear in his eyes.

'Yes,' he said, and gripped his agemate's arm reassuringly. 'That's all that matters.'

Fleet woke to a dazzling shaft of sunlight. It streamed in through the roof to douse the mound with white fire and send spectral images swarming from the cavern's corners. Fleet cried out and threw up her hand and then, mercifully, the sun shifted and the spectres vanished. Unnerved, Fleet scrambled to her feet.

Her shoulder throbbed and it took her a moment to steady. The daylight revealed the cavern to be the size of Fleet's tur, but it would have proved useless as shelter; its sides pocked with openings. Some were as large and airy as berian dens while others were little more than cracks.

The scent of berian was strong and Fleet searched for signs of them, relieved to find scats and coarse hair at one of the larger openings. The scats weren't fresh but she remained cautious as she peered in. The light showed a tunnel that stretched away into darkness but Fleet had no idea how long it was or whether berian lurked around the first corner.

Fleet was no stranger to journeying at night, for hunters roamed far, but star-sheen intruded even under the densest leaf-roof or She the Moon's light, while here there was nothing. Fleet moved restlessly but her choices were clear: stay where she was and die of starvation, or go into the darkness, *and still die*, a voice in head sneered. Despair threatened but then she tossed back her hair. She was a hunter! Hunters tracked scent to its end, no matter how long, no matter the cost!

With a last glance at the light-filled cavern, Fleet set off down the tunnel and, as the darkness closed in, used her right hand to guide herself along the wall. The stone was smooth under foot but a fear grew it that might suddenly give way to a chasm or water-filled pit.

Fleet couldn't swim and as a Little Sister had watched in horrified fascination as snowmelt's first waters thundered down the empty streambeds. The torrent carried everything before it, including the unwary, and Fleet couldn't imagine a more horrible way to return to the void.

She came to a stop, having to keep her foot wedged against the wall to prevent her losing direction. The silence was absolute and she wondered if death were like this and then bizarrely, whether she *had* died in her plunge into the cavern. It would explain the spectral forms, she realised in horror, but then the smell of berian pulled her back to the sunlit world above and woke a determination to return to Berian-tur.

She must atone for her breaking of Talabraith, she reminded herself, and slumped against the wall. The darkness pressed in and then she straightened. The void would reclaim her when it saw fit, she decided, and she wouldn't pre-empt it by being reckless. She retrieved an arrow from her quiver and tapped its barbed head experimentally on the floor. It gave a pleasing ring and she went on, tapping the floor in front of her.

She ate when she was hungry and slept when she was weary but mostly she walked. Sometimes she was seized by a fear she would never again feel the bite of snow-fresh air on her face, and then she drew on every shred of her hunter strength to keep walking. Berian had found a way through, she repeated like a mantra, and she would too.

It was sometime after her fourth sleep that Fleet sensed the air shift. She felt like sobbing in relief but forced herself not to hurry, knowing she could still be overtaken by some catastrophe. The wall of the tunnel twisted sharply and then she was dazzled by light. If berian had been there, her momentary blindness might have proved fatal, but what confronted her now was just as deadly. The tunnel ended in a *solid wall of stone.*

13

*F*leet stared at the wall in dismay. It held no gaps big enough for even a murrow to squeeze through, let alone a berian, and the light source, a narrow opening in the tunnel's side, was too small as well. She must have missed the main exit in the dark but she dismissed the idea of retracing her steps. There was no guarantee she wouldn't miss the exit a second time *and* lose the berian scent.

She turned back to the light source. The opening also delivered fragrant air and desperate to escape the clammy darkness, Fleet pushed her pack inside and clambered in after it. The tunnel was even narrower inside and the circle of light at its far end seemed a long way off. She inched along on her back, using her arms to shove her pack along ahead of her, while the tunnel walls scraped and skinned her.

It was hard going and she was almost to the end when a terrifying thought brought her to a stop. What if the tunnel exited high above the ground? Or from a cliff-face? There were dark openings on Ashali's sheer sides visible during snowmelt and so high only gyars and snowhawks nested there. What if this tunnel were the same? Its ice-brittled edges ready to send her hurtling into space?

If she *did* fall, she had a better chance of grabbing onto something if she were on her stomach but her injured shoulder made grabbing onto *anything* unlikely. Even so, she decided to turn over, which was far from easy.

Her shoulder and hip hit the roof and she was horrified to feel the stone shift. Fleet held her breath as grit rained down, and then there was a sharp crack and the floor pitched downwards, and Fleet began to slide.

She clawed at the stone but her pack disappeared out the

end and with a choking cry, Fleet followed it. Her flight was mercifully brief and ended in a scrubby tree just below. The branches held her cradled and then, one by one, gave way so that Fleet descended in a series of undignified lurches to the ground.

She lay on her back amidst the woody wreckage and laughed in relief and at the sorry spectacle she must present but then her surroundings intruded and she rolled up into a crouch and drew her knife.

The air was unseasonably warm and so sweet she expected to see talith in full flower but she recognised nothing. Small green birds darted amongst bushes bright with snowmelt foliage, and purple fruit glowed on a scatter of darker shrubs. Fleet straightened but kept her hand on her knife. There were groves of ashin and fyr downslope, but in full bloom, and she frowned in confusion. Ashin and fyr didn't flower for another moon. And then her skin woke.

She crouched and turned as she would had a scinton been near and for a moment, had no idea what she looked at. And then she gasped. Ashali soared above her, familiar and yet *unfamiliar*. It was Ashali's *western* face! She had crossed the mountains!

Fleet staggered in shock. Was Siah to be proved right then? Was she to have Scead after all? A gyar called to the east, high and keening, and Fleet's chaotic thoughts swung to the Great Turrel. Meat would be roasting there *if* the hunter had killed; *if* the beast had been Willing; *if* Talabraith had been served. Understanding swamped her, as bitter as the snowcome winds. She might have crossed the mountains but nothing had changed at all.

Fleet spent the night in the familiarity of the ashin and fyr groves and woke to a breakfast of errem disks. She ate slowly, hoping to fool her belly into believing more food was coming, and tried not to think of how she would feed herself if her shoulder didn't mend.

One of the small green birds watched her, its beak opening and closing in a parody of eating, and Fleet smiled despite herself. Her debt to Talabraith remained unpaid but it was impossible to feel bleak when sunlight dappled the forest and honeyed-scents filled the air.

She left a crumb for the bird, hefted on her pack, and set off west. The fyrs and ashins were huge, their branches filled with green *and* yellow birds squabbling in the leaf-roof or tussling on the forest floor. Fleet found their antics distracting and was almost in the open before she realised the trees had given way to bushy grassland.

She drew back. The forest's abrupt ending was strange, as was the land that lay ahead. It ran away in a series of undulations and held an openness Fleet distrusted, but her waterskin was almost empty and she could hear the chime of water somewhere below.

She scanned and tasted the air before she left the trees *and* as she picked her way down, but the sight of the water scoured all thoughts of caution from her mind. It rushed along as if in late snowmelt, its force so great that it carved the banks away to expose the rough faces of boulders. Some had even tumbled into the streambed to form a natural crossing place.

Fleet must cross the stream to continue her journey west but she feared the water's force and there were other reasons she hesitated too. The stream was like a barrier between her and Scead, and between her and those she loved in Berian-tur. Fleet paced along the bank, knowing she must cross but decided to delay the inevitable by filling her waterskin first.

Tel stood with hands on hips as he stared back along the Sunwash's empty bank. 'The lone traveller is always the swiftest,' he muttered, having to stamp his feet to keep warm. Islan had been just behind him but had disappeared. Off chasing some creature or other, supposed Tel, as he paced up and down.

Only three seasons separated him from Islan but the gap seemed many times bigger. He needed Islan's help to manage the corral but he also craved the male friendship the early death of his father had robbed him of.

Time stretched and when Islan didn't appear, Tel decided to

wait for him at the ford, one of the few places that accessed the eastern bank. Tel had gone there often as a boy, hoping to see the dark shapes of bears roaming in the snowy distance. The sight had thrilled him but they hadn't stayed in the snowlands and he had been forced to devise the stinking traps.

His stomach tightened at the memory of the first bear his traps had caught. It had been little more than a cub, its eyes small and blind, its snout crusted with blood and it had taken Tel two clumsy attempts with his knife to end its suffering. He had vomited afterwards and sworn never to return and yet here he was again, having given in to Islan's badgering to search for bears.

Fleet filled her waterskin as quickly as possible, her gaze on the smoother flow of water at the stream's centre. It shone like ice, reflecting the ragged outlines of bushes on the opposite bank, but robbing them of form and colour. They reminded her of the phantoms burned neri bark roused and she hurried stoppered her waterskin, pushed it into her pack, and hefted it on.

The pack woke the pain in her shoulder and she hesitated. Even as a Little Brother, Scead had warned of the risks of unwashed wounds and while Fleet had no idea how bad her injury was, she couldn't afford to sicken. She slid off the pack, then her jacket and unbuttoned her shirt.

The actual wound was slight, unlike the bruising, which covered most of her shoulder, but her shirt pulled the scab away and the wound bled. Fleet laved chill water over it then glanced back to the stream and froze. The reflections had changed! Her hand went to her knife and she slowly raised her eyes.

A man stood on the opposite bank, as tall and strong as any Sceadu man, but without earth-name, air-name or marriage—the faceless man of her dreams! Fleet's hunter self screamed at her to flee but his gaze held her immobilised and then someone called to him and he half turned, breaking the nexus between them.

Fleet swept up her things and fled back up the slope, plunged through a dense stand of bushes and crouched motionless. *A moving beast is a seen beast* but when there were no sounds of pursuit, she crept back into the safety of the trees.

Was it really a man she had seen? He had been full grown but unpatterned. How was he connected to the void? To the sun-lit world? Had he been cast out for breaking the law of his place? For breaking Talabraith? The void swirled closer and Fleet's hands balled into fists. She hadn't been cast out! She was Scea-du, earth-named and . . .

Fleet drew a steadying breath. She had to cross the stream but the stranger made it too dangerous here and nor would he be the only stranger she might encounter. There could be many peoples between here and the *great tarn* Siah had spoken of, *if* such a tarn existed. Fleet swallowed dryly. Siah had said Fleet would return but Siah didn't know Fleet had broken Talabraith, and that changed everything.

She turned east again to follow the stream upslope to where its bed would narrow and while it was galling to backtrack, the detour might save her time in the long term. The day drew on and by dusk she was tired and dispirited. The stream showed no signs of narrowing and the next morning she reluctantly turned west again.

The sun had set before she reached the tumble of boulders and she waited out the last of the light in the trees' shelter. The stranger was probably long gone but Fleet wanted the cover of darkness to cross. She scanned the open slope while she waited and stilled. There was a berian path! Fleet's eyes narrowed.

The path was faint but ran from the trees behind her, through the scrubby bushes, and disappeared in the direction of the stream. Fleet hefted on her pack. So much was strange here that the berian path filled her with excitement, and she followed it down, careful not to trespass on it.

The pungent scent told her it was still in use and she hadn't gone far when she heard a growl. Fleet knew the berian voices for pleasure, hunger and warning but this growl made her skin crawl. She went on, careful to keep downwind and as the stench of scats filled the air, the bushes gave way to a circle of smashed wood.

Fleet gasped in horror. A great she-berian lay at its centre, her bloodied entrails strewn across the ground, her snout agape in agony. Old and weak beasts were vulnerable to wolf attack but this berian was neither and then Fleet saw its rear leg was caught by something dark and jagged.

Once on hunt, Fleet had come across the skeleton of a massive scinton. Its ribs had been scattered but its skull intact, each curved tooth in its jaw as perfect as She the Moon in crescent form. The teeth that held this berian were shaped the same but larger, stronger and made of metal. They were anchored too by heavy chains so that the berian *must* fall prey to wolves or hunger or thirst.

What man would do this? What hunter? None who bowed to the laws of Talabraith! Fleet winced, shamed by her own wasting, and pledged the berian a quick death for a slow one. The arrow was swift and true and, for once, she didn't retrieve it.

14

Tel stretched his long legs to the fire and sighed, pleasantly full after his meal of roasted white-root, berrem and stewed honeyapples. Inkala had fallen asleep on the rug at his feet, and he contemplated her rounded face and golden skin. They were very different to the woman's at the ford. Even without her tattooed cheeks, the woman's white skin and clothing marked her as a stranger *and* one that roamed east of the Sunwash, *where the traps were.*

'You look troubled,' said Tanalan.

'My muscles are sore,' muttered Tel, keeping his gaze on Inkala.

'Ah well, that will soon be mended. How long will you stay with the Meduin?'

'I haven't decided,' said Tel. In truth, he had forgotten he must pause his journey at the Meduin Stead to pay his respects.

'Take me with you.'

Tel looked up in surprise. Tanalan knew women didn't journey; that the gardens needed their labour. 'Your place is here.'

'My place is with Kanan. I want to see him to arrange my marriage rites.'

He had agreed to Tanalan's betrothal to Kanan, a member of their Meduin kin, but it was *his* prerogative to decide when the marriage took place. 'I will inform you when it's time to arrange any marriage rites,' he said coldly.

'And when might that be?'

Tel rarely lost his temper but Tanalan's challenge added to his anxiety over the stranger and he sprang from his seat. '*If* you marry, it will be at a time of *my* choosing,' he thundered, 'and you will *not* raise the matter again!'

He strode from the stay, startling Inkala who started to grizzle. Tanalan lifted her little sister onto her lap but, in truth, it was *she* who needed comforting. Tanalan stroked Inkala's hair as she considered Tel's outburst.

His anger was out of character, as was his threat to prevent her marriage. Islan had told her Tel called out in his sleep and had taken to early morning forays, sometimes as far as the ford. Tanalan scowled. Whatever bothered her elder brother wasn't helping her to see Kanan again! It was nearly two seasons since their pledge but circumstances had kept them apart since and now Tel forbade her from journeying, the very thing he intended to do himself!

Tanalan seethed at the injustice and then calmed. Once Tel had left, Islan would be in charge of the corral *or so he thought*. Her *little* brother could order the gardens and orchards however he liked, but he certainly wouldn't be ordering *her* about. With Tel gone she would be free to go as well.

Her eyes shone as she thought of Kanan. 'Soon, my love,' she whispered. 'Soon.'

Tel was a long way from sleep, thanks to Tanalan's impudence. He had cared for those of his corral since he was a boy and Tanalan's selfish wish to gratify her own desires infuriated him. The stranger added to his angst and he remained haunted by the sight of her fleeing *up towards the traps*.

She had to be going west, for the east held only empty snowlands, and that meant she had to cross the Sunwash at the ford, for there was nowhere else. Now that he considered it, she had probably been about to cross when he had frightened her away and had probably waited until he and Islan had finished their fruitless search for bears, then crossed and gone on her way. In fact, she was probably halfway to the Terecleft by now while he lay there fretting.

Tel's tension eased and he rolled over to face the door. He liked the wash of cool night air on his face and was considering the forage available on his journey to the Okianos when he slipped into sleep.

Fleet battered her bloodied hands against the thing that held her but its teeth had driven through the hide of her boot, the flesh of her ankle, and perhaps through the very bone itself. It wouldn't release her. Soon wolves would come for her as they had come for the she-berian and horror at its mutilation leant Fleet new strength. She clawed her way forward over the ground but then the chain jerked her leg taut and she screamed in agony.

Tel was woken by savage snarls. The corral was full of marauding bears: their eyes wild and deep, their claws long and sharp as they destroyed everything he had worked for. He hurled himself at them and one turned on him and sliced his shoulder to the bone. The pain was horrendous, but not as horrendous as knowing he had failed those in his care.

Tel's shame was so intense it woke him. He knew the bear attack was a dream but his sense of urgency grew and he barely responded to Islan's sleepy enquiry as he dashed from the stay and across the corral.

Then he was sprinting east along the path to the Sunwash. At some point he realised he'd brought no waterskin and that Islan followed, but whatever had driven him from his stay forced him on.

The next time awareness intruded the sun was high and Islan a long way behind him. Tel forced himself to wait but paced up and down in agitation. 'Did you bring a waterskin?' he demanded, as Islan drew near.

'I didn't think to,' said Islan, red-faced and resentful.

'We'll drink at the ford then,' said Tel, and ran on.

When he reached the tumble of boulders, he scrambled down the bank and scooped the water to his mouth, then dunked his head under its cool flow. Islan did the same and shook himself like a washrat.

The water seemed to quench whatever had taken possession of him and Tel stared up at Ashali in a desperate attempt to reclaim normality.

Birds circled, dark against the snowy slopes, and Islan followed his gaze. 'Carnon,' he said. 'Something dies in the ragwort.'

'Most likely a bear in the traps,' said Tel. He wished he'd forbidden Islan from coming but he had been in no state to forbid *anything*.

'I would like to see a bear living or dead,' said Islan.

That was because Islan had never seen the latter, concluded Tel sourly. 'Stay close,' he ordered, and made his way across the boulders. He selected a piece of washwood from the detritus, then led the way upslope, probing the bushes for traps.

They were about twenty lengths from the river when the bushes exploded and a pale shape flashed past. 'A wolf!' cried Islan in excitement.

Tel said nothing. The stench of rotting meat marked a clear trail and a little further on the ragwort gave way to flattened foliage. The scavengers had been busy, noted Tel in disgust. The bear's empty eye socket glared back at them and its bloodied rib cage showed stark against the black of hair and hide.

'Look at this,' said Islan. He was crouched over the bear's head and Tel joined him, trying not to draw the fetid air into his lungs. An arrow protruded from the bear's neck. 'That isn't a Sunnen arrow,' said Islan.

'No,' agreed Tel, but could think of nothing else to say.

Then Islan gripped his arm. 'Listen!'

Tel heard the Sunwash's mutter below and the carnons' discordant song above, and then he heard a long shuddering groan. Islan's horrified eyes came to his but Tel pushed past him. He didn't want to go on but he could no longer go back.

Fleet sensed the approach of a beast, drawn by her blood. Her quiver and bow were lost to the pain-filled darkness, but her knife was trapped beneath her and she laboriously worked her fingers towards it until her hand closed over the haft.

The beast's footfalls drew nearer and then it was turning her, testing her Willingness to die. She *wasn't* Willing! With the last of her strength, Fleet plunged the knife upwards.

Tel threw himself sideways but too late! The blade caught the arm of his shirt, hit flesh, and re-appeared slicked with blood from a rent in his shoulder. The pain was shocking but he slammed the woman's wrists into the ground and the knife spun away into the ragwort.

'Get her arrows *and* the knife,' he grunted, holding her pinned.

Islan scurried forward, dragged the quiver and bow from her, then searched the ragwort for the knife. He found it sticky with blood and dust. The woman was limp but Tel still held her, wondering if her quick surrender were some sort of trick. His brain had slowed, unlike the blood that streamed from his sleeve, to join the blood already there on the woman's jacket.

Islan was suddenly beside him. 'I must see to your shoulder, Tel. You're losing blood. Tel! You can let her go. She's fainted.'

Tel blinked hard in an attempt to clear his vision. 'I need to free the trap,' he said hoarsely.

'Shoulder first,' insisted Islan.

Tel was dully surprised by how surely Islan had taken charge and he watched as Islan tore strips from his shirt to bind the wound, but it seemed to make no difference. Dizziness swirled him around like a leaf in the Sunwash and then his vision failed completely and the darkness carried him away.

It was dusk when Tel came to himself, weak and shockingly thirsty. Islan still crouched beside him and Tel managed to sit up. 'Take the woman's waterskin back to the Sunwash and fill it,' he rasped. 'Use the stick as I did before. And take care, Islan.'

Islan nodded and disappeared through the ragwort but time dragged and Tel feared he had murdered his brother too. The woman lay motionless and he crawled closer. The trap had caught her ankle and her boot and trousers were dark with blood. He could scarcely bear to look at them but look he must. It was the only way he could remember how the trap worked.

If only he weren't hurt as well! He wanted to sleep, not tackle some long-forgotten mechanism. He ran his hands over the plate and pressed tentatively, but nothing happened and he drew back, desperate not to inflict more pain.

The woman's breathing was harsh and as he watched, her skin silvered, as if in death. Tel's heart lurched but it was just the moon, clearing the trees. The woman watched it too.

And then she opened her hands, palms upward *as if in surrender*. 'She the Moon,' she whispered. 'I am Willing . . .'

Tel recognised the gesture for what it was and sprang forward. 'Don't die!' he cried in panic and, seizing the plate, forced it downwards. The trap's teeth tore themselves free and the woman screamed, clawed her way upright, and collapsed back. Tel scarcely noticed; holding the plate down took all his strength.

And then Islan was suddenly there. 'Drag her clear!' gasped Tel.

Islan scrambled to comply and the trap sprang shut with a metallic clang. The pain in Tel's shoulder beat with a ferocity that returned blotches to his eyes and then, in the silence that followed, a wolf howled.

'We can't stay here,' whispered Islan, wide-eyed.

'No,' gasped Tel. He took a swig from the waterskin and offered it to the woman but she turned her face away. 'Take . . . her things,' he said to Islan. 'I'll carry her first . . . and then . . . you carry.' He turned back to the woman. 'We go to . . . our place now,' he said, trying to gentle his voice. 'We will carry you. You won't be hurt.'

She gave no sign of having heard and Tel managed to heave her over his good shoulder and struggle to his feet. The world swayed and bile filled his mouth but he followed Islan down to the ford and staggered onto the first of the boulders.

Then the woman gripped his arm. 'What is it?' he rasped.

'Leave me here.'

Tel's sluggish brain struggled to make sense of her words. She spoke Sunnen but strangely accented. 'Leave you here?' he slurred. 'But you'll die.'

'Leave me here!'

Tel hadn't the strength to argue and hoped she wasn't about to fight him but thankfully she made no further protests and he reached the opposite bank, lowered her down, and collapsed beside her. Islan passed him the waterskin but he was too nauseous to drink.

The woman didn't drink either and Islan lay his fingers against her cheek. 'She burns!' he exclaimed. 'What if she dies, Tel? What if—'

'Merala's skilled in curing fever,' rasped Tel. 'She'll cure this woman's too.' He took the woman's pack and weapons and Islan hoisted her over his shoulder but while Islan was close to Tel in height, he wasn't in strength. He wove from side to side and when he came close to dropping her a second time, Tel slid her back onto his own shoulder. She felt familiar to him now, as if he had carried her many times.

Tel trudged on, resting when he could go no further, then walking again, and it was with sunlight not moonlight that they reached the corral. Tanalan emerged from her stay, yawning as she braided her hair and stopped open-mouthed, but Tel brushed past her, going on to Merala's stay and lowering the woman onto his father's bed. He wanted to issue precise instructions but the night air had stolen his voice and the floor was rising to meet him.

'Send for Sekwana,' he croaked, and that was the last thing he remembered.

15

$\mathcal{T}$el was aware of chanting, the voice gravelly and the words hard to understand, and he focussed on the puzzle of light instead. He had returned at dawn but now it was dark. He slid back into sleep and the next time he roused, painful jabbings kept him wakeful.

It was Sekwana who chanted and who plied a needle, but he stopped when he saw Tel's eyes were open. 'It is unwise to tangle with bears,' he said dryly.

Tel said nothing, having to concentrate on not crying out. He distrusted the old Wiseman's influence over the more gullible Sunnen, but Sekwana was skilled at mending injuries, and Tel was grateful for his aid. The pain increased, as if the needle plunged into the very heart of the wound and as Tel gritted his teeth, Sekwana shifted the dish of smouldering tinqua closer. Its fumes numbed pain, but Tel turned his face away.

Sekwana eye him shrewdly. 'There can be no aid unless you allow it,' he said.

Tel was thankful to feel sleep steal over him again and drifted until he heard the chink of Sekwana gathering his tools. Someone spoke and Tel was unsure whether the words came from Sekwana or from a dream but they were clear, however they came: *the woman will live—if she chooses.*

Merala didn't return to the corral until late that night, having spent another long day treating Sharli's birth-fever. Her neighbour had safely birthed a little boy but had been ill ever since and it had taken all Merala's skill to douse the fire that burned her. Now as Merala set her bag of herbs on the table, she felt the cost of those days.

The injured woman lay motionless in Barin's bed and Tanalan still kept watch. Her face was pale with exhaustion and Merala mixed her some honey-water and waited for some colour to come back before she spoke.

'What did Sekwana say about the woman's injury?' she asked. Tanalan shrugged and Merala took a deep breath. 'And about Tel's shoulder?'

'He said the wound was clean,' muttered Tanalan, 'but that Tel was weak from loss of blood. He said other things too.'

'What things?'

Tanalan shrugged again. 'I didn't really listen.' There was a pause and then her face contorted with anger. 'How could *she* do that to Tel? He was helping her!'

'Islan said there were wolves nearby. He thinks she mistook Tel for one of those.' Tanalan glared at the still form and Merala sighed. It had been a dreadful day, the worst since news had come that Barin wouldn't be returning. 'Sekwana said the woman would live, *if* she chose to,' said Tanalan abruptly. 'What did he mean by that?'

As Merala contemplated the woman's foot, swollen twice the size of its companion, the Wiseman's words seemed only too clear. 'He meant she might not *want* to live.'

'How could she *not* want to live?'

'She might lose her foot and see no reason to go on.' Tanalan's shoulders slumped and Merala drew her into her arms. 'Time for sleep, my love,' she said, and kissed her on the forehead.

Tanalan went slowly from the stay and Merala took her seat. The woman's face bore the marks of the Sceadu, which was extraordinary, but not as extraordinary as her eldest son's behaviour. Tel had rushed off to a place he rarely visited, *before* dawn, without taking as much as a waterskin with him. It was the sort of impetuosity worthy of Barin, a man who Tel had spent his entire life striving *not* to emulate.

Merala went to the cooking place and prepared a fever-reducing tincture and some honey-water for herself and sipped it as she settled down to wait. The night drew on and Islan came in to report that Tel slept but he didn't linger; he looked exhausted as well.

Merala slipped into the type of sleep she snatched when she watched over the ill and when the woman woke, she quickly roused and offered her the tincture. The woman seemed too befuddled to drink but when she roused a second time, and still didn't drink, Merala knew her refusal was deliberate.

Merala continued her vigil until silvery light invaded the stay then rose and stretched and wandered to the door. Ashali's peak floated like a shining island above the mist and her eyes narrowed as she considered her dead husband's tales. Barin's knowledge of the Sceadu came from his father and had fed a wanderlust that led to Barin's untimely death.

She remembered an argument too that, in some odd twist, involved Sekwana. Barin had been keen to expand the Sunnen's gardens but Sekwana had argued against it, insisting the Sunnen maintain some of their older hunting ways. Barin's response had been scathing. *Are we to live as Sceadu hunters? Forced to chase each meal across the mountain tops, grubbing up what best we can, and going hungry when we can not?*

Merala hastened back to the bed and examined the woman critically. Her arms were as muscular as any man's and she was tall and lithe, making her swift, as a hunter should be but then Merala's gaze reluctantly slid to the woman's ankle. The wounds were deep and cruel; she would be fleet no more *if* she survived.

Was this the reason behind the woman's refusal to drink? Merala's mouth hardened. So it was with the young! Things must be all one thing or all another! When Barin died, she had wanted to follow him into death but that way was closed to her. She owed care to her children, those already born, and the one still in her belly.

And so she had worked the gardens and kept the stays and, in the end, they had brought her great joy, but not the freedom to make her own path as Barin had, and as Tel and Islan one day would.

Yet Barin was dead and she endured so who was to say her path had been the lesser? This woman must be made to see this too and not to turn away from life.

Fleet didn't want awareness to return but it did, with a storm of searing pain and all-consuming thirst. She had believed she would pay her debt to Talabraith in the Whitelands, or in the darkness under the earth, and in the agony of the trap she had finally been Willing, but the faceless man had taken her to a tur filled with other faceless people who harried her with syra-flower-tinted water. Fleet refused it for she sensed in her growing fever the chance to at last atone for breaking Talabraith.

'Why won't you drink?'

The old woman spoke Sceadu words but bent out of shape like the tur's walls, that shimmered and blurred. Her hair was as grey as Ket's and her face as kind, and Fleet wanted to explain the necessity of Willingness but the words were dust in her mouth. It didn't matter; nothing mattered any more.

Light and dark chased each other around the tur until Fleet found herself in the dreamscape of the Drylands. Desiccated sands stretched away and there was nothing kind or gentle there. Fleet's hunter self harangued her to turn back to the world of light and water but she was determined to hunt the void. It was hard though; each step sinking her deeper into grit and the air filled with dust.

She felt dead already; the husk of herself rolling along before a scorching wind. Memories of love and life receded and thought withered, and then, as the dark swirl of the void loomed, with its promise of absolution through dissolution, Fleet fell to her knees and, lacking the strength to rise, crawled forward.

Scead placed a gentle hand on his wife's brow but she was still too warm. The distillation of sourslip had been too green and until the earth warmed, he had no chance of finding any riper.

He eased himself away so as not to make the mattress rustle, and all but succeeded. 'Be at peace, Scead.'

'I am,' he lied.

'You worry about me too much,' she said, her hot hand finding his.

'I mainly worry about my poor healing skills.'

'You shouldn't. They are the best amongst the Sceadu.'

Scead knew that being *the best amongst the Sceadu* might not be enough. 'Don't fear for me, Scead. I simply do what every Siah before me has done.'

'How can I not fear for you? How can I not fear I will lose you, that I . . .' he stumbled to a stop.

Siah's grip on his hand tightened, bone against bone, surprisingly strong. 'You knew I was a Siah before we married. You knew what it meant.'

'I knew you were a Siah,' said Scead, steadying. 'But I didn't know what it meant.'

Unexpectedly, Siah laughed. 'I didn't know what it meant either,' she confessed. 'I can travel the void and see all manner of beginnings and endings but am blind to my own shortcomings. I think the void must have a sense of humour.'

'You have no short-comings, beloved.'

'The Circle doesn't trust me, yet they trusted the old Siah. I fail to make myself clear.'

'I doubt they trusted the old Siah when she was your age,' said Scead. 'Trust takes time. The fault isn't yours that you've yet to be given it.'

'Then there's Chant. I should have better prepared her for what was to come. I saw hunter death and hunter journey but was too unpractised to unpick the weave of time. Firn died and Ashin was stolen and Chant lost two agemates in a single instant. I doubt she will ever forgive me.'

'That which is given freely can never be deemed stolen,' said Scead, gathering Siah close. 'Chant will see that one day.'

'I hope so, Scead, for I lost two agemates in that moment too. Firn is gone but Chant can still return. Yet I fear for her.'

Scead wondered if Siah had foreseen Chant's death but they had an understanding he would ask no questions about her dream-visions. It wasn't his task to join Siah in the void, even if he could, but to comfort, heal and make her whole on her return, but dread built he couldn't even do that.

Suddenly Siah stiffened. 'I must leave you,' she gasped.

'What—' he began, but she was already beyond him, her body rigid, her eyes unseeing. He would have believed her seized by a catastrophic illness except for her words, but even so, the hair on the back of his neck rose as he watched her tremble and twitch.

It was the change in the air that stopped Fleet. She was beyond reason but the vestiges of her hunter self sensed a shift. A sere wind whipped her hair about her face, but what loomed from the darkness remained untouched by it.

Then its voice filled her head. 'This was not where I sent you. Turn back to your task.'

It was Siah but Fleet felt neither anger nor surprise at Siah's presence, or at her ability to extract Fleet's thoughts as if on a thread. *I wasted the gift, I broke Talabraith, now I must atone.*

'Your Willingness is atonement enough,' said Siah.

A gift wasted is a gift owed.

'Do not dispute the laws of Talabraith with *me*! Turn back to your task,' thundered Siah.

I won't turn back.

'Turn back for the Sceadu!'

No!

For a long moment all Fleet heard was the wind's moan and then Siah's voice sounded again. 'Will you turn back for Scead?'

Scead is yours.

'Complete your task before the fourth moon passes and I'll relinquish him *if* that is what you choose.'

Fleet's awareness grew, fed by the understanding there could be no subterfuge in this place of swirling sands. *I choose.*

The darkness was suddenly empty of Siah's presence but Fleet felt no hope; only Siahs could visit the void and return to the world of light. Then, in the empty, scoured places within her, something stirred. It filled her like meltwater filled the streambeds at snowcome's end and it carried with it the will and strength to turn away from the darkness and claw her way back to life.

16

$\mathcal{T}$el struggled through the scrubby growth of Sekwana's corral, sourly concluding it was as unruly as the man himself. Tel's wounded shoulder added to his discomfort but not as much as his reluctance; Sekwana's corral was the last place he wanted to be.

I can cure the woman's fever if she allows it, Merala had said last night, *but I cannot cure her wish for death. Only Sekwana can do that.*

Merala had never ordered Tel to do anything since he'd become head of corral and she hadn't last night, but she may just as well have. Her meaning had been clear: do nothing and the woman dies. Tel's lip curled as he contemplated the offerings on the stay's weathered doorstep: disks of freshly baked berrem, hanks of flax, and pots of honey; gifts from the grateful *and* gullible Sunnen.

A love potion perhaps or a glimpse into the future? Sekwana could be relied upon for both and now Tel must make his own offerings: dried honeyapples, berrem flour, and a grudging heart.

Movement at the window alerted him to Sekwana's presence and he forced a neutral expression as the Wiseman beckoned him in. The stay was thick with fug from herbal brews and Tel breathed shallowly as he settled on a mat, bowed his head, and offered his gifts. Sekwana put them to one side but said nothing, not even in response to Tel's brief greeting, and Tel pressed on, determined to get the visit over with as quickly as possible.

'My mother asks . . .' he began, and stopped, aware he sounded like a little boy on an errand. '*I* ask that you come to our stay and help the injured woman there.'

'I have already helped her.'

'You have indeed,' said Tel hurriedly, 'and I thank you for it and for the aid you rendered me.' Sekwana regarded him unblinkingly and Tel's annoyance grew. 'The woman is fevered but refuses all drink,' he said bluntly. 'Unless she takes water soon, she will die. My mother is a skilled healer but she cannot cure this woman's wish for death.'

'It is as you say but I can offer no aid.' Tel went to rise but Sekwana gestured him back. 'There are many paths to tread and each of us must choose our own. To answer the dream or to turn away; to journey alone or to walk with the many; some would even choose the path of death. I cannot choose for this woman any more than I can choose for you, nor can I change her mind. Each of us must carry the burden of our own decisions.'

'I thank you for your words,' muttered Tel and with the briefest of nods, strode from the stay and struggled back through the tangled yard. He set off back along the path but he went on past his own corral to the small hill that overlooked the Stead. It took him a long time to climb it and when he reached the top, he collapsed against a tree.

Sekwana's allusion to dreams had raked up unwelcome memories of his sprint to the traps *and* fears that he'd become unhinged for a time. Curse the old Wiseman! The simpler Sunnen might find magic in his mumblings but all they did was disguise Sekwana's complete lack of useful potions.

Tel's shoulder throbbed and he stifled a groan. It made no sense the woman would choose to die, unless *she* was unhinged, which would explain her solitary wandering. But as Tel recalled how her eyes had met his at the Sunwash, with a gaze as pure and bright as Ashali's snow, he knew that whatever the reason, it wasn't that.

It was fully dark before he stumbled back to his corral, so weary he could scarcely put one foot in front of the other. He feared the woman had died in his absence but she remained in his father's bed and Merala stitched a shirt by the fire. Her needle flashed in the firelight and he winced, reminded of his own stitching.

Merala put aside her sewing and prepared a drink for him. 'It aids healing,' she said with a smile, and when Tel made no move to take it, added, 'you're not going to be less cooperative than our guest, are you?'

'She's drinking?' asked Tel incredulously.

Merala's smile broadened. 'Indeed, she is.'

Tel was so relieved he hardly noticed the bitterness of the potion he gulped down. With his mother's healing skills and the woman's willingness to be helped, there was a chance he hadn't murdered her after all.

'What did Sekwana say?' asked Merala.

'Nothing. Just his usual ramblings about—' Islan flung open the door, tossed his pack to the floor, and crammed disk after disk of berrem into his mouth. His boots were caked with mud and Tel's relief over the woman was wiped away by his usual irritation with Islan's childish habit of hunting.

He listened with exaggerated politeness as Islan described the massive prin he had been on the verge of taking when Mirsin's blunderings had scared it away and how, to add insult to injury, he'd had to wade into the mosslands to retrieve his arrow.

'It's disappointing you lost the prin,' said Tel with mock sadness, when Islan had finished. 'I was looking forward to roast meat.'

'In that case, take up Sal's invitation,' snapped Islan.

Tel straightened. 'What invitation is this?'

'I came across him high in the orchards and he was very pleased to see me too. Said I had saved him a long trek here.' Tel's eyes narrowed and Islan swallowed and hurried on. 'He plans to extend his stonestreams and has gathered kin in readiness but seeks your guidance. And given the distance, he invites you to be his guest during the construction.'

Tel's hard gaze stayed on Islan but his heart quickened. The prospect of laying out new stonestreams excited him and Sal's pretty daughter, Nasala, would provide a pleasant distraction, not that he'd give Sal any reason to demand marriage of him.

It meant postponing his journey to the Okianos but that was a small thing and he considered the other implications of his absence. The injured woman would consume much of Merala and

Tanalan's time which meant Islan must give up wasting his days in chases through the garron.

It would actually be a good way for Islan to begin his duties as head of corral because if something *did* go amiss, Tel could be back from Sal's in less than a day. There was another reason Tel was keen to help Sal, that he barely admitted even to himself. Being absent from his corral meant not having to witness, day after day, the horror of what *his* traps had inflicted.

Fleet's days drifted past without order or pattern. Fever consumed her and she was only vaguely aware of a Little Sister and two women, one as old as Ket and the other near her age-set. They plied Fleet with potions heavy with syra-flowers and Fleet's befuddled brain struggled with why they used the pretty bloom as a cure-herb, but sleep reclaimed her before she found answer.

Fleet had no idea how much time had passed before the fog cleared and she woke properly. The Little Sister and younger woman were there and while the Little Sister might be too young to be earth-named, the woman's bare face reminded her of the faceless man at the crossing place.

What kind of people were these unpatterned, *unconnected* strangers? She recalled the older woman's kindness and that they had cared for her, but she still tensed when the younger woman loaded errem disks on a platter and approached the bed. The Little Sister came too but the woman ordered her away, then set the platter on the cover and, grasping Fleet's arm, hauled her into a sitting position.

'You must build your strength if your ankle is to heal,' she said, but Fleet found even lifting a disk to her mouth exhausting.

The Little Sister was busy dropping remnant dough onto the firestones and her squeals as it sizzled, reminded Fleet of the Sceadu Little Sisters and her tension eased.

'My name is Tanalan,' the younger woman said, 'and that's Inkala,' she added, nodding towards the Little Sister. 'What are *you* named?'

The question was simple enough but Fleet didn't know how

to answer. Even *if* her ankle healed, she would never be fleet again. Even more shocking was the understanding that another part of Siah's vision had unfolded.

'Have you forgotten?' asked Tanalan impatiently.

Fleet swallowed dryly. 'I am named Chant,' she whispered, and closed her eyes.

'She's called Chant,' Tanalan told Islan the next morning as they breakfasted. 'I'd have thought *wolf* would have suited her better,' she added, as she flipped berrem disks.

'Since we know nothing of her, apart from her being our *guest*, it's hard to judge,' said Islan coolly.

'I'm sure Tel would agree she's more of a stabber than a singer,' goaded Tanalan, looking sideways at him. She loaded the last of the berrem disks onto a platter and put them aside. Merala was gathering and Inkala still slept. 'You're minding Inkala today,' she added cheerfully.

'I hadn't forgotten.'

Tanalan collected her gather-sling and went out and Islan glowered at the still form in his father's bed. Caring for Inkala was women's work, as was preparing berrem and white-root *and* setting the fish in the smoke-stay, all of which he now must do. His only escape was netting at the Silverwash but he must take Inkala with him and her ruckus gave him little chance of seeing washrats.

He stalked to Tanalan's stay to confirm Inkala still slept and then to his own stay and threw himself on the bed. The woman's pack still lay in the corner where he'd tossed it on that fateful day and he hauled it onto the bed and pulled out her weapons. Her arrows and bow were finely crafted, and he stroked them admiringly, but her knife was still sticky with Tel's blood. He stared at it and then went to Tel's clothing chest and retrieved Tel's knife.

Tel forbade him from handling it but he laid it on the floor next to the woman's knife then grinned. He rarely took his elder brother by surprise but he wagered he was going to this time and he was still grinning as he cleaned the knife and stowed it with her bow and quiver at the bottom of his clothing chest.

Tel ordered that the woman, *Chant*, not have access to her weapons *or* be left alone with Inkala, which was understandable, given her attack on Tel, but Islan didn't believe she posed a threat to anyone, especially as she had yet to leave her bed.

As the days passed, Chant stayed wakeful longer but the ferocious throb of her ankle continued unabated and she was haunted by the fear she would never walk again. And what use would she be to the Sceadu if she couldn't even forage? And to Scead? Was that why Siah had promised him to her? Because she knew Chant would never be able to claim him?

Merala changed the bandages each evening and reassured Chant the wound healed, but pain made it hard to think of anything, let alone unravel her mysterious meeting with Siah in the void, and Chant distracted herself by watching those of the tur. Apart from Tanalan, Inkala and Merala, there was a man called Islan.

He shared Tanalan's sulky expression and Chant guessed they were all Merala's children despite only Tanalan and Islan sharing Merala's brown curly hair and straight nose. Inkala's face was finer and her mouth fuller so she probably looked like her father who had yet to appear.

Merala had explained that Chant was with the *Sunnen*, in the *corral* of someone called *Tel*, and that it formed part of the Sunnen *Stead*, but Merala hadn't explained what *gardens* were even though, according to Inkala, Merala and Tanalan spent their days there. Chant didn't know what a *corral* or *Stead* were either, but she guessed they were probably like Turrels.

Islan was certainly happier when Tanalan was at the *gardens* but like Tanalan, he clearly resented Chant's presence, although *unlike* Tanalan, he managed to hide it most of the time. Only Inkala was genuinely friendly but Islan and Tanalan ordered her away whenever she sidled up to Chant, leaving Chant with nothing to do but dwell on the possibility she would never walk again.

One morning when Chant woke, it was Tanalan and Islan who were absent, and Merala who remained, and with her, she had a length of wood, padded at one end to make a crutch.

'I think it's time the hunter walked again,' she announced.

Chant's hands tightened on the cover. Even having the bandages changed was agony but Merala waited and Chant eased herself to the edge of the bed and, with Merala's help, fitted the crutch under her arm, and came upright. The tur rocked sickeningly and only Merala's strong hands stopped her from falling. Her sound leg was as weak as her wounded one and her wounded one throbbed with exquisite jabs of pain.

'Islan must find you a longer crutch,' said Merala, peering up at her. 'Would you like to go outside?'

Chant nodded. She longed to see Ashali's snowy crest again but when she finally reached the doorway, the Sunnen's turs and fences were so strange she almost forgot to look.

'It must be very different to the Sceadu lands,' said Merala, her keen eyes on Chant.

'You know of the Sceadu?' asked Chant, startled.

'My husband's father was a great traveller and journeyed to many lands. He went west to the seas *and* east over Ashali.'

Chant's heart missed. '*Over* Ashali?'

'The ice was less then,' said Merala thoughtfully. 'My husband's father spoke of a people who lived below Ashali's eastern slopes, who kept no gardens, and who lived by what they found. He said they owned no stays and knew no kin.'

'It's not as he said!' exclaimed Chant, angered by the suggestion the Sceadu cared nothing for each other.

'I meant you no insult,' said Merala mildly. 'The stranger sees always with a stranger's eyes. When my husband's father visited the Sceadu place, he looked upon *your* people with Sunnen eyes, even as you look upon *us* with Sceadu ones. The Meduin do not see the world as we do either, nor do the Okianos, yet both share our blood. And everyone knows that men and women see the world differently,' she added with a smile.

In the following days, Chant devoted all her strength to mastering the crutch. It was awkward and painful, and infuriatingly slow, but to reclaim Scead, she must walk again. Merala encouraged her but Tanalan remained aloof and Islan only seemed interested in escaping the tur.

They continued to keep Inkala away from Chant and so Chant found it odd one day when Islan took his nets and left, and then Tanalan hurried off after Merala, without so much as a backward glance.

Merala was a healer and the woman who had appeared at the tur that morning had been agitated, so Chant guessed the summons had caused Tanalan to forget Islan netted. It didn't matter. Chant took Inkala to a sunny spot behind one of the turs and spent the day teaching her the string games played by Little Sisters and Brothers.

Chant enjoyed the day as much as Inkala. The Little Sister snuggled in Chant's lap and her chattiness distracted Chant from her ankle *and* her interrupted journey. The Little Sister was a quick learner too and had just managed a murrow burrow, one of the hardest of the strings, when Islan returned.

She leapt into his arms and squealed as he dropped his sling of fish and threw her into the air. Then he set her down and glanced about in puzzlement. 'Where's Tanalan?'

'Gone,' said Chant.

The change in Islan was instantaneous. He cursed, took several paces towards the corral gate, swung back, cursed again and launched into a tirade that didn't stop even when Chant told him Tanalan had gone with Merala. His outburst included people called *Kanan* and *Tel* and the shocking news that *Tel* had ordered Chant must never be left alone with Inkala.

Chant struggled upright. 'Is it because I broke Talabraith?' she asked hoarsely.

'What? No, it's because you stabbed Tel . . . at the traps,' he added. Chant stared at him blankly. She remembered little of that time beyond a storm of pain. 'Tel ordered it before he went away, before he had the chance to know you as we do,' added Islan uncomfortably. Chant continued to stare at him as she tried to make sense of his words, and he reclaimed the fish and stalked off.

'I don't understand,' muttered Chant.

'Tanalan says you shouldn't waste time trying to understand brothers,' said Inkala gravely.

Chant glanced down at the Little Sister's earnest face. 'What else does Tanalan say?'

'Oh, that Tel's bossy, and it's unfair he can go off wandering whenever he feels like it while she has to stay here, and that Islan thinks he's a man whereas he's just a silly boy who can't even hunt without ruining his best boots in the mosslands . . .'

Chant grinned despite herself. 'I've caused Islan a lot of extra work though,' she said thoughtfully, as they made their way back to Merala's tur.

'Tanalan says it's good Islan finds out what a woman must do,' said Inkala.

Islan was already hunched over the grinding stone when they reached the tur. The flour danced in the air as it had in the girls' Turrel and Chant's eyes burned. She hadn't appreciated how happy those days had been.

Inkala's small hand stole into hers. 'Don't be sad, Chanty,' she whispered.

Chant blinked, aware Islan had stopped grinding and watched her too. Everyone had their tasks in the girls' Turrel, even hunters who returned from long hunts. 'I'll grind the errem for you,' she said to Islan. 'Then you can sort the fish.'

'It's *berrem* and the stone's too heavy. You've yet to regain your strength.'

'I'll regain it by grinding.'

Islan eyed her doubtfully but moved aside and Chant took his place and started the stone turning, concentrating on a smooth rhythm, and she had almost forgotten his presence when he spoke again. 'Was this your task amongst the Sceadu?'

'When there was a need, and I hunted, and I cleaned fish,' she added, looking pointedly at the sling at his feet.

Unexpectedly Islan grinned and with a nod, disappeared out the door.

17

*G*rinding errem was hard, as were her endless laps of the corral, but as the days passed, she was rewarded with the gradual return of her strength. The crisp mornings merged into mild ones and into days that were almost hot. It was nearly a moon since she had trekked into the Whitelands expecting death, and she guessed it would be another before she was strong enough to continue her journey. That left barely two moons to find the thing Siah said would unlock the snowcome ice, return it to Berian-tur, and claim Scead.

Siah's vision still made no sense, nor did her claim that, in being Willing, Chant had repaid her debt to Talabraith. Time would tell whether that were true, concluded Chant grimly, but she *had* crossed the mountains and become Chant, so she had to believe that in the end, Scead would be hers again too.

It was close to the end of another warm day when Chant ceased her circling of the corral and collapsed onto a seat under the eaves of Merala's tur. Blue-black clouds had built all day and the air's tightness made Chant's skin shift and flick.

Thunder rumbled and as the air took on a peppery scent, odd drops of rain fell then increased until rain pelted down. Narrow streams zigzagged across the yard and Tanalan bellowed from the doorway for Chant to come inside, but Chant's attention was fixed on the mountains.

Something strange and terrible unfolded on Ashali's slopes. As the clouds dragged their ragged skirts of rain up the mountain, they faltered and then spun out as fine as flax, *empty of water*.

'Chant?' It was Merala. 'Come inside,' she said firmly. 'You're soaked.'

'It doesn't rain on the Sceadu,' whispered Chant. 'Why doesn't it rain on the Sceadu?'

Merala came to her side and followed her gaze. 'The winds bring the water from the oceans but they lack the strength to carry it far beyond the Stead,' she said. 'Even the Sunnen lands are drier now. Come inside,' she repeated.

She helped Chant change into a set of Tanalan's clothes and then they ate together but despite the tur's food and warmth, Chant found it impossible to settle. The sight of the clouds shedding their precious rain on the *western* side of Ashali forcibly reminded her of the Sceadu's plight.

Despite her naming, she was a hunter and hunters brought meat to the Great Turrel, not wasted their days in idleness! And even when her ankle was strong enough for her leave, she couldn't because her weapons had disappeared.

The fire collapsed into a tumble of coals and Merala carried a sleepy Inkala away but Chant fidgeted. She would have demanded Islan tell her where her weapons were but he dozed in his chair and her attention flicked to Tanalan. The Sunnen woman stitched intricate patterns onto a skirt and probably wouldn't tell Chant anyway, even if she knew. Ket had gifted the bow and quiver and Chant's breath hissed.

'What troubles you?' demanded Tanalan in irritation.

'Where are my hunting weapons?'

'Somewhere you won't find them—on Tel's orders.'

Chant glared at her. 'What is he? Some sort of thief?'

'How dare you! Tel's the head of the corral! He's—'

'Your weapons are quite safe,' said Islan, jerking awake. 'I'm sure Tel will return them when he comes back.'

'So, my journey has to wait on the *mighty* Tel, does it?' she sneered, and hobbled from the stay.

'Let her go,' said Tanalan. 'The night air will soon cool her temper.'

Islan surveyed his sister sourly. 'You've never liked her, have you, and you've made no attempt to disguise it. I shouldn't need to remind you that Chant is our guest.' Tanalan kept her attention on her stitching and Islan went out, slamming the door behind him.

Chant's prints were clear in the rain-softened earth and he followed them around to the back of the corral. She was hard up against the fence, staring up at Ashali, her longing clear.

He hadn't been much friendlier than Tanalan, he conceded; having seen Chant as a nuisance who curtailed his freedoms. 'Chant . . . I'm sorry,' he said awkwardly. 'Tel will be back soon and then I'm sure he'll return your weapons.'

'I *must* have them for my journey,' she said, her gaze still on the mountains.

'Where is it you go?'

'To a great tarn in the west.'

'Do you mean the ocean?' Chant's intense black eyes fixed on his face. 'It's like an immense lake that goes on and on until the horizon,' he explained.

'You've seen it?' she whispered.

'No, but Tel has.'

Her anger surged again and Islan cast about for a distraction. 'I'm netting at the Silverwash tomorrow,' he said quickly. 'Why don't you come? It will make a change from the stay and Inkala would enjoy having you there.'

'Is it far?'

'No further than your travels around the corral,' he said and managed to dredge up a smile.

She seemed to see merit in the idea because she nodded and he was so relieved, he slipped his arm around her to help her back to the stay.

Merala and Tanalan had already left for the *gardens* when Chant breakfasted the next morning and Islan left soon after, assuring Chant that Inkala knew the way and they could come at their own pace.

Inkala rummaged under her mother's bed and emerged with a pair of sandals that she put on, but Chant had no idea where her boots were. Maybe Tel had stolen them too!

'Is the path rough?' she asked, wondering if she could go

barefoot.

'Shoes must always be worn to the Silverwash,' intoned Inkala. 'Yours are there, Chanty,' she said, and pointed to sandals under Chant's bed. They looked new.

'Are they Tanalan's?' she asked in confusion.

Inkala shook her head. 'Merala had them made for you.'

Chant's throat tightened. Merala, like Ket, seemed to know when to nudge Chant in the direction she must go. She slipped one on but her foot was too swollen to take the second one despite the wound having healed. The scar sat like a raised purple bracelet around her ankle and Chant hid its ugliness under a bandage.

She would carry the scar for the rest of her life but to take her place amongst the Sceadu again, she *must* regain her hunter's speed.

Inkala danced along beside her as they made their way west but their progress was slow; the path a lot rougher than the corral. Chant scanned as she struggled with the crutch, needing to familiarise herself with the lands she would soon journey alone.

Inkala kept up a steady stream of chatter about her favourite places at the Silverwash but Chant barely heard her, distracted by the strangeness of all they passed. Fences of sharpened stakes formed patterns as complex as honeycomb and hid turs with roofs just visible above the stake-points. Occasionally she heard voices but was relieved that no one appeared, dreading confronting more *faceless* strangers.

The corral fences gave way to trees awash with the green and yellow birds Chant had seen earlier. According to Inkala, the green ones were pipers and the yellow ones sallowfaces. The trees thickened until they crowded the path and Fleet regretted her lack of weapons. Inkala's carelessness added to her worries. The Little Sister seemed less aware than a child half her age.

Chant asked Inkala about dangerous creatures that might be nearby but Inkala could only name the whitesnake and before Chant could question her further, she suddenly sped off. The crutch gouged Chant's shoulder as she struggled to catch up and then the trees gave way to a sweep of sand and a glittering expanse of water.

Inkala jigged around Islan who sorted his nets on the shore but Chant only had eyes for the Silverwash. It was as broad as the Fine, Ige and Ruthvin streambeds combined and she hobbled forward. The sand made the crutch even more awkward and Islan helped her the last of the way to the water.

'Why is the stream so large?' she asked, unable to drag her gaze from it.

'The Silverwash is a river, not a stream,' said Islan, 'and small compared to the Sunwash. The Sunwash is so mighty it's cut a gorge through the Teresas Mountains.'

Chant blinked. She couldn't imagine anything bigger than this *river* and Islan smiled. 'Inkala usually plays on the boulders while I fish,' he said. 'You can sit there too, if you like. Merala says resting your foot in the water will ease the swelling.'

Merala's words proved to be true and Chant accompanied Islan whenever he netted. After a while the second sandal fitted and her ankle took more of her weight but her growing strength wasn't the only reason she enjoyed their netting expeditions.

She was fascinated by the Silverwash's ever-changing colours and the games she and Islan played to amuse Inkala, amused her as well. Islan's aloofness gave way to a good-natured friendliness that reminded her of Firn and she looked forward to their times together.

Islan found himself enjoying her company too. Chant didn't rain biting criticisms down on him like Tanalan and since her ankle had healed, her smile appeared more readily. It lit her whole face and he found himself searching for ways to see it more often.

He had wanted to introduce her to his friends but Merala had advised against it. Chant had enough to deal with between her injury and being far from home, she had said, without enduring their curiosity as well.

As the days grew warmer, Inkala took to playing in the shadier areas further along the shore, but Chant remained at the boulders. They jutted into the Silverwash's flow and she loved the current's chill tug over her feet.

The day was almost hot when Chant clambered onto her usual perch and dipped her feet in the Silverwash's green-brown slide. Tiny fish flashed silver and her attention shifted between them and Inkala, who built miniature turs in the river sand. Islan netted nearby and when he dunked his head to cool off, shining rivulets of water zig-zagged down his honeyed skin.

Chant watched them in fascination and then Inkala screamed. A seresnake reared, ready to strike and Chant threw herself into the water and forced her way through its flow. She reached the sand, sprinted along the shore and scooped up Islan's bow and arrow. Islan shouted warning. If the arrow went astray it would kill Inkala but there was no time to lose. Chant dropped to one knee and fired.

Then time seemed to slow. She saw the arrow pass through the snake's neck, a spurt of dark blood, and then the snake carried forward almost to Inkala's feet. Islan dashed past and scooped up his little sister, holding her while she sobbed, but Chant was too dazed to move. The snake had been Willing and that meant she *had* atoned for breaking Talabraith, as Siah had claimed.

Chant struggled to her feet, cut the arrow free, and carried the snake back to the river. Then very gently, she let the water take it. By the time she returned, Inkala had quieted and Islan had donned his shirt.

'You're a hunter,' he said. It was a statement, not a question and Chant nodded, freed at last from the guilt of the burned aperion pelt. 'Why did you put the whitesnake in the Silverwash?' he asked curiously.

Chant glanced at the crevices in the nearby bank. 'She died keeping her young safe,' she said. 'It's a fine place for nestlings and she was a fine mother. The water will shelter her.' Islan frowned as he struggled to make sense of her words, and she looked back at the river. 'Your nets have been swept away.'

'I'll find them tomorrow.' He retrieved her crutch from the sand but instead of handing it to her, hurled it into the trees.

'You ran, Chant; you've no more need of it.' Then he knelt and unravelled the sodden bandage from around her ankle. 'You've no more need of this either,' he said.

Chant looked down at the scar. 'It's so ugly,' she said, but as Islan straightened, his face held an expression she hadn't seen before.

'There's nothing ugly about you, Chant,' he said softly.

Islan's words played over in her mind as they made their way back to the corral and, for the first time since leaving Berian-tur, she thought of Tor. He had looked at her the same way and she felt a little thrill of happiness. She was to wed Scead, she reminded herself, but the feeling remained.

Fright robbed Inkala of her usual chatter and as soon as they reached the corral, she broke free and disappeared into Tanalan's tur.

'At least today should make her more wary,' said Islan, as they made their way across the yard.

'Don't you teach your young the ways of the seresnake?'

'*Whitesnake*,' corrected Islan. 'We teach them to keep away.' He paused. 'I haven't thanked you for saving my sister's life.'

His eyes held the same expression as at the Silverwash and Chant's heart quickened. 'There's no need for thanks.'

'Wouldn't the Sceadu give thanks for such a deed?' he asked, stepping closer.

'The Sceadu . . .' said Chant and faltered. Thoughts of Tor had reminded her how far she was from them and when Islan drew her into his arms, she stayed there, savouring his warmth and comfort.

'No fish today?' a voice asked dryly.

Islan released her and excitedly embraced the man who lounged in the tur's doorway. 'Chant, this is my brother Tel,' he said, grinning hugely.

The faceless man from her dreams! The man who thought she would harm Inkala! The man who had thieved her weapons! Chant managed to nod but his expression was as cold as Tanalan's and then, as his eyes slid to her ankle, it turned to disgust.

Islan had made her feel whole again today, even beautiful, but Tel's revulsion had destroyed it in an instant. She limped away to Merala's tur where the day's errem waited to be ground but had scarcely started the grindstone when Tel appeared in the doorway. He didn't speak or enter, just watched her, and she let the grindstone slow to a stop.

Tel waited for the woman, *Chant*, Islan said she was called, to stop grinding berrem before he spoke. Sweat still slid down his back at how close Inkala had come to death and he must thank the woman formally.

'Islan told me what you did—' he began, and then her furious face was suddenly a hand's span from his.

'You wear *my* knife!' she hissed.

Her fierceness contrasted sharply with Nasala's gentle affection and he was shocked to realise *this woman* actually matched him in height. 'Are you calling me a thief?' he asked icily.

'It's *my* knife!'

'It was my father's.'

'Do you think me a fool not to recognise my own?' she demanded, refusing to take a backward step.

Tel eyed her calmly but he was incandescent with rage. How dare this savage inveigle her way into Islan's affections and then challenge *him*, Tel, the head of corral!

'Perhaps it's you who thinks *me* the fool,' he said softly. 'My brother is unpractised in the ways of women and is easily duped into thinking the first who weeps in his arms would make a worthy wife but I am not so easily deceived.'

Her face contorted with pain but it was so brief, Tel half thought he'd imagined it. There was no mistaking her contempt though.

'You needn't fear I would make Islan a *poor* wife,' she sneered. 'I am already pledged,' and with that she pushed past him out of the stay.

Tel was too astonished to move. What kind of man allowed his future wife to go off, unprotected, on her own? To cross Ashali, of all things!' Tel's mouth twisted. Given her nature, she had probably gone *without* his permission! His angry thoughts swung to Nasala's gentle sweetness. Now she was as a woman should be. If he did one day marry, it would be to Nasala, or someone very like her.

Islan was sprawled on his bed when Tel returned but jumped up. 'You've spoken with Chant?' he asked eagerly.

'Spoken with her? Shouted, more likely,' said Tel, pacing around the tur. 'She accused me of stealing her knife, of all things!'

Islan grinned and Tel watched in mystification as he retrieved a bundle. The shape told Tel it was the woman's weapons but his breath emptied at the sight of her knife. As a boy, he had crept into the garron to hold and dream on a knife from a father lost to Tel before Tel had grown to know him. And now this savage had come over the mountains bearing the same knife and Islan had fallen in love with her!

'You know she's pledged,' he said, watching his brother carefully.

'Pledged? Then why in Ashali's name isn't her future husband with her?'

Islan showed none of the hurt of a disappointed lover and Tel wondered whether he'd mistaken Islan's feelings. 'Maybe the man is as reckless as her,' said Tel, throwing himself onto the bed.

'Where's Chant now?' asked Islan.

Tel shrugged, still smarting from their exchange. 'I don't know and I don't care.'

'She's owed our hospitality, no matter how grudgingly some of this stay would bestow it,' said Islan and went out.

Islan was right to rebuke him, conceded Tel, but he wondered whether Islan's concern stemmed from more than a sense of duty. He yawned and pulled off his boots. Walking through the night had left him weary but he was glad he hadn't delayed his return. His corral needed to be brought back to order and over the next few days, that was precisely what he would do.

18

$\mathcal{C}$hant was well down the path to the Silverwash before her temper cooled enough to think. Not only had Tel stolen her knife but he'd had the gall to deny it! He probably intended to keep her arrows and bow too, which left no way to feed herself on the journey ahead.

Once she had quenched her anger by running until exhaustion claimed her but her ankle prevented it and she forced her way into a dense tangle of sappy stems. She had crawled into bowers as a Little Sister to enjoy the closeness of other creatures and they calmed her now as they had then.

Jewelled beetles clung to the undersides of leaves and redlegged ants marched in endless processions. The bower muted the birdcall outside and amplified the rustle and creak of things that grew, gave birth to new life, and decayed to dust. There were so many worlds, some of bud and bark, others of husk and hollow; so many worlds beyond the mountains *as Siah had foretold*.

Her stomach started a familiar churn and she crawled back onto the path and grimaced at her grass-stained trousers. Tel would think her even less worthy now, not that she cared. Her ankle had healed enough to walk so there was no reason to delay *except* she had no weapons!

She tensed at the sound of running but it was Islan. 'I thought you'd left,' he panted.

'Not without my knife and hunting weapons.'

Islan smiled. 'Tel didn't take your knife, Chant. He wears his own. It just happens to be the same as yours.'

'That's not possible!'

'It probably is,' said Islan thoughtfully. 'The knife came

from our grandfather who was a great traveller so it's likely he once visited your lands. He gave it to his son Barin, our father, and Barin to Tel.' Islan paused. The knife is special to Tel, so when you accused him of stealing it . . .'

Chant could well understand Tel's anger but her antagonism remained. Hunting knives cost metal-smiths many days to craft and should never be squandered on strangers.

They turned back towards the corral and were almost there when Islan brought her to a stop. 'Tel told me you're pledged. Why isn't your future husband here with you?'

'It wasn't his task to journey,' said Chant, and felt her face warm. Twisting the truth with Tel was one thing but deceiving Islan, who had shown her kindness, quite another. Not that it *was* deception, given she *would* be pledged to Scead on her return.

'He should be here with you,' persisted Islan.

'He's the reason I must continue my journey,' said Chant and faltered as she realised she journeyed to aid the *hungry* Sceadu. If Scead were anything at all, it was a reward or *bribe*.

'At least stay for Giving,' said Islan.

'Giving?' repeated Chant, struggling with the revelation.

'It's at the full moon. There'll be music and feasting with our kin and Sekwana will lead a ceremony to offer thanks for good weather and the like.'

Chant was horribly aware of the time her ankle had cost her but it would be safer to travel under She the Moon's *full* light and, if this man Sekwana gave thanks for the void's gifts, he might be able to offer guidance.

'Another few days won't hurt,' cajoled Islan.

'I'll wait,' said Chant, but even as Islan smiled in relief, she wondered whether the delay could be the difference between claiming Scead and losing him forever.

Islan gave her a quick hug, his touch re-awakening her need for comfort. She must get used to doing without Islan's company, she told herself; to being utterly alone again. 'Inkala will be pleased you're staying for Giving too,' said Islan eagerly. 'She will miss you when you leave, Chant; we all will.'

Chant knew Tel and Tanalan wouldn't, but she kept her silence.

The days leading up to Giving were filled with food preparation and the reorganisation of turs in readiness for guests. Chant's bed was shifted into Tanalan's tur, much to Inkala's delight but not Chant's. However, Tanalan proved uncharacteristically friendly.

Chant guessed her good mood was due to the imminent arrival of her Meduin kin. Tanalan told her they dwelt beyond the Teresas Mountains which was a three-day journey *unless* the Sunwash flooded and closed the cleft and then no one journeyed, for it was the only way through. The last piece of news was worrying because Chant could ill afford another delay.

'We have kin in the far west too,' said Tanalan, as she rummaged through her clothing chest. 'Merala's sister Turai married an Okianos man but we rarely see them. It's too far for them to come for Giving.'

'How many days journey is it?'

'I'm not sure. Tel's visited them; you should ask him.'

Chant had no intention of asking *that* man anything. Islan had said the Sunwash flowed to the ocean and so she would simply follow it. Then she forgot about the Sunwash *and* Tel, as Tanalan lifted a necklace of disks from the chest. Chant had never seen anything like them. They glowed like miniature moons.

'What are they?' she gasped.

'Taka—from the sea,' said Tanalan as she draped them across her breasts. 'I'll wear them at Giving when I marry Kanan.'

Chant blinked in surprise. Tanalan had never mentioned anyone called Kanan or being pledged but Chant recalled the name from Islan's tirade when he'd believed Tanalan had gone.

'Kanan and I pledged two seasons ago but he hasn't been to Giving since,' explained Tanalan. 'Firstly the Terecleft flooded and then last Giving, his father died and he became head of corral. But he's coming this Giving.'

'Why didn't he visit some other time?'

'He owes care to his corral first,' said Tanalan, as she carefully restowed the taka in the chest.

'Then why not go to him?

'Because Tel's forbidden it!' She snapped the chest lid shut and glared at it, then glanced back to Chant. 'Islan's told me you're pledged too. What of the man you're to marry?'

'He's called Scead,' said Chant reluctantly.

'Scead?'

'It means flesh of the Sceadu,' said Chant. If the Siah were of the void's darkness, her husband must be of the sunlit world. But what of a Siah who broke her marriage? Chant could think of no precedent. All she knew was air-names couldn't be changed.

'What's Scead like?' pursued Tanalan.

'He's tall,' said Chant distractedly, 'though not a hunter . . .' What *was* Scead like? What were his deepest wishes, his darkest secrets, the hidden parts of his soul? She didn't know because they had never been close. The revelation was akin to pain and Chant faltered.

'You must miss him very much,' said Tanalan gently.

'I do,' choked Chant, but all she could think of were Scead's tender glances at Siah during her naming ceremony. Scead *did* love Siah, so why had Siah pledged to relinquish him, on the edge of the void, *where there could be no deception*?

The first of Merala's kin arrived the next morning and Inkala's face shone with excitement as she dashed between the turs to tell Chant each newcomer's name. Chant was soon thoroughly confused and Tanalan was no help, taken up with food preparation, while Islan had disappeared.

On hunt, Tanalan told Chant, rolling her eyes as she hurried past. Tel was absent too and, according to Inkala's breathless account, was busy showing *Nasala* the orchards. Chant was grateful for his absence. It was hard enough enduring the visitors' curiosity without his animosity as well.

She escaped their gazes by volunteering to tend the smoke-stay. It had the advantage of taking her to the quietest part of the corral and the disadvantage of giving her plenty of time to dwell on why Scead would break his marriage.

Perhaps he would stop loving Siah in Chant's absence but Scead's loyalty was one of the qualities Chant loved about him. It was equally unlikely Siah would cease loving Scead and before Chant had any hope of solving the mystery, she must find the mysterious thing that returned water to Berian-tur's stream-beds.

She still had no idea what she searched for or how long the search would take and regretted her pledge to wait for Giving. At least Islan had returned her weapons, which meant she could feed herself once she did set out and before she left, repay Merala for her kindness too.

Chant left at dusk and headed east into a breeze bright with the scent of snow. Her ankle throbbed with every step but she threw back her head and drew the air deep into her lungs. It was almost as if she were back in Berian-tur, when Firn still lived and Ashin was still hers.

She cut off the thought and turned onto a steep overgrown path. It led upwards and she needed to get her bearings. Her ankle made the climb hard but the hill gave surprisingly good views of the corrals and of the *gardens* and *orchards*, where the Sunnen grew their rows of forage plants. The last of the sun lit what looked to be lines of water too and Chant strained into the gloom, but the failing light defeated her and she stared skywards instead.

Early stars glittered like ice shards and she wondered if Scead watched them as she did, and whether Siah did too. Her mouth hardened, and setting an arrow, she set off into the trees.

It was past half-night when Chant limped back to the corral and despite the pain in her ankle, she felt like singing as joyously as the Sceadu did at snowmelt. The aperion was the best she had taken and she was still admiring its beauty as she slid it to the ground outside Merala's stay.

'Where in Ashali's name have you been?'

Chant whirled, angered not just by Tel's tone, but by her failure to sense him. He was less than a length away, feet planted, knife drawn.

'I've been hunting,' she said.

'I thought you were an intruder,' he said, sheathing his

knife.

'Perhaps I am.'

'Those of my corral must be within in its fences before moonrise,' he said, ignoring her words.

'I'm not of your corral.' There was a tingling silence.

'While you are a *guest* here, you will do as we do.'

Chant resisted the temptation to retort that she would *never* do as he did, but as she went to move past him, he blocked her way. 'You have blood all over your shirt,' he said.

'It's the blood of the beast.'

'You should wash.'

Why? To hide that she was a hunter? To be like him and his kin who forced their forage to grow in lines and not as seedfall dictated? Her chin came up and she considered him coldly. 'The beast was Willing,' she said. 'I am proud to wear its blood.'

19

The first day of Giving dawned fine and Islan opened his eyes with a sense of joyful anticipation, dampened only by his failure on hunt. He stretched and yawned and then, inexplicably, the stay was invaded by the odour of roasting meat.

'What . . .' he began, but as usual, Tel's bed was empty.

The smell of roasting meat was stronger in the corral and he hastened to Merala's stay. The central fire had been lit and an enormous prin roasted on its coals.

'The corral has a hunter at last,' said Tanalan, busy scraping white-root.

Islan hurried to Tanalan's stay and peered in but Chant's bed was empty too. He knew she was a hunter but it hadn't occurred to him there was a lot she could teach him and now it was too late. He scowled as he recalled he had yet to net and set off for the Silverwash, glancing anxiously at the sky as he went. The air hummed as if storms brewed and he hoped Giving wasn't to be ruined by rain.

There would be feasting at the corral after Sekwana's ceremony and dancing in the Stead, and he hoped Chant delayed long enough to join in. He imagined her travelling alone, sometimes in light but more often in darkness. It would be dangerous too and his happiness ebbed as he realised just how much he wanted her to stay.

Chant rose early and went to the Silverwash to bathe, then changed into her Sceadu clothes and settled on her usual boulder. Mist curl over the silvered water and the river seemed lonely now without Islan's jokes and Inkala's laughter.

She would miss Islan and Inkala, *and* Merala, who had shown her so much kindness but mostly she would miss their turs' safety. Her ankle meant she couldn't outrun attackers, human or beast, and while Siah had claimed Chant would return, there might be worse dangers ahead than the trap.

Chant shivered as she wondered whether Siah had foreseen her maiming and if so, why Siah hadn't warned her, and she was still considering Siah's motives when Islan appeared with his nets.

'You're not leaving now, are you?' he asked, eyeing her Sceadu garb. Chant shook her head. 'I saw the prin you killed but I've never got close enough to one to take proper aim. There's so much you could teach me about hunting, Chant, but I need to net. Will you stay for a while?'

Chant agreed, in no rush to return to Tel or the stranger-filled corral. She watched Islan sort his nets and as he fished, described how Little Sisters and Brothers were instructed by elders skilled in the youngster's interests, and how Ket had guided her.

'I've had no one to teach me such things,' said Islan, when she fell silent.

Chant shrugged. 'The Sunnen garden.'

'At least we don't hunger *or* are forced to risk ourselves in journeys over mountains,' he retorted .

'I've not been *forced* to risk myself,' said Chant, annoyed in turn.

Islan tethered his nets and clambered up onto the boulder beside her. 'So, you're telling me you *chose* to risk yourself while the man you're to marry chose *not* to risk himself?'

'The journey's mine alone,' said Chant, stung by Islan's words.

He snorted and Chant regretted not having returned to the corral after all. 'Tell me I'm wrong,' he said more gently and leaned closer. 'Stay here with us, Chant. Stay here safe in our corral.'

'I'm pledged.'

Islan snorted. 'In name only! What man allows his future wife to go off alone into danger?'

'The Sceadu's ways are different,' she mumbled.

'The love between a man and a woman is the same whichever side of the mountains they dwell,' he retorted.

The truth of his words slammed home and then she was in his arms, his kisses igniting a hunger she scarcely knew she had. She answered him kiss for kiss before she tore herself free, clambered back to shore, and fled.

He called after her but Chant ran on, overwhelmed by unanswered questions: could she make a home for herself here; abandon the Sceadu; relinquish Scead? Then, as she neared the corral, Tanalan burst through the gate, dressed finely but with an angry, tear-stained face. She hesitated when she saw Chant and seemed about to speak but turned and set off swiftly towards the Stead.

Chant was still staring after her when the gate was thrust open a second time, this time by Tel, dressed as finely as his sister and just as angry, but unlike Tanalan, he stopped and his gaze swept over Chant coldly. 'At the celebration of Giving, the Sunnen wear their finest clothes. I'm sure Tanalan can provide you with something more . . . suitable.'

Chant flushed. 'You look beautiful enough for both of us!' she flung back.

Tel took a furious step towards her and she dropped into a crouch and drew her knife. 'Is this how the Sceadu settle arguments?' he sneered.

Tel might be obnoxious but Chant wasn't about to repay Merala's generosity by causing upset, especially on this special day, and she straightened and sheathed her knife. 'Violence isn't the Sceadu way,' she said curtly. 'I leave this night and so thank you for the shelter and care that you, as head of the corral, have accorded me.'

Tel looked taken aback. 'I . . . there is no need for thanks. 'I'll have food prepared for your journey.'

'Don't trouble yourself,' she said, and stalked past him into the corral. But as Chant thrust her meagre possessions into her pack, she feared she had just traded days of hunger for a moment of point scoring. At least she could thank Tel for reminding her of her obligations to the Sceadu *and* for her leaving the Sunnen

123

in the same sorry way she had left the Sceadu: in anger and without formal farewells.

Chant spent the remainder of the day ensconced in a bower that overlooked the Silverwash. She dozed in the sun's warmth and, as the wind grew and the light faded to night, heard the chant of a single voice. She sat up and peered through the leaves. A procession emerged from the trees led by the chanter; an elder Chant guessed was Sekwana. The procession came to a halt at the river and Sekwana's chanting quickened as She the Moon edged over the mountains.

He knelt awkwardly, cupped water in his hands and scattered it over the land, then cupped it again and tossed it into the air, and the third time, gave it back into the river. He thanked the earth, air and water, and Chant's heart lifted, reminded of the Sceadu's welcome of snowmelt.

Sekwana took up the chant again but his voice was weary now and Chant made her way down as the gathering drifted away and She the Moon glided higher into the warm, storm-filled air.

Startled, he peered up at her. 'Why do you stay?' he asked.

'For the same reason you do; to give thanks.'

They waited together until the water caught She the Moon's fire and then Sekwana took pieces of bone from the pouch at his neck. 'The earth gives thanks to the beast that gifts itself,' he said, and there was a plop as the bone shattered the circle of light.

The light fragments reformed and Sekwana tossed a second piece of bone into the water. 'The air gives thanks to the beast that gifts itself,' he said, and waited for the circle to mend. 'The water gives thanks to the beast that gifts itself,' he finished, and tossed in the last piece of bone.

Then he dragged his gaze from the water to Chant. 'You are a foreteller?' he asked. Chant shook her head. 'What are you named?'

'Chant.'

'Ah,' said Sekwana. 'A time will come when you *will* tell.'

'I don't have the strength . . .' she confessed, afraid suddenly.

For a moment his eyes mirrored the fiery water. 'You won't do it alone, although you might wish to,' he murmured, and then roused. 'Remember the way of the hunted beast,' he added, and shambled away.

A sudden gust of wind whipped her hair around her face and Chant shivered. Had Sekwana foreseen her death? The dark offered no answer except the prospect of a storm and she pulled her jacket close and set off along the shore.

20

$\mathcal{C}$loud devoured She the Moon and plunged the river into darkness but Chant struggled on, fighting the wind's buffet, then stumbled to a stop. Something lurked at the water's edge and her heart thundered. Was this what Sekwana had foretold? The beast sent to deliver her to the void?

The wind roared and lightning cracked, its yellow light revealing what the darkness had hidden. 'Tanalan!' gasped Chant.

'Kanan hasn't come; there's illness in his stay. Will you take me with you?'

Tanalan's voice was as empty as her face and she carried a pack, but Chant shared nothing with this Sunnen woman except animosity. 'Sceadu hunters travel alone,' she said shortly.

Tanalan's face twisted. '*Sceadu* hunters are fortunate to have no brothers to make prisoners out of *them*!'

The wind whipped up stinging showers of river sand but Chant's thoughts were on Tanalan's *arrogant* elder brother. It might be good for the *mighty* Tel to discover his *wondrous* corral couldn't confine everything and *everyone*.

'Come if you wish,' she said grudgingly and flinched as a branch crashed down. The trees bent and thrashed and Chant heard another crack. 'We need to find shelter!' she bawled.

Tanalan gestured ahead and they fought their way on through the wind until Tanalan ducked into a deep cleft in the bank. Chant followed and they had scarcely wedged themselves inside when the rain began.

'When will he know you've gone?' asked Chant, as the rain lashed the stone outside.

'If he's with Nasala, not till dawn.'

Then he would come after her, realised Chant. The idea of

kin hunting kin was repellent but at least they had a full night's start on him. 'Did you farewell Merala?' she asked suddenly.

'I left the same way you did,' said Tanalan tartly. 'Inkala sobbed when she found out you had gone.' The rain's pound filled the silence before Tanalan's voice sounded again. 'Merala knows my heart. She will understand.'

Chant just hoped Ket had too.

The rain eased to plinks and they went on, picking their way over the slick stones at the water's edge and then through the sodden grass on the bank. The air was full of the scent of drenched foliage and their trousers and boots were soon soaked. They went steadily, despite Chant's worsening limp and, at dawn, perched on some river stones to breakfast. Tanalan had brought enough food for two, which meant Chant didn't have to hunt, although Tanalan seemed more concerned about the river than Tel catching them.

'If this rain keeps up, the Terecleft will flood, and we will have to turn back,' she said.

'I won't be turning back.'

'You haven't seen the Terecleft,' said Tanalan darkly.

The rain *did* keep up, making the journey miserable, but they reached where the Silverwash joined the Sunwash as the sun westered. Chant dropped her pack to the ground and simply stared. The rivers' muddy waters came together in mighty clashes that churned up foam and seeded roiling whirlpools. The void surged closer and Chant dragged her eyes from the water to the Teresas Mountains. They were scarcely better; a wall of peaks soaring skywards capped with dirty yellow snow.

'Mighty slabs of stone, not snow,' said Tanalan, following her gaze. 'The Meduin call it the Giant's Grin because it looks like teeth. You see why there is only one way through. Do you think your ankle will manage the climb?'

'It will have to,' said Chant.

They endured a second wet night before they snatched some

sleep under a shallow overhang and went on in silence through another drizzle-filled day, reaching the mountain's foothills as low cloud stole the daylight. They stopped to rest; Chant's ankle almost too painful to stand on. At least the leaf-roof kept the worst of the rain off but they needed to find somewhere dry to sleep.

'Are there caves nearby?' she asked.

Tanalan shook her head. She had huddled against a tree, her gaze on the ground and Chant grimaced and limped back to the Sunwash. She trawled about for washwood and wove it through the branches of a broad scrubby bush to fashion a shelter. It was rudimentary but surprisingly snug.

It was too wet to set a fire but the shelter seemed to make Tanalan more sociable and she spoke about her growing in the Stead. Chant nodded occasionally, her attention on the night outside. The rocky slopes could be berian haunts and while she had seen no spoor and taken no scent, the rain might have washed both away.

'I'm curious about the lines on your face,' said Tanalan, after a while. 'Do all Sceadu have them?'

Chant glanced back to her. 'Not before Inkala's age. The child's nature must be known before they receive their earth-name and first patterning. Then as they approach marriage, they receive their air-name and second patterning.'

'So, the lines mark each name?' Chant nodded. 'What was your first name?' asked Tanalan.

'Fleet.'

There was a long pause. 'I'm sorry,' muttered Tanalan.

'It isn't your fault I stepped in the trap.'

'It was the head of *my* corral who set them.'

Chant wasn't surprised Tel had concocted such cruel devices but she still couldn't blame him for her own stupidity. 'It's not his fault either,' she said grudgingly, her gaze on the night-shrouded trees again. 'I shouldn't have been so . . .'

'So what?'

Chant swallowed dryly. 'Side-blind.'

They set off as soon as there was light enough to see but the rain continued a steady patter on the leaf-roof. Tanalan didn't speak of the Terecleft being flooded again but her tension infected Chant. If the cleft *were* flooded, the water could take days to subside and Tel would catch them, not that Chant cared; her only concern was losing Scead.

The valley narrowed as they climbed, forcing the Sunwash between its stony banks, so that it roared along below them. They clambered through an under-storey of thorny bushes and rotted logs, the ground oozing and slicked by the rain, and every slip jarring Chant's ankle.

'Is this the way your kin travel?' she finally asked, sleeving the water from her eyes.

Tanalan shook her head, her face pale in the gloom, her wet hair plastered to her forehead. 'There's a path somewhere. It must be further up the slope.'

Chant peered up at the dense growth. Low cloud obscured the way ahead and the river's thunder masked sound. It was berian territory but all Chant could smell was rain. 'It's safer to stay near the river,' she said.

Tanalan shook her head. 'I'm sick of this stinking tangle,' she said. 'I'm going up.'

Chant's skin roused and she scanned, desperate to pierce the gloom, and when she glanced back, Tanalan had all but disappeared through the growth. 'Tanalan, wait!'

Tanalan gave no sign of having heard and Chant struggled after her, using her hands to haul herself up. Her breath heaved in and out and then she broke through a wall of bushes onto a path. It was smooth and edged with stone and Chant stared at it in surprise.

Tanalan had settled on a boulder overlooking the Sunwash and was rummaging in her pack. 'I *told* you there was a path,' she said triumphantly, as she pulled out food. 'Come and eat. I'm ravenous.'

Chant's skin still flicked and she peered down. They were on a narrow spur that jutted into the Sunwash and forced the river to all but turn back on itself to clear. From Chant's viewpoint, it looked like a seresnake *ready to strike.*

Chant's skin shrieked warning and she whirled. The trees behind Tanalan trembled, as if stirred by a breeze, *except the air was still*! And then, Chant felt a vibration through her boots. The whole slope was moving!

Chant flung herself forward, wrenched Tanalan from the boulder, and threw them both backwards. The noise was horrendous as a slurry of earth, stone and trees grated down the slope, taking Tanalan's former resting place with it. The mess of broken trees and stone disappeared from view and there was a hiatus, and then a roar as it crashed into the Sunwash and was swept away.

Chant sat up and wiped the mud from her eyes. Tanalan was plastered with mud too. 'My pack,' she sobbed. 'It had the taka.'

'Kanan will love you with or without the taka,' said Chant, as gently as she could.

'What would you know?' demanded Tanalan furiously. 'You who have left the man you're *supposed* to love on the other side of the mountains! Don't lecture *me* about love!'

Tanalan was distressed but her words stung and knowing she might have brought about Tanalan's death, simply to spite Tel, added to Chant's upset. Ket had once called her side-blind, but it was Tor's description of her as arrogant that returned to haunt her now.

The path made their travel quicker but the rain showed no signs of easing and, as the day wore on, the slope steepened to a cliff-face. The Sunwash's roar grew too, until it boomed like thunder and Chant stared about fearfully.

'The Terefall,' muttered Tanalan.

Chant had no idea what a *terefall* was and Tanalan's sullen face didn't invite questions. The vegetation gave way to the slabs yellow stone they had seen from a distance and then the path descended in a series of steps cut into the cliff-side. The descent tested Chant's ankle but what stopped her wasn't pain; it was the surge of muddy water over the path.

'How deep is it?' she asked, but Tanalan had slumped against the stone like a sulky Little Sister.

The cleft was several lengths wide and while the flow was gentler nearer the cleft walls, great chunks of trees were swept along in the middle. Chant swiftly considered her options. If they waited, she would have to hunt because their food had gone with Tanalan's pack. Tel would carry food so Tanalan could share his on their return journey, but it might take Chant days to find a Willing beast; days she could ill afford to lose.

'I'm going on,' she said, 'but you should stay here. Thwarting Tel is no reason to risk your life.'

'Neither is proving your *Sceadu* independence,' retorted Tanalan.

Chant didn't bother replying. She removed her boots, aware that Tanalan did the same, and stowed them in her pack. 'If you *are* coming, stay close behind me,' she said. 'If you get swept away, I might have a chance to catch you.'

'And what if *you're* swept away?' challenged Tanalan.

'I'll drown for I can't swim.'

Tanalan's eyes widened. 'Then we *must* wait!'

'For what? The river to rise? Your brother to catch up?'

Chant stepped into the water and crept forward, searching for hand holds in the stone. The water was cold and as leaves slapped against her legs, she tried not to think of what would happen if something bigger hit her.

The murky water edged up her thighs but she forced herself on, sweat oozing down her back. How much further? A jut of stone obscured the way ahead, sending the water into dizzying eddies and, as sparks erupted on the edge of Chant's vision, she lost her grip on the wall.

Water cut off Tanalan's shriek and Chant struck out, found nothing, and kicked with all her strength. She got her mouth clear but her pack dragged her down again and then the current turned her over and over and carried her away.

Tor slid the scinton from his shoulders and eased his aching muscles. He was grateful for the beast's Willingness but it didn't make carrying it any easier or the journey home any shorter. He had been absent from Serest for five days and was determined not to make it six.

Tor smiled, the only shadow over his happiness Serest's continuing delay of their marriage. He guessed her reluctance stemmed from her mistake over Snowhawk's feelings and he had tried to be patient, but all he wanted was to add the marriage line to his face and proclaim to all of Berian-tur that Serest was his wife.

He took a swig from his waterskin and eyed a clump of frost-burned syra-flowers. The Whitelands had been bitter too but as he journeyed on, his thoughts were on Serest rather than snowmelt's delay.

He pushed himself hard and by the time the sun lit Ashali, he had gifted the scinton to Siah, and hurried the last of the way to his tur. It was empty and the firestones cold which meant the fire hadn't been lit for days. Tor hadn't expected Serest to remain alone during his absence but he *had* expected her to welcome him back, and his thoughts went to Reed and Shale who Serest had kept company with before. Neither were married.

Tor needed to eat, bathe and rest but first he must gather windfall, for Serest had exhausted the supply. He was too tired to go far, just collected cones from around the tur and set the fire, warmed some water and washed himself down. Then he changed into clean clothes and prepared a stew. He made enough for two but Serest didn't appear and he ate alone.

His tur was furnished with a clothing chest, a bed, a table, and two chairs he had fashioned from glice and spent long evenings ornamenting. He had fired cups and platters too and been gifted pelts from Willing beasts to make his tur snug. He had been content here but now all he felt was emptiness.

The new day brought no sign of Serest and Tor went about his chores half-heartedly. Sometimes he worried she had come to harm and sometimes he was irritated by her apparent selfishness but after a while, both feelings gave way to a belief she had sought the company of the man who had been friends to them both and, as the midday sun dispatched the last of the frost, he set out for Snowhawk's tur.

No one answered his knock but smoke came from the vent and Tor pushed the door open. Serest was curled in Snowhawk's bed and, as Tor noted the rumpled covers on the mattress's other side, his happiness shattered like ice under a boot.

Serest stirred as he remained transfixed in the doorway. 'Tor,' she murmured. 'You're back.'

'Yes.'

'Join me,' she invited sleepily, flipping back the cover to reveal her nakedness.

'In Snowhawk's bed, in Snowhawk's tur? Hardly an act of friendship.'

'Snowhawk won't mind,' said Serest. 'He's off playing Uncle to Mist.'

'And that makes it acceptable to betray him, does it? As you've betrayed me?'

Serest propped on her elbow and smiled. 'I've betrayed no one, Tor. We've all slept together countless times before.'

'Fully-clothed for warmth!'

'It was like that this time.'

'You're naked!'

'Have you ever slept with a scinton pelt against your skin?' she asked, stroking it languidly. 'It's delicious.'

Tor wanted to believe she had gone to Snowhawk to sate her loneliness and that Snowhawk had sated *only* that but *wanting* to believe and *believing* were different things and he blundered away through the trees.

Hunter instinct kept him safe as he struggled to concoct a palatable explanation for Serest's actions. It was possible she had only enjoyed Snowhawk's friendship but if not, it meant they were lovers, had probably *always* been lovers, and that Snowhawk had lied about being happy in Tor and Serest's partnering.

But why bother *unless* Snowhawk only wanted Serest as a casual lover and Serest had used Tor to arouse the *handsome* Snowhawk's jealousy. It would explain her delay of marriage too.

Crystaleyes broke cover and Tor slipped deeper into the trees, in no mood for polite conversation, and then his heart missed as a tall, dark-haired figure emerged from the fyrs. For a moment he thought it was Chant but it was Mist and Tor stepped back into the open. Mist started and again Tor wondered why the Uncles had released Mist into a *hunter's* care. His name was puzzling too. Mist's blue eyes, dark hair and fair skin made names like Night or even Sky a better fit.

'I greet you, Tor,' said Mist.

'I greet you,' replied Tor. 'I thought Snowhawk was with you,' he added, wondering if Serest had lied.

'He was but then he was going to hunt. I've heard since another hunter killed a scinton so maybe Snowhawk won't have to hunt after all.'

'I gifted the scinton.'

'Oh,' said Mist, and coloured.

'If you're returning to the boys' Turrel, you've strayed too far west,' said Tor, and gave Mist directions for the safest route back. Mist blushed again as he thanked Tor and, as Tor continued his journey, he recalled how awkward he had been at Mist's age *and* how uncertain. He was still uncertain about Serest, he conceded, but even in the boys' Turrel, he had known his path as a hunter, while Mist didn't seem to know anything.

In the days that followed Serest's desertion, Tor spent as much time as possible in the Whitelands. The effort to survive its frigid emptiness gifted him a dreamless, exhausted sleep, but nothing gifted him back his contentment. He wondered sometimes whether it would have been better to have never tasted the sweetness of her love. He hadn't been happy alone but he hadn't been miserable either and he'd had Snowhawk and Serest's friendship, whereas now he had nothing.

His self-imposed exile increased the beasts he gifted to Siah and his reputation grew, but the admiring glances of younger hunters reminded him too keenly of Chant. Even if Serest hadn't returned to him, the void had reclaimed Chant too swiftly for love to grow.

The last time Tor had gifted a beast, Ketwing had taken him aside and assured him Chant *would* return and Tor hadn't upset his former guide by arguing, but common sense told him Chant would never frequent Berian-tur again.

His thoughts were on her again as he neared his tur at the end of another long hunt. The beast was in Siah's keeping but his shirt was stiff with blood and he wore the sweat of the journey. He gathered windfall as he went, looking forward to bathing, cooking a simple stew and sleeping, but when he pushed open the door, Serest lounged at the table.

Hope flared but resentment did too and held him for a moment, like a black-moth in a web. Then he went to the fire circle, dropped his load of windfall, and rubbed the resin from his hands. 'Why have you come?' he asked.

'To see you of course,' she said, tilting her head.

She had looked at him like that as she had tugged him into bed, and desire surged. 'I don't think that's a good idea,' he said, mechanically setting the fire.

'As you won't come to Snowhawk's tur, I think it is an excellent idea.' She was perfectly at ease as she came to him but Tor found even the mundane task of striking spark hard.

'You've chosen Snowhawk and as Snowhawk knows I desire you too, it's best I stay away.'

'I don't want to mean less to you than Snowhawk does,' she pouted, sliding her fingers down his cheek. 'I want to mean *everything* to you and for that, you must trust me. It's your suspicion that drives us apart, Tor, not Snowhawk. I delayed our marriage because you don't believe Snowhawk and I aren't lovers. I can't marry you until you give me your trust,' she murmured. 'I need your trust, Tor.'

Tor knew he should send her away and get on with his life but her nearness fired the longing of all his nights alone. 'I want to trust you,' he said thickly.

Unexpectedly, Serest laughed. 'I suppose that will have to do for now,' she said, and was still smiling as she peeled off his shirt.

'I want to trust you,' repeated Tor, but there was more pain than pleasure in his voice, and then Serest's sweet mouth ended further speech.

21

Tel trudged on through the night cursing the mud, the murk and the endless rain. He had forgotten what it was like to wear dry clothes, to sleep, and to wake in comfort. The gardens needed rain but why in Ashali's name must it fall now? Chant! She was the root cause of all his problems and while he grudgingly conceded she hadn't brought the rains; her pernicious influence had encouraged Tanalan to run off after Kanan.

The only good thing to emerge from his corral's upheaval was the discovery of just how fast he could travel when he had the need. He had reached the Teresas in less time than he dared hope possible, and then . . . Tel shuddered and the sense of foreboding washed over him again.

He had followed the path almost blindly, the clouds hiding all from view, and then the path had disappeared, wiped away by a landslide. And then, as he had peered down at the river, he had seen a pack snagged on a submerged tree. It had to be Tanalan or Chant's, but had the river taken one of them or both or just the pack?

The awful question seemed to have been answered when he reached the cleft. It was flooded, as predicted, and while Chant might have tried to pass, out of ignorance or spite, Tanalan would have waited, but neither were there.

He had shouted himself hoarse and searched the surrounding slope and then braved the surging waters himself. As head of corral, it was now his terrible duty to inform Kanan that his future wife had drowned. But what was he to say to his mother and brother and little sister? Merala had already endured the loss of her husband; must she now mourn a daughter as well?

Chant yearned for death as the water pressed in, cold and crushing, but as the void swirled closer, her flailing hand connected with something warm and rough and clamped shut. It tossed her back to the surface, and she vomited bile and water but held on.

It was a tree root that had unwound from the bank and, shuddering with cold and shock, Chant hauled herself along it back to the wall. She was terrified it would break off and send her back into the river's icy depths but her heel touched the path and she stood. She had no idea whether Tanalan was in front or behind or had been swept away too but she *did* know that, to escape the water, she must let go of the root.

She unclamped her aching fingers and, panting with fear, edged along the submerged path and around the next bend. Ahead of her, the path emerged from the river and Chant staggered up it. Watery footsteps followed her and the last thing she remembered, before darkness closed in, was the horror of being hunted by the water.

There was the stench of rot and mud, and the kinder smell of smoke and Chant opened her eyes. It was all but dark and Tanalan had her back turned, bent over a sullenly smoking fire.

'The wood's wet,' croaked Chant and struggled to sit.

Tanalan swivelled. 'Thank the mountain! I thought you had drowned. I thought . . .' She brought a shaking hand to her mouth.

Chant retched and spat dirty water. 'How far . . . to the . . . Meduin?'

'We could be there before dawn if you weren't ill,' muttered Tanalan.

It was understandable Tanalan resented being caught so close to the man she loved and Chant struggled to her feet and swayed as her surroundings tilted.

'You need to rest,' said Tanalan, scrambling up.

Chant's stomach roiled again but she swallowed down the bile. 'We need to . . . go on.'

Tanalan stared at her in disbelief but stamped out the fire and they set off, Chant clutching at passing bushes to stay upright. The path left the river and a thunderous roar grew as it zigzagged its way down. Chant wondered if the river had damaged her ears but Tanalan beckoned her from the path and Chant stumbled after her and stopped in shock. An immense column of water bellowed from the night sky, smashed onto the rocks below, and billowed up in great clouds of fume.

'The Terefall,' bawled Tanalan, 'where the Sunwash drops to the valley floor.'

Chant nodded, too overwhelmed to speak. They went on but every step was an effort, her muscles cramping, and her belly throwing up bile.

'There's a shivering fever near the sea,' said Tanalan, on one of their many stops, 'but I've heard of no illness that afflicts the Sunnen or Meduin here.'

Chant sat on a log, her head in her hands, too ill to dispute that Sceadu weakness was somehow to blame. She had swallowed a lot of river water and a host of dead things had been washed into its flow. 'You . . . go on,' she panted.

'I can't leave you here alone.'

Chant managed to raise her head. 'I won't be . . . alone . . . for long.'

Tanalan's wide eyes searched the darkness behind them. 'I'll send my Meduin kin back for you,' she said hurriedly.

'Don't. I'll . . . come . . . with Tel.'

Tanalan gave an awkward nod and hastened away and as soon as she had gone, Chant slid from the log onto the ground. Lying down was easier than sitting, and closing her eyes, easier still.

The rain had stopped and it was close to dawn but Tel barely noticed, fighting to keep his mind empty as he strode along; the words he must say to Kanan and later to Merala, too painful to contemplate. And then someone moved on the path ahead and he jerked to a stop.

Meduin lands were peaceful but he braced himself and then the predawn light revealed the long loose hair. Chant; alone, and the last of his hope guttered. 'Where's Tanalan?' he asked hoarsely.

'Gone.'

Tel seized her and shook her savagely. He wanted to inflict real pain but managed to thrust her away. 'You've done this!' he snarled. 'Tanalan would *never* have left but for you! *You've* killed her!'

'She's gone to Kanan.'

Chant's knife flashed as he took a step towards her. 'I saw her pack in the water!'

'It went when the slope collapsed but she didn't go with it.'

Chant had no reason to lie but doubt gnawed. 'You'll come with me,' he said, and went to haul her up, but recoiled as the knife nicked his hand.

'Touch me again and I'll add to that scar on your shoulder!'

It wasn't the Sunnen way to lay hands on a woman and Tel fought to subdue his anger. 'We need to keep moving,' he said.

She seemed to agree because she clambered to her feet. 'You lead,' she said.

She obviously believed he would attack her again and shame at his loss of control added to his temper. Having to screw his head around to speak to her didn't help either. 'How long since Tanalan left?' he demanded.

'She will be with Kanan by now.'

'If Tanalan is foolish enough to *be* with Kanan, her reputation will be beyond repair,' he growled and, as head of *her* corral, his would be too.

'You think Kanan is unworthy of her?'

'His worthiness is irrelevant,' spat Tel, incensed by the ignorance of the question. 'Tanalan needs *my* permission to take a husband because unlike *your* people, who care *nothing* for *their* women, *we* protect *ours*. Tanalan remains in *my* care until *I* decide otherwise.'

'You obviously care nothing about her happiness.'

'I care about her safety!' retorted Tel, 'and it's usual for Sunnen women to *respect* those who care for them, *unlike* Sceadu women, who obviously treat *their* carers with contempt.'

Chant stopped and Tel was tempted to leave her to sulk alone but as he glanced over his shoulder, she staggered and fell to her knees. He hastened back and stopped as she drew her knife again. She was soaked from head to toe and his blood chilled as he realised she must have lost her footing in the Terecleft.

'Why didn't you tell me you were ill?' he demanded, keeping a careful eye on the knife.

'We didn't get . . . to that part of . . . the conversation.'

Tel grunted and glanced up at the brightening sky. If he were to discover whether his sister still lived, he must help this savage walk. 'Unless you want to spend the rest of your days here, you'll have to accept my aid,' he said.

She looked up and he was taken aback by the anguish in her face. What she muttered made no sense either. *You won't do it alone, although you might wish to.*

'What?' She ignored him but at least she sheathed the knife and he passed her his waterskin, gratified to see her drink. 'When did you last eat?' he asked.

'Tanalan's pack had the food.'

He passed her some berrem and though her hands shook, she took only small bites as if to prolong every mouthful. So it was with those who chased beasts across the lands to fill their bellies!

She ignored his proffered hand and struggled to her feet, but she was so unsteady he brought his arm round her. He half expected to feel the knife plunge into him a second time but she didn't react; either too ill to notice or having given into common sense.

She was his height which made her easy to hold, unlike Nasala, who barely reached his shoulder, but her limp reminded him of the traps and he forced his thoughts back to Kanan. Tel liked the Meduin man but Tanalan's defiance had prevented her proper transfer to Kanan's corral and may have fatally complicated her pledging.

Chant had sagged against him by the time they reached the rise above the Meduin Stead and Tel lowered her down and offered her his waterskin again, and berrem and fish.

She ate in silence, her gaze on the Stead. 'It's like Berian-tur,' she said, after a while.

'Berian-tur?'

'My home,' she said, still intent on the Stead. 'They have a Great Turrel and smaller turs but fences like yours.' Her black eyes came to his in puzzlement. 'What are they for?'

'The fences? They protect the stays and show ownership.'

'Ownership? Like you owning Tanalan?'

'Care isn't ownership,' snapped Tel, his thoughts on his looming meeting with Kanan again.

The Meduin man was well-respected and since the death of his father, head of his corral. His gardens were large and fertile too. The Meduin still wasted their time hunting but marriages between them and the Sunnen were common. Tanalan would be far from lonely, *if* she still lived, *if* the marriage proceeded.

'Time to go,' he said brusquely, and helped Chant up. She was still unsteady and he kept a grip on her arm as they descended, but she slowed as they passed ponds set amongst the trees. 'For hunting,' he said briefly, and hauled her on.

'The Meduin *hunt* the water?' she asked in confusion.

'You can't *hunt* water,' said Tel impatiently. 'The Meduin hunt the reed-ducks the water attracts, although they'd be better served using the water for their gardens,' he added.

22

Tel's descent of the scrubby slope was too fast for Chant who wanted to curl up somewhere and sleep. Tension radiated from him and Chant hoped his coming meeting with Kanan went well, for everyone's sake. And if it didn't? Tel would drag Tanalan back to the Stead, or fight Kanan, *or* both.

There must have been watchers for people emerged from the turs as they entered the corral. There was a stocky, powerfully built man; two younger men about Islan's age; and a woman bent double with hair as white as Ashali. There was no sign of Tanalan.

Tel released Chant so suddenly she clutched the fence to stay upright, and then he advanced across the yard to meet the powerfully built man Chant assumed was Kanan. They reminded her of the he-berians that circled each other at snowmelt. Combat didn't always follow but was deadly when it did.

No good could come from a fight between Tel and Kanan, for even if Kanan won, Chant suspected he must still seek Tel's permission to wed Tanalan, and Tel would hardly be likely to grant it. And if Tel won, his mean-spiritedness meant he might deny Kanan a wife anyway.

Tel came to a stop and Kanan bowed. 'Welcome to my corral, Tel,' he said.

Tel nodded briefly, consumed by a single question. 'Is Tanalan here?'

'Your sister rests in my mother's stay.'

The knot in Tel's stomach loosened but his anger rekindled. 'This meeting is not of my choosing, Kanan. My sister had no right to leave the Sunnen Stead without my permission, nor to risk herself in the journey here.'

Kanan inclined his head but held his silence and Tel paused. He stood in Kanan's corral, confronting not just Kanan, but Kanan's kin, likely soon to be his and whatever came of this meeting, as head of a corral, he was obliged to maintain cordial relations.

'My anger is not for the husband my sister has chosen,' he said more quietly, 'but for the *manner* of her choosing. Her behaviour has been anything but proper.' Still Kanan said nothing, which showed both restraint and goodwill but an important obstacle remained: Tanalan's reckless behaviour had prevented the proper confirmation of the match.

'It has been two seasons since you last saw my sister,' continued Tel. 'It is a long time to be apart and much may happen over so many moons. I would deem it no insult if your heart has changed since you pledged.'

'My heart hasn't changed,' said Kanan, 'nor my desire to have your sister as my wife. As you say, it has been two seasons since we pledged, a commitment made in accordance with Sunnen and Meduin customs. You have been rightly angered by what has followed but I ask that the pledge be honoured and that you pass your sister into my care.'

Tel considered the other man and Kanan met his gaze steadily. 'The pledge is honoured,' said Tel finally. 'I welcome you, brother.' Kanan's face split into a broad smile and they embraced, and then the others crowded forward, Tanalan amongst them.

Chant had no idea how long she slept after Kanan, or was it Tel, helped her to a tur, and the white-haired woman plied her with sweet drinks, stripped off her wet clothes and eased her between bed covers, but she woke feeling much improved.

Tanalan sorted clothes nearby but stopped when she saw Chant was awake. 'You are feeling well?' she asked. Chant nodded, relieved the nausea had gone. Tanalan looked very different. Her clothing was clean, her expression soft, and her eyes shining. She even blushed when she told Chant her wedding was to take place in three days.

Chant congratulated her but her smile felt wooden. Love seemed to come so easily to others: Scead and Siah, Tanalan and Kanan, and Tor and Serest had probably married by now too.

Chant willed Tanalan to leave so she could find her clothes and escape, but Tanalan perched on the bed instead. 'The wedding's been brought forward, because of the . . . way I arrived here,' she said, and smoothed down her shirt. 'I . . . I've yet to thank you for saving me when the land slipped. As for what I said afterwards . . . I was wrong and beg your pardon.'

'You weren't wrong,' said Chant, and cleared her throat. 'I'm not pledged yet. It won't happen until I return home.'

It was a measure of Tanalan's newfound happiness that she wasn't angry at Chant's deception but she warned Chant that Tel would be. 'He hates deceit,' she said.

And I hate bullies, thought Chant, but she held her tongue. She was leaving that night anyway and wouldn't have to endure Tel's loathsome company again. But Tanalan was horrified when she voiced her intentions. 'You can't leave! I *must* have female kin with me on my wedding day.'

'I'm hardly that,' said Chant, startled by Tanalan's reaction.

'No, but you lived with us for several moons and it would be even more *improper* if no woman from the Sunnen Stead witnessed my marriage. You *must* stay, Chant,' she repeated, and caught Chant's hands. 'If it weren't for you, there would be *no* marriage. Please, Chant. I need you here.'

Tanalan was on the verge of tears but Chant had already postponed her journey for Islan. 'It's only three more days,' begged Tanalan, and was so distressed that Chant reluctantly agreed. 'I'll see what clothes Kalia can find for you for the ceremony,' she said eagerly.

'I don't need—' began Chant, but Tanalan had already gone.

They ate together that night in Kalia's tur. Kanan's ancient mother reminded Chant of Merala and of the happier times she'd spent in the Sunnen Stead. She was surprised how much she missed Merala, Islan and Inkala given their early strangeness.

The conversation ebbed and flowed around her and she glanced at the cooking pots gleaming on the shelves and the patterned mats on the walls. The tur held an air of plenty, like Merala's had, not because the Sunnen and Meduin laboured harder than the Sceadu, but because the rains gifted them time to do other than search for food.

Kanan and Tel sat together in quiet speech but the rest of the gathering noisily exchanged news of harvests, the building and letting go of gardens, and of those who had settled in other Steads.

Chant found the idea of far-flung kin strange but the Sceadu songs and chants told how the Sceadu had crossed Ashali from the west and that meant she probably had kin elsewhere too. Tarish hooted with laughter over something and she roused. He and Simien were taller than Kanan, despite being younger, and as rangy as Firn had been.

Even as she considered them, Tarish caught her eye. 'Tanalan tells me you hunt,' he said. Chant nodded; aware the other conversations had quietened. 'Simien and I hunt too,' he said.

'What beasts—' began Chant, but Tel interrupted. 'Were the Meduin to spend more time on their gardens, they'd have no need to waste their strength in chases through the trees.'

Kanan smiled good-naturedly. 'The Meduin don't seek to emulate the mighty gardens of the Sunnen,' he said. 'We seek the beasts the Groves grant us as well.'

'Or *don't* grant you,' said Tel.

'Beasts will be granted if the gift isn't wasted,' said Chant tartly.

Tel's sardonic gaze came to rest on her. 'The Sceadu have *no* gardens at all, such is their faith in what the land offers or *fails* to offer.'

Chant drew breath to retaliate but Simien broke in excitedly. 'Your hunters must be very skilled indeed!'

'Skilled they may be but are so few they even risk their women on hunt,' said Tel.

Chant turned on him angrily. 'It's true we aren't like the Sunnen,' she said. 'We don't *own* others or force a girl-child to be this, or a boy-child that. To come to know the earth, our children are gifted earth-names. To come to know themselves and their life task, they are gifted air-names. All Sceadu carry these naming lines,' she said, touching her face, 'except the girl who has yet to become a woman, and the *boy* who has yet to become a *man*.'

Her gaze on Tel made it clear who the jibe was aimed at but before Tel could respond, Kanan broke in smoothly. 'It is well you are here then, Chant,' he said, 'for we have a marriage feast to prepare.'

'Simien and I hunt this night,' said Tarish eagerly. 'Will you come?'

'She's been ill,' said Tel sharply.

'You leave at moonrise?' she asked, keeping her attention on Tarish. Tarish nodded. 'I will be ready.'

23

$\mathcal{T}$el completed another round of the cooking place and paused to peer out the window. The dew was long gone and he grunted with frustration. Waiting for Chant to wake had seemed preferable to the meetings that preceded Meduin marriage rites, but Tarish and Simien had breakfasted and departed some time ago.

He threw himself into a chair then wondered whether Chant's illness had returned. Then he cursed as he recalled that illness haunted the flat valleys near the sea *and* was at its worse this time of season!

He had planned to continue to the Okianos after Tanalan's wedding, rather than return home and set out again later, but common sense dictated he do exactly that. His breath hissed he and resolved to find out why Chant hadn't bothered to appear.

Quick strides took him to the stay she shared with Tanalan, and he knocked once and thrust open the door. She still slept, her clothes strewn over the bed, the pale skin of her back visible under a tumble of blue-black hair.

Tel knew his presence was improper, but something held him there. She looked younger asleep and more vulnerable but, even as he watched, she gave a violent gasp and came awake. Her black eyes met his as they had at the Sunwash before the traps, but mussed with sleep and, as they focussed, he gave a small bow.

'There is food for you in Kalia's stay,' he said. 'I'll await you there.'

Chant was so relieved to escape the dream she barely registered Tel's presence, but she certainly registered her hunger and hastened to Kalia's tur. Tel lounged by the fire but filled a bowl for her from the cooking pot. The stew was a tasty mix of spicy meat and greenfood and she savoured every mouthful.

'Kanan begs your pardon for his absence,' said Tel. 'He is taken up with his wedding preparations.' Chant nodded. 'He would normally congratulate you on the prin you killed as well.'

'It was Tarish's beast,' said Chant, intent on the stew.

'Tarish said *you* killed it and Simien called you *the best hunter in all the Meduin lands*. You seem make a habit of impressing *young* men, Chant.'

'The wind changed just before Tarish loosed his arrow,' said Chant, ignoring Tel's mocking tone. 'But he took its scent first and tracked first.' She finished the stew and rose.

'There is more if you hunger,' said Tel quickly, but she shook her head and moved towards the door. 'And what do you intend to do today?' he asked.

Chant reluctantly paused. 'Explore the Groves.'

'That would be unwise. A stranger near the Stead will elicit suspicion, for the Meduin rarely see strangers. Normally Kanan would provide a stranger such as yourself with an escort but as he's otherwise occupied, I am willing to escort you.'

'Don't trouble yourself,' said Chant, annoyed Tel had called her a stranger three times in so short a speech. 'I'll stay in the corral.'

'Let me know if you change your mind. The corral's likely to prove monotonous for someone who's accustomed to wandering at will.'

Tel's prediction proved correct and Chant soon regretted her promise to wait for the wedding. Tanalan was absent anyway, as were Kanan and Tel, and only Kalia, Tarish and Simien shared the evening meal. Kalia dozed, her bent frame as fragile as snowmelt ice, but Tarish and Simien made up for their mother's silence, and Chant learned more about the Meduin marriage rites.

The couple spent time with the Meduin Elders being instructed in their responsibilities to each other and to the Stead, for the marriage pledge couldn't be undone, no matter how ill the union.

The idea seemed ludicrous to Chant. 'The Sceadu understand the young sometimes make mistakes and allow a marriage to be broken in its first season,' she said.

Tarish and Simien were astonished. 'It's a shame Tel's with the Council discussing the setting of gardens,' said Tarish. 'He has great interest in the ways of different peoples.'

Chant snorted. 'Tel has no interest in the Sceadu.'

'You're mistaken,' croaked Kalia, coming awake. 'Tel is curious about strangers no matter who they are. He's journeyed to the far west, unlike most Sunnen, and Tanalan tells me he's to journey there again once the marriage festivities are complete.'

Her rheumy eyes contemplated Chant. 'I understand you journey that way too. It would make sense to travel together.'

Chant stifled a retort as she recalled Tel would soon be Kalia's kin. 'Sceadu hunters travel alone,' she muttered, but had an uncomfortable feeling Kalia knew exactly how she felt.

Tanalan returned later that night as Chant checked her arrows. They seemed unaffected by their dunking in the Sunwash, unlike Chant, who never wanted to go near a river again.

'Tel's to visit our kin in the west after my marriage rites,' said Tanalan. 'It would be safer if you journeyed with him.'

'Sceadu hunters travel alone,' she said, but Tanalan proved harder to put off than Kalia. 'Tel's been there before. It would make your journey easier.'

'Tel hunted you all the way here,' said Chant in exasperation, 'and would have forced you back to his corral, had he caught you, and yet you want me travel with him?'

'You don't understand Sunnen ways,' said Tanalan.

'I understand them enough to want no part of them!'

Chant expected a nasty retort but Tanalan looked more discomfited than angry. 'Tel acted as a head of corral should,' she said. 'Our father died when Inkala was a baby and Tel little more than a child himself, but he's looked after us since. I understand why he wanted me safely in the Sunnen Stead, better now Kanan's discussed it with me. Tel acted correctly,' she repeated. Chant said nothing and Tanalan's voice softened. 'Even in the

149

Sceadu lands, it must be safer to travel in company than alone, isn't it?'

'Sometimes,' muttered Chant, recalling the horror of the serest.

Tanalan softened her voice. 'Whatever Tel's faults, he would never desert you.'

'I might desert him,' said Chant tartly.

'I don't believe you're that kind either,' said Tanalan. 'Think on it, Chant. Kanan and I wed tomorrow evening, and Tel leaves soon after. It would be a relief to know you travelled with him.'

Giving relief to Tanalan wasn't Chant's priority but she held her tongue.

Tanalan was absent again when Chant woke, in fact, Kalia seemed the only person in the corral and Chant spent another tedious day alone and was relieved when the sun finally westered. No one came to the tur and her spirits rose at the possibility she'd been overlooked and she was considering whether leaving early broke her pledge to Tanalan, when Kalia appeared with an armful of clothes.

Chant's heard sank as she laid them carefully on the bed. 'They belonged to my daughter,' said Kalia, as her gnarled fingers gently smoothed the cloth. 'I lost her to childbirth and the babe too.' Her face crumpled and Chant waited uncomfortably for her to steady. 'I'm sure there is something here to suit you,' she said, and hobbled to the door. 'I'll be back soon and we can go to the ceremony together.'

Kalia's grief reminded Chant of Tel's when he'd thought Tanalan lost. It seemed the way the Sunnen and Meduin lived, with each family sequestered in its own corral, led to this burden of feeling, where the death of one person was the loss of all love. Chant had been heartbroken when Talith had died, but there had been love aplenty from her ageset, the Aunts and Uncles, and the elders.

Chant wished again she hadn't agreed to wait, but there was no escaping her pledge, and she selected a blue dress and trousers. The clothing looked well enough, she supposed but she resented pleasing Tel by looking more Sunnen.

Kalia returned clad in pale green with yellow flowers in her hair and carrying a garland for Chant of vivid crimson blooms.

Chant groaned inwardly but bent obediently to allow Kalia to set it on her head. 'I hoped the colours would suit you,' said Kalia, squinting up at her, 'and they do. If Tel doesn't see your beauty now, he's even blinder than I thought.' Kalia smiled at Chant's expression. 'I've always enjoyed a little match-making and I'm good at it. Kanan wouldn't be marrying this evening if it weren't for my skills.'

Kalia clung to Chant's arm as they made their way out of the corral, her frailty making their progress excruciatingly slow and giving her plenty of time to tackle another uncomfortable topic. 'Tel's told me you're pledged and Tanalan's told me you're not,' she said, her rheumy eyes surprisingly shrewd.

Chant's face warmed but she decided against describing the complications of her air-naming and instead, gave the answer she hoped would end Kalia's questioning. 'I lied to Tel. We were arguing.'

'There's much that can be said in the heat of argument and yet you claimed to belong to another man. I think you told Tel that to keep him from you.'

Chant gaped at her. 'He despises me!'

'Tel chips away at you until you respond in kind,' said Kalia, 'but he's not a man to waste time on things he despises.' Chant's head filled with a long list of things that rebutted Kalia's claim but then Kalia spoke again. 'Tanalan says your limp was caused by one of Tel's bear-traps.'

'The accident was caused by my blindness,' said Chant tightly.

'We have bears in the Meduin lands too but we don't use traps,' said Kalia. 'We are wary and the bears the same.'

'Not like the Sunnen,' muttered Chant.

'Different peoples have different ways,' said Kalia mildly. The steepening path robbed Kalia of the breath to speak for which Chant was grateful and, after a while, the path forked and Kalia steered Chant along the northern one. 'The women's path,' she rasped. 'The southern one belongs to men.'

'Why don't they use the same path?' asked Chant curiously.

'Men tread the earth differently . . . with less feeling, some women say. Whatever their ways . . . men journey in the manner they must . . . just as our journey is . . . true to *our* natures. But in the end, men and women . . . must journey together . . . or else the world . . . would be forever broken in two and . . . never made whole.'

Chant's thoughts swung to Siah and Scead: the spirit of the Sceadu and the flesh of the Sceadu, together making the Sceadu whole. But where did that leave the hunter? And more troublingly, where did it leave *her*?

Tel sat cross-legged on a mat with Tarish next to him, then Simien, followed by men who stretched away in a loose circle in kinship order. The kin-linked women made up another circle inside theirs, and both circles enclosed the podium where the marriage rites would take place.

There was a gap in the women's circle where Kalia would sit but there was no sign of her yet or of Chant. Tel wondered if Kalia were ill again and Chant had stayed with her, or whether Kalia still made her way to the ceremony and Chant had departed. His lips thinned. Chant breaking her pledge to Tanalan would be no surprise at all. His fingers drummed the mat and he would have returned to the corral to check on her whereabouts had it not risked missing the ceremony.

The hubbub quieted and Tel swivelled as the Meduin Elders appeared in solemn procession, followed by Tanalan and Kanan. Tel's heart swelled with pride as Tanalan moved past, her beaded dress flashing red and yellow in the last of the sunlight and her loose hair crowned with white and red blooms.

The Elders took up position on the podium, Tanalan and Kanan kneeling before them, and Tel glanced back to see Kalia and Chant had taken their places too. Both were finely dressed but Chant was luminous. The blue beads of her dress echoed the blue-black of her hair and a garland of crimson flowers formed a halo around her face.

The Elders began the rites but Tel was struck by the contrast with Chant's usual wild demeanour and his attention remained on her. She sat with her head down and after a while, Tel realised she was distressed. The ceremony probably reminded her of her *absent* future husband and contempt for the man rose like gorge in Tel's throat. If he had any doubts about Kanan's ability to care for Tanalan, he would stop the ceremony even now, but Kanan's face held only the most steadfast commitment.

Tel found Kanan's expression reassuring but also disturbing. To bind yourself to another person for life seemed a shocking gamble and Tel couldn't imagine doing so, even with Nasala. Merala's long grieving for his dead father, when Tel had heard her cry herself to sleep night after night, proved how foolhardy it could be.

The ritual words ended and Chant helped Kalia to her feet. Chant was desperate to be gone from where lovers reinforced her own aloneness but drums and pipes started instead. The women began to sing, their voices as light as the breeze, and then to dance, small rhythmic steps in time with the music. Chant danced too, keeping a steadying hand on Kalia's shoulder as she tottered in front. The men sang and danced as well, as did the Elders, and in the centre of the moving circles, Tanalan and Kanan danced entwined.

Chant kept her face towards the newly married couple, aware of Tel's tall shape as he danced past behind her, and of Tarish and Simien's grins as they followed. Then the music ended and the circle of men turned to face the circle of women.

Chant knew Tel's sweet-water scent, the arrogant tilt of his head, the flesh where she had plunged the knife. Once she would have raised her face in challenge but not this night. The music had blasted a way through her, tearing her open for all to see, and she turned and fled into the darkness—and Tel followed.

Tel called to Chant to stop but she didn't lessen her pace and as his heaving lungs forced him to slow, worry for her turned to anger. Her departure from the ceremony was discourteous in the extreme, as was his own, and he was in high temper by the time he reached Kanan's corral. But as he stormed across the yard, he heard sobbing. It reminded him of the terrible time at the traps and guilt added to his anger.

Chant lay face down on her bed but sprang up when he entered, her hand going to the empty place at her hip. Always the knife, thought Tel sourly, which at least left no doubts about her feelings. Even so, as a former guest of his corral, he owed her *some* protection.

'What has upset you?' he asked formally. She didn't answer but the catch in her breath reminded him of Inkala at her most distressed and he had to quell the impulse to comfort her. That right belonged to the stinking man on Ashali's other side, in fact,

the man's absence gave Tel the chance to discharge his debt for her injuries. 'I'm to continue west after the wedding festivities and understand your journey lies that way too. I've journeyed there before and am willing to guide you.'

'I leave this night.'

'You pledged Tanalan to stay for her marriage rites!'

'I've fulfilled my pledge.'

'The rites end after the marriage feast and that's tomorrow,' pointed out Tel.

'Tomorrow? But I've delayed too long already,' she said in alarm.

'Given how urgent your journey is, I presume you know the *quickest* route to the sea?'

Chant's chin came up. 'Islan said I only need to follow the Sunwash.'

'Following the Sunwash *will* take you to the sea—in about a moon. The route I know takes a third of that time.' Her uncertainty was clear and he pressed home his advantage. 'You can travel *swiftly* with me, *if* you delay until the morrow's feast, or leave now and travel *slowly* on your own.'

'I'll delay,' she muttered, making no effort to hide her resentment.

'A victory for common sense,' he couldn't resist saying, but as he made his way across the corral, the reality of journeying with the Sceadu savage struck home. It wouldn't be a pleasant trek but he predicted it would be far from dull.

24

$\mathcal{C}$hant was shocked by the quantity of food consumed at the marriage feast. As well as the aperion she had hunted, there were roasted birds, boiled birds' eggs, toasted nuts, baked whiteroot, errem pats swathed in honey, fruits pickled in syrup, and fermented drinks that made the men sing, and later, stagger. What would have sustained the Great Turrel for many days was eaten in a single sitting, and those who gorged even complained of feeling ill from their greed.

By sunset she was desperate to offer her thanks to her host and complete her formal farewells. She tried to ignore Tanalan's delight that she was to travel with Tel after all and the gleam of Kalia's eyes as she kissed Chant on each cheek and wished her a safe journey.

Tel was glad the first part of the trek took them through the Groves where the paths were well marked. It had been many seasons since he'd been to the Meduin lands and he was grateful for Kanan's instructions. The paths would take them to the end of the trees and then they would follow the Sunwash until they reached the Old Stead. Kanan's knowledge went no further, but Tel was confident his memories would become clearer as they went on.

They walked through the night and it was dawn before Tel called a halt. He glanced about as if his only concern were a suitable resting place but, in truth, he was bone-achingly weary. He would have stopped earlier but Chant hadn't complained and he was keen to prove his strength was equal to hers. She refused his offer of a sleep-shelter with her usual lack of politeness, pulled out some rough sort of sheet, and curled up with her weapons. Tel settled nearby and when he woke, Chant had gone.

So much for Sceadu pledges, he thought angrily, as he shoved his sleep-shelter into his pack and then he sensed movement behind him. His heart thundered at the possibility of bears and he drew his knife and slowly turned.

It was Chant, her hands loaded with wildfruit. 'I've found us some breakfast,' she said.

'I've enough food for both of us,' he clipped out, still rattled. She wordlessly set half the fruit on the ground and stalked off and he followed, aware he'd been discourteous. 'Perhaps it's best we keep my food for later. I thank you,' he added.

Chant ignored him *and* his attempts at conversation as they went on and Tel sourly concluded it would be a long and dreary trip if she continued to sulk.

The path became more overgrown as the trees thinned and then gave way to grasslands. The Sunwash gleamed in the distance but was further than it looked and it neared dusk before they reached it. Tel thought it would be pleasant to eat on its banks but Chant refused, and he bad-temperedly led the way to higher ground.

'Where will we be by this time tomorrow?' she asked as they ate.

'Perhaps two or three days from the Old Stead.'

'*Perhaps*? You said you knew the way.'

'I *do* know the way,' he said tersely. 'The Old Stead is three days from the Groves; the Marshlands four days from the Old Stead; the sea two days from the Marshlands.'

'The sea . . .' she murmured, her gaze on the Sunwash's soft grey.

'Why are you journeying there?' asked Tel.

'You can't possibly be interested.'

'You're mistaken,' he retorted, annoyed by her rudeness. 'I am *fascinated* by Sceadu practices where a man lets his future wife go off, totally unprotected, on a long and perilous journey alone.'

Chant scrambled to her feet. 'I agreed to travel with you to shorten my trip, not to put up with your insults!' she said and strode off along the bank.

Tel took a steadying breath. If he wanted to keep her with him, he was going to have to keep his thoughts to himself. The next day he made an effort to be pleasant but Chant remained unresponsive though she seemed preoccupied rather than angry.

As night fell, they collected windfall and he set a fire and prepared white-root. She sat in silence, her gaze on the flames. 'Hungry?' he asked, wanting human speech even if it were an argument. She shook her head and he tried again. 'I've noticed you eat very little.'

'The Sceadu don't gorge like the Meduin.'

'It was a wedding feast,' he said in surprise.

'Squander the Willing beast's gift and the void will send no more. Then hunger will—' she stopped.

'The Sceadu hunger?'.

'There's less food when snowmelt's late but we have enough,' she muttered, keeping her gaze on the fire.

Tel bit back a comment about hunting's vagaries and asked about the Sceadu seasons instead. 'There are two: snowcome and snowmelt,' she said briefly.

'They're equal in length?' asked Tel, as he grappled with the notion of only two seasons.

'They were, but snowcome can last up to eight moons.'

'That must make your first harvest very late,' he said in shock. 'Ah, I forgot you prefer to scrounge what grows wild and kill what your arrows reach—or don't reach,' he couldn't resist adding.

'At least we don't leave beasts to suffer slow, agonising deaths in traps,' she retorted.

'The traps protect us from bears,' said Tel stiffly.

Chant's face hardened. 'What *you* call bears have as much right to forage as we do. They are *never* Willing.'

'In which case, I suppose your intended husband is happy for you to be killed by some beast, because as a hunter, you kill them.' He passed her the baked white-root but she refused to take it. 'Eat,' he said impatiently. 'I don't have time to slow my journey if you fall ill.'

'You won't have to! I'm not putting up with your obnoxious company a moment longer!'

She swept up her pack but Tel was just as angry and caught her arm. She pulled back, and when that didn't free her, twisted violently to break his grip and thrust her knife up between them. 'Stab me in the other shoulder this time and even things up,' he goaded, refusing to step back.

Her expression suggested she might just do that but then she sheathed her knife. 'I thank you for your guidance thus far,' she coldly, 'and wish you a safe journey to your kin.'

She strode off but Tel hurried after her and barred her way. 'I apologise for insulting your people,' he said quickly. Her face remained mutinous and he tried again. 'Stay, Chant. It's safer for us to travel together.'

'I've never sought safety!'

'No, but you've sought speed and I know the way. I would welcome your company,' he added. It was obvious she didn't believe him but her need for speed seemed to trump everything else and she came back to the fire.

Chant woke knowing it had been a mistake not to leave the previous day. Had she walked through the night she would be far from Tel now and closer to Scead but as the day progressed, Tel seemed like a different person.

He named the trees they passed, the birds that skimmed the river's surface, and the fish that flashed in its depths. He shared his knowing of the way ahead too, describing how the Sunwash would soon swing wide to skirt the Old Stead, a rocky outcrop of ruined stays.

'Once we reach the outcrop, it's quicker to leave the Sunwash and head straight west to the Old Stead,' he said. 'It's a hard climb, despite the path, and we can take the easier route along the river banks if you wish.'

'We'll take the quicker route,' said Chant, keen to compensate for her earlier delays.

They reached the outcrop as the light ebbed, taking the fine weather with it. 'It *would* rain now,' muttered Tel, as they started to climb.

'Rain is the void's gift and always welcome,' said Chant.

It was too wet to stop and Tel passed her berrem as they climbed. The path grew steeper and more overgrown, and Chant's ankle throbbed. The path didn't look like it had been used for seasons, *at least by people*, and Chant flared her nostrils. The rain washed the air clean of scent and she scanned. Fissures opened in the stony slope above and she stopped.

'We need to keep moving,' said Tel impatiently.

'It's berian country,' said Chant. 'We should leave the path.'

'Berian?'

'What you call bears.'

'Kanan said nothing about bears and the path is the quickest way up.'

Chant unclipped her bow and fitted an arrow. The low cloud made it harder to see. 'It was *your* choice to come this way,' said Tel. 'We need—'

There was a long, low growl and they froze as a massive black bear materialised from a fissure above. 'Get down!' ordered Chant.

'What—'

'Get down!' she repeated. She seized Tel's arm and forced him almost to his knees. 'Now, backwards,' she ordered, stepping off the path and dragging him with her into the bushes. 'Don't look up!' she hissed, as they floundered backwards down the slick slope. 'Keep going, keep going,' she instructed. 'Don't look up!' They scrambled on, scraped by stones and lacerated by branches, and were deep in the trees before Chant stopped.

'Why didn't you shoot it?' whispered Tel, half expecting the bear to burst through the bushes.

'I won't kill without need.'

'I wouldn't like to see a time when there *was* need!'

They crouched in silence, the only sound the drip of rain from the trees. 'We must find another path,' said Chant eventually.

'There *is* no other path.' Chant said nothing and Tel sleeved his eyes. 'The bear's probably gone. We can use the path again.'

'The path belongs to the berian. It will kill anything that moves on it.'

'It didn't kill us,' he pointed out.

'We submitted to it and were no longer a threat. Berian don't kill without cause; only men do that.'

Tel scowled at the implied insult. 'If we can't use the path, we'll have to force a way through the scrub.'

'We can't use the path.'

He started back up the slope and Chant followed, the sodden mesh of vegetation so dense in places, he had to hack a path with his knife.

'Are there caves nearby?' she asked, as they stopped to draw breath. It was completely dark and they were drenched.

'Kanan didn't mention any.'

'We could spend the night here,' she said. 'I could build a shelter.'

'The Sceadu might be content to curl up on the wet ground like animals but the Sunnen aren't,' he snapped.

A new scent intruded and Chant flared her nostrils. 'Is the Old Stead's stone different from the stone here?'

'Yes. Why?'

'Then it's more to the north.'

He shrugged but veered north and the slope gave way to an extraordinary sight. Immense stones towered over her or leaned against each other at drunken angles. Others had collapsed and lay half hidden in the undergrowth.

Chant shivered. 'Who lived here?' she whispered.

'No one knows. It's been deserted in the Meduin's memory and their memories are long indeed.'

'But why would they leave such a place?'

'Nothing lasts forever, especially when things change. There's less risk to people who grow their food than to those who hunt and forage,' he added.

'There's nothing to say these people weren't gardeners,' said Chant.

'I see no evidence of gardens.'

'Nothing lasts for ever,' she retorted and hugged herself. 'I don't like it here. I don't want to stay.'

'We need shelter.'

'Not the Sceadu. We're content to curl up on the wet ground

like animals.'

Tel sighed. 'I beg your pardon for saying that. I was annoyed with myself for guiding you badly.' He forced a smile. 'I know of a snug place where I can set a fire. Then I'll bake some white-root and toast berrem, and we'll both feel better.'

Chant followed him through the stones, glancing about uneasily. The Old Stead reminded her of Tarchen-tur despite the lack of bones and pyres. Tel stopped where stones had collapsed against each other to form an angular cave. It was dry inside and full of windblown twigs and branches, and he soon had a fire set and white-root baking.

Chant stared out at the triangle of rain-striped sky as Tel toasted errem. 'You did well to smell the stone,' he said, as he handed her some. 'You must be one of the Sceadu's best hunters.'

'Tor's more skilled,' she said, taking a mouthful of errem. 'He's hunted the Whitelands for five or six snowmelts whereas I've just started.'

'So Tor's the Sceadu's best hunter?' said Tel, retrieving white-root from the coals.

'Tor *and* Snowhawk. Between them they bring most of the meat to the Great Turrel.'

'How old are they?' asked Tel, setting the white-root on a platter between them.

'About twenty-three. They're in the same ageset.' Tel's face told her he had no understanding of *ageset* but his next question was about *Chant's* age. 'I'm eighteen,' she replied, brushing errem crumbs from her shirt.

'You're too young to be so far from home!' he exclaimed, looking genuinely upset.

'I'm air-named,' she said, surprised by his reaction.

'That changes nothing!'

'It changed everything,' she murmured and, for a while, only the fire's crack filled the silence.

'I would like to know more of the Sceadu,' said Tel eventually.

Chant doubted it, given his disdain for her ways, but it seemed churlish not to oblige and she described the turs and the

Great Turrel, how Little Sisters and Brothers were earth-named, and the air-naming and assigning of life tasks. She described Siah's guidance of the Sceadu too, but while Tel's interest was genuine, he couldn't hide his contempt for Siah's visioning of her journey.

'And this man you're pledged to; he agreed to you being sent away?'

'I chose to go.'

Tel leaned forward. 'Freely and without coercion? I find that hard to believe.'

'What you believe or don't believe is of no consequence to me,' said Chant. 'I granted you the courtesy of answering your questions and now, as I'm tired, I'm going to sleep.'

Chant slipped quickly into sleep and Tel stretched his legs to the fire. He couldn't believe she had set off into terrible danger because a woman called Siah had experienced a dream. Even given the Sceadu's bizarre practices, there had to be more to it than that.

His gaze moved over the curve of her shoulder and hip to her scarred ankle and he winced. At least he'd kept her with him to prevent further harm. The fire was pleasantly warm and his eyelids drooped but then she spoke and he roused. 'What?' he mumbled, then saw that she still slept.

She spoke the word again and then a third time before she settled. *Scead*; the longing in her voice left no doubt as to who *Scead* was. Tel's mouth twisted in distaste. He had a name now for everything he despised.

25

The rain drifted away overnight to leave the Old Stead bright with sunlit pools and the musical drip of foliage. It was beautiful but Chant couldn't wait to leave. The stones whispered of the Sceadu's fate if she failed her quest and the understanding made her skin crawl.

Tel looked grim too although his mood probably resulted from her refusal to use the path. They scrambled down through the scrub again but unlike the outcrop's eastern face, its western one was infested with briars. Tel used his knife to clear a path but they were soon badly scratched.

'I'll take the lead for a while,' said Chant, but Tel shook his head.

'You're already bleeding,' he said.

He tipped water into his hand to wash her scratched cheek but Chant stepped back. 'We're the same height and carry the same knife. What difference does it make who leads?'

'*I* lead,' said Tel.

'Why? Because you're head of corral?' she sneered.

'No, because I can protect you from even more scratches, unlike Scead, the stinking man you're pledged to.' Chant gaped at him. 'You called his name in your sleep,' said Tel, 'but I hardly think he deserves you.'

'Scead's not—'

'Here? Precisely! Like the rest of the Sceadu, he's abandoned you to Siah's ridiculous dream. Well I *am* here and I'm not about to abandon you to anything, including these thorns. Now stay behind me.'

'I'm not staying anywhere near you!' she fumed.

'Now's not the time for your foolish notions of Sceadu independence—'

Chant didn't wait to hear the rest of Tel's diatribe but began to hack her own path and, infuriated by Tel's mocking regard, ducked beneath the tangled growth. It was easier lower down anyway, she discovered, for small beasts had made runs through the mesh. Tel called to her but she struggled on until she stumbled out into the open. The Sunwash was thirty lengths away and Tel nowhere to be seen.

Her shirt was torn and blood beaded scores to her hands and arms but when she reached the river, she searched for signs of sudden flood before she washed her wounds. The rents reminded her of Firn after the first berian attack; of Ashin's interest in the healers' treatment of him; and of Spark's prediction he would live.

Scead and Siah had known their life-paths even then, while she had known nothing, *still* knew nothing. Grass seeds swirled on the water's surface and the sunlit world blurred, and then footsteps crunched over the grass and Chant blinked.

It was Tel, so badly scratched she felt sorry for him. 'I beg your pardon for insulting the man you're pledged to,' he said formally.

'I'm not pledged to Scead,' said Chant, her gaze on the water again. 'He's Siah's husband.'

There was silence and Chant glanced up. Tel's confusion was obvious and Chant felt scarcely better. She *would* marry Scead so to all intents and purposes they *were* pledged, except Scead was married to Siah and had never offered himself to Chant in marriage.

'At least we've reached the Sunwash,' said Tel, staring about. He peeled off his shirt and sluiced the water over his chest and torso. The scar on his shoulder was obvious and Chant glanced down at her ankle. They each bore scars inflicted by the other and would continue to injure each other with anger and argument while they remained together.

'I've decided to continue my journey alone,' she said, her words falling like stones through the sunny air.

Tel was busy drying himself with his shirt. 'I won't allow that.'

No amount of arguing was going to alter Tel's strange belief he was responsible for her and Chant didn't bother, just hefted on her pack and set off. He followed, keeping a constant distance behind her, and she had just decided to put more distance between them when he broke into a jog and caught up.

'We need to cross the Sunwash here,' he said, as if they'd been walking companionably all day. 'Those trees mark the beginning of Tirsad lands. They don't tolerate strangers but we'll be safe enough on the other side.'

Chant peered up and down the river. 'There's no crossing place.'

'It's an easy swim,' said Tel. 'I'll collect washwood to float our packs across. It worked well enough last time.'

Tel trawled about for wood and wove it together but Chant felt like she watched him from beneath tarn ice. Everything seemed distant, except for her heart, which roared in her ears.

Tel finished the raft and came back to her. 'Give me your pack and weapons, *and* your jacket and boots, unless you're intending to swim in them,' he said. Chant numbly handed them over and they joined his belongings on the raft. Then he set it on the water and waded in after it.

She didn't move and he glanced back impatiently. 'Are you ready? Night draws near.' Chant still didn't move and he sighed. 'I've explained to you why we need to cross. We—'

'I can't swim.'

Tel stared at her in disbelief. 'But you passed through the Terecleft *in flood*!'

'I was swept away. I almost drowned. I—' She drew a shuddering breath. 'I won't cross.'

Tel's mind raced. He had seen Chant angry and contemptuous, and at the traps, had witnessed her agony, but he had never seen her frightened *until now*. Her face held pure terror.

'I'll take the packs across first,' he said calmly. 'The current is gentle here and quite safe. I've swum it before with no problems. It will be easy for me to swim it again while you hold to my shoulders and float behind. It's quite safe.'

He managed to smile but he was in turmoil. They *must* cross the Sunwash and to do so, she *must* trust him, and nothing in their time together suggested she would. He pushed off and swam slowly, then made his way carefully up the bank, knowing it would be disastrous to slip and go under. Then he swam back.

Chant was exactly where he'd left her and he held her eyes as he came up the bank. 'Come,' he said, and extended his hand. She didn't move. 'Trust me, Chant,' he said softly and she placed her hand in his.

Then, keeping his pace even, he led her into the water. When it was chest deep, he stopped and turned to her. 'Join your hands around my neck, Chant. You must hold to me.' Her face was rigid, her eyes unblinking. 'Put your arms around my neck, Chant,' he repeated. 'Let the water take you.'

Let the water take you . . . Tel's voice came from afar, as if swallowed by the void. The water had taken her at the Terecleft and now it threatened to take her again. Tel's voice sounded again, pulling her back to the sunlit world and she managed to drag her arms from the water and encircle his neck. Then he pushed away and all solidity vanished.

Memories of the Terecleft's suffocating filth slammed back and the darkness swarmed with spectres. For once she let them come, their horror preferable to the water's dissolution. Tel spoke to her as he swam, but it was his warm skin and the pulse beneath that tethered her to life.

'We're across, Chant. You can stand.'

She opened her eyes but her aching fingers refused to unlock and Tel turned in the circle of her arms. The water flowed between them, tugging at her as if to tear her from the sunlit world, and she clung to him.

Tel held Chant close as he held Inkala when some fright sent her running to him but Chant wasn't Inkala. Her body fired his senses and he was glad her knife was on the bank in case she decided his arms were the last place she wanted to be.

'You did well,' he said conversationally, when her shaking had eased, and led her from the water. 'We need to change into dry clothes and eat. There's a good campsite further on with plenty of fuel and shelter.'

They turned their backs to change and went on, the stars silvering the river and the mild night air fragrant. The sandy bend was as he remembered and he set their fire in the lee of a massive tree washed down in a flood.

Chant remained quiet and the firelight revealed a softness to her face he hadn't seen before. It might be the residue of fear but he hoped it was something else. Holding her in his arms was infinitely preferable to fighting her.

When they set off again the next morning, Chant's determination to journey alone had vanished. For the first time she felt something other than antagonism in Tel's company, and found it easier to share her life amongst the Sceadu.

'I can't believe you ever returned from hunting with nothing,' he chided, after she described her early expeditions.

'I once hunted for four days and didn't loose an arrow. After the first three, I was angry and hungry, for I'd only taken food for two, but no beast gives itself to an angry hunter.'

'And were you often angry, Chant?'

Chant hesitated. 'In my last days in Berian-tur I was. Angry I had been misnamed; angry the Circle believed Siah; angry Siah sent me to my death. The Sceadu know there's no way over Ashali.'

'Yet still you went,' said Tel, unable to hide his exasperation.

'Because I broke Talabraith,' said Chant.

Leaves fell and buds breached bark; she-aperions dropped their calves onto a detritus of death; young shard-spiders ate the husks of the old. For the void to give, it must take back, but how was she to explain the hunter's law to a man with no understanding of hunting.

'Talabraith must be extraordinarily important if the price of its breaking is your life,' said Tel, as the silence stretched.

'It's hard to understand unless you're a hunter.'

'As the man you're pledged to obviously is, or he wouldn't have agreed to you being condemned.'

Chant forced a smile. 'I'm not dead, as you can see, and I was wrong to doubt. Siah said I would cross the mountains and I did. Siah said—'

'Did she warn you of the trap or of the Terecleft?' interrupted Tel.

'She said there was a great tarn in the west and you've said the sea is there, and she said I would find something to unlock the snowcome ice *and* return home. Siah has spoken and so it will be.'

Tel snorted. 'No one can change the seasons, Chant.'

Only the day before, Chant would have delivered a stinging rebuttal but now she held her silence. She had surrendered herself to Tel to cross the Sunwash and he hadn't failed her. It had changed something between them *or* changed something in *her*.

'There are other ways to live,' he said more calmly. 'I could come to your lands and show you what they are.'

'We have no need of gardeners.'

Chant hadn't meant her words to be so blunt but even if she were prepared to risk Tel in the dark journey through Ashali, there was no point. The void's task was hers alone.

26

*K*etwing pulled her jacket close as did Must beside her; the wind chill as it keened through the trees. Siah and her husband led the procession to Tarchen-tur but the rest of the Circle obscured them from Ketwing's view. Turan walked immediately in front partnered by Prin, and beyond them were Win and Talin, and Nima, who walked alone.

Her usual partner, Sai the song-smith, followed at the back. It was Sai's final journey, made in the manner they would all make one day: wrapped in shoat pelts and carried by those who loved them best.

The pipe was as mournful as the wind and the drumbeat as slow as Ketwing's feet, but for once she didn't fret over delaying those who followed. Siah set the pace and she was just from her bed.

The wind scattered the scent of burned neri bark and Ketwing raised her head to better taste it and caught sight of She the Moon. It was close to three moons since Chant's naming ceremony and Chant might already be where Sai journeyed, yet Ketwing's heart refused to believe it.

The procession came to a stop and its members took up position around the pyre, bowing as Sai was gently laid on the wood. Then Siah stepped forward and Ketwing's breath caught. Siah's eyes were hollow and her skin stretched tight across her bones. Scead was pale too and Ketwing's hunter gaze took in his stiff shoulders and face.

It was usual for Siahs to suffer illness but to recover swiftly, especially younger Siahs, yet this Siah showed no signs of recovery and Scead, *the Sceadu's best healer*, was frightened.

The rest of the Circle showed none of the alarm that pounded through Ketwing's veins but they might not realise the danger went *beyond* losing another Siah so quickly. The void had gifted Siah the means to break snowcome's grip and so Siah had sent Chant away, but if *this* Siah were lost, then Chant might be too.

A cry sounded, long and piercing, and Chant stopped and scanned. There were few trees to obscure her view and she saw nothing untoward but then a strange scent intruded and she drew her knife.

'A marsh-hover,' said Tel, coming to a stop beside her. 'A bird,' he added, in response to her blank look. 'They're common in the Marshlands but I'd forgotten they frequent the grasslands too.'

'And the smell?' asked Chant, continuing to scan. 'Is that them too?'

'That's the sea.'

A stiff breeze flicked her hair back and rolled the grasses in shining undulations. Tel said they were like the sea's waves, except the sea was blue not green, unless the weather was foul, then it was as dark as storm clouds and flung foam inland to burn all that grew. Tel preferred the Sunnen valley to the flat valleys of his kin, and Chant was certain she would too. The sea sounded too much like the Terecleft's churn.

The breeze grew as the light waned and although it wasn't cold, its buffet was relentless. Chant wrapped her shelter-sheet around herself that night as she ate errem and smoked-fish and listened to Tel's description of the Marshlands. Their grasses were taller than a man, he said, and the earth as soft as water and he seemed worried they would reach them when She the Moon was small.

'The last time I was here, I set out at dawn but it was still dark before I reached the Marshlands' westward side. The moon was full then, so I had plenty of light, but this time there'll be none. We *must* clear them before dusk, Chant.'

'How long is it since you were here?' she asked.

'Close to five seasons.'

'Perhaps they've improved.'

Tel shook his head. 'The Marshlands don't improve, in fact, Septim thinks they're spreading. He's the husband of my kin, Turai,' he explained.

'And you visited them because, as head of your corral, you had to pay your respects?' asked Chant, testing her understanding of Sunnen ways.

'Yes, and to find out how my father died.'

'Islan told me he was a great traveller,' said Chant.

'He was.'

'So, you're like him,' she murmured, wondering what traits Brin had passed to her.

'I'm not like him at all! I journey to fulfil my kinship obligations but my father visited the Okianos only the season before and had no reason to return so quickly.'

Chant looked at him startled. Tel's face held more anger than grief and he wrapped himself in his sleep-shelter and lay down. 'It's best we rest now,' he said shortly. 'Tomorrow will be a long day, and the next day, longer.'

They woke to rain and a squalling westerly wind, ate a quick breakfast of errem, and set off. There was no sunrise, thanks to the cloud, and the rain-laced wind meant they must go with their heads down. It wasn't helpful to conversation but Tel was uncommunicative anyway. The gloom slowly lightened and the rain eased but not the wind, and silver-plumaged birds dipped and wheeled on its back.

'Gulls,' Tel told her, as he passed her dried wildfruit. 'And the dark line ahead is the edge of the Marshlands. We'll be there by dusk and then the grasses will give us shelter from this stinking wind. We can have a fire and some warm food then too. Would you like that Chant?'

There was something in his expression that reminded her of Tor in the snow cave and she stared up at the gulls. 'It will be good to be out the wind,' she said.

The dark line in the distance resolved itself into tussocks of tall coarse grass and as a dank reek filled the air, Chant understood why Tel disliked the Marshlands. Shallow pools of water appeared, gleaming dully in the last of the light, and swarms of biting flies hovered above their murky surfaces.

'The ground dips like a bowl and the Sunwash loses its way for a time,' said Tel. 'The earth is so wet that beasts drown in it like water.'

'Then how are we to cross?' asked Chant in dismay.

'We use the tussocks. They are deep-rooted and will bear our weight but the earth in between won't, which is why we need the light to keep us safe.' Chant felt far from reassured and Tel smiled to lighten his words. 'We'll find somewhere pleasant to eat and spend the night.'

Tel led the way to an area sheltered by a dense wall of tussocks, and they dropped their packs, then went back to the Sunwash's shores to hunt for fuel. 'Rivers flow more powerfully on their outer bends and have the strength to carry washwood,' said Tel, as they searched the river sands. 'Which is why you find washwood on the *inner* bends,' he added. And of course, they were on an outer bend.

They collected what they could and set the fire, and Tel prepared a stew. The fire smoke blocked the smell of decay, which was a relief, as was being out of the wind.

'Once we clear the Marshlands, it's a two-day journey to the sea,' he said, as he hefted the last piece of wood onto the fire.

Chant hugged her knees, still having no idea what she sought. It might be like Tanalan's luminescent necklace of taka that in the hands of a Siah, took on special powers, or like neri bark that when burned, guided the spirit back to the void.

'You're quiet,' said Tel after a while. 'Thinking of the man you're pledged to?'

'No.'

'You've never spoken of him and yet with Tanalan it was *Kanan this, and Kanan that* non-stop for two seasons. Will you at least tell me his name?'

'Scead,' said Chant reluctantly.

'The man you said was married to Siah? So, this is a different Scead?'

'It's the same one. We will pledge on my return.'

'He's married to Siah but will pledge to you,' said Tel slowly. 'Are you saying Sceadu men have more than one wife?'

'Of course not! It's just that . . .' Chant took a steadying breath. 'The Sceadu recognise the young sometimes make mistakes when they marry and so the Circle allows unhappy marriages to be broken in their first season.'

'I suppose there's a certain logic in that,' said Tel, his voice heavy with disapproval. 'How many mistakes are the Sceadu allowed to make?'

'Mistakes?'

'How many times can you marry and then *un*marry? Three, four, five times?'

'Twice,' said Chant defensively, 'and even that's unusual.'

Tel's face had hardened and she saw how carefully he chose his words. 'I'm not going to pretend what you've told me is easy to accept, Chant. The Sunnen believe marriage binds us for life, no matter what may come. But if I understand you correctly, Scead is to marry you because he no longer loves Siah.'

Chant shook her head helplessly.

'Then because Siah no longer loves him?'

Chant shook her head again. Tel wouldn't understand her meeting with Siah in the void even if she found the words to explain it.

'So, you're not pledged to anyone at this moment?' he said.

'No,' she muttered, before she recalled Tanalan's warning that Tel hated deceit. But rather than looking angry, Tel looked almost cheerful.

'Make sure you wrap your sleep-shelter securely over yourself tonight to keep the stingers off,' he warned. 'And sleep well, Chant,' he added softly.

Not even the gulls had roused when they set off the next morning. The day was still but Tel knew the wind would build again. It hammered the flat valleys so relentlessly the walls of his kin's stays were twice as thick as those of the Sunnen.

He rubbed his neck as he walked. He hadn't slept well and

173

wondered if it were due to Chant's bizarre revelations. She loved a man who clearly didn't love her, in fact, the man had married the woman who had sent Chant away. And Chant had accepted her banishment because she believed this woman, *this Siah*, dreamed the Sceadu's future.

Tel suppressed a snort. Even less explicable was Chant's belief that Scead would break his marriage to wed *her*, even though Scead loved Siah! It was an astonishing form of blindness that had endangered Chant before but would never endanger her again, not while she was under *his* protection.

The sun brought the stinging clouds of flies but Tel didn't stop. He leapt from tussock to tussock and Chant followed, landing precisely where he had stood a moment before.

It wasn't hot but he sweated and a headache set up a dull thud behind his eyes. He swigged down water and passed Chant berrem and fruit, but as the day wore on, his headache worsened until, as the sun's westering rays glanced off the fetid pools, he was forced to stop.

He swayed and Chant's hand fastened on his arm. 'You're ill,' she said.

'No, I—' he began, but his legs buckled and it was only Chant's strength that stopped him tumbling into the mud. She lowered him down and crouched beside him, the sun gilding her face and running along each strand of glistening hair.

'You're so beautiful,' he murmured, at a loss to know why he'd never noticed it before, and then the darkness closed in.

Chant stared at Tel's unconscious body in dismay. Tel's kin were still two days away but where exactly, she didn't know. She wedged her feet into the softer mud at the tussock's edge, extricated his shelter-sheet, and tucked it over him to keep off the flies. There was scarcely enough room for one on the tussock, let alone two, but she stayed put, terrified he would slip into the mud.

The last of the light gave way to night and the marsh-hovers' cries echoed across the desolate expanse. The Sceadu were far from her now as were the Meduin and others who might aid them. Tel shivered and him calling her *beautiful* suggested he was already fevered. The night deepened and as Chant's weariness grew, she locked her arms around Tel's shoulders, braced her feet against the tussock, and slept.

27

Tel was woken by an intense thirst and his befuddled brain took a moment to make sense of his surroundings. He was still in the Marshlands! He fumbled for his waterskin and slid sideways and then Chant's strong arms brought him to a halt. She held him as she passed him a waterskin and as he drank. He wanted to tell her it was unnecessary but he'd never felt so weak in his life.

'Do you know what ails you?' she asked.

'Marsh fever,' he whispered with a terrible certainty.

Septim had described it to him on his last visit: a headache followed by a strength-sapping fever, followed by a sleep with no awakening. Tel couldn't recall how quickly death came, but given how weak he felt, it might only be a day or two.

His vision ebbed and Chant's voice was suddenly harsh in his ear. 'Tel! Listen to me! We're going on together. You can rest when we reach the end of the Marshlands but not before.'

Protesting took too much effort and he allowed her to haul him up and felt her arm come around him. 'We'll step in unison,' she instructed. 'I'll count to help you keep pace.'

Tel lacked the strength to even keep his eyes open and used the little he had left to concentrate on Chant's counting; on how the muscles in her side bunched in readiness to leap; on how her grip on him tightened as they leapt together. Only her strength kept him upright and increasingly, only her strength of *will* kept him with her. He was beyond exhaustion and could smell Chant's sweat too and feel the flex of her ribs as they heaved in and out, but she didn't stop.

Tel had no idea how long it was before she ceased counting and spoke, but the only word he made out was *rest*. He smelled dry grass and stalks prickled his cheek but after that, there was nothing.

Chant collapsed beside Tel, heaved the shelter-sheet over them both and slept. It was dusk again before she woke and Tel was so still that, for a horrible moment, she thought him dead. She shook him and when he didn't stir, gritted her teeth and slapped him sharply across the face. He groaned and she held the waterskin to his mouth, thankful that he swallowed.

But getting water into him wasn't the only thing she needed. 'Your kin's stay, Tel,' she said urgently. 'Where is it?' Nothing. She shook him savagely. 'Where is it, Tel?'

'On river; nearest marshes.'

His reply was barely decipherable but she had what she needed. 'I'm going to fetch aid,' she said. 'I'll leave you the waterskins, packs and food. Don't try to walk, Tel. I'll come back for you.'

Tel made no sign of having heard and Chant propped the packs to shield his face from the sun and set the waterskins near his hand, along with most of the food, taking only small bundle for herself.

There was no reason to delay yet she lingered. Tel had brought her across the Sunwash, keeping her safe from the void's empty swirl, and she knelt and touched his cheek. 'I *will* come back for you,' she said with sudden fierceness. 'I pledge.'

Only speed could save Tel but Chant could no longer use the easy lope of a hunter. Instead she had to shorten her steps to compensate for the limp. The gait was unnatural and painful, and when she could bear it no longer, she slowed until the pain eased, then sped up again.

She quenched her thirst at the Sunwash but as time went on, it carried the same tang as the air and Chant realised it was salt. She was too weary to solve the puzzle or rejoice in the dawn, just snatched some sleep at midday and again at dusk and ran on through a second night.

The new gait gave way to a stagger and her ankle to a boiling gob of pain, and thirst tormented her, the Sunwash now too salty to drink. Another dawn sent a sky brilliant with golds and gulls that flashed like metal and Chant stumbled on, devoid of thought and reason, her head filled with images of Siah and Scead and Tel.

Signs of a settlement appeared and she blinked the sweat from her eyes. For a long moment she simply stared and then, with a choking cry, she fell to her knees. The tur, and the aid it held, were on the other side of the river.

Islan sat sprawled against the smoke-stay's wall, enjoying the gentle warmth of evening. The gardens grew well, the smoke-stay was full of fish, and the day's berrem was ground. All was in order and he'd even had a chance to hunt with Rist and Mirsin. The prin had disappeared into the garron before he'd loosed an arrow but it hadn't mattered; it had been good to be with his friends and to catch up on the Stead's happenings.

There had been precious little time since Tanalan and Tel had gone and it had been hard for Merala too, even with Inkala's help, to tend Tanalan's garden as well as her own. Nor would it get easier. Tanalan's continued absence must mean Tel had been forced to let the marriage proceed.

Islan winced even at the memory of Tel's fury. Tel had been in a good mood when he'd brought Nasala back to the corral after Sekwana's little river side ritual but had discovered Tanalan's absence and stormed off after her.

It had been left to Islan to escort Nasala back to her own corral and an uncomfortable journey it had been, not that Nasala had suffered for long. Rist had told him she kept company with Tarak and that both families approved the match.

'Islan?'

Inkala hesitated at the edge of the stay and when he smiled, sped forward and settled in a warm jumble of arms and legs in his lap. She wriggled about as she always did and Islan hugged her close, lay his head back against the stay and closed his eyes.

'A murrow burrow,' she chirruped, after a little.

'What?' He dragged his eyes open to see her holding up an elaborate weave of strings.

'Chanty showed me how to make it—before she went away.' Inkala heaved a sigh. 'I wish she was here, and Tel, and

Tanalan. Everyone's gone away.'

'I'm here,' he said, kissing the top of her head, 'and Tel's coming back.'

'With Chanty?'

'I don't know,' he said honestly. 'If Chant finds what she's looking for, she might return this way. I think it's the shortest way home for her.'

'I want to see her again,' said Inkala.

Islan thoughts went to their times together at the Silverwash. 'I want to see her again, too,' he said.

Chant remained slumped on the ground, too weary to move and after a time, a small breeze lifted her hair and she managed to raise her face. The Sunwash's broad sweep flowed on past the tur and disappeared around pale hills, beyond which she sensed lay the sea, and the end of her quest.

A tumble of thoughts rattled through her exhausted brain. She could continue on her side of the Sunwash, retrieve what Siah had sent her to find, and turn east again. She knew how to cross the Marshlands, find her way back to the Old Stead, and pass through the Terecleft. Then she could skirt the Sunnen Stead and follow berian scent back through Ashali's heart *to Scead.*

It would be madness to try to cross the Sunwash. The void's grace had delivered her from drowning once but it wouldn't a second time and, if she failed her quest, Berian-tur might fail too. As for Tel, he had journeyed westward and, like his father, hadn't returned. No one would know the *strange* Sceadu woman had abandoned him—except *she* would know she had condemned him to death.

Chant struggled to her feet, her gaze on the tur. It looked deserted but she waved and shouted, rested, then waved and shouted again. No one appeared and she trudged eastward. It was galling to retrace her steps but she found what she searched for on the next bend.

The branch was large and she struggled to drag it back into the water. It floated and she pushed it under experimentally, reassured when it bobbed back to the surface. It would keep her afloat but her hands shook as she struggled out of her jacket and boots, stowed them with her pack on the bank, and waded into the water.

The branch was knobbed which made it easy to grip but Chant's hands were greasy with sweat. She pushed off and panic seized her as the branch dipped and then she remembered to kick. She moved away from the bank but the river's flow was quicker in the middle and she picked up speed.

The tur swept past and she was carried on towards the small hills and then a horrifying understanding stilled her legs. She was going to her death in the great tarn Siah had foreseen.

28

*T*or reached the snowline and lowered the chet carcass to the ground, ate a simple meal of errem, and trudged on. It was five days since he'd set out but two days was the limit of Serest's willingness to wait. Then she was off with Snowhawk, or Shale, or Reed. Tor didn't know which and he wasn't permitted to ask.

If you want to know my every movement then it's clear you don't trust me, Tor, and how can I marry you, if you don't trust me?

Tinsel-flies glittered but Tor's thoughts were on Serest's likely companion. Tor hadn't sought Snowhawk out since he'd found Serest in his bed and tellingly, Snowhawk hadn't sought Tor out either; proof their hunter bond was no more.

Perhaps it was always destined to end thus, for what friendship can withstand the want for the same woman *or* man, for that matter? Perhaps Siah had resolved she and Chant's competition for Scead by sending Chant away but to believe so denied Siah's guideship of the Sceadu. And yet, the void's gifting of Chant's life task had been very convenient indeed.

Sunlight striped the ground before he reached the Great Turrel and his mood lifted as he heard the squeals of Little Sisters and Brothers at play around the walls. He propped his weapons near the door but as he straightened, he caught sight of snowhawks over Ashali and his good mood vanished.

The hall was filled with the smell of stew and his belly rumbled as he continued through to the Seeing-Place, lowered the chet to the floor, and knelt. He usually didn't have to wait long before Siah appeared to accept the gift and thank the hunter, and he heard footsteps almost immediately. But it wasn't Siah's voice he heard, but Scead's and Tor was so shocked he broke protocol and looked up.

'Siah thanks the beast, Siah thanks the hunter, Siah thanks the void,' recited Scead solemnly. Tor's thoughts raced. A Siah *always* officiated when a beast was gifted. 'Siah is too unwell to accept the gift in person,' said Scead. 'I hope my words suffice.'

'Of course,' said Tor, and was still shaken as he made his way out.

It had been dim in the Seeing-Place but the strain on Scead's face had been clear, and Tor's mouth settled into a grim line. The Sceadu had a Siah too ill to perform even the most mundane of duties and a husband who already wore the mask of mourning!

Tor snatched up his weapons, turned and collided with Ketwing. His hand shot out to steady her but her sombre face silenced his apology. 'You've seen Siah?' she asked.

'I've seen Scead. Siah was too ill to accept the gift.'

The lines around Ketwing's mouth deepened. 'Siah sends to the Aunts in search of a child who dreams as she does, but I fear there's no one here to replace her.' Ketwing drew a shuddering breath and Tor took her arm and helped her to the seat in the clearing. It was deserted making it a good place for private conversations.

'What else do you fear, Ketwing?' he asked, as he settled beside her.

'I came upon Scead last moon deep in the Redlands. He spends every waking moment in search of a cure for Siah's fever.' Ketwing's black eyes came to his. 'Exhaustion might have caused the slip or he might have intended me to know. He said that Chant *must* return by the full moon after this or all will be lost.'

Her knobbed hand fastened on Tor's arm; her grip surprisingly strong. 'Can you keep your hunter's gaze trained for her? She might be exhausted or injured; she might need help to complete the last of her journey. You've hunted with her, Tor; you know the way she might come. Will you watch for her?'

'Of course.'

Ketwing's face eased and he nodded his farewell and set off

for his own tur. There was a certain irony in the way things were turning, he mused, as he wove his way through the trees. If Siah died and Chant returned, Chant would gain her heart's desire, but if both Siah and Chant died, Scead would be left lonely.

His own name might be apt but Scead's name meant flesh of the Sceadu, and what became of the flesh when the spirit departed? It withered, as they all would without a spirit-guide, without the beneficence of the void, without the gentle rains of snowmelt.

His tur was empty of Serest *and* fire-fuel and as he debated whether to collect windfall or eat errem again there was a rap on the door. Tor knew better than to hope it was Serest but Mist was the last person he expected to see. He surveyed him coldly as he wondered whether Snowhawk had used him as a messenger: *Sorry Tor, but Serest's mine.*

'What do you want?' asked Tor.

'I waited for you to come back,' said Mist, looking everywhere but him. 'It's Snowhawk. He's gone on hunt and hasn't returned.'

Tor half shrugged. Mist should know how inexact hunting was. A five-day expedition could double or, if the beast were Willing, halve. Yet Mist was so anxious he shook and Tor beckoned him in. 'Sometimes a hunt takes longer than planned,' he began. 'The beast—'

'No! Snowhawk tells me *exactly* how long he will be and it's always as he says, even if he must come back without a beast. Something's happened to him . . .' Mist's voice cracked. 'You're his closest friend, Tor. That's why I've come to you.'

Tor grunted. To believe that Snowhawk would *abandon* a hunt just to be with him . . .

'Please, Tor. We need to search.'

Mist's slender hand gripped his arm and Tor felt its tremble through his jacket. Tor sighed. 'Which way did Snowhawk say he hunted?'

'Southwest between the Fine and Ruthven streambeds.'

The way Chant would return, *if* she returned. All Tor wanted was rest, preferably next to Serest's naked body, but he'd promised Ketwing to scout for Chant and Mist looked ready to collapse.

'Return at dawn with enough food for five days, a shelter-sheet *and* warm clothing,' he instructed. 'We'll reconnoitre.' Mist's relief was palpable but Tor interrupted his babble of thanks. 'Is Serest at Snowhawk's tur?'

'Serest doesn't go there anymore,' replied Mist. '*I'm* with Snowhawk now.'

Mist was proud Snowhawk had chosen to teach him rather than spend time with Serest; being selected by the *handsome* hunter obviously gave him a level prestige few of his ageset could match.

But as Mist disappeared back into the night, Tor realised he actually preferred Serest to be with Snowhawk, rather than the arrogant Shale or humourless Reed. At least Snowhawk was worthy of her.

The river swept Chant on and on but as the sound of the sea grew louder, her hunter self roused and she kicked with renewed ferocity. The other bank drew closer and then her knee struck something solid. She was still some distance from the shore but there was a ridge under the water and she braced her feet against it, heedless of its sharp edges, and found purchase.

She struggled along it, cutting her feet and still clinging to the branch, and only relinquished it when the water sank below her knees and then, sobbing with relief, she crawled up the bank and collapsed on the sand. A watery mix of blood oozed from her feet but Chant was beyond caring. She lay with her chest heaving and, when she was able, limped back along the shore to the tur.

Despite her exhaustion, she set an arrow and approached the stone building in a crouch. It sheltered two smaller turs, she discovered, and a smaller version of the Sunnen gardens, set between them and a thick stone wall.

Chant turned towards the largest tur and jerked her arrow up as a snarl erupted beyond it and a strange beast appeared. Its head was heavy and blunt and its forequarters more powerful than its hind. Chant aimed at the point below its jaw but didn't release the arrow; the beast was angry or frightened, but it wasn't Willing.

A man appeared from the same direction and stopped. 'The dog will do you no harm,' he said, and ordered it back. The beast slunk behind him but its yellow eyes continued to glare.

The man was short with massive shoulders and equally watchful. 'Who do you seek?' he asked.

'The kin of Tel of the Sunnen,' croaked Chant.

The man's shaggy brows rose. 'Turai? She is within. Come with me and leave your weapons outside. You've no need of them here.'

Turai wondered at Septim's words but put aside her stitching and followed him into the cooking place. *There's a Sceadu hunter here asking for you and she's had a hard journey*. And there she was, like one of Barin's tales come to life: long black hair, white skin, and patterning lines across her nose and cheeks. But her eyes were hollow and she was soaked and streaked with blood.

'I'm Turai,' she said, 'sister to Tel's mother Merala, and this is my husband Septim. What is it you want?'

'Aid for your kin, Tel. He's ill, a day and half from here, on the Marshland's western edge.'

The Sceadu's claim was preposterous but it was Septim who found his voice first. 'It's not possible to travel so far in so short a time.'

The woman's black eyes flashed. 'I'm a Sceadu hunter! It's as I've said!'

'What's the nature of Tel's illness?' asked Turai quickly, rueing her husband's bluntness. She hoped it was something minor but her heart filled with dread as the woman listed Tel's symptoms.

'I'll ready the boat,' said Septim grimly, and went out.

Septim would need kina, which took time to brew and the Sceadu woman needed aid too. 'Sit and rest yourself,' said Turai, fearing she would soon be lifting an unconscious body from the floor.

The woman continued to pace in agitation. 'We must go

185

now! I've left him unprotected.'

'Preparations must be made,' said Turai, careful to keep her voice calm. 'We can't rush off without the means to help Tel.' *If he can be helped*, she thought. 'And you must eat and rest if you're to guide Septim back.' The woman sat but her anxiety was plain and Turai ladled soup for her. 'What's your name?' she asked, as the woman ate.

'Chant.'

'Well Chant, Septim will fetch his brother Dargil to help him with the boat but they can't leave until the tide turns.'

'I've abandoned him,' muttered Chant.

'Seeking help isn't abandonment,' said Turai soothingly, as she set water to boil. 'Only grass-skippers and sivets roam the grasslands and neither are dangerous.' Turai pulled out her store of bitter-flax, sour-hip and sea-strap. If the marsh fever had entered its third or fourth day, Tel would need a mix heavy with bitter-flax, not that he'd welcome its effects. Tel liked to be in control of all things, *at all times*, especially his emotions.

On Tel's previous visit, he'd seemed as set in his ways as a man twice his age. *As solid as sea-swelled log and just as predictable*, Septim had scoffed, and Turai had reluctantly agreed. The last thing she expected was a return visit, in marsh fever season, with a *Sceadu* woman.

The kina bubbled and Turai strained it off and filled the skins, then fetched some salve for Chant's cuts. Chant's explanation of how she'd injured herself added to Turai's astonishment; it suggested a bond that went beyond friendship.

'What—' she began, but Septim came in and Chant scrambled to her feet.

'We leave now,' he said, as Turai handed him the skins.

'Try to sleep in the boat, Chant,' said Turai, and then they were gone.

Septim carried a large pack but went without urgency and Chant jostled at his shoulder. 'The tide's yet to turn,' he said gruffly, and when Chant stared at him blankly, added, 'it's best to journey with the flow.' Chant still had no idea what he meant, only that he dawdled while Tel lay dying.

Septim continued unhurriedly along a sandy path to a wooden structure and, secured to it by a rope, was the *boat*: a bigger, more sophisticated version of the raft Tel had used at the Sunwash.

A man sat in it who Septim introduced as his brother, Dargil, then Septim swung his pack and the skins down to him, and Dargil extended a hand as big and meaty as Septim's.

Chant stayed where she was. 'We go in that?' she gasped.

'We do if you wish to travel as swiftly as you claim,' said Septim dourly.

Chant had no choice but to take Dargil's hand and his strong grasp steadied her until she was seated. 'Have you not been in a boat before?' he asked kindly.

Chant shook her head, too terrified to speak, and then the boat plunged sickeningly as Septim clambered in. Chant gripped the sides and screwed her eyes shut, then sensed the boat move forward and slitted her lids. Septim and Dargil pulled rhythmically on long pieces of flattened wood to drive the boat through the water and they sped along many times faster than Chant had journeyed.

Dargil smiled sympathetically as she loosened her grip and flexed her aching knuckles. 'There's nothing to fear,' he said. 'Septim is the finest seaman of all the Okianos and they're fine indeed. And I'm the second finest,' he added, making Septim grunt. 'You've not told us your name,' he continued, his small eyes expectant. He was a younger, less grizzled version of Septim.

'Chant.'

'Ah,' he said, 'I like that name. Now tell me Chant—'

'Watch that oar,' interrupted Septim, and Dargil rolled his eyes and brought his attention back to his task. The land slid into darkness and Chant nodded as the rhythmic slapping of the oars went on. She was vaguely aware of Dargil wrapping her in the warm folds of his jacket and easing her into the bottom of the boat and the next thing she knew it was the dewy quiet of dawn.

'The river breaks soon,' said Septim, and Chant struggled from the jacket's warmth, dull-headed with sleep. She didn't recognise the lands and flared her nostrils to better taste the air. 'There!' she croaked and pointed.

Septim and Dargil expertly brought the boat around and as soon as it reached the shore, Chant scrambled out and ran drunkenly towards the motionless shape ahead. She half thought she rushed towards a corpse, for Tel lay exactly as she'd left him, but his cheek was hot to touch. Septim thumped down beside her, seized Tel by his jacket, and rained blows on his face.

'Stop it!' she shrieked and drew her knife.

Septim was suddenly very close. 'If you want him to live, you'll hold him,' he said.

Chant panted with fury but she obeyed and Septim's massive hand clamped Tel's jaws around the spout of the skin. Tel gagged and thrashed but most of the kina went down his throat.

'Hold him still,' ordered Septim, as he unplugged the second skin.

Chant did as Septim bid but she would have gladly killed him at that moment. Septim emptied the second skin down Tel's throat and Chant lowered Tel gently back to the shelter-sheet.

Septim grinned. 'It's good that he fought. It shows he has strength.' Chant glared at him but he seemed not to notice. 'Take the skins and packs back to the boat and send up Dargil,' he ordered. Chant did as he bid and held the boat secure until Septim and Dargil reappeared carrying Tel between them. His head lolled back and his fingers skimmed the water as they lifted him in.

They settled him in the bottom of the boat and then Dargil reached over and, with his mighty arms, lifted Chant in. She thanked him shakily, knowing she hadn't the strength to clamber in by herself. 'Rest,' he said. 'There's nothing more you can do for him.' Chant wanted to sit in watch but her weariness was so great she lay down beside Tel and slept.

Turai sat by the fire and stitched a skirt, her gaze on Tel as often as her work. The cooking place was the warmest room in the stay and Septim had set a bed there under the window. Tel was motionless but at least he still lived. Turai had seen many victims of marsh fever but it was shocking to see her kin so ill.

Septim had done well to get two skins of kina into him but Tel had been fortunate to have had such a swift travelling companion. Or was Chant his lover? Turai's needle paused. Tel's attraction to the *unusual* seemed to be a family trait and she just hoped it wasn't to cost him his life too.

Tel was so careful! It was incomprehensible he had forgotten marsh fever was at its worse now and that meant Chant *must* have something to do with his journey. But what?

Turai jabbed her needle through the cloth. She knew impatience served no purpose; Septim had told her often enough, and she knew Chant's deep sleep meant there would be no answers until the morrow but knowing didn't make the waiting easier.

29

The first things Chant saw when she woke were her pack and weapons propped beside the clothing chest, along with her jacket and boots. Septim must have fetched them for her and then her thoughts swung to Tel and she scrambled out of bed.

The tur was strange but she followed the scent of smoke back to the cooking place and saw Tel lying motionless on a bed. She hastened over and lay her fingers on his cheek. Thankfully it felt cooler.

'He's mending,' said Turai, making Chant start. The Okianos woman was sewing but put her work aside. 'Come and sit,' she said, and fetching a bowl, filled it from the pot. A delicious odour invaded the tur and Chant thanked her and ate; the soup thick with fish and greenfood.

'You're a long way from home,' said Turai, after a little.

'I'm looking for something near the sea,' said Chant and braced for the questions and incredulity that inevitably followed, but Turai seemed more interested in why Tel was with her.

'Is he helping you with your search?' she asked.

'He had planned to visit you so it made sense to travel together.'

'Not in this season,' said Turai. 'Tel knew marsh fever was at its worse.' Her gaze was intense but Chant was too surprised to say anything. 'You haven't looked upon the sea yet, have you?' said Turai.

Chant shook her head, still puzzling over Tel's motivations. Maybe he had simply forgotten about the illness.

'She lies just beyond the dunes. All you need do is follow

the Sunwash.' Chant glanced at Tel uncertainly. 'He'll sleep for a good time yet,' said Turai. 'Go.'

Chant made her way along the path she had last taken with Septim. His boat bobbed on the Sunwash and looked no safer than it had before. The day was fine but Chant barely noticed; she shouldn't have needed Turai to remind her of her quest. Tel was safe and she must retrieve what Siah had sent her to find and turn east again.

The path left the Sunwash and snaked off between the small hills Chant had seen from a distance. Turai called them *dunes* and Chant soon discovered they were huge piles of sand. They looked like a yellow version of the Whitelands' snow and were just as hard to navigate. She struggled on and then, as she cleared the last of them, she stumbled to a stop.

The world had turned to water. An endless glitter of ever-moving blues and greens stretched unbroken to the horizon and waves, capped with brilliant white, broke upon the land to draw back and break again. Chant dropped to her knees and bowed her head to Siah's visioning.

It took a long time to rise and then she stumbled down to the bubbling surge and scooped the water to her mouth. It was salt! Siah had sent her to a vast tarn of salt! Clever Siah, and clever, clever Chant for coming so far. Chant's chest heaved but Siah hadn't said the *tarn* would unlock the snowcome ice, but something *near* it.

Chant shaded her eyes and peered up and down the shore. The sand curved away to either side like a giant scinton claw, terminating in rocky headlands north and south and, even from a distance, she saw spume hurled high as waves beat against them.

Chant set off along the shore. Here were the tracks of a beetle and there a polished stone. A gull's silver feather rolled before the wind and a toss of waterweed glistened, but nothing sent a thrill of recognition through her. She was still weary from the journey and the sea's vastness made her feel as small as the grains of sand and she turned back to Turai's tur.

Septim gutted fish by the fire. 'And how do you like the

sea?' he asked.

'I don't like it,' she said tersely. 'It's salt.'

'It's well known the sea's salty,' he said, his small eyes glinting with amusement. Chant made no reply, suspecting Septim's suspicion of her had given way to belief she was a fool. She stared across at Tel, willing him to wake. He might be contemptuous of her beliefs but at least his gaze was familiar, but Tel didn't stir.

Septim was busy cleaning the next day's catch when Tel roused and Septim put aside the chopping board, wiped his hands, and went to him. Tel's eyes were shadowed and it was a while before Septim saw a spark of recognition.

'Septim,' croaked Tel.

'It's me all right,' said Septim, and grinned. There had never been much warmth between him and his wife's kin but he was genuinely pleased to see Tel awake. 'About time you joined us,' he added. Tel's gaze drifted past him and Septim saw him try to make sense of the room. 'It's been nigh on five days since that Sceadu woman of yours appeared and demanded we come to collect you,' said Septim.

Tel's expression changed to alarm and he tried to pull himself up but Septim pushed him back. 'Don't go tiring yourself now or Turai will have me for wairbait,' he said. 'The Sceadu's safe enough. She's on the sand where she spends most of her time when she's not staring at you *or* threatening me with that knife of hers.' He paused. 'I've got some soup on the flame; you should have some.'

He fetched a bowl but by the time he returned, Tel had slipped back into sleep.

Septim shook him awake. 'Up you come,' he said, hauling him up and pushing pillows behind him. 'It's food you want now, not sleep. You must eat if you want your strength back.'

He held the bowl close to Tel's mouth and gave him the spoon, but Tel had taken only half of it before he was too weak to continue. Septim put the bowl aside and cleaned Tel's face.

'Ah, I'm sorry Septim to cause you this trouble,' said Tel.

'Sorry, so sorry.'

'We're always glad to have our kin visit but what possessed you to come now? Had you forgotten the marsh fever?'

'Chant wanted to come. Women shouldn't travel alone, should they, Septim? Not alone, Septim.'

Tel's eyes closed and this time Septim let him sleep. The bitter-flax would take a few days to wear off and Tel's over-blown emotions settle, and then Septim might be able to get some sense out of him.

He went back to his fish cleaning and was all but finished when Turai returned with her harvest of greenfood. 'He's woken?' she asked, taking in the pillows and half-eaten soup.

'That he has,' said Septim, filleting methodically.

'Well?'

'He woke, I gave him soup, and now he sleeps.'

Turai snorted and sat down. 'Did he say why he came in this season?'

'He didn't want the Sceadu to travel alone.'

'What else did he say about Chant?'

'Nothing.'

'Even after the bitter-flax?' pursued Turai.

Septim shook his head and Turai's eyes flashed with irritation, but Septim simply scraped the tailings into a bucket, wiped his knife and went to the door. 'We might try the river tonight,' he said, and went out.

Turai sorted the greenfood with quick impatient movements. Nothing fitted her memories of Tel at all. Septim held that all Sunnen were as fixed in their ways as their gardens were to the earth; a result of living too distant from the cry of the gulls and the restless ever-moving sea, but that was a waterman's prejudice.

Instead, Turai suspected Tel saw Barin's restless spirit as a flaw and, to atone for hi father's waywardness, had bound himself doubly hard to Sunnen ways and *that* made his appearance at the Okianos Stead, in marsh fever season, with a *Sceadu* woman, even more intriguing.

Chant came in and went to Tel first, as she always did, then settled at the fire beside Turai. Chant's cheeks glowed from the sun, giving her a wild unkempt beauty, and Turai glanced down regretfully at her own weather-beaten hands. Chant hadn't proved very communicative but now she was full of questions about the sea, especially why the water invaded the land and at other times, stayed away.

Turai described how the tides followed the moon's waxing and waning and how it was the manner of all things to come and go. 'The wair run from the south, and then the silverfin, and then it's the darts' turn,' she said. 'It's the same with greenfood, as you know. It sets seed, sprouts and dwindles and when the rains come, grows again.'

'But what if the sea were to go and not come back?' asked Chant, her face troubled.

'The tides turn in a day, but it takes many seasons for the silverfin to grow strong,' said Turai. 'All things that go, return but it might not be in the time we've been given.'

'But if there's no way to bring water to the Sceadu . . .' murmured Chant. 'But Siah said there was!'

Barin had spoken of the Sceadu's Siahs and Turai dredged her memory. 'Your Wisewoman sent you here to find something?' she asked tentatively, and Chant nodded. 'Something that would bring the Sceadu water?' Another nod.

The notion that an object could bring rain was ridiculous and she instinctively glanced at Tel. Her kin had never hidden his contempt for those claiming otherworldly knowledge.

'And have you found anything?' she asked lightly.

Chant extended her hand and Turai's breath caught then she smiled as Chant revealed a collection of azurine. Turai had collected the iridescent shells when Septim had first brought her here, but she was surprised a Sceadu hunter did the same girlish thing.

Turai filled some bowls from the pot and as they ate, asked Chant how she came to be with the Sunnen. Chant's description of being caught in one of Tel's traps was shocking enough, but when she described how she'd travelled west through the Tere-cleft with Tanalan, *but without Tel*, Turai all but choked on her soup.

'Tanalan had long wanted to marry the Meduin man

Kanan,' said Chant matter-of-factly, 'and Tanalan told me Tel had given his blessing. It was a small matter to go to Kanan's corral without him.'

Turai refrained from listing the many reasons why it *wasn't* a *small matter*, and the Tel she knew would have put as much distance between himself and Chant as possible, not risked marsh fever to guide her here. He *had* to be courting her, as extraordinary as the idea was.

But Turai recalled from Barin's tales that a Sceadu Wise-woman's demands took precedence over everything else, including any love Chant might have for Tel, and she wondered whether Tel had realised that yet.

Chant dreamed of the void that night but instead of offering her Scead in return for completing her quest, Siah offered herself. Chant woke with a start. It was still early and she went to the window and pushed the shutters wide. The air was cool and the pre-dawn light painted the Sunwash silver. There was so much water here but all she wanted was to be back in Berian-tur.

If only she knew what she searched for! She was thirsty again too, as if the salt had soaked into her skin. She pulled her waterskin out of her pack, but it was empty. There was a water-pot in the cooking place, she recalled, and she eased the door open and tip-toed out so as not to disturb Turai and Septim.

The fire glow lit the cooking place but she could find no cups and filled a bowl instead.

'Chant?'

It was Tel, awake at last. The growing light revealed his pallor but he seized her hand with surprising strength. 'You saved my life,' he said hoarsely. 'You could have abandoned me but you didn't. You sought help instead. You saved me!'

'I fetched Septim, that's all,' said Chant, taken aback by his fervour. 'It was Septim and Dargil who brought a boat and Septim who got the potion into you. Septim and Turai have looked after you since.'

'You saved me when all you wanted was to go straight to the sea. Have you seen it yet? What do you think of it? Is it as you imagined?'

'I could never have imagined anything so vast; no Sceadu could, except Siah perhaps. And it's salty. You didn't tell me it was salty.'

'I didn't think to. I'm sorry.'

Tel's intensity was unsettling and she extricated her hand. 'It doesn't matter,' she said. 'Siah said I would find what I seek near it, not *in* it.'

'There's no such thing, Chant. Only the sun and rain can melt ice and you have no power over those. Give up your search and stay with me on this side of the mountains.'

Chant stared at him in astonishment. 'I can't do that!'

Tel heaved himself onto his elbow. 'Forgive me, I phrased that badly. I'm asking you to stay here as my wife, Chant. I'm asking you to marry me.'

'I'm to wed Scead!' she said wildly. 'Siah promised him to me.'

'Is he a net of fish to be traded?' demanded Tel. 'And if he's content to be passed from one woman to another, who's to say he won't move onto a third wife when he tires of you?' Tel gentled his voice. 'The Sunnen aren't like that, Chant. *I'm* not like that. You will have my love *and* loyalty, and my care and protection to the end of my days. Marry me,' he repeated softly.

His face held the same tenderness she had glimpsed in their last days of travel together and her heart raced. Tel wanted her, *unlike* Scead, but the Sceadu remained in snowcome's frigid grip. 'I have to find the thing that unlocks snowcome's ice,' she said unsteadily.

Tel slumped back but his gaze held hers. 'There's no such thing, Chant, and you know it. Soon you'll be forced to give up your hopeless search and, when you do, I will be waiting.'

30

*C*hant spent the day in her usual search along the shore but Tel's proposal made it impossible to concentrate. He was a gardener, she reminded herself, but his face held love and she could no longer pretend leaving him behind would be easy, despite Siah's promise of Scead.

Is he a net of fish to be traded? Chant shook her head in frustration; she had no answers either. Her hands came to her hips as she stared up and down the shore. She had searched this stretch many times but Turai said all manner of things were tossed up when the *tide* was high and it would be highest in two days when She the Moon was full.

But She the Moon's fullness also reminded Chant she had a bare fifteen days before she *must* start for home. Her gaze went to the headlands. They held the same oppressiveness as the Old Stead and to reach the southern one meant crossing the Sunwash again. Chant turned in its direction anyway, eyeing the river anxiously as she drew closer.

It was very different to where she had crossed before, she saw in relief, both broader and shallower, with sunlit spangles throwing shadows on its sandy bed. She waded through, pleased it barely reached her knees, and hurried off along the sand keen to search the headland and re-cross as fast as possible.

But there was a second, smaller river hidden by a dip and, as Chant stared at it in dismay, figures emerged from the dunes and turned towards her. She reached for her knife but her belt was empty, and she cursed. She'd stopped carrying her weapons because there was nothing to hunt but fish, and she had no interest in taking them.

She considered fleeing back to the Sunwash but the figures resolved themselves into the solid shapes of Septim and Dargil, laden with nets and carrying a sling of fish between them.

'It's good to see you again,' said Dargil, as they came level. 'How are you liking the Okianos lands?'

'They're very different to my own,' said Chant politely. In truth, she was heartily sick of the ever-moving sea, strident gulls, and over-lay of salt.

'That they must be,' said Dargil. 'Yours are east of the Sunnen lands I hear and have mountains. What fish do you—'

'The tide's on the turn,' broke in Septim. 'Speak as you walk.'

Chant fell into step and Dargil explained that the smaller river was the Tramm and the southern headland Trammel Head. 'You need to start early to pass the Tramm at its lowest,' he said.

Beyond Trammel Head lay another bay such as theirs but shallower. It had been Myrali but the Myrali's fish runs had dwindled and they had dismantled their turs and shifted south.

'And the northern headland?' asked Chant, her gaze on the dark jut in the distance.

'Skeardin? It's Vulturi land. Their fish runs have dwindled too.'

'Why is there less fish north and south of you?' asked Chant.

'There's less fish everywhere but our bay's deeper and we have the Sunwash,' said Dargil. 'The Vulturi have shallows and the Ecanwash, which is scarce more than a trickle.'

They reached the Sunwash and Septim took the fish and went on ahead. The flow was faster now that it rushed in from the sea and Chant was grateful when Dargil took her arm. 'Nothing to fear here,' he said reassuringly. 'Not like the Heads where Tel's father drowned.'

They waded through and turned east along the path, then stopped where a second path ran off northward. The brothers divided the fish and Dargil bade them farewell and headed off towards a scatter of turs. Chant and Septim went on in silence and she was just considering that one brother had inherited *all* the sociability when Septim spoke.

'The sea flows changed when the clouds started to shed their water elsewhere,' he said. 'Sand grew in some places and dwindled in others. The water-grass died and the fish that fed on it. The Mirali shifted south and we built extra boats and fish the river more. But the Vulturi . . .'

Septim looked at her sideways, his eyes all but hidden under his shaggy brows. 'There's no love for anyone or anything amongst them. They scour the shore for what the sea brings and for the small offerings of the Ecanwash. What is found belongs to the man who found it and is shared with no one.

'I've heard tales of fights between brothers over dead sivets washed down in floods or boil-weed tossed up by storms. A man might kill his brother over such things and fill his own belly before he fills the bellies of his wife or child.

'I know you seek something to cure your peoples' lack but don't seek it that way. The Vulturi have forgotten what it is to be kind to each other and they never had that knowing for strangers.'

Tel tottered to the fire and carefully lowered himself onto a seat. Soup simmered on the coals, as it had on his first visit, and he wondered whether the pot was ever emptied. The Okianos diet was rich in fish and greenfood but lacked variety, for the sandy soil and salty winds allowed no orchards, berrem or whiteroot. If they built their stays further from the sea, they could enjoy these things too but when he had suggested it on his first visit, Septim had said it wasn't the Okianos way.

Tel's mouth watered at the smell of soup but he couldn't remember where the bowls were kept; his last recollection was of speaking with Chant. By the mountain! He had declared his love and asked her to marry him! Tel's breath failed him and then he all but swooned in relief as he recalled she'd refused.

The door opened and he started, but thankfully it wasn't Chant but Septim, his arms loaded with washwood. 'It's good to see you from your bed,' he said, as he deposited it on the hearth. 'I'll serve you some soup.' Tel numbly watched Septim fetch bowls from a side shelf. 'How do you feel?' he asked, as he ladled the soup.

'Much better, I . . . I thank you.'

'Bitter-flax is a powerful antidote for marsh fever but has a loosening effect on the tongue,' said Septim, passing him a bowl. 'People tend to spit out what's closest to their hearts.'

Tel's face burned. 'Has Chant spoken to you?'

'That she has,' said Septim, his shrewd gaze on Tel. 'She asks about the tides and the land beyond the Heads, and about what the sea shows or hides in its shallows.'

Chant obviously hadn't told Septim of his proposal and Tel felt relieved but also oddly disappointed. 'She searches for something that can't be found,' he said sourly.

'Chant's a Sceadu hunter,' said Septim, as he filled his own bowl. 'Your father told me they go on until the death of the beast or their own.'

'She's no fool. In the end she will realise her search is hopeless and turn aside.'

'How long do you intend to be away from your corral, Tel?'

The implications of Septim's question were obvious but Septim didn't know that Chant's need to be back in her own lands was urgent too. 'I'll be home by the end of this moon,' he replied and, to keep Chant safe, he would take her with him, at least as far as the Sunnen Stead, and after that, he couldn't bear to think.

Chant left early over the following days to search the rocks at Trammel Head but she found nothing except rockpool creatures that opened and closed like miniature hands, and shelled creatures that scuttled sideways out of reach.

Each tide tossed new things onto the sand but Chant no longer believed they would send what she sought and time was running out. The only place she hadn't searched was Skeardin Head and, given Septim's warning, she had no intention of searching its stones, just the shore nearby.

She completed her usual reconnoitre of the Sunwash and, as the sun westered, turned north. The headland's seaward side resembled a brooding face and her skin flicked. It was just the haphazard strew of stones, she told herself, but then something or *someone* moved on the rocks and Chant stopped.

She strained into the gloom but now all that moved were the waves. She could taste nothing but salt but her skin continued to flick and she turned back. The sun painted a fiery path across the waves and, as shadows crept down the sand, she scanned behind her. The shore remained empty and her thoughts turned to Tel.

She knew he blamed himself for her injury, which was probably why he'd risked marsh fever to guide her here, but that obligation, if it *were* an obligation, had been discharged. He owed her nothing now, least of all marriage.

She was going to marry Scead anyway, and yet … even the memory of Tel's words of love sent a warm pulse of pleasure through her. She hadn't had a chance to speak with him since because he'd either been asleep or with others, and when she reached the tur, Septim and Dargil were there again.

Tel was in conversation with Septim, which was probably why he barely acknowledged her, and it was Dargil who greeted her with real warmth. 'You'll turn into a proper Okianos, Chant, spending so much time on the shore,' he said. 'Have you found anything this day?'

Dargil's eyes gleamed expectantly and Chant dug into her pocket and pulled out another handful of azurine. The beautiful iridescent shells were her only compensation for her long days of searching.

'I'll thread them for you,' said Dargil, and Chant emptied all but one into his massive hand.

As soon as Tel's conversation with Septim paused, she offered it to him. 'This is for you, Tel, as you've yet to reach the shore,' she said with a smile, but he made no move to take it.

'Best keep it with the rest,' he said, and turned back to Septim.

Chant was glad the dimness hid the heat in her face. Her gift seemed childish now and she forced a smile and gave it to Dargil. Tel continued his speech with Septim but his exclusion of her now seemed deliberate.

Turai returned with a basket of greenfood and Septim rose to serve the soup and, as soon as the meal was finished, he and

Dargil went out. *To fish the river*, Dargil said and then with a wink, invited Chant to join them *in the boat*. Turai delayed very little afterwards before she bade them a good night and went to her sleeping room.

The door closed behind her and Chant stared at the flames, for the first time feeling awkward in Tel's company. The silence stretched and she cleared her throat. 'I'm glad you've recovered enough to leave your bed,' she said politely.

'As I am. I've lost too many days to illness but should soon be strong enough to start for home. Then we must leave.'

Chant's heart quickened but his face held no tenderness; he simply planned how quickly he could resume his duties. His marriage proposal must have been an aberration caused by the fever, in fact, he might not even remember making it.

'I have eleven more days before I must leave,' she said evenly.

'You need to come with me. It's too dangerous to journey alone.'

'I know the way now,' she said curtly. 'There's no danger.'

'How will you cross the Sunwash?' he persisted. 'Remember you must cross it a day from the Old Stead.'

'I'll use washwood as I did to reach here.'

'It's too risky. That's how my father drowned.'

'No it isn't. He drowned at the headland.'

'Who told you that?'

'Dargil,' she said. Tel's frown deepened and Chant hoped she hadn't caused some sort of upset. 'Perhaps Dargil got mixed up.'

'Or told the truth.'

Tel glowered into space and Chant wished him a good night, but as she pulled the door closed behind her, she suspected he didn't even know she was gone.

Tel slept poorly, disturbed by Chant's revelation, and wasted no time the next morning broaching the subject with Turai, but she simply reiterated that Barin had drowned.

'Where exactly?' he pursued.

'At Skeardin Head.'

'*Skeardin* Head? What was he doing there?'

Before Turai could answer, the door opened, admitting a blast of salty air and Septim with a bag of fish. The stay was filled with the splash and gurgle of his ablutions and then he thumped down on a chair next to Tel.

'We were speaking of Barin's death,' said Turai, but Septim's attention was on the soup. He filled a bowl and asked Tel whether he had eaten, but Tel was more interested in answers than food.

'Was my father trading with the Vulturi?' he asked.

'Barin had no interest in trade,' said Septim, between slurps.

'Then why go there?'

'Your father found them interesting,' said Septim.

'But the Vulturi are dangerous. You said so yourself.'

'As are the spine-fish that lay on the sea bottom, *if* you tread on them.'

'So . . . my father went there and was washed off the rocks on his return journey?'

'We found his body in the water at Skeardin Head,' confirmed Septim, taking up the ladle to refill his bowl.

'Were there signs of injury?' asked Tel.

'You've seen how the sea strikes the stone; how shells are smashed and weed ripped from its roots. All things that go into the water are injured.'

Septim ate in the same placid way as he did everything else but Tel's disquiet grew. He'd believed his father had been caught by the Sunwash's tides and he wondered why he hadn't been told the truth on his first visit.

But when he asked Septim that very question, Septim simply shrugged. 'It would have served no purpose,' he said. 'One way or another, Barin drowned.'

31

el's weakness meant he had plenty of time to mull over his kin's deception. He didn't have the strength to leave the stay until the following day and then he only just reached the shore before his legs gave way. He crawled into the lee of a dune and lay propped there, his gaze on the sea. It was pleasantly warm out of the wind and the sea as beautiful as he remembered.

During the journey, he had imagined standing here with Chant, enjoying her amazement, but he had been carried the last of the way to his kin like a piece of washwood. And then, thanks to the bitter-flax, he'd blurted out his feelings for her. Tel's jaw clenched as he recalled tales of men similarly afflicted, who had stumbled into marriages they had spent the rest of their lives ruing.

Chant's confusion last night had been clear but it was better she was confused than regretful and yet . . . his heart kept producing arguments to thwart the cool reason of his head. The struggle added to his weariness and he decided to doze for a little and then wander along the shore to aid his recovery.

Tel had no idea how long he had slept before the cold woke him. The sunshine had given way to dark scudding clouds and a gusting wind that filled his clothes with sand. Thunder cracked and as lightning danced across the sky, he heaved himself upright. Storms made the shore hazardous but there was a figure in the distance. It might be an Okianos fisher caught out by the weather *except* the Okianos knew their lands' moods too well. It could only be Chant.

Rain pitted the sand but Tel lacked the strength to run for shelter even when it sheeted down, and Chant didn't run either. She came from the direction of Skeardin Head and would have gone on past him had he not caught her arm. 'You should have sought shelter,' he said.

'So should you,' she retorted, shrugging him off and striding on. Tel struggled to keep up, anxious to confirm she knew the dangers of the Vulturi. 'Septim told me,' she tossed over her shoulder, but Tel was far from reassured.

'You're not to go near Skeardin Head,' he ordered.

'*Don't* tell me what I can or can't do!' she said, rounding on him.

'Someone needs to. When you're on your own, you—'

'But I'm *always* on my own, Tel! You and I share nothing!'

She strode off but Tel remained where he was and not only because his legs had ceased to function. The impact of his earlier rash words was clear and yet it was actually he who should be aggrieved. He had made an honorable proposal of marriage and Chant had refused it because she refused to give up a man *who was already married*.

It took Tel a long time to reach the stay and he was glad his bed had been shifted to a sleeping room. It gave him the privacy to strip off his wet clothes and struggle into dry ones. By the time he returned, Septim and Dargil had joined Turai in the cooking place and they ate together.

The rain eased to a patter on the roof, but Chant didn't appear. 'Has Chant gone to her bed?' he asked finally.

'Not that one,' said Dargil, starting on his third bowl of soup. 'She's gone hunting.'

'Hunting?'

'Yes. Arrived ahead of you, asked about sivets and grass-skippers, took her weapons and left.'

'You let her go out, on her own, on a night like this?' asked Tel incredulously.

'The storm's blown through,' said Dargil. 'Never last long

when they're westerly. She'll come to no harm.'

'How do you know that?' demanded Tel. 'She might fall and injure herself, be attacked by—'

'She's Sceadu,' interrupted Septim, his small eyes fixed on Tel. 'Not kin by blood or marriage. We owe her the hospitality we owe *any* stranger and she owes us honest dealings. She has no need of our permission to do this or that and nor do we demand it.'

'Chant's more than a stranger to me,' retorted Tel, and as the stay quietened, he dropped his gaze to the fire. 'She's a friend,' he muttered.

'It didn't look like it on the path this afternoon,' said Dargil.

Turai eyed Dargil sternly. 'Even friends have disagreements sometimes,' she said.

Chant was glad to be on hunt, to feel her quiver snug on her back, to test the air for a beast that *could* be hunted. She was tired of searching for what Siah sought and weary of the salty air. She longed for the Redlands' crystaleyes and whisper-owls; its stands of ashins, lart and fyr; its deep woody places strung with webs.

The Okianos lands were flat and clad only in coarse grasses, now drenched by the storm which meant her boots and trousers were too. According to Dargil, she must walk through the night and part of the morrow to reach where sivets foraged, and she had been so keen to escape Tel, she hadn't thought to bring food.

Had she hunted the Redlands, she would have gathered sherenberries but there was nothing here and even if she found a Willing beast, she wouldn't be back at Turai's tur for three days.

She had gone hungry as a young hunter and in Berian-tur, hunger lurked in snowcome's depths, but she had grown used to a full belly since. The Sunnen ate twice a day, *every day*, as did the Meduin. The Okianos seemed to eat even more often; soup always bubbling away in the cooking place. Her mouth watered even at the thought.

The cloud drifted away and Chant grew weary but she pressed on and, as the night deepened, her skin roused. Turai had said the grasslands held nothing dangerous but her skin told a different story and she set an arrow. She crept on but the night revealed no threat and her skin ceased its flick.

The sweep of grasslands lightened and it was dawn when she smelled droppings and came to a dip in the riverbank. A drinking place, but closer to the Okianos Stead than Dargil suggested sivets roamed, so maybe grass-skippers drank here. Chant decided to wait and as the new sun warmed her, curled up in the grasses and slept.

She woke suddenly, the sense of threat palpable, and peered through the stalks. There was a man some twenty paces off. He carried a spear and wore no shirt, the sinewy muscles of his back plain, and then he swivelled and Chant gasped; his face was patterned! But he had the hardest eyes she had ever seen and his features were spare, as if formed from too little flesh. She shrank back as his gaze swept over her hiding place and, after what seemed an age, he moved off northwards.

Chant remained crouched in the grass. The man fitted Septim's description of the Vulturi although Septim hadn't mentioned patterning. Perhaps the man was Myrali *except* if the Myrali had shifted southwards, they wouldn't be wandering about in Okianos lands, *if* these were Okianos lands.

She remained vigilant but thankfully, the man didn't return. The day drew on and then, as dusk reclaimed the land, the grasses stirred and a beast akin to a small aperion appeared. It snuffed the air then came down the bank, and others followed until a group of seven drank at the water's edge.

Chant set an arrow and crept forward. The beasts finished drinking and one by one disappeared back into the grasses until only a single beast remained. Chant loosed the arrow. She felt it hit, sensed the void's sudden swirl, and then the beast leapt away into the darkness.

Chant stared at the empty space in disbelief, then scrambled down the bank and sped after it. But she hadn't gone far when she heard a soft panting and saw its wraith-like form prone in the bank's shadow.

The beast fell silent but as she crouched to retrieve her arrow, it gave a final convulsive kick and caught her just above the eye. Pain exploded and Chant reeled back, clutching her face, then staggered to the river's edge and scooped cool water over it. Her eye burned making it hard to complete Talabraith's rites, and stars had filled the sky before she heaved the carcass over her shoulder and set off.

Before long, her eye had swollen shut and, to add to her misery, her belly ached with hunger. She trudged on, having to hold her head at odd angles to see and dawn was close again when her wounded ankle twisted and she almost fell.

She set the beast down and collapsed beside it. Far away, the Sceadu still slept, safe in the Great Turrel, while the Okianos slept too, snug in their stone turs. She cradled her head in her arms and tears coursed down her cheeks. She was tired of journeying and of carrying the Sceadu's burden, but most of all, she was tired of being alone.

32

*T*el cursed his weakness as he pushed himself to complete another round of the cooking place. Turai would wake soon and Septim and Dargil return from their night's fishing, and then the stay would fill with their easy conversations. It had been so last evening and the evening before: Turai, Septim and Dargil, but no Chant.

Tel stopped at the window and peered east. Dawn streaked the sky but the river was as empty as his heart. He managed another round of the room and sagged onto a chair as Turai appeared securing the end of her braid. She wore it in a single plait, unlike Chant, whose hair was an unconfined sweep of blue-black.

Turai wished him a good morning, filled a pan from the waterpot, and shifted the soup pot deeper into the coals. It was bubbling by the time Septim and Dargil thumped in, carrying the smell of the river. They washed noisily and, as they ate, Dargil recounted a comical tale of how he had all but tipped up the boat.

Septim bellowed with laughter and Turai joined in but Tel found it hard to even smile. Chant hadn't eaten for two nights now; Septim said she'd taken no food and there was none where she went. Being Sceadu meant she had probably grown used to hunger, but knowing she suffered tore at his heart.

Chant set the beast down outside Turai's tur and was sluggishly considering whether to leave it there or take it to the cooking place, when Septim came out. 'That's a nasty bruise,' he said, and led her inside.

Tel was there but Chant's only concern was food. She gulped down the soup Septim passed her and when he refilled the bowl, emptied that one too. She ate the third more slowly and, as Septim disappeared through to the sleeping rooms, let herself drift.

'I'll see to that bruise,' said Septim, making her jump. She tilted her head and his thick fingers worked a cool paste around her eye. He was surprisingly gentle for such a strong man. 'How did you manage this?' he asked.

'By hunting badly,' she mumbled, her speech slurred by exhaustion.

'Does your head ache?' he asked.

'Yes.'

Septim stoppered the paste. 'I don't want to see you on the shore for a couple of days,' he said.

Chant didn't argue but as she struggled to her feet, Tel rose too, his sweet-water scent waking her need of him, not of *him*, she amended angrily, of *Scead*. He seemed about to speak but she brushed past him and went to her room. The anger he had roused added to the throb of her head and she crawled into bed, pulled the cover high and slept.

The sivet leant the tur a festive air and Septim wasted no time in inviting his kin to share the feast. In the two days Chant had been confined to the tur, Turai had prepared huge pots of fish and greenfood, and even a bowl of honey-apples. Given the excitement over the beast, Chant wondered why the Okianos didn't hunt more often but when she asked Dargil, he had told her they were fisher folk.

It seemed a poor reason but she couldn't question him further because he had gone off with Septim and Tel to collect washwood. Septim planned to roast the sivet in the yard where there was ample room for his kin. Chant dreaded having to deal with more strangers but at least her eye had opened.

210

Bruised as black as night, Dargil had told her cheerfully, a description Turai had confirmed. But Turai had also reassured Chant that, despite her blackened eye and Sceadu patternings, Septim's kin would be far more curious about Tel.

'For a Sunnen to come all this way is virtually unheard of,' she said. 'Septim's kin *and* many of the Stead are keen to see what sort of man he is.'

Chant had managed not to smirk. Knowing Tel was about to discover what it was to be an object of curiosity gave her a perverse sense of pleasure that even eased her anxiety over her interrupted search.

Turai and Septim greeted their guests near the fire that evening, Turai wearing a magnificent, many-stranded necklace of taka and Septim an enormous disk of it at his throat. The newcomers were introduced to Chant but she didn't bother to keep track of them, preferring to watch Tel try to and fail. It was a Sunnen custom to differentiate between kin, not a Sceadu one, but Tel had never been among so many unfamiliar kin at once.

Septim had arranged mats and chairs around the fire and set large pieces of washwood for extra perches and, before long, the yard was full of a cheerful hubbub. The gathering reminded Chant of snowmelt's celebrations when the girls' and boys' Turrels mixed. She and Spark had ignored their agemates' teasing to join Firn and Ashin and, as the snowmelts had passed, her trysts with Ashin had become so predictable her ageset had taken no notice.

And then, one day, she had gone on hunt and Ashin had married Spark, and nothing had been predictable since. Her gaze settled on Tel on the other side of the fire. There was nothing *unpredictable* about *his* life. How pleasant it must be to have corral fences to include everything you wanted and exclude everything you didn't; to have plants grow in rows instead of how seedfall dictated. Why, he even controlled the water's flow and how proud he was of that! The mighty Tel, who could *bring the water* . . .

Septim rose to formally welcome his guests and Chant rose

too, but instead of listening politely, stumbled away towards the shore where thought might be possible.

It couldn't be Tel! She had met him moons ago; met him *but not recognised what he was,* until now, beside the great tarn, *as Siah had foretold.*

There was movement behind her and she spun. It was Tel, wearing an expression she knew all too well. 'Why have you left the gathering?' he demanded. 'You deserted the celebration of Giving; you disrupted the marriage of Tanalan; and now you insult your hosts here.' Chant stared at him dumbly, dazed by her discovery. 'Are the Sceadu *utterly* bereft of respect for the ways of others, or is it just that you are?'

'At least the Sceadu aren't deceitful like the Sunnen,' she choked out. 'We don't pretend love for those we despise.'

'Don't accuse *me* of deceit! It was you who—'

Dargil's voice sounded from the yard's direction, summoning Tel back to the feast and as he glanced back, Chant turned and ran. He called after her but she had always used exhaustion to escape pain and she pushed herself on and on, long after her muscles shrieked at her to stop.

It was the sense of something looming from the darkness that finally brought her to halt. Skeardin Head, she realised in shock and as Septim's warning sounded in her ears, she swung back and all but collided with a man. For a moment, she thought it was Tel but this man was shorter and then something flashed and a spear blade pierced her shirt.

'We go,' he said.

Chant recoiled. 'No,' she said, and tried to move past him but the blade stabbed again, deeper this time and Chant gasped as blood oozed from her breast.

He raised the spear again and she flinched. 'We go,' he repeated, confident now he had her, as well he might to be, concluded Chant, bitterly regretting not wearing her knife. He marched her north along the shore but she slowed as they neared the headland's feet. 'Keep going,' he ordered.

'There's no way through.'

The spear stabbed again, into her shoulder this time and she stumbled forward then stopped as foam showered her. The man grabbed her by the hair and dragged her onto the rocks, and Chant screamed as her legs were washed from under her. He wrenched her upright, leapt onto the next rock and yanked her after him. Salt blinded her and sometimes water, but the man dragged her on. Fear was a more potent weapon than any spear and Chant had no idea how long it was before the rocks gave way to sand.

He gave her a violent shove that sent her sprawling and then threw back his head and bellowed. Chant had heard a he-berian bellow after it had torn the jaw from its adversary. It had been a bellow of triumph and a warning to would-be challengers.

The man was back in his own lands, sure of himself *and* of her. He lowered the spear and traced the outline of each breast with its blade, drew it over her belly and smiled as he slid it between her legs. Then he wrenched her upright and held her so her face was close to his. 'You're mine now,' he said. 'I found you; I hunted you; I claimed you.'

His aggression was as sour as his breath and Chant wanted to spit in his gloating face but she daren't risk the beating that would follow. She forced her shoulders down and dropped her eyes and didn't retaliate even when he dealt her a stinging blow that split her lip. The man enjoyed inflicting pain but the greater her injuries, the lesser her chances of returning to Berian-tur.

He ordered her on and the dim outlines of a ramshackle settlement emerged from the gloom. A dog barked and Chant smelt the rot of refuse. Siah and her assurance Chant would return were a long way away now, unlike Septim, Dargil and Tel. But Chant was kin to none of them.

Septim wouldn't seek trouble with the Vulturi and Tel couldn't compromise his corral's protection by risking his life, even if he wanted to. Her only hope lay in avoiding injury by pretending compliance but as the Vulturi turs closed in, it was a hard to hold onto any hope at all.

33

The the Moon's small light made it a poor time to look for anything except a fire site, concluded Tor sourly, as he chafed his hands. To add to his ill temper, he suspected Snowhawk was ensconced in his tur, while he and Mist roamed the chilly Redlands in search of him. Yet Tor couldn't return to his tur while there was a chance Snowhawk had indeed suffered an accident.

There had been unexpected compensations travelling with Mist. He gathered windfall for the fire each night, found ripe sherenberries in the most frigid of places, and pointed out herbs Tor hadn't noticed before. But it was his affection for Snowhawk that gave Tor the patience to tolerate his nervous starts. Even the tussle of ketwings made Mist jump and he continuously asked whether berian were near.

'We need to go east,' said Tor, as Mist drew level. 'It's too exposed for a fire here,' he added, having developed the habit of explaining the most obvious of things. Tor moved off but Mist didn't follow.

'We must go to the Ruthvin streambed,' said Mist suddenly. 'Snowhawk would have gone there.'

'The Ruthvin's too stony even for murrow to frequent,' said Tor, as patiently as he could.

'He would have gone for lave-flower, not for beasts.'

'Lave-flower?'

'It gives a purple dye. Snowhawk knew I had run out.'

Tor suppressed a grunt. It seemed convenient Mist suddenly knew where Snowhawk was and his suggestion Snowhawk wasted hunting time to search for dye plants was even less believable. 'It's too dark to go there now,' he said shortly.

'Can we go at first light then?'

'Yes, but then we return to Berian-tur. I've wasted enough time already.'

Mist fidgeted through the meal and his impatience was many times worse by the next morning. Tor became increasingly irritated by his reckless rushing ahead and, as they neared the Ruthvin, Tor ordered him back. The streambed grew deeper with every snowmelt and its brittle banks were treacherous. He approached cautiously and scanned its length: there was no sign of Snowhawk.

'Any other suggestions?' he asked, but Mist suddenly sprinted off along the bank, oblivious to the shower of stones in his wake. 'Mist,' cried Tor in alarm, but Mist's attention was on something ahead and, as Tor hastened after him, he saw it was a pack. And then, before Tor could stop him, Mist launched himself over the edge. Tor cursed but Mist completed the descent safely on his backside and Tor wasted no time in following.

Snowhawk lay at the bottom, his perfect face motionless in death. Grief was like a knife in Tor's heart and he staggered, while Mist sobbed out endearments and covered Snowhawk's face with kisses. Swamped by his own agonising loss, Tor barely registered what he saw and then, beyond hope, Snowhawk's eyes flickered open.

There was no awareness in them but Mist's sobs turned to exclamations of joy. More of his kisses found Snowhawk's mouth and Snowhawk turned so that his lips met Mist's. The kisses of lovers, not friends, realised Tor, unable to look away. Mist's cheek pressed to Snowhawk's and his fingers twined in Snowhawk's hair, and there was such tenderness in Mist's embrace that Tor's eyes burned. This was what he had wanted with Serest, *craved* with Serest, but it wasn't what she wanted with him *or* it appeared, enjoyed with Snowhawk.

Snowhawk's awareness grew and as Tor stared into his

eyes, it seemed he knew nothing of his agemate. Snowhawk neither lessened the intimacy of his embrace with Mist nor broke his gaze with Tor. *This is what I am*, Snowhawk seemed to say, and more troublingly: *Am I still deserving of your friendship? Of your love?*

Then Snowhawk's eyes closed and Tor gave Mist a shake. 'Come,' he said urgently. 'We need to see to his injuries.'

Mist released Snowhawk and Tor saw what Mist's body had obscured; the lump of shattered stone that pinned Snowhawk's ankle to the streambed. The detritus provided a cushion but his ankle might still be crushed. Tor's jaw clenched. Hunters died from such injuries or lived out their days as cripples.

Snowhawk wore no jacket and his shirt was saturated and when Tor lay his fingers against his cheek, he was horrified by its iciness. Snowhawk *must* be warmed but first he must be freed. The stone was heavy though not beyond him or Snowhawk to shift. But it sat snugly between juts of rock that had made it impossible for Snowhawk to pull it towards him or push it away. If Mist hadn't insisted Tor search, Snowhawk would have died of cold or berian strike.

Tor heaved the stone away and slid his fingers inside Snowhawk's boot, relieved to feel no breaks. He splinted the ankle just in case, then removed his own jacket and managed to get Snowhawk into it. Snowhawk didn't warm but Tor soon shuddered with the cold.

'I'll fetch Snowhawk's pack,' said Mist. 'He must have his shelter-sheet.'

Mist was right but Tor shook his head. 'The bank won't hold you.'

'It won't hold *you* perhaps but there are advantages to being skinny apart from Snowhawk loving a slender body.'

Mist spoke unselfconsciously and Tor frowned as if he weighed the risks of climbing the brittle bank, but Mist didn't wait. He clambered up the stone with surprising agility, heaved Snowhawk's pack over the edge, and followed it down in the same manner as before.

'That was well done,' said Tor, as he extricated Snowhawk's shelter-sheet. Mist helped him wrap Snowhawk in it and

Tor donned Snowhawk's jacket himself. 'We'll make camp as soon as we clear the Ruthvin,' he said.

Carrying Snowhawk was hard, the pot-holed streambed littered with rubble and branches from the last snowmelt's flood. The streambed ran east, which at least took them deeper into the Redlands, but the night had turned before they found a dip in the bank to haul Snowhawk out.

Tor built a fire while Mist hurriedly collected an enormous pile of windfall so it would burn hot all night, and then Mist supported Snowhawk's head while Tor tried to coax water down his throat. But no matter how they held him, the water trickled from his mouth.

'He's going to die, isn't he?' said Mist.

Tor remained silent, gripped by the same dread. Snowhawk reminded him of the tinsel-flies caught in snowcome's ice; their glittering beauty preserved until snowmelt released them to decay.

'He's going to die!' shrieked Mist, and Tor's head came up.

'Don't—' he growled, and grabbed Mist's arm. In his own weariness and fear, all Tor wanted was quiet but the next moment, Mist was sobbing in his arms and Tor muttering words of comfort. Mist felt different to Serest, harder but somehow more fragile, the type of body Snowhawk liked, no, the type he *loved*. And Mist's kisses had roused Snowhawk before!

'We need to give Snowhawk reason to come back to us,' he said urgently.

'I don't understand,' said Mist, wiping his face.

'The child's first warmth is skin to skin with its mother, but it's not just warmth, Mist, it's scent and heartbeat, breath and love. We'll put Snowhawk between us, skin to skin, heart to heart. We both love him. If our warmth doesn't draw him back, perhaps our love will.'

Mist smiled tremulously. 'And if he leaves . . . if he returns to the void, I'll go with him. He'll go safely with my love.'

'Snowhawk wouldn't want you to give up your life,' said Tor, but his thoughts were on Serest, who wouldn't even give up a few days for him.

Mist's slender fingers caressed Snowhawk's cheek. 'We know what it is to be alone, Snowhawk and I, and what it is to be as one. The void holds no fear for us after that.'

Scead came out of the Great Turrel into the pale light of the new day and lifted his eyes to Ashali. It seemed an age since he had last noticed its shining peak; the shimmer of the Redlands' leaf-roof; the chill spike of air on his skin. Siah's fever had ebbed and Scead felt as joyous as if snowmelt had begun.

He knew the reprieve might be brief, that tomorrow might bring another fever to drain her dwindling strength, but that was tomorrow and now he could stand in Berian-tur's quiet beauty and pretend that all was well.

His peace was short-lived. There was the sound of running feet and then Tor burst from the trees. Ketwing had asked Tor to watch for Chant's return and Siah's delirious mutterings held their agemate's name, but Tor was grim-faced and Scead wondered if he brought news of Chant's death.

'What's amiss?' asked Scead.

'I have . . . need of aid . . . for Snowhawk,' panted Tor.

'Snowhawk? Has he suffered berian strike?'

Tor shook his head. 'He . . . fell and spent nights . . . in the open. We've . . . managed to warm him and . . . get him back to his tur. He can barely take water . . . he's so weak.'

'Do you want me to come?'

'No. We . . . I can care for him. I've left a friend with him and come directly here. If you . . . can give me something . . . a restorative . . . I'll take it back.'

'Then you must rest,' said Scead, as he hurried back into the Great Turrel. 'You're exhausted.'

Tor deposited his weapons at the door and followed him in. 'It was a hard journey, but . . .' Tor smiled. 'The Sceadu can't afford to lose our best hunter.'

'The Sceadu can't afford to lose *any* hunter,' corrected Scead grimly. 'No matter how far from us they roam.'

34

*C*hant leaned back against her ramshackle prison and winced as her wounds smarted. Dawn was close and she was parched, having drunk nothing since the previous evening. Her captor had secured the door and gone but he would be back.

Chant gave the walls another violent shake but more out of frustration than any belief she could break free. The walls might be of odd pieces of washwood and the roof of thatch, but they were lashed together with close-set leather thongs, and the uprights driven deep into a ground so hard that Chant doubted she could dig her way out, even had she a shovel.

She couldn't escape through speed either. The man would catch her at Skeardin Head, its surging waves as much a prison as her present one. The alternative was to flee inland but other Vulturi would join the chase and Chant had no stomach for what would follow.

Voices approached and she tensed as she recognised her captor's then the door was flung open and she was dragged out. She kept her head low as a cub would before a he-berian but her captor seized her hair and wrenched it up. Showing off his trophy, realised Chant, as she struggled to control her anger. The second man was taller and more muscular but shared the same scraped features, and his roughened fingers gripped her chin as he appraised her. The men's patterning made their brutality even worse.

'I thank you *little* brother for finding me such a handsome prize, *if* a little damaged,' the second man said.

He captor snatched her back. 'She's mine by right of finding!'

'If she were a dart or bloater-fish, perhaps, but women go to the strongest seed. You should know that, *little* brother. The Vulturi don't want weaklings planted in their women's bellies. Strength is in the first-born.'

Her captor shoved Chant behind him and pulled a notched blade from his belt, but the second man seemed unconcerned. 'Don't be more of a fool than you already are, *little* brother,' he sneered.

Her captor lunged and the second man stepped nimbly aside, caught her captor's wrist and forced him to his knees. 'The strength is in the *first-born*, *little* brother,' he goaded, as he pushed her captor's face to the dirt.

Chant toyed with the idea of making a dash for it after all but a crowd had gathered: bent, grey-haired elders, sullen younger men and stony-eyed women clutching skinny children. All were patterned and Chant sensed the women's animosity. If Chant were something men were prepared to fight over, they might share food with her and that meant less for them and their children.

A gruff command sounded and the gathering pulled back. The brothers stopped their fight too and her captor struggled to his feet, glaring at his brother. He still held his knife but made no attempt to use it. A white-haired man appeared through the throng; his sinewy chest thrust forward. He carried a spear but more as a badge of office, thought Chant, than as a weapon. He looked even more ancient than the weathered elders, but his bearing and the taka at his throat reflected power.

'My sons fight in the dust for you,' he said, his eyes as sharp as blades. 'But then, my sons fight in the dust for washwood.'

The gathering tittered but hushed as the man spoke again. 'Shargen, tell me why she's here,' he said, his gaze fixed on Chant.

'Karesh brought her.'

'I found her on the shore,' said her captor *Karesh*.

'North of Skeardin?'

The question made the crowd uneasy and Karesh hesitated. It was the first time Chant had seen him other than arrogant. 'South,' he muttered, 'but loose, and loose there a time before. In the lands above the Sunwash, she was loose too. I hunted well. She's mine by right of finding.'

'But not by right of birth, *little* brother,' said Shargen.

The older man seemed to be losing interest in his sons' quarrels. Perhaps he would let them fight it out *or* share her and Chant gulped down air. 'My husband will be angry I've been taken,' she said wildly.

The man's eyes narrowed. 'Your husband is Okianos?'

'He's Sunnen but kin to the wife of Septim.' The man's jaw tightened at the mention of Septim, but Chant didn't know whether his animosity boded well or ill.

'Your husband's a careless man to leave you loose.'

'He's ill and forced to his bed. I . . . I like to wander. It makes him angry. I cost him a lot of . . . taka when he . . . traded for me. I come from beyond the mountains and have caused him trouble before. He will be very angry,' she repeated.

The older Vulturi would understand a man's wrath at losing a possession and she wanted to plant the idea that, having traded for her once, her husband might trade for her again. The Vulturi wore a small disk of taka and Chant knew it was greatly valued amongst the Okianos, *and* here, she hoped.

'I think you lie,' said the Vulturi. Chant's heart migrated to her throat and she became aware of the gatherings' silence; even the children were mute. 'You say you come from beyond the mountains yet your face is patterned. I think you are kin. What are your people named?'

'The Sceadu,' choked Chant.

'They're not known to me. They must have departed in the time of my forefathers when many of lesser strength left.' He glared at her as if she were responsible for their weakness and when he spoke again, his voice held anger. 'Leave her be for two days,' he ordered his sons. 'We will wait to see what fortune the wind and water bring.'

'She's mine by—' Karesh began, but there was a blur as the old Vulturi's spear flashed to his throat, then a jab, and a trickle of blood.

'Kablar has spoken!' Karesh bowed, and with a final glare, Kablar strode off.

The crowd wandered away too but Shargen remained. 'Two more days, *little* brother, then she's mine. If you want to enjoy her, best do it soon.'

Karesh thrust Chant back into her prison and then horrifyingly, seemed about to join her, and Chant's determination to survive at any cost fled. She knew how vicious his intimacy would be and would kill him first or be killed, before she endured that.

But as Karesh wiped the blood from his throat, he seemed to reconsider. He flung the door shut and leather scraped as he secured it, and then there was silence.

Tel had the cooking place to himself the next morning, despite the sun being well up. The feasting had lasted deep into the night but Tel's strength had given out far earlier and he had taken to his bed. Chant hadn't risen either which added to his frustration. He wanted to speak to her without the presence of others *and* the antagonism of their last exchange.

At least the Sceadu aren't deceitful like the Sunnen, she had spat at him. *We don't pretend love for those we despise.*

The trouble was he hadn't *pretended* love for her. Thanks to the bitter-flax, he had blurted out his feelings and then been left to undo the damage. A poor job he had made of it too. It had been cowardly to pretend no words of love had been spoken and naive to believe his want of her would fade.

But last night had convinced him her place was with the Sceadu and his with the Sunnen. Before the feast, he had harboured hope she could find happiness with him in the Stead, but she had chosen the moment of Septim's speech to destroy that hope. By storming off, she had unambiguously demonstrated her contempt for the Okianos and, as his kin, for him too.

He had briefly wondered whether there was another explanation for her behaviour but hadn't had time to find out. He was kin *and* from afar, and the meat couldn't be carved in his absence. But the Okianos hadn't delayed the feast for Chant, despite Chant having provided the meat. His lips thinned. The lack of respect flowed both ways, he perceived.

Sick of his endless machinations, he decided to have it out with her, but her sleeping room was empty. At least her pack and weapons were there which meant she hadn't gone off on another ill-fated hunt *or* started east without him, but her untouched bed made him uneasy and he followed the path down to the shore.

She had run from him after their argument and, although the tide was higher, there were enough wide-spaced prints to tell him she had still been running hard as she had headed north towards *Skeardin Head.*

Tel's blood ran cold as he wondered whether, in her anger and upset, she hadn't realised her direction or whether she hadn't cared. He trudged off towards the headland and when he neared it, collapsed onto the sand to catch his breath.

The waves crashed against the stones with such violence he knew Chant would have stayed well clear of it and he struggled to his feet. The waves had scoured most of Chant's prints away but as he turned south again, he found another set, and a single, larger print. Tel felt as though a dead hand had brushed his skin and he stared at it for a long moment, then hastened back along the shore.

Septim sat with his gaze on the fire as if he had nothing pressing to do and all the time in the world to do it. Tel's fingers drummed the chair. He had described what he had found *and* his fears and it was only Turai's warning glance that held him silent.

'I think you might be right,' said Septim finally. 'Chant is most likely in Vulturi hands.'

'Then we must go and demand her release,' said Tel.

Septim drew the chopping board back onto his lap and resumed his interrupted filleting. 'It isn't as simple as that.'

'Why not? We both know Chant was on Okianos land when she was taken and that means the Vulturi trespassed to abduct her.'

'That would be difficult to prove,' said Septim. 'What we

do know is that Chant is neither Okianos nor our kin, and that she was alone. Such things strengthen the finder's claim.'

'*The finder*? She's not a piece of washwood to be snatched up and carried away!' Septim said nothing and Tel glared at him. 'Well I'm not willing to abandon her, even if you are.'

Septim's head came up but it was Turai who spoke. 'No one's speaking of abandonment, Tel, except you,' she said quickly. 'But I'm puzzled by your willingness to risk your life for her. When she came seeking aid for you and later, when she sat by your sick bed, I thought you shared love, but there's been nothing but animosity between you since.

'Septim is right. Chant isn't kin and although she helped you, you can't risk your corral's protection for her sake. And be very clear, Tel. If you go to the Vulturi demanding her return, they *will* kill you, as they killed your father.'

Tel stared at her in shock. 'They killed my father?'

'Along with three of our men,' confirmed Septim. 'The Vulturi lost several times that number and the last of their boats.'

'But why? What caused the fight?'

'A pretty Vulturi girl,' said Septim, tossing the tailings into a bucket and setting the chopping board aside. 'But she didn't start it and neither did Barin's willingness to enjoy her charms; they were simply the spark. The fuel had built for seasons beforehand and, when the spark jumped, the fuel burned.'

Tel ran his fingers through his hair as he struggled to make sense of Septim's words. 'What happened?'

'Barin met her on his first visit but on his second she decided to join him on our side of the headland. The Vulturi give nothing away, although they're happy enough to steal. We had tolerated their incursions for some time, for we have enough and they have little, but the girl's desertion tempted them to not only reclaim her but take Okianos women *and* anything else they could carry off.

'The Vulturi attack was predictable. They brought boats up the Sunwash but the Sunwash isn't the Ecanwash. Its flows are stronger and there are bars and stone reefs. Two boats broke up in the current and we burned the last to the waterline.'

'My father was killed during the fighting?' asked Tel

hoarsely.

Septim shook his head. 'When the fighting was done and the girl gone, he believed he could retrieve her through stealth. I thought I had talked him out of it but he went off in the night. We found his body the next day, in the water, at Skeardin Head.'

There was a long silence. 'Why didn't you tell me this on my first visit?' asked Tel.

Turai's leathery hand closed over his. 'My sister had lost her husband and you had lost your father. These things couldn't be undone but their hurt could be worsened.'

'Yet you tell me now.'

'So you don't repeat your father's mistakes,' said Turai gently. 'Chant is no kin to you, Tel, but those who wait for you in your corral are. Go back to those you love.'

Tel smiled grimly. 'I've spent my entire life ensuring I *don't* act like my father and yet, here I am, sitting in your stay as he did, speaking of how to retrieve a woman stolen by the Vulturi. Yet I am *not* my father. I haven't married a woman only to deceive her *and* the children she bore me. And you are right to tell me to go back to those I love, because I love Chant, and for that reason, I won't abandon her.'

Tel expected to see disapproval in Turai's face and contempt in Septim's but Turai's face had softened and Septim's expression eased. 'Men have been known to do strange things for love,' he said, his gaze on Turai. 'Take some soup, Tel, for you need to build your strength and then we'll discuss what might be done.'

35

Tel moved steadily along the sand, his gaze on the sea. The tide would be at its lowest soon and Skeardin Head easiest to pass. Then, if all went well, he would be rounding it again, with Chant, before the tide turned. *If all went well.* He refused to think of what would happen if it didn't go well.

Septim had given him dried wait, a fish rare in Vulturi waters, and taka, prized by peoples the length and breadth of the shore. To retrieve Chant, he must trade for her, and what he offered must exceed her worth to the Vulturi many times over.

They might take his trade and kill him anyway, but his kinship link to Septim lessened the risk. Tel didn't know the part Septim played in the fighting, but he had hinted Kablar wouldn't want that kind of trouble again. Tel assumed that if the Vulturi *did* kill him, Septim would exact bloody revenge, but it wasn't exactly a comfort.

He set his face in a scowl, which given the circumstances was easy, and strode purposefully on. He was still in Okianos lands but there might be watchers and he must play the part of the wronged husband. According to Septim, Tel's best chance of recovering Chant *and* keeping his life, was to think and act like the Vulturi. Their men exerted absolute authority over their wives and expected absolute obedience; in short, he must be as brutish as them.

Tel worried Chant wouldn't understand her part in the charade and fight back, and if she did, he would really have to hurt her. It was a worry Septim hadn't shared. *Hunters understand how the weaker beast might outwit the stronger*, he'd said.

Tel reached the headland and clambered onto the first of the broken stones. The waves spent their fury further out but he was still showered with spume and the strews of slime-weed made the going treacherous. It distracted him but there was a real possibility he was going to his death and Septim's farewell had been grim. He patted his knife, its presence reassuring, despite knowing he couldn't retrieve Chant by force.

According to Septim, the Vulturi Stead was strung out behind the first line of dunes and Kablar's stay big enough to accommodate many people. The Vulturi congregated there in the hope of picking over Kablar's cast offs.

The first of the stays came into sight and Tel struggled not to stare. Their walls were washwood and so crooked their windows and doors sat at strange angles. Women crouched around cooking fires with their children, and sullen men propped against doorways, their faces patterned like Chant's.

Septim believed the peoples between Ashali and the sea were linked because they shared a common tongue, but Tel refused to accept he shared *anything* with these people. Those he passed fell in behind him but Tel strode on, his gaze on the biggest stay, and he was almost to it when a man barred his way.

Tel swaggered to a stop. 'I'm kin to Septim of the Okianos and have business with Kablar,' he said.

The man eyed Tel's knife but gestured him forward and Tel entered the stay. It was dim inside and thick with the reek of too many bodies. People crowded around the walls and a grey-haired man sat on a pile of pelts at the stay's centre. Tel's escort gestured him to sit and Tel settled on the floor in front of the man.

He presumed it was Kablar and bowed in the way Septim had instructed, then set the bag of fish and taka on the floor and waited.

The man's eyes gleamed as he looked at the bag but Tel stared straight ahead. 'I am Kablar,' the man confirmed. 'What is your business?'

'I am Tel of the Sunnen, *kin* of Turai, *wife* of *Septim* of the Okianos,' said Tel. 'I visit my Okianos kin as part of my obligations as *head* of my stay. With me I brought a wife, lately traded, but a curse she's been, despite her cost.' Tel spat to one side. 'Three nights ago, she wandered. That's why I've come.'

'What makes you think she's here?'

'I followed her prints to Skeardin Head. There's nowhere else she could be.'

'My younger son recently found a woman. He's long sought a wife and doesn't want to trade her.'

Tel frowned, as if confused. 'Septim tells me *you're* the Vulturi leader,' he said. It was dangerous to question Kablar's authority but Tel had to ensure he dealt only with the Vulturi leader, whose greed Septim had described in detail.

'Septim is correct,' grunted Kablar.

'Ah,' said Tel, and forced a smile. 'Then it's with you I trade.' Kablar made no reply but his attention shifted to the bag. Tel loosened the drawstrings but didn't open it. 'As I've said, the woman cost me much, but she is young and strong and will give me children. However, I understand her foolishness made her appear loose . . .'

'What is it you trade?'

Tel opened the bag and Kablar leaned forward as did the gathering. 'Septim is a fine fisherman and, as a gesture of friend-ship, he sends you wait.' Tel passed the fish to Kablar who put it to one side, his attention on the bag. 'For my wife, I trade taka,' said Tel, and emptied the shining pile onto the floor.

Kablar's eyes widened and there was a collective gasp. It was a rich prize indeed and Kablar knew it, as did those present.

'It's a *fair* trade,' reiterated Tel.

Kablar nodded and the knot loosened in Tel's stomach but then a voice broke in, and pretending irritation, Tel turned. It belonged to his escort and as the man vented his displeasure, Tel realised it was Kablar's son, *the man who had snatched Chant.*

'My son doesn't wish to lose his wife,' said Kablar.

'The trade is with *you*!' said Tel, no longer needing to feign anger.

'My son has taken a liking to your knife.'

Tel kept his face a glowering mask but Septim's warning

was stark in his head: *If they judge you the weaker, they will kill you.*

'Bring the woman,' growled Tel. 'I want proof you hold her.'

Kablar's son left and Tel glared into space as if he reflected on the man's insolence but he was in turmoil. Handing over his knife rendered him weaponless and the temptation to kill him would be irresistible. Septim would retaliate but Kablar wasn't thinking beyond the treasures before him and any regret would come later, if at all, and too late for he and Chant.

Kablar's son returned, dragging a woman, and Tel sprang to his feet. It *was* Chant and Tel wrenched her from the Vulturi's grip and dealt her a blow across the face. 'I curse the day I ever traded you,' he roared, and slapped her again. Men guffawed and Tel gave her a violent shake and turned back to Kablar. 'I've given you fair exchange,' he snarled, 'but have urgent need to be back in my stay. Take the knife, for I've no more time to haggle.'

He flung the knife at the son's feet and strode from the stay, yanking Chant after him. It was a gesture of contempt *and* strength, but Tel didn't pause or look back. He passed swiftly between the crooked buildings, cuffing and cursing Chant as he went, while his heart raged against what he did. He was terrified she would fight back and horrified when she didn't, fearing the Vulturi had brutalised her beyond retaliation.

'I have to do this to get us away,' he hissed, but she gave no sign of having heard him.

Shadows held the shore and as he turned towards Skeardin Head, there was movement in the dunes behind. It seemed Kablar's son, or his friends, weren't satisfied with the trade after all. Tel guessed the attack would come at the headland, where the rocks provided cover and which was far enough away for Kablar to retain his honour. Tel's body would be found later, in the water, like his father's.

But they had a start on their attackers. 'They follow,' he whispered, and shifted his grip to her hand. 'Run!'

They fled along the hard sand at the water's edge stride for stride and, even with the old injury to her ankle, she was fast. Tel had to use every shred of his failing strength to keep up but she slowed as they neared the headland.

'I can't cross,' she panted. 'I can't.'

'You must! They will kill me if you don't!' She stared at him wild-eyed. 'Go now! Go!' he ordered.

He pushed her forward and she clambered onto the rocks. The waves beat on the seaward stones and water surged and sucked about their ankles. Where he could he steered her into the shadows but he had no time to look behind him; any pause would cost his life. Chant's ragged breaths were audible above the waves and he was no better; the remnants of marsh fever eating his strength.

Then she stopped and he blundered into her, the way ahead a surge of water. A spear clattered off the rocks to his left and he grabbed her hand and leapt, taking her with him. A second spear passed so close the air whispered but they clambered on, keeping to where the stones provided shelter. The desperate scramble seemed endless, with Tel expecting a spear in the back at any moment and then blessedly, open sand stretched before them and they broke into a run again, forcing themselves on until the shore provided no more hiding places.

Tel clutched his knees to catch his breath but Chant kept on going and he hastened after her. She allowed him to turn her, as she had allowed him to beat and berate her, and he gently smoothed the hair from her face. Blood trickled from a cut to her lip but he didn't know whether he had caused it or the Vulturi.

He scooped up seawater and gently cleaned it. 'This might sting a little,' he said tenderly, then caught the flash of her eyes before the blow took him full in the face. He was sent sprawling and when he touched his throbbing mouth, found blood.

'Try the seawater, although it might sting a little,' she sneered, and strode off.

Tel scrambled up and lunged after her, his hand fastening on her arm. 'Of all the ungrateful . . .' he began furiously, but Chant turned on him with fists, elbows and knees.

She had always been close to him in strength and now her wildness made her impossible to subdue. Their fight ranged up and down the shore as he struggled to ward off her blows and then, as they stumbled into the shallows, he drove his hip and shoulder into her and threw her backwards.

The water was less than thigh deep, but cold and Tel gasped, and staggered upright. Chant remained limp under him and he wrenched her back to the surface and carried her up to the drier sand. Her eyes were shut and her hair plastered to her battered face and, as Tel crouched over her, blood from his mouth dripped onto the blood on her shirt. His blood had mixed with hers at the traps and they had inflicted more wounds on each other since, sometimes in spite but more often in ignorance.

At the traps, the full moon had lit Chant's face in all its alien beauty but now the moon was slight and Chant's features bathed in shadow. It didn't matter; he didn't need to see her face to know her.

'Chant?'

Her eyes opened and for a long moment, they regarded each other. Then she reached up and touched his bleeding mouth. 'It wasn't you,' she whispered. 'It wasn't . . .'

Tel caught her hand and kissed it. 'I know,' he said. 'I understand your anger at what they did. I'm sorry I had to act like them too. It was the only way to bring you back.'

'Why didn't you just leave me there?'

Tel settled on the sand beside her but kept her hand in his. The sea was a moving pit of darkness but its voice was gentle. 'Because I love you,' he said.

Chant tried to withdraw her hand but Tel tightened his grip and she sat up. 'I don't believe you.'

'I can understand why. I professed love for you before and asked you to marry me. It was the effects of the bitter-flax, one of the ingredients of kina. When my head cleared, I pretended the words had never been spoken.'

'So, you've drunk kina again,' muttered Chant, staring at the water.

Tel gently turned her face to his. 'Bitter-flax doesn't make you lie, Chant, quite the reverse. It reveals what you really feel. But afterwards, I realised your obligations to the Sceadu and mine to my corral made being together impossible.'

'Nothing has changed.'

'*Everything* has changed, at least for me. The Vulturi made

231

my choices very clear: give you up or fight for you.'

Chant dropped her gaze to the sand. 'I can't abandon my quest for you.'

'I know. I'll help you complete it in any way I can. I'll search for this thing you seek and I'll be there for you if Scead stays with Siah, or you decide you don't want him anymore.'

Chant half shook her head. 'But none of this is fair to you,' she cried. 'You can't delay returning to your corral for me, and as for Scead . . . I don't understand what Siah meant *or* what Scead feels . . . or what *I* feel. Merala and Inkala need you and . . .' she trailed off.

The fact that Chant was torn between her obligations to Siah and what appeared to be feelings for him gave Tel hope. Time was on his side too. They still had a journey of many days to reach his corral, and he intended to use every one of them to convince Chant of the benefits of life on the *western* side of the mountains.

'Come,' he said, getting stiffly to his feet and helping her up. 'Things will seem better after we've changed into dry clothes and had some of Turai's fish and greenfood soup. Or is it greenfood and fish soup? Sure to be one or the other,' he quipped.

They started back but Chant's face remained troubled and, as Tel glanced at her blood-stained shirt, hatred for Kablar's son burned anew. 'Are you in pain?' he asked.

'My back hurts where it's cut and my face,' said Chant, 'but there's something I must speak of.' She avoided his eyes and Tel's throat tightened as he considered the full depth of violence the Vulturi might have inflicted.

'I've found it, Tel.'

'What?'

'The thing that brings water. I've found it.'

'But . . . when? Where?'

'On the night of the feast, beside the great tarn in the west, as Siah foretold.' She smiled sadly and Tel's mystification deepened. 'It's you, Tel.'

'Me? I can't unlock ice or cause rain, Chant.'

'No one can. That wasn't what Siah meant. But you can bring the water with your stonestreams; you can bring the water.'

Tel stared at her in bemusement. 'But you knew that back in the Sunnen Stead.'

'Yes, but I was blind to it. I had to come here to learn to see, just as I had to lose my swiftness to become Chant. Fleet the hunter, for all her skill in tracking the beast, couldn't have found it, nor could she tell of it, only the chantress could.'

Much of what Chant said was incomprehensible but one thing was clear: Chant believed he was the object of her quest. Of all the arguments Tel had considered to convince her to stay with him, this was the most powerful and the only one he hadn't thought of. He smiled and then, as its full implications sank in, threw back his head and laughed.

Septim had left a lamp burning at the door but neither he nor Turai had gone to bed, and he sprang up and enclosed Tel in a rib-cracking hug. 'You've done it, man!' he exclaimed and then his expression darkened as he turned to Chant. 'And I see they've made a fine mess of you,' he said, then beamed at Tel once more. 'You've defeated them in their own stinking lands and few can claim to have done so.'

Turai eyed them shrewdly, the soup already on the coals. 'Dry clothes, then food, then rest,' she ordered, and led Chant away.

Septim waited until the door had closed before he spoke again. 'I see you've fought, Tel. Take no insult if I say I'm surprised you lived to return.'

Tel touched his mouth. 'That was Chant,' he said.

Septim's eyebrows rose. 'It doesn't seem much of a reward for your efforts.'

'She's safe,' said Tel. 'That's reward enough.'

36

$\mathcal{A}$ll Chant wanted to do the next morning was start for home but Tel had gone off with Septim, and Turai insisted she rest. Chant was too unsettled to rest and after eating two bowls of soup and refusing a third, she wandered back to the shore and settled in the lee of a dune. The sand was pleasantly warm and she stared up at the clouds while her fingers played over her knife. Never again would she be fool enough to venture out without her weapons.

Finding the object of her search hadn't brought her the relief she expected, just another set of complications. Tel owed his kin before the Sceadu and the journey through Ashali was perilous. If no berian had passed that way lately, their scent would faint and, if they had, they might still be lurking in the darkness.

Chant had no idea where the tunnel exited in Berian-tur either. If it were high in the Whitelands, Tel mightn't survive its frozen emptiness to pass his skills to Siah. And even if she and Tel *did* reach Berian-tur safely *and* the Circle accepted Tel's advice, the day would come when she must bid him farewell. His place was as head of corral, on the Sunnen side of Ashali, and hers was as a hunter for those of Berian-tur.

Tel's retrieval of her had rekindled her feelings but Siah's promise of Scead remained and, given that every other element of Siah's foretelling had unfolded, this last part must too.

'Turai said I would find you here,' said Tel, making Chant jump. He looked relaxed as he settled beside her, despite his swollen lip.

'I'm sorry I hit you,' she said.

'We've already exchanged apologies and given how many times I hit you, you owed me one at least,' he said lightly. He took her hand and a little thrill moved through her. 'It's nice here in the sun,' he said. 'I've been helping Septim prepare the boat. Tomorrow he and Dargil will take us up the Sunwash to the Marshlands. It will make the first part of the journey easier.'

'I'd rather walk,' said Chant dourly.

'Dargil thought you might say that. He said to remind you that he's the finest seaman among the Okianos *apart* from Septim. And I'll be with you,' added Tel, bringing her hand to his lips.

'You were with me last time and it was an awful journey.'

'Being unconscious doesn't count,' said Tel with a smile. 'This trip will be better, I promise.'

The last of the stars still glittered when they set off the next morning. Septim and Dargil rowed and the boat was pushed along by the incoming tide. Septim was his usual uncommunicative self but Dargil's chatter helped distract Chant from the boat's terrifying lurch. Tiredness eventually overcame fear and she dozed and then she and Tel slept, Tel's offer to take a turn at the oars declined.

The sun was rising over the mist-swathed waters when Septim steered the boat to the bank and they unloaded their packs. Septim embraced Tel and then kissed Chant on each cheek. 'We part under happier circumstances than we met,' he said, and she nodded.

Dargil hugged her next and handed her a small bundle. 'Thank you . . .' she began, but Dargil had already turned to Tel.

'Take good care of her,' he said brusquely, and with a nod, clambered back in the boat. Chant watched them manoeuvre it into the flow and then, with a wave, they were gone.

'Aren't you going to unwrap Dargil's gift?' asked Tel.

Chant unwound the cloth to reveal a gleaming bracelet of azurine. Dargil had cleaned and polished each shell, made a neat hole, and threaded them onto a fine, shining yarn. It was a labour of many days and Chant wished she had thanked him properly.

'I think Dargil had more affection for you than he showed,' said Tel. 'His wife died before my first visit and he hasn't remarried. Some people only love once,' he said, his face intent.

Chant pushed the bracelet into her pack. 'We should make a start,' she said.

'Yes,' said Tel. 'Best get the stinking Marshlands over with.'

Tel took the more northerly route Septim had outlined for him and while jumping from tussock to tussock was no easier, and the stench and flies no more pleasant, the journey *was* quicker. By the time the first stars glinted, they had cleared the last of the fetid pools and reached the grasslands. Tel built a fire to celebrate but they were weary and spoke little before they slept.

It was different the next day when Tel kept up a constant stream of conversation. Chant said little, troubled by the understanding that for Tel to go to Berian-tur, he must abandon Merala, Islan and Inkala, the very people who had shown Chant kindness.

Sometimes as they walked or as they sat by the fire at night Tel took her hand and, in their more light-hearted moments, kissed it but he sought no further closeness. Chant guessed he gave her time to recover from the Vulturi, but Tel wasn't like them. His face held tenderness while theirs had held only a hard wanting.

It was evening when they reached the place where they must cross the Sunwash. Tel had spoken of it earlier in the day and of how he would make a raft for their packs, then return and float her across as he had before. He sought to prepare her for the crossing but fear was like a scinton's jaws tightening on her throat.

'I'll need your knife to cut some greenwood,' he said, as they took off their packs. Chant looked at him blankly. 'It's more flexible than washwood and holds the raft together,' he explained. Chant handed him her knife, overcome by the memory of him flinging his own knife at her captor's feet. The air had been so thick with threat she hadn't recognised the significance of the gesture but she did now.

Tel had traded his most precious possession for her and she closed her eyes, overwhelmed with the understanding Tel's commitment was neither shallow nor temporary.

He finished the raft and loaded their gear on. 'I'll take it across and come back for you. Soon we'll both be on the other side and, if you wish, we can make an early camp.' He smiled reassuringly and Chant watched him set off, reach the other side and start back. She walked down to meet him, placed her hand in his cool wet one, and let him lead her into the water.

When it was shoulder high, she looped her arms about his neck, closed her eyes and let the water take her. She thought of those who lived together in loving companionship in the Great Turrel, and in the Sunnen, Meduin and Okianos turs. No one lived alone.

Tel stopped swimming and Chant opened her eyes as if awaking from a dream. 'That was easier than last time,' he said in relief. 'You did well, Chant.'

His face was close and as the Sunwash intensified his sweet-water scent Chant brought her lips to his. Her hunter senses fired and she slid her hands down the smooth undulations of his ribs and flank.

Tel breathed as if he'd run and Chant's breath fell into the same rhythm, as if there weren't enough time to taste the essence of him, but then he pulled away. 'This is too soon,' he said. 'We must be married first, properly, in the Sunnen way.'

'I'm Sceadu,' she said, seeking his mouth again. 'I love you. I want you now.'

'No, Chant. *I* need to do this properly. And we need to change into dry clothes, not spend the rest of the night up to our chests in the Sunwash,' he added, with forced lightness.

He led her from the water but Chant wrenched her hand free as soon as they reached the bank and Tel turned in surprise, his gaze going to where her wet shirt had moulded itself to her breasts.

Chant flushed, made awkward by his rejection and by what the Vulturi had done. 'Turn your back,' she ordered, and when he'd done so, she changed into dry clothes and thrust her wet clothes into her pack.

'Do you want to set camp here?' he asked, as he fastened his shirt.

'No,' she said, and strode off along the bank.

They went on in silence, Chant humiliated by wanting Tel more than he wanted her and incensed by his assumption they would marry in the Sunnen way. Thoughts of Scead added to her turmoil and as night fell, she wondered whether Tel had used Sunnen customs to extricate himself from his marriage offer. He had proposed under the influence of kina, reneged, then renewed his commitment, but each day must make the pull of his corral stronger.

'It's too dark to go on,' he said eventually. 'We'll set camp here.' Chant dropped her pack and was about to collect wash-wood when he caught her arm. 'Never doubt my love for you, Chant.'

'But it isn't enough, is it?'

'What do you mean?'

'My task is to hunt for the Sceadu and yours is to head your corral. I'll take you through Ashali to speak with Siah of the stonestreams, but then—'

'*Through* Ashali?'

'There are tunnels,' said Chant, and described how she had followed berian scent to the Sunnen lands. Tel was clearly shocked by her words but when he flipped out his sleep-shelter next to hers, he didn't speak of tunnels but of Sunnen marriage rites.

'They prohibit men and women from love-making until the marriage is celebrated so any child born of the union knows the man who owes them protection.'

'I'm not Sunnen.'

'The Sunnen rites give women and children protection,' persisted Tel. 'What protection is there in the Sceadu custom of breaking a marriage in its first season?'

'Your special Sunnen rites didn't stop your father wandering off, did they?' she retorted.

'I'm not my father!'

'I didn't say—'

'You implied I would be unfaithful!'

Chant turned over and pulled the shelter-sheet high. It was pointless arguing over Sceadu and Sunnen marriage rites when Tel owed his kin first and she owed the Sceadu. She had remembered that now and she wondered when Tel would remember it too.

The following days passed with only the most mundane of talk and Chant dropped back so Tel's scent was less intense. She wanted to avoid rousing the feelings that had overtaken her at the Sunwash and told herself it was for the best, but her heart thought otherwise.

They reached the Old Stead without incident and Tel didn't argue about avoiding the path, although he did ask to share Chant's knife, which she declined; hacking through the briars distracted her from the complications ahead.

They sheltered in the cave of collapsed stones again but the night was mild and they didn't light a fire which Chant soon regretted. The shades of those long since departed drifted closer and she wondered whether the Old Stead's fate had infected her senses. As the night deepened, she abandoned her struggle to sleep and sat up.

Tel must have heard her for his shelter-sheet rustled. 'What troubles you?' he asked.

'I can sense those who were once here.'

She expected a snort of derision; Tel only believed in things as solid as the surrounding stone but it never came. 'They crafted a mighty stead,' he said, 'but when things change, people sometimes prefer to leave rather than change too. That's what the Myrali did who dwelt south of the Okianos.'

'And the Vulturi stayed,' said Chant grimly.

'And became as they are.'

The horror of that time was still fresh and Chant scrambled

upright, but there was no comfort in the surrounding stones.

Tel's footfall sounded behind her and she turned away and hugged herself. 'I know Sunnen customs are strange to you, Chant, but it will be easier in the Stead if you accommodate them,' he said gently.

'I've never said I would live in the Stead.'

'I'll come to your lands and show your people how to set stonestreams and orchards and gardens, but they might choose not to. When the runs of fish dwindled, the Okianos offered the Vulturi aid but Vulturi pride refused it.' Tel paused. 'Septim believes the Vulturi are kin to you, given you share patterning.'

'The Sceadu share *nothing* with the Vulturi!'

'Denying the truth doesn't alter it,' said Tel quietly. 'Why did your Siah send you to find me?'

'You don't believe in Siahs!' she retorted.

'Why, Chant? Because she knows the Sceadu can no longer live by hunting alone. If your season of cold is as you describe, and your streams don't flow, it takes no mystical skill to know the old ways must fail. Then the choice becomes to eke out a living at the cost of care for each other, as the Vulturi do; leave, as the Myrali and those who built this stead did; or change, as the Okianos and Sunnen have. We built the stonestreams when the rains began to fall elsewhere and while the rains might return, our gardens need water *now*.'

Tel's words were true but scarcely bearable and Chant took a shuddering breath.

'Chant?'

She didn't want him to know she wept but his fingers skimmed her cheek and felt the wetness, and he drew her into his arms. 'I love you,' he said, 'and that won't change. Nor will my wish to marry you. I'll come to your lands and tell your Siah how the Sceadu might live differently but whatever your Siah decides, you and I will have our own decisions to make.'

Tel's words brought Chant comfort but dread built again as they neared the Meduin Stead. Tanalan wouldn't welcome Tel's abandonment of his duties, no matter how temporary. Chant's feet dragged and Tel took her hand as they entered Kanan's corral and he tugged her after him into Kalia's tur. He sought to reassure her but she also sensed he wanted to announce their relationship.

Tanalan took her meal there with Kalia and Tarish and, with a cry of delight, flung her arms around Tel's neck. Tarish was on his feet too, smiling broadly and Tanalan released Tel and hugged Chant. 'It's *so* good to see you both,' she said, wiping away tears.

'Carve some more meat, Tarish,' ordered Kalia. She looker even frailer than Chant remembered, but her eyes had lost none of their shrewdness as they darted between Chant and Tel. Tarish handed Chant a platter of meat and she thanked him as she settled beside Tel, grateful the meal wasn't fish.

'How goes Turai?' asked Kalia. 'Is she well?'

'She is indeed and much the same as on my last visit,' said Tel. 'She and Septim pass on their regards to you and to the rest of Kanan's corral.'

'Merala will be pleased to have news of her sister too,' said Tanalan.

'We're *all* pleased,' said Kalia. 'Not many venture west and those who do, like Turai, often don't return. Yet you've come back, Tel, and brought Chant with you. Are we to witness another wedding?'

Tanalan's head swivelled and Chant tensed but Tel's voice was calm. 'If there's to be a wedding, it will be in the Sunnen Stead so regretfully, you will be unlikely to witness it.'

'*If?*' pursued Kalia, not put off.

'We must visit the Sceadu lands first,' said Tel. Chant kept her gaze on her meal, glad Tel had acknowledged that any marriage wasn't certain.

'Turai and her Okianos husband are well, you say?' prompted Kalia, her eagerness for news overcoming curiosity about Tel's marital intentions. Tarish was keen for news too and pulled his chair closer as Tel described their visit.

The talk passed back and forth and Chant snatched a glance at Tanalan, not surprised to see her earlier warmth had vanished. Chant doubted her welcome at the Sunnen Stead would be any better either. Tanalan saw Chant as robbing the corral of its protector and Merala would see her as stealing her son and, unless Chant agreed to live in the Sunnen Stead, both charges would be true.

37

Tel spoke with Kanan long into the night. He wanted to strengthen their kinship ties but he found Kanan's company enjoyable too. Marriage certainly suited him and news that Tanalan carried their first child added to Tel's envy. He craved the certainty of Chant being his wife, living safely with him in his corral and, sometime in the future, carrying *their* child.

He considered the impediments to him being in the same happy state as they continued their journey the next morning and they were formidable. He must trek through Ashali in utter darkness; overcome Chant's attachment to Scead; persuade her to marry him; *and* convince her to live in the Sunnen Stead. He had survived his encounter with the Vulturi, he comforted himself, and nothing could be worse than that.

Chant said little but the occasional caress of her hair on his arm reinforced the breach between them. Aborting their lovemaking at the Sunwash had undermined her confidence in his commitment and he had missed the opportunity to make her truly his. There might be other rivals for Chant's affections in the Sceadu lands apart from Scead, whereas here there were none.

They reached the Terecleft close to dark and, as Kanan had predicted, the path was clear. Even so, the cleft made the Sunwash turbulent and the narrow path meant they must cross in single file.

Chant stared down at the boil of muddy water. 'We don't have to pass through now,' said tel. 'We can set camp and go on at first light.'

'But it will still be here, won't it?' she said, with a poor imitation of a smile. 'You go first.'

Tel set off and she watched him reach the other side and turn, then took a deep breath and followed. She kept her eyes fixed on his and his love was like a bridge that excluded all else, even the spectres that swirled like the water below, and when she reached him, she collapsed into his arms.

The strong beat of his heart calmed her and then his arms tightened and his mouth sought hers. Her first impulse was to pull away, still raw from his earlier rejection, but his nearness quickened her blood.

'Do you want me?' he asked softly.

His sweet-water scent and body, hard against hers, held the spectres at bay. 'I want you.'

He led her off the path into the trees and spread his sleep-shelter where the ground was soft with leaf litter, and Chant peeled off his shirt and her own and lay atop him, delighting in the feel of his skin against hers. His strength and tenderness escalated her own need and her passion built in tune with his until they were doused in a sweet, satiating pleasure.

Afterwards she slept curled against him but Tel didn't sleep, his awareness of Chant so potent he imagined it was how a hunter sensed the world. But he was no hunter, as Chant had often pointed out, and he wondered again if he would be enough for her once they reached her lands.

Scead wasn't a hunter either, he reassured himself, and nor had Scead taken Chant in love. Tel tightened his arms around her and she stirred and murmured a name. Not his, nor Scead's, but Siah's.

The only shadow over Chant's happiness in the following days was the nearness of the Sunnen Stead and her likely reception there. Merala had nursed her back from a fiery fever and Chant was to repay her kindness by stealing her eldest son.

It was a measure of the accord between them that Tel sensed her unease. 'All will be well,' he reassured her, when they finally reached his corral.

Inkala was the first to know of their arrival and she reached Tel in a mad sprint and squealed as he hoisted her high into the air. Then she wriggled free and leapt into Chant's arms, staying there only a moment before dancing off across the yard.

'Tel's home, Tel's home,' she sang.

The smoke-stay door flew open and Islan appeared, grinning incredulously. 'Tel! It's good to have you back! And Chant!' He embraced Tel and gave Chant a hug, then embraced Tel again, and laughed. 'It feels like you've been gone an age.'

'Close to two moons,' acknowledged Tel, 'and I think you've grown. You are as tall as I am now.'

'Hardly,' said Islan, but he looked pleased. Chant didn't think Islan was taller but he *was* more assured.

'Merala's here?' asked Tel.

'Still at the gardens,' said Islan. 'Come and eat.'

They followed Islan into Merala's tur and as soon as Tel sat, Inkala clambered onto his lap and clung to him. Tel smiled as he stroked her hair, and Islan flipped errem disks as Tel described his time away, but Islan's flipping paused when Tel recounted Tanalan's wedding. Chant guessed Islan remembered Tel's reaction to Tanalan's disobedience but it all seemed a long time ago now.

'Septim gets gruffer with age,' said Tel, as he handed Chant an errem disk and juggled a hot one himself. 'I think Chant found him a bit off-putting at first,' he added, smiling as he briefly touched her knee. 'But we were all good friends in the end.'

Islan's eyes narrowed at the gesture but before he could speak, Merala appeared with a bulging sling of white-root. Her eyes widened and she hugged Tel and then Inkala squealed until she was pulled into the circle of arms. Chant watched them uneasily and caught Islan's speculative gaze on her.

The hubbub quietened and Merala turned to Chant. 'You look very well,' she said. 'The journey seems to have suited you.'

'It suited us both,' said Tel quietly, and took Chant's hand. 'I've asked Chant to be my wife.'

Merala faltered but recovered quickly to kiss Chant on each cheek and welcome her formally. 'It will be a happy occasion to have a wedding here given Tanalan's rites were held at the Meduin Stead,' she said.

'We are to go to the Sceadu lands first,' said Tel, 'and may marry there.' Merala stared at him in shock. 'Over the mountains? But it's too dangerous!'

'We'll go *through*,' said Tel. 'It's how Chant journeyed here.'

'There are tunnels under Ashali?' broke in Islan excitedly, and Chant nodded.

'I've never heard of such things,' said Merala. 'Is the way is well-marked?'

Chant shook her head. 'No, it's—'

'Then why go there, Tel?' she demanded. 'A woman joins her husband's corral on marriage, not the other way around.'

'I *will* go there first,' said Tel.

Merala's face hardened. 'Would you walk away from your corral, *from us*, so easily?'

'I will only be gone a short time.'

'That's what Barin said when he insisted on revisiting the Okianos,' said Merala tartly.

'I'm not my father! I've cared for this corral since I was little more than a child but now I've found someone I love; I don't intend to lose her like you lost Barin.'

'Don't speak of things you of which you know nothing!'

'I don't,' retorted Tel. 'I—'

Chant sprang to her feet. 'Please don't argue! I won't take . . .' she stopped. She *had* to take Tel back but Merala was right to fear. Siah had said *Chant* would return; she made no mention of any companion.

The void surged closer and Chant stumbled from the tur, desperate for the earth's rich scent to reclaim herself. She took refuge behind the smoke-stay as she had before and, as the sunlit world re-asserted itself, a new scent intruded. It was Islan with Inkala on his hip, but she turned away, not trusting herself to speak.

'Do you remember how we argued over your weapons and

you stormed out here?' he asked lightly.

'It seems a long time ago now,' she said thickly.

'So will this one day.'

'I don't want trouble in your corral, Islan.'

Islan snorted. 'It's the way of people to have trouble, Chant. For a long while it was Tanalan with her incessant talk of Kanan and threats to run away, and now it's Tel with his love for you.'

'He should stay here.'

'And be miserable? What's the point of that? No, Merala will see he is serious and she knows what it is to lose one who is greatly loved. I'll let a garden go for a time; there will be fewer mouths to feed in any case and we can reclaim it when you and Tel return. You *will* return, won't you, Chant? I missed Tel when he was gone and I want you here permanently *as my wife.*'

Chant gaped and Islan grinned. 'But as Tel has prior claim and *is* head of the corral, we'd better make that as my sister,' he added.

Inkala's chubby hand reached out and stroked Chant's hair. 'Sister,' she echoed solemnly, and Chant smiled.

Tel was glad when Islan followed Chant out and took Inkala with him. He didn't want Chant alone or Inkala upset.

Merala remained stony-faced and Tel took a deep breath. 'I was wrong to speak to you of Barin and for that I beg your pardon. I have no way of knowing how it was for you, only how it is for me.'

'And how is it for you?' asked Merala coldly.

'As if the world is at last made whole.'

Merala patted the seat beside her and Tel sat. 'I don't understand why you must go to Chant's lands,' she said. 'Is Chant insisting on Sceadu marriage rites?'

'She hasn't agreed to *any* rites yet,' admitted Tel. 'The Sceadu's foreteller sent her to find something to bring the Sceadu water and because of my skill with stonestreams, Chant believes it is me.'

Merala's eyebrows rose. 'But you've never had any faith in the spirit-sighted, Tel.'

'It's what Chant believes that's important. It means she is willing to take me with her.'

'Into the darkness, never to return, like Barin,' said Merala grimly.

Tel leaned forward and took his mother's hands. 'Chant is a skilled hunter, Merala. If I didn't think she could find a way through, I wouldn't let her go.'

Merala snorted. 'And how could you stop her? I've never seen her bow to your will. She's Sceadu, Tel, not Sunnen. Her ways aren't our ways. It would have been better had you chosen a Sunnen wife.'

'You're probably right but that isn't the way things turned. Your sister has been happily married to an Okianos man for many seasons and I intend to be happily married to Chant.'

'At least stay for a time,' she said. 'Inkala missed you terribly and Islan has need of his brother for a while.'

'We can only rest a few days,' said Tel. 'Chant must be back in her lands before the full moon.'

'Only a few? Is she to be the head of your corral or you?'

'The Sceadu don't have corrals,' said Tel with a smile, and sobered. 'It's only for a little while, Merala, no more than a moon. Then we'll be back.'

His mother looked at him sadly. 'Perhaps,' she said.

38

The brazier's ash was cold; the brazier hadn't been lit since She the Moon had waxed. Siah couldn't bear even the lightest covering over her burning, wasted body. She lay in a thin shift, her breath as sere as firn winds and Scead sat and watched her. He felt as empty of life as the brazier, yet it was Siah who died, not him. Every breath she exhaled bled him of strength; every flutter of her heart, robbed him of hope. He was a lover whose body scorched rather than soothed; a healer who couldn't heal.

He no longer searched for herbs to quench Siah's fever, for there *were* none, and the Circle no longer searched for a young woman or Little Sister to take her place, for none existed. There were many Sceadu who now dreamed of darkness, but these dreams weren't markers of the next Siah, but seeded from dread at Siah's slow slide into the void.

When he could, Scead coaxed honeyed-water down his wife's throat but he spoke as rarely as she did. His grief added to her distress and he hid it by staying silent. He left her side only to accept a gifted beast or to speak with the Circle, but the Circle's summonses had grown rare. There was no cure for Siah, no one to replace her, and in the end, nothing to say.

The person he saw most, when he did venture out, was Ketwing, and then she spoke of Chant, the single slender hope that remained. Siah had once spoken of Chant too, before fever had eaten her voice, and Scead knew the full moon was at the heart of Siah's visioning. Yet Siah's strength dwindled as She the Moon grew, and Scead feared the full moon marked Siah's death as well as confirmed Chant's.

Six more days, he thought in despair. Tears coursed down his face but he made no sound. Siah's slow dying had taught him many things including how to weep in silence.

Tel swore as he squirmed down the narrow tunnel. He had used his last days in the Stead to prepare himself for darkness, not for being skinned alive. His elbows and knees stuck wetly to his clothing and the heels of his hands stung as he clawed his way forward and then, thankfully, out into the larger tunnel where Chant waited.

'It gets easier,' she assured him, as he cranked himself upright. 'That was the narrowest part.'

She set off and Tel's heart quickened as the darkness closed in. 'Wait!' he called, and heard her footsteps stop. 'What if we lose each other?'

'Don't you know my scent?' Tel knew the delicious odour of her in their most intimate moments but he could hardly track her by that. 'I know yours,' she said, and when he didn't answer, added, 'I won't lose you, Tel.'

She went on and he followed, trying to concentrate on her footfalls but fancying he heard bear-claws instead. Sweat oozed down his back; the prospect of being pursued through the darkness by bears almost too terrifying to contemplate. Time passed but it was impossible to tell how much. 'Do you think that it's night outside?' he asked eventually.

Her footsteps stilled. 'Do you want to rest?'

'I'm thirsty,' he said, but what he really wanted was quiet to listen for bears.

'We may as well eat but then we need to go on. We don't have much time.'

He heard her settle on the floor and searched his pack for the berrem. 'Do you think there are bears here?' he asked as they ate.

'Their scent is faint. I don't think they've been here recently.' Tel swallowed his berrem in a single, painful lump. It was bear scent that must guide them! They ate in silence and he heard her get to her feet. 'Are you ready?' she asked.

'Yes,' he replied, although the last thing he wanted was to go deeper into the dark.

They walked and ate and slept in dreary sequence, the feel of Chant in his arms each *night* the only thing that made the dark tolerable. But as they finished what Tel calculated must be their fifth day of travel, the tunnel still showed no signs of ending.

'We might have missed the exit in the dark,' said Chant, echoing his own fears as they settled on the dusty floor to eat. 'We *must* be back before She the Moon reaches her largest,' she added anxiously. 'It was a mistake to delay at the Stead.'

'It was only five days, not many considering how long I had been absent. I'm head of my corral, Chant. I can't just walk away as the whim takes me and we needed to rest.' Chant said nothing. 'If we've been in the tunnels five days, there is still five days until the full moon,' he added. Still silence. 'I've never understood why being back by the full moon is so important,' he tried again. He heard Chant's breathing quicken and his own followed suit. 'Tell me, Chant.'

The silence was so long he thought she wouldn't answer. 'A beast gifts itself to a hunter on the understanding its gift isn't wasted,' she began slowly. 'But I dishonoured the gift. It was the reason I left Berian-tur and expected to die high on Ashali.'

'Yet you survived and arrived in the Sunnen lands,' prompted Tel, familiar with this part of her story.

'And stepped in the trap. A fitting end to the hunter Fleet,' said Chant, mockingly. 'You took me from the trap to your mother, a skilled healer, and my repayment to the void was thwarted again.'

'So, you sought death by refusing water,' said Tel, as understanding dawned.

'Yes, and I came so close. But then . . . you might call it a dream, Tel, but Siah came to me on the edge of the void and demanded I complete my task.'

251

'And so you accepted the water Merala offered.'

'No, I refused Siah's demand.'

'But—'

'Then Siah offered me something I desired above all else; something I could only have if I completed my quest and returned in a certain time.'

Tel's heart sank as he realised what confronted him couldn't be outwitted like the Vulturi or endured like the darkness. 'Scead,' he said heavily.

'Yes.'

'Will you take him?'

'I don't know.'

Tel would have liked to stride away but he hardly knew the direction they had come from, let alone the way out. The darkness confined him but at least it hid his humiliation.

'There *must* be a reason why I must be back before She the Moon is full or Siah wouldn't have offered me Scead for she loves him too.'

She loves him too; there it was, stark and undeniable. 'That's why you haven't accepted my marriage proposal, isn't it?' he said.

'Yes ... and no.' He heard her sigh. 'If we're to marry, one of us must spend our lives on the wrong side of the mountains. Are you willing to live amongst the Sceadu, Tel?'

Tel hesitated. His intention had always been to instruct their Siah in stonestreams, then take Chant back to the Sunnen Stead. A woman joined her husband's corral at marriage—a Sunnen, Meduin or Okianos woman, that is.

'Are you saying you won't live with me in my corral?' he countered.

'You've told me that Sunnen marriage rites are binding. We *both* need to be very sure of *everything*, if we are to marry.'

Tel was so taken up with this new set of complications he only realised how tired he was when Chant halted and he blundered into her. 'Do you want to stop for the night?' he asked, although he guessed the night had long gone.

'I've lost the scent.'

'What?'

'I've lost the scent! The thing that guides us, that allows us to escape this stinking darkness, that takes us home! I've lost it!'

'I've got tinder,' said Tel, more calmly than he felt. 'It might help to see what lies around us.'

'Light won't help,' she said dismissively, but Tel fumbled in his pack, set a pile of oil-soaked leaves on the floor and struck spark. Flame blossomed, sending their shadows leaping up the walls and revealing a scatter of crevices, one of which was angular.

'Someone's worked the stone,' he said excitedly, as the darkness closed in. It meant others had come this way and there must be a way out. But which crevice led to the world of sky and sun he craved?

Chant's footsteps sounded, stopped and sounded again. She examined the crevices, he realised. 'Can you smell anything,' he asked.

'Only the smoke from the tinder.' There was another long silence but Tel forced himself to wait. 'It must be close to dawn in Berian-tur,' said Chant finally, 'which makes it our sixth day of travel yet it only took me four days to reach the west. Either we are wandering in circles or we are going to exit in the Redlands.'

'They're below the snowline?'

'Yes, which means we need a descending path.'

'Possibly,' said Tel, although he no longer knew *what* was possible. 'Let's try the opening that's been worked. We can count our steps in case we must return.'

'And try the next one and the next one until we've got nothing left to try,' said Chant, again voicing his fears.

'When I followed you into the darkness, I knew there was a chance I wouldn't come out,' said Tel. 'Yet I would prefer to end my life here with you, than to live it alone in the bright sunshine of the Sunnen Stead.'

Her mouth came to his, hard and passionate. 'I'm a Sceadu hunter,' she said fiercely. 'I *will* find a way through.'

Her kiss robbed the darkness of its intensity and Tel's hope rekindled. 'Let's go then,' he said.

39

They set off through the angular-shaped opening but hadn't gone far before the tunnel ascended. 'I don't think I've chosen well,' muttered Chant, then gasped.

'What is it?' hissed Tel.

'Berian fur, snagged on the stone, *and* berian scent,' she whispered. 'They're close.'

Tel's heart lodged in his throat and, as they crept on, a pungent smell filled the air. The darkness faded and Chant's outline emerged. She had set an arrow and Tel wiped his sweaty palms on his trousers. There were droppings and broken branches, and the smell of bears was so thick he breathed through his mouth.

Chant gestured him to halt and crept on alone around the tunnel's curve. Tel clenched his jaw as time stretched away and he had resolved to follow her, no matter the consequences, when she reappeared and beckoned urgently. They edged past a nest of leaves and branches to the mouth of a cavern and then Chant caught his hand and they set off upslope in a crouching run. The air was crisp and the stark, hilly landscape very different to the Sunnen valleys

The slope steepened but they didn't stop until they reached its heavily forested crest but, as Tel sagged panting against a tree, Chant suddenly gripped his arm. Brownish shapes moved on the slope below and Tel looked around wildly for some sort of weapon. Chant's bow came up but then she lowered it; they weren't bears but men.

There was a shout as the men saw them and came swiftly

up the slope. There was no mistaking their or Chant's excitement and Tel wondered if one of the three were Scead. One had striking snow-white hair and intense blue eyes, the second had black hair and equally blue eyes, while the third was darker and powerfully built.

Tel straightened, aware of his unpatterned face and Chant's grip on his hand tightened reassuringly as she introduced him. 'This is Tel of the Sunnen people who dwell on Ashali's *western* side. I bring him to Berian-tur in fulfilment of my air-naming task. Tel, this is Snowhawk and Tor, Sceadu hunters, and this is Mist.' Tel nodded to each. 'It's uncommon for hunters to hunt together,' she added.

'When we hunt the beast,' agreed Tor with a smile, 'but Ketwing sent us to hunt *you*. We searched north of the Fine but came down to the Ruthvin at first light.'

'Ket would be anxious for me,' murmured Chant.

'She is indeed,' said Tor, 'but her main concern is Siah. Ketwing asked us to bring you to the Great Turrel immediately if . . . *when* you returned.'

Chant looked at him in bewilderment. 'Siah?'

'Siah is dying,' said Snowhawk.

'Dying?' gasped Chant. 'But how? Why?'

'Siah has never been robust,' said Snowhawk, 'and her spirit-journeys have spawned a fever without a cure. Scead's scoured every grove, slope and streambed for cooling-herbs in the moons of your absence but he hasn't been seen abroad of late. It's said his grief is so great he will accompany Siah back to the void.'

Chant's legs gave way and Tel lowered her to the ground and crouched beside her.

'Are you unwell?' asked Snowhawk in alarm.

'We've had a difficult journey and are weary,' said Tel, his anxious gaze on Chant.

Chant sat with her head in her hands overwhelmed, not with exhaustion, but with understanding. Tears ran unchecked down her cheeks and yet she smiled as she looked up at Tel. 'I know why Siah sent me to you and came to me in dream-vision. I know, Tel,' she said tremulously.

She cradled his face and kissed him gently on the mouth, ignoring those who watched. Then she struggled to her feet and dropped her pack to the ground. Her weapons followed. 'I need go with Tor and I need go swiftly,' she said. 'Snowhawk will take you to my tur.'

'We will take you to *our* tur,' said Mist.

Snowhawk nodded. 'An empty tur is no welcome for a stranger. You will be our guest until Chant returns.'

Tor's pack thumped to the ground beside Chant's but he kept his weapons, his waterskin and a bundle of food. He nodded his farewells and set off and, with a final glance at Tel, Chant followed.

They sped through the trees, pausing only to sip water and eat errem. Weariness made Chant's limp more obvious but she dismissed Tor's concerns *and* his questions about Tel; explanations would have to wait.

'We must detour east,' she panted, when they paused to drink. 'Unless you know of syra-flowers the way we go.'

'Syra-flowers? Why—'

'Because I need them.'

They ran on and when the pepperminty scent of glice freshened the air, Chant trawled her memory for the right mix of sunlight and shelter. Syra-flowers were vulnerable to frost-burn and she daren't risk weakening the concoction. She found a clump that was all but spent, and another, yet to flower, then blessedly, a patch in full bloom.

She harvested quickly and stumbled as she rose. 'You need to rest,' said Tor, but Chant shook her head. 'Your stubbornness hasn't changed,' he added.

'Nor have your manners.'

Tor grinned. 'Can you run again?'

'No. But I will anyway.'

He took her hand and Chant didn't object; her legs had divorced themselves from her body. She had run like this to aid Tel and now she ran to aid the other man she loved.

The day grew old and by the time the Great Turrel emerged

from the trees, only Tor's grip kept her upright. 'Tell Scead I'll meet him in the clearing,' she gasped.

Tor's eyes narrowed but he disappeared inside and Chant forced her trembling legs to the seat and collapsed. The seat was striped with shadow and Chant's sweat-soaked shirt began to cool.

You can have Scead, if you choose.

If Chant *chose* to hide what she had discovered in the Sunnen Stead, Siah would die and Scead would be hers. Siah had foreseen her need for a cure and if that failed, the need to find other ways for the Sceadu to live. In sending Chant to retrieve Tel, she had prepared the Sceadu to continue without her or *any* Siah, for the Sunnen didn't use visioning to fill their bellies but neat gardens and stonestreams.

But in promising Scead in return for Chant completing her quest, Siah had taken a terrible risk. Chant was her rival for Scead's affection and they had parted in anger. And while Siah may have visioned Chant's feelings for Tel, she may not have visioned how Chant's feelings for Scead would rekindle on her return. Knowing Scead might die had changed everything.

Scead came out of the Turrel and Chant rose. A lingering shaft of sunlight caught his honeyed hair and his gaunt face was alive with the joy of seeing her. Then she was in his arms, enveloped in his sweet scent, and wetted by his tears.

They stood entwined and then Chant cradled his face as she had cradled Tel's. 'I love you Scead,' she said, and then she brought her forehead to his and softly told him of her time in the trap, of her wish for death, and of how a Sunnen healer used syra-flowers to quench a fever fiercer than fire.

'I think Siah meant me to find a cure for her and bring it back,' she said and, as Scead's liquid eyes widened, Chant slid the harvest of blooms from her shirt and pressed it into his hands.

Chant remained in the clearing long after Scead had hurried away, shaking with cold, but too weary to even keep her eyes open.

'Put this on,' said Tor's voice in her ear. He wore a jacket now and helped her into another one. Then he sat beside her. 'You gave the syra-flowers to Scead,' he said. 'Why?'

'Because a concoction of them cured my fever in the Sunnen lands.'

'Syra-flowers,' breathed Tor. 'Who would have thought? If you're right . . .' He half shook his head. 'Ketwing wept with joy when she learned of your return. Come, I'll take you to her.' Chant shook her head and Tor stared at her in mystification. 'You know how hard it is for Ketwing to come outside,' he said.

'I'm not entering the Great Turrel,' said Chant, her gaze on the trees, and heard Tor sigh.

'We'll go to my tur, then. It's closest.' He helped her up and had to steady her as they walked. She was beyond exhaustion and wondered if it was why she felt so little joy in being back.

'Do you realise you're the only Sceadu to have journeyed beyond Ashali?' he asked, as they threaded their way through the trees.

'Siah has on dream-quest,' mumbled Chant.

'But no Siah's ever brought a man back. Do you intend to marry him?'

'Tel has kin to care for on his side of Ashali,' she said, and paused. 'I expected to see the marriage-line on your face by now, Tor.'

'I promised to wait for you, remember?'

'That was before . . . I thought Serest would have returned to you.'

'Snowhawk told me you came upon he and Mist,' said Tor, 'although I wish it had been me. As for Serest . . .' The lines deepened around his mouth, making him look older. 'Serest isn't content with one man, Chant. I would wed her tomorrow but that wouldn't keep her with me and I can't bear her to be with others.' He made a poor attempt at a smile. 'Maybe jealousy is one of my flaws. Does your Sunnen man want you all to himself?'

'Yes, and I won't share him either.'

'Yet you're prepared to let him go back to his lands?'

'He's not going anywhere for a while,' said Chant, refusing to be drawn. They walked in silence for a time, the Redlands steeped in the quiet that came before whisper-owls roused. 'Do you need windfall?' she asked, as they neared his tur.

'I have a good supply.'

He soon had the fire going and a batch of stew bubbling and, after their meal, he made her a snug bed of pelts. Serest was a fool to pursue other men when she could have Tor, thought Chant drowsily, as she snuggled under the cover. And maybe she was a fool too. She had yearned for the life she'd had before her air-naming and now she was back, she wondered if that life could somehow be reclaimed.

40

$\mathcal{S}$leep came upon Tel so swiftly he remembered little after the meal Mist had served him. It might have been the stay's warmth or the softness of the bed Snowhawk had put together for him or knowing that, at least for a while, he was safe from bears.

He drifted to wakefulness to the sounds of Mist and Snowhawk's murmured conversation and sleepily concluded Mist's stay must be nearby. 'I hope you rested well,' said Snowhawk politely, when he saw Tel was awake.

'I did indeed,' said Tel, and winced as he flexed his shoulders. Having to carry Chant's pack as well as his own, had woken a whole new set of muscles.

'If you need to relieve yourself, it's best done to the east of the tur,' said Snowhawk. 'To the west you'll find the spring we use for drinking and bathing water.'

'Chant told me the Sceadu lacked water,' said Tel in surprise.

'The springs are fed by seep-water; it's meltwater we lack. Without it, the streambeds remain empty of fish and we must rely on what hunters bring.'

Tel pondered Snowhawk's words as he relieved himself, then searched for the spring. It was easy to find; the run-off marked by a green sward. He surveyed the surrounding lands, considering how gardens could be set, and how the spring could be used to feed them. The trees grew closely and his gaze shifted to where Ashali's peak loomed, its eastern face shockingly different—like the Sceadu.

Chant had asked him whether he was willing to live amongst the Sceadu but he was no closer to answering that question and he grimaced as he recalled standing in the clearing above the Sunnen Stead and yearning for the unknown. But yearning for the unknown and living it were very different things.

Chant didn't appear and as the day drew on, Tel wondered whether Siah *had* died and Chant seized the opportunity to wed Scead. He had no idea how complex Sceadu marriage rites were and the more he fretted, the more remote their earlier intimacy seemed. His dread was exacerbated by Snowhawk's observation that if Chant weren't with Scead, she would be with her *fellow hunter* Tor, and when Chant finally emerged from the trees, she *was* with Tor.

They walked closely and as she smiled at something Tor said, Tel recalled how contemptuous she had been at his lack of hunter ways. Her greeting of him was brief too, her attention on transferring food from Tor's pack to her own. She thanked Tor, and then Snowhawk and Mist for gifting Tel their hospitality, and Tel nodded awkwardly and they set off into the trees.

'It would be best if we reached my tur before dark,' she said, and Tel's unsettled thoughts swung to bears. They crossed a rock-strewn gully Chant called the Fine streambed but it didn't look like it had held water for seasons. Chant remained uncommunicative and Tel wondered if ill news awaited him. 'We're close,' she said at last, and started to gather windfall.

Tel gathered it too as he followed her up a rise to a small building. The stay looked like Snowhawk's from the outside but while Snowhawk's had been snug, with shelves loaded with cups and platters, colorfully dyed coverings on the bed, and ample furniture, Chant's stay held a single table and chair, and shelves empty of platters. There was no bed either, just covers and pelts, piled in the corner.

'Is this where you live?' he asked, taken aback.

'I stayed here briefly before I left,' said Chant, depositing wood in the fire circle. 'It was my mother's tur. I never thought I'd be here again.' She paused, as if lost in thought, then retrieved flints from the shelf.

'You saw Siah?' asked Tel, unable to contain his impatience any longer.

'No, Scead,' she said, striking spark.

'And?'

Chant huffed the flicker of flame into life. 'Siah's illness complicates things.'

'I'd have thought it simplified them. If Siah dies, you can marry Scead. Isn't that what you want?'

Her black eyes flashed to his. 'I've never wanted Siah dead or Scead's heart torn out!'

'But you want Scead.'

'I *want* Scead to be happy.'

'So what did you say to him?' pursued Tel.

Chant rubbed the ash off her hands. 'Very little. I simply gave him the syra-flowers.' Tel looked at her blankly. 'It's what your mother gave me. If a potion of syra-flowers can't cure Siah's fever, nothing can.'

Tel's breath emptied. Chant had destroyed her chances of having Scead. 'Chant,' he said softly. Their kiss was long and sweet, as was their lovemaking that followed, tangled in the covers on the floor. Chant cried afterwards, from exhaustion or Scead's loss, Tel didn't know, but he kissed the saltiness from her cheeks, and then they slept.

News of their return prompted a string of visitors. As Tor's food dwindled, Mist arrived with a fresh supply and with pots of dye he used to stencil their sleep covers. Then Snowhawk appeared in the company of a wood-worker who, over the following days, constructed several more chairs and, much to Tel's relief, a bed.

The wood-worker had scarcely departed when Win arrived with cooking pots, and then Chant took Tel to the clay-pits where they spent a happy day working clay into cups and platters to harden in the fire coals. She took him gathering too but there was one place Chant refused to go, and that was to the Great Turrel.

Each visitor brought news of Siah's gradual return to health and Tel expected members of the Circle to visit to thank Chant and, when they didn't, reminded himself *again* the Sceadu's ways were different.

But just how different was brought home to him when Chant announced she was going on hunt. Tel knew hunts could last many days but Chant assured him she would be back in four. He resisted the urge to argue against her going, or ludicrously, to accompany her as some sort of protector, but as she disappeared into the trees, he was overwhelmed with longing to be back in Sunnen lands.

At least Siah should soon be well enough to receive him and then he could instruct the Sceadu on how to set gardens and channel water from their springs. He had no idea how they would repel bears but he guessed it wouldn't be with traps.

It was dusk on the second day after Chant's departure and Tel sitting on the doorstep staring at Ashali's *eastern* side, when an elderly woman appeared on the slope below. Her progress was painfully slow and he hastened down to help her.

She accepted his aid but declined his invitation to enter. 'If you bring me a chair, I will rest here. I am Ketwing the hunter and although I can no longer hunt the Whitelands, I still enjoy their view.'

Tel fetched a chair and she grunted as she lowered herself onto it. 'Chant has spoken of you,' he said, resuming his perch on the doorstep.

'But she hasn't spoken of *you* because she refuses to come to the Great Turrel,' said Ketwing tersely. 'What I know of *you* I've had to glean from others. Where is she now?'

'Hunting. She said she would return in four days.'

'She's not gone far then, no doubt to spare you from being alone in so strange a place.'

Tel's lips thinned at the implication he lacked the attributes to be left alone and he wondered what exactly Ketwing had *gleaned* about him.

'I know you're of a people called the Sunnen who dwell on Ashali's western slopes,' said Ketwing, as if she guessed his thoughts, 'and that you have skill in directing water to grow food plants, *and* I know you're Chant's lover.' Her face hardened. 'I am not familiar with Sunnen customs but the Sceadu complete the marriage rites *before* they share a tur.'

'I would have gladly married Chant before we came here,' said Tel tightly.

'Then why didn't you?'

'She wanted to test her feelings for Scead first.'

Ketwing's gaze became measuring. 'And you accompanied her despite that?'

'I had no need to test *my* feelings.'

'No, I can see that you didn't,' said Ketwing more gently. 'I spent much time with Chant after her mother died, or *Fleet,* as she was then, and later trained her to hunt. Her happiness is important to me but she left with no proper farewells and while she has reconciled with Scead and brought cure for Siah, she refuses to honour Siah as she must.'

'Considering what Chant suffered on Siah's behalf, it's Siah who should honour *her,*' retorted Tel.

'Anything Chant suffered has been on behalf of *all* Sceadu,' said Ketwing sternly. 'We are Siah and Siah is us. You need to understand this if you're to make your home here.'

'I don't intend to make my home here. After I've offered my skills to Siah and the Sceadu, I intend to take Chant back to my own lands. There's no hunger there *or* suffering.'

Ketwing's gnarled hand touched his arm. 'I do not mean to sound ungrateful, Tel. If Chant hadn't completed her quest, *with your aid*, and turned aside from old hurts, Siah would have died. We endured great anguish when we thought she *would* die, for no new Siah could be found and Chant was far from us. Will you tell me how she spent that time?'

Tel nodded, and recounted the little he knew of Chant's journey before he had seen her at the Sunwash, careful to omit her breaking of hunter law in case she was punished in some way. He described her injury and illness afterwards, her journey to the Meduin with Tanalan, and her determination to reach the sea. He spoke of his illness and the aid she rendered him, of her being taken by the Vulturi, and of their journey back to his lands.

The sun had sunk behind Ashali before he finished his tale and, as the air chilled, he helped Ketwing inside and set the fire. 'You've endured much together and for each other,' said Ketwing thoughtfully. 'And yet Chant still felt the need to see Scead again.'

'Because of what Siah told her in dream,' said Tel, as he tossed cones on the flames.

'In dream?' said Ketwing sharply.

Tel rubbed the resin from his hands. 'After she was caught in the bear—*berian* trap, Chant was gravely ill and said Siah came to her in the place you call the void.' Tel shrugged. 'Chant was delirious.'

'What did Siah say?'

'That Chant could have Scead in exchange for completing her quest.' Tel settled on the chair next to Ketwing. 'I've no belief in foretellers, Ketwing, but Chant has. When she learned of Siah's illness, she interpreted the dream to mean she could have Scead *if* Siah died.

'My mother is a skilled healer and used a brew of syra-flowers to cure Chant's fever. It would have been an evil thing for Chant to withhold the cure and of course she didn't.' Ketwing's expression was so grim Tel's heart faltered. 'Chant acted as she should,' he reiterated.

'Indeed she did,' said Ketwing, her gaze on the fire.

'Then what troubles you?'

'We are gifted from the void into this world and are taken back at death. Only Siahs can visit the void *and* return in a single lifetime.'

Tel stared at Ketwing in mystification and then gasped as understanding dawned. 'Surely you're not suggesting—' he began, but Ketwing had struggled to her feet.

'When Chant returns, tell her this: if she has *any* love or respect for her hunter guide Ketwing, she is to come to the Great Turrel.'

Ketwing hobbled away into the darkness and Tel threw the door shut in disgust. Of course, Ketwing didn't want to lose the young woman she had cared for, but to suggest Chant was a Siah to keep her here … Tel fumed as he paced around the stay but as the night deepened, his anger was replaced with a fear that, despite all they had endured together, he might lose Chant after all.

el slept poorly that night, troubled by Ketwing's visit and by the empty place in the bed beside him. He even missed Chant's sleep-talk, which now occasionally included his name as well. The night was chill and as morning neared, he rose to put more fuel on the fire, then wedged the shutters open, and peered out.

Ashali glimmered palely above the black silhouettes of trees and then he caught movement in the lart below. His heart quickened as something headed in his direction and then slowed as he recognised Tor.

At least it wasn't a bear but such an early visit was unlikely to herald good news and Tel wrenched the door open before Tor had a chance to knock. 'Has Chant been injured?' he demanded.

'Chant? I thought she was here with you.'

'She's gone hunting.'

'Hunting holds risks but Chant is skilled,' said Tor, which Tel didn't find particularly reassuring. 'I've just presented a beast to Siah,' continued Tor, 'and she asks that you meet with her and the Circle at dawn. As Chant is absent, I will escort you back.'

Tel beckoned him into the stay's warmth and gestured to a seat. 'This is a lot more comfortable than when I last visited,' said Tor, as he stretched his hands to the fire. 'The first task of an ageset when they quit the Turrels is to furnish their turs but Chant went hunting instead.' He paused. 'Hunting's always been the most important thing to her which was why she found her air-naming hard.'

'*Chant* isn't a hunter's name,' said Tel.

'No, it's a messenger's name and in bringing you here, Chant confirmed the truth of Siah's visioning, though I've hoped Siah was mistaken in my own case,' he added.

'Mistaken?'

Tor shrugged. 'You're fortunate to have Chant, more fortunate than us. The Sceadu can't afford to lose any hunter, let alone one of Chant's skills.'

'Yet you sent her off into terrible danger.'

'And she returned, as Siah foresaw.'

Tel bit off a retort. Arguing over Chant's treatment wasn't going to help him deal with Siah. 'What will happen when we reach the Great Turrel?' he asked instead.

'You will be shown to the Seeing-Place where the Siah and her husband

reside. You will also meet with the Circle who represent the elders. Then afterwards, Siah will seek guidance from the void.' He smiled. 'Whatever Siah directs us to do, you will be welcomed if you choose to stay. Chant would be happiest here too, where she can hunt.' Tel made no response and Tor glanced out the window. 'Dawn is close,' he said. 'We should start back.'

Tel considered Tor's powerful physique as he followed him down the slope. Tor was old enough to wear the marriage line and, as a hunter, seemed like a natural pairing for Chant. Snow-hawk was a hunter too, recalled Tel, and like Tor, bore only two lines, and he wondered whether men married later in the Sceadu lands or whether, for some reason, hunters did.

'Did you and Chant hunt together before she left?' he asked, as the slope lessened.

'It is usual for hunters to hunt alone, but yes, we hunted together. Chant was reckless and needed guidance,' said Tor. His gaze was on the trees and Tel saw how he scanned and how, like Chant, he flared his nostrils to better take scent.

Chant's risk-taking hadn't changed but Tel was more concerned by Ketwing's bizarre suggestion Chant was some kind of Siah. 'I've been thinking of what I might say to your Siah,' he said, as they made their way through the trees. 'Chant has described how Siahs guide the Sceadu but I'm not clear how someone becomes a Siah in the first place.'

'Not *someone*, Tel, Siahs are *always* women. As the old Siah's time in this world draws to an end, she searches the void for her successor. The Aunts are vigilant too. It's common for Siahs to be ill as Little Sisters, as if the void already drains their strength and once they are a Siah, the physical strain is even worse. No woman chooses to be a Siah; the void chooses *them*.'

'So, the present Siah was ill as a child,' said Tel, relieved as he considered Chant's speed and strength.

'Very ill, which might explain why she came close to death so early in her time as Siah. No successor could be found and there is great joy Siah has been granted longer in this world.'

'But surely there was a time when a Siah died without a successor?'

'Never, which means there must be a Siah amongst us or one soon to be born. Sometimes Siahs are hidden for a time. The healthy child might sicken or start to dream of the void. It's not always clear. Chant was once as fragile as Siah and being ill together bound their friendship, but then Chant grew strong and competition over Scead tore them apart.'

Tel struggled to keep his face expressionless but he saw now why Ketwing wanted Chant in the Great Turrel. Tor wanted her too for her hunting skills, if not for other reasons, and of course, he wanted her as his wife. The only unknown in this whole complicated situation was what Chant herself wanted.

Chant shaded her eyes. The rise gave a good view over the land below. A breeze rippled the ashin crowns and away on Ashali's slopes, a gyar called, but Chant's attention was on a stand of lart in the distance that sheltered her tur and the man within it.

In four days she had taken no scent and loosed no arrows but she hadn't hunted the Willing beast but the life she had left behind, and the hunt had ended in failure. Siah had plagued her dreams and Chant knew that if she remained in Berian-tur, Siah would plague her waking times too. Chant must bend her knee to Siah each time she brought a Willing beast to the Great Turrel and, to marry Tel in the Sceadu way, she must bow to her again.

Ashali shone above her and she considered those on its western slopes. If she married Tel in the Sunnen lands and hunted there, she would never again have to endure Siah's presence but it meant leaving everything familiar behind *and* robbing the Sceadu of meat.

The world darkened and Chant staggered and then the ashins' rustle intruded again. Tel had kept her from the Sunwash's dissolution and his love had kept the darkness at bay since and, as the understanding washed over her, she set off down the slope.

Tel felt like many days had passed, rather than just one, by the time Tor escorted him back. Tor looked weary too and declined Tel's invitation to share a meal, and Tel rebuilt the fire and collapsed onto a chair.

The Great Turrel had looked disconcertingly like Kablar's stay and the crowded interior had reinforced the impression but that was where the similarity ended. The Turrel had held a sense of community and kindness, not meanness and threat.

Ketwing had guided him through its dim interior and a hush had fallen over the Sceadu, except for the children, whose happy chatter Tel had found reassuring. The Turrel was large and he had reached the end before he realised there was a second room.

It smelled of tinqua and was crowded too but with members of the Circle. Ketwing had introduced them and, while Tel had responded politely, his attention had been on Scead, the man Chant had risked everything for. He wasn't as handsome as Snowhawk or Mist *until* he smiled, and then it was as if a lamp had been lit.

Scead's warm welcome had eased Tel's tension *until* Tel had turned to Siah. She barely reached her husband's shoulder but her first utterance lifted the hair on the back of Tel's neck.

He was unsure now whether it was power of her voice or the strange glitter of her eyes, but his answers had seemed inconsequential, as if she extracted what she sought by other means.

He had spoken of the manner of Sunnen life, and of the

stonestreams and gardens, and she had questioned him intensely about everything. Occasionally one of the Circle had queried some point but it had been his and Siah's voices that had filled the room and it had been Siah who had brought the interview to a close.

'We thank you for making the difficult journey to Berian-tur,' she said, 'and for sharing your wisdom with us. We thank you too for the aid you rendered Chant in completing the task the void ordained. Chant is dear to us, *to me*, and we rejoice in her safe return.'

Tel considered Siah's parting words as he poked at the fire. They seemed sincere and yet Chant refused to speak to her one time friend. It was puzzling, given Chant had relinquished any claim on Scead, and it made her time in Berian-tur increasingly awkward. Ketwing's longing to see her former pupil was obvious and there must be others in the Great Turrel who loved Chant too.

Tel started as the door was flung open and Chant rushed into his arms. Her fragrance reminded him of just how much he had missed her. She panted from her run and he waited until her breathing steadied. 'Your hunt was successful?' he asked.

'No.'

'It doesn't matter,' he said, smoothing her hair back. 'Tor told me he had killed. He came here, you know, as did Ketwing. She's called on your love *and* your respect for her, to visit the Great Turrel.' Chant stiffened and he forced a smile. 'I've spent the entire day there with the Circle and Siah, and a long day it's been too. I've told them everything I can about our stonestreams and gardens.'

Chant dropped her head and Tel brought his fingers under her chin so she must look at him. 'Siah said you were dear to her, Chant, and I think she meant it. Meeting with her would make things easier for Scead *and* others in the Great Turrel like Ketwing.'

'I'm not going there!'

'I know Tanalan gave you no welcome when you first came to my stay, but in the end, you had some level of rapport. While you and I . . .' He smiled. 'You and I, my love, fought over everything, but now you are dearer to me than life itself. I've been told you and Siah were close once. Can't you at least be civil to each other?'

'You don't know what you ask!'

There was such despair in her face that Tel's heart missed. 'This isn't just about Siah, is it?'

'No.'

'What *is* it about, Chant?'

'The void.'

42

$\mathscr{C}$hant waited until Tel was asleep before she slipped from the bed and dressed. Then she paused to look down at him. How familiar he was to her now: the scent of his skin; the shape and taste of his lips; the silken sense of him during their lovemaking. Yet if she bowed to Siah, she would lose him forever.

She collected her weapons and quietly pulled the door shut behind her. She the Moon was one day from full but Chant didn't need Her light to go where she had journeyed countless times before.

It was close to half-night before she reached the Great Turrel and, despite the icy air, loitered outside. She felt as hollow as a shard-spider husk, as if what waited inside, had already claimed her.

She started to shiver and, propping her weapons by the door, stepped inside. Those within slept but as she picked her way forward, someone struggled to their feet. Their scent was of open skies, of guidance and love, but of forcing Chant to her knees during the naming ceremony. For a long moment they simply regarded each other and then Ket opened her arms and Chant went to her.

Ket held Chant enclosed then kissed her on each cheek and released her. 'Come back to me afterwards,' she whispered.

Chant nodded and continued to the Seeing-Place. The smell of burned neri bark roused the wraiths she had long fought and she dropped to her knees and bowed her head.

'Welcome, Chant,' came Siah's familiar voice. Chant kept her gaze on the floor and Siah's voice sounded again. 'Leave us, Scead.' It was an order and Scead's sweet scent moved past her out of the room.

'What is it you want?' demanded Chant, refusing to raise her face.

'You *know* what the void wants. It has told you many times.'

'I am a hunter. I won't spend my life a prisoner of the dark, confined places!'

'All Siahs are hunters, Chant. The void doesn't offer up its sparks of the future as generously as clouds toss snow to earth.'

Chant's head snapped up. 'I *won't* do it! I won't surrender to you!'

'To *me*?' Siah's face hardened. 'We were *both* there, Chant, though you've chosen to forget it. Siah's last breath held space for only one name, but we were *both* there!'

Chant flinched as spectral forms swarmed closer then dissipated as Siah spoke again, her voice weary now. 'The void has been generous to you, Chant, more so than to me. In obeying its summons to gift *me* cure, it gifted *you* time. You can marry your Sunnen man and live with him on the western slopes of Ashali. You can bear his children, suckle them at your breast, have the joy and blessedness of their love. I will have none of these things.'

'You have Scead!'

Siah smiled sadly. 'For a little while.'

Silence stretched and when Siah spoke again, business-like now. 'The Circle has decided against setting stonestreams. We will go to the water, not ask the water to come to us. The void offers me this guidance, but it might offer you different guidance when the time comes. Our song-makers and chanters thank your Sunnen man for his words. They won't be forgotten.'

'When will I know?' asked Chant thickly.

'I will greet and farewell you in dream, as every departing Siah greets and farewells the new.'

Chant's fists clenched. 'I might not come! I might abandon the Sceadu!'

'You didn't abandon your quest, Chant, nor your Sunnen

man as he lay dying in the place where earth became water. Even when caged and beaten, you didn't abandon hope. You won't abandon the Sceadu.'

Chant stumbled back to the comfort of Ket's arms and the old hunter held her until the storm of tears had passed. Then she pulled the cover over them both, enclosing Chant in her warmth and love, as she had so many times before.

'You knew?' asked Chant, when she was able.

'I suspected. I was with the last Siah in her final moments.'

'I don't want to do it; I don't have the strength.'

Ketwing stroked her hair. 'You will be older when the task comes to you. The world is different through older eyes, Chant. You come to see that all living is a taking and a giving back. The void took my swiftness and the straightness of my bones—'

'But what did it give you in return?' demanded Chant.

'These precious moments with you, the love and friendship of Must and of the last Siah, and many more snowmelts than Talith to see you grow to be a hunter, and a chantress, and to find love yourself.'

Chant sighed. 'I have a favour to ask.'

'What is it?'

'Not of you, of Must.'

'Will it wait until dawn?'

'Yes.'

'Then let it,' said Ket, and yawned. 'Old eyes might see more truly, but they get tireder than young ones.'

Tel spent the day convincing himself that waking to an empty bed wasn't a sign of impending ill fortune. Chant had simply done what he had urged her to do and gone to the Great Turrel to make her peace with Siah. But why slip away while he slept? And even the bitterest of quarrels shouldn't take an entire day to resolve.

Her confession that the breach involved the void added to his worry. The void was a place he understood to mean death but

274

meant far more to the Sceadu. He wished he had insisted Chant explain herself more thoroughly last night, but he had been distracted; making love tended to do that.

As the day dragged on, he was tempted to set out in search and he might have done had Berian-tur not been pathless. He wandered about outside the stay but had settled in his usual spot to watch the stars birth when she emerged from the lart below.

He hastened down the slope and was almost to her when she raised her face. Seared across her cheeks was the third of the patternings: the marriage-line. For a ghastly moment, he thought she had wed Scead after all, but her expression of tenderness was unmistakable.

She slipped her arms around his neck and kissed him. 'I love you,' she murmured. Tel said nothing, fearing the answers to the questions that crowded his mind. She led the way back to the stay and as they settled by the fire, took his hands in hers. 'Siah has refused your offer of stonestreams, for the moment,' she said.

Tel didn't know whether to feel relieved they were free to leave, *if* Chant agreed, or angry at Siah's intractability. Then Chant's last words sank in. '*For the moment*? Are you saying Siah might change her mind?'

'This Siah has decided that Sceadu ways remain unchanged. The void might guide the next Siah differently.'

It was better news than Tel had hoped for. Chant had fulfilled her obligations by bringing him here so the Sceadu had no further call on her. As for the next Siah . . . Once Chant was part of his corral, all contact with the Sceadu would cease.

'You wear the marriage-line,' he said carefully. 'Does that mean you are ready to marry me?'

'Yes. I've made my farewells.'

Tel's heart quickened. 'You will marry me in the Sunnen Stead and live with me in my corral?' he asked incredulously. Chant nodded and Tel laughed with joy but her face remained grave. 'What is it you haven't told me, Chant?'

'That there will come a time when I must return to live out the rest of my days here.'

'But why? You did as you were asked. It isn't your fault

Siah has refused aid. There's no reason to return.'

'*This* Siah has refused but we have both seen the Vulturi, Tel, and the next Siah won't risk the Sceadu suffering the same fate. If snowmelt isn't gifted again, she will be forced to tread a different path.'

'That's not your concern!' Chant's black eyes came to his, the firelight making them glitter and spark, and Tel's blood ran cold. 'No Chant! You're not a Siah. They can't make you do this!'

'You're right, Tel. They can't *make* me do it. But when the time comes, *if* it comes, I must make a decision.'

'Chant—' he began urgently, but she placed her fingers on his lips.

'Whatever happens, my love for you won't change, Tel. Nothing will change my love for you.'

'I've seen what that sort of life does to people,' said Tel desperately. 'Tor told me too. I don't want to lose you, Chant. I *refuse* to lose you!'

'The previous Siah was an elder before the void reclaimed her,' said Chant. 'And the present Siah has always been frail. I am not as she is.'

Tel sat with his head in his hands and Chant recalled Ket's final words to her. *Your hunter skills have twice allowed you to pass through Ashali. There is nothing to prevent you from returning when you wish, or when there is need for you here.*

In choosing to live with Tel in the Sunnen Stead, she wouldn't be deserting the Sceadu nor, if she received the void's summons, would she completely leave her Sunnen life behind.

A whisper-owl gave voice and Chant went to the window. She the Moon hung above Ashali and Chant drew the gold-frosted air deep into her lungs, then Tel's scent intruded as his arms encircled her with his love and protection.

'She the Moon shines on both sides of Ashali,' she said, 'and we know the way between your place and mine.'

'Yes,' said Tel quietly, and tightened his grip. 'We know the way.'

End of Heart Hunter

I hope you enjoyed *Heart Hunter*. **Authors need reviews!** It's how our readers find us. I would love you to leave me an honest review on Amazon, Goodreads or another of your favourite reader sites. Enjoy **free** short stories? Visit my website, sign up for my newsletter, and read *The Gift* and *The Tale of Prince Anura*.

Works by KS Nikakis

Available on Amazon KDP and a range of digital platforms

Non Fiction

Journey: Seeking the Sacred, Spirit and Soul in the Australian Wilderness – *For fans of Joseph Campbell's hero journey*

When we set out into the wilderness, what is it we *really* seek?

Do we seek new sights or do we seek new selves? And are we really on one journey or on two?

Journeying fifteen thousand kilometres into Australia's blood-red heart, Nikakis discovers that every journey is perilous, for travellers risk carrying the clutter of their outer lives with them; a clutter that blinds them to the other journey they crave; that of the inner *soul-journey* into a deeper understanding of self.

To enter Australia's vast Outback wilderness, is to enter a place of endless horizons; a place doused with brilliant gold dawns and dazzling sunsets; a place silvered by star-encrusted night skies and, most importantly, a place of hidden sacred places in whose deep stillness our inner journeys can at last unfold.

In the spirit of travellers like Robert Macfarlane and Scott Stillman, Nikakis asks what it is we really see, feel and understand when we follow in the steps of those who have gone before us deep into the wilderness.

Drawing on her Ph.D. in Joseph Campbell's hero myth, and using original poetry and novel extracts, Nikakis takes us on this second journey; a journey of the sacred, spirit and soul, where our inner selves finally have the time and space to gift us richer and more fully-realised lives.

Fiction

Angel Caste 5 Book Series – available complete in one book or as five individual books: Angel Blood, Angel Breath, Angel Bone, Angel Bound, Angel Blessed.

Angel Caste – Complete 5 Book Series – *A modern female hero on a timeless quest*

A troubled half-angel, a beautiful angel guide, a binding promise . . .

Viv is on day release from jail to attend the funeral of the thug she thinks is her father, when she comes face to face with her real father, the powerful angel Archae Kald. If finding out she's a half-angel isn't shocking enough, Viv discovers her mother isn't dead after all but lost somewhere in the tangle of worlds called the Rynth.

Determined to find the only person who has ever truly loved her, Viv transits to Kald's angel world where he appoints the beautiful Thris as her guide. Thris is kind and caring, unlike the males Viv has known before, but after living on the streets, Viv finds it impossible to trust.

Friendship grows as Thris trains her to travel the rifts, but the Rynth is a dark and dangerous place, even for angels and, as Thris grows increasingly tempted by Viv's emerging angel traits, disaster strikes.

Viv journeys on alone and stumbles into a war zone where she finds a lost child, who she pledges to take to safety but, as the war rages on, deciding who is friend and who is enemy becomes a deadly game of chance.

Bound by his promise to guide Viv to her mother, Thris embarks on a desperate search for her, but a greater threat confronts them both and, in the end, they must fight not just for their own lives, but for the lives of those they love.

The Kira Chronicles 6 Book Series - available complete in one book or as six individual books: The Whisper of Leaves, The Silence of Stone, The Secrets of Stars, The Thunder of Hoofs, The Crying of Birds, The Music of Home.

The Kira Chronicles – Complete 6 Book Series – *traditional fantasy with deep forests and high stakes*

A gold-eyed Healer, a prophecy, two brothers at war.

In seasons long past, twin gold-eyed princes sundered a kingdom. Rejecting his brother Terak's warrior ways, Kasheron led his people deep into the great southern forests and established the healing settlement of Allogrenia. The Tremen flourished, upholding Kasheron's legacy of peace and healing, and protected by the vast, trackless trees.

All Tremen delight in the healing arts, but Kira is the greatest Healer of them all.

To the north of Allogrenia, drought ravages the Shargh's land and, as their suffering escalates, the chief's younger brother seizes on an ancient prophecy to snatch the chiefship for himself. The prophecy links the Shargh's doom to a gold-eyed Healer, and Kira has gold eyes.

The Shargh attack with devastating consequences and Kira must fight to save the wounded, but the Shargh wounds rot, no matter her skill, and Kira finds herself in a deadly race against time. As the slaughter continues, she makes the horrifying discovery that the Shargh hunt *her*. To halt the attacks and save her people, she sets off for the North to seek aid from her long-sundered warrior kin.

But the dangers beyond the forests exceed even the Shargh attacks. The Tremen detest their warrior kin but Terak's descendants have inflicted a worse fate on the Tremen. Kira's newfound love is torn apart by ancient hostilities and when trust turns to betrayal, it risks everything she has fought for.

As the battles rage on, Kira becomes increasingly sickened by the bloodshed and, desperate to end the suffering once and for all, she sets out on a quest that could cost her everything and everyone she loves.

The Emerald Serpent – *the Celtic Fae, in a fight for survival*

Book trailer: https://www.youtube.com/watch?v=bGpKxnp-CEMg

Betrayal, torture, death: Etaine lives on only to destroy those who robbed her of everything she loved.

Seven years before, Etaine met a fellow Ranger, Cormac, the he-Eadar she believed was her longed for true-mate. Emerald-eyed, white-skinned, and black-haired, the Eadar had formed Ranger bands to fight the Fada, invading religious zealots determined to replace the Eadar's Serpent Goddess with their own gods of stone.

The pure blood of the ancient Eadar runs strong in Etaine and Cormac's veins, and their joining had the potential to open the Emerald and Serpent Ways to them, old worlds only true Eadar can enter, but their love affair goes tragically amiss, with catastrophic consequences.

Etaine flees and as the years pass, slowly rebuilds her life, but the Fada attacks grow ever more ferocious, and the Eadar are forced to fight for their very existence. When the Fada mass to commit yet more bloody slaughter and the bands join in a final, desperate effort to defeat them, Etaine comes under Cormac's command, the very last Eadar she wants to see again.

Together they have a weapon that can destroy the Fada, but to use it, Etaine must learn to trust again and Cormac to Remember.

And time runs short: the Serpent rises.

The Third Moon – *Science fantasy with a very human quest*

Where does the past end and the future begin?

Warrain is haunted by inherited memories of his people's dispossession and the theft of their children, and when he is just twelve years old, the nightmare repeats. But Warrain isn't living on Earth in the 21st Century but on the planet Imago in the far flung future.

Five years before, Station One's Mech's got high on the opioid arrash and, in the bloodshed that followed, Warrain's scientific community were expelled from the Station, his father murdered, and his mother and unborn sibling lost to him.

The scientists carve out a rudimentary Station high in Imago's ranges and Warrain's friends get on with their lives but not Warrain. He climbs the Tors to stare down at Station One, dream of his mother and sibling, and plot revenge.

And then one day, everything changes. A third moon appears in the sky, one of Imago's life-forms calls him by name, and disease breaks out at Station One.

When Mechs visit to seek help for their ill, Warrain seizes the opportunity to deal them a blow they will never forget. But the third moon brings changes that threaten them all and, to aid the life-form whose kind is being dispossessed and slaughtered, he must turn his back on the hate that has long sustained him and find another way to live.

Messenger – *a dystopic future filled with hope*

In a world made deaf by hatred, who will hear the messenger?

Severine's world ends the day her Traveller family is murdered. Being raised in their loving gay community marked her as an outsider, but being female doubled the danger. Women are scarce, precious, and hunted.

When chance brings Severine face to face with the father she has never known, he assigns, Jeph, the son of his murdered friend, as her guard. They soon clash and Jeph is glad to deliver her to the Enclaves, the sanctuary her father carved out for his community's women and children.

But there is no safety in a world broken by war and sickness and when violence follows her, Severine sets out for the northern city of Andhaka, in search of a home among her mother's people. Pledged to protect her, Jeph follows, but the north holds nothing for him except terrible danger.

It's been years since Andhaka welcomed outsiders with anything but bullets, and to survive and protect Jeph, Severine must learn to use her enemies' weapons against them.

As the stakes rise, she comes to understand what drove her father north seventeen years before and his quest becomes her quest. But she hasn't counted on the savage legacy war and sickness have left behind, or on falling in love.

I Heard the Wolf Call My Name – *gender-fluid shifters in search of home*

Finalist Best YA Novel – 2019 Aurealis Awards

Jax is just twelve years old and in bird-form high above his island home, when it explodes, killing everyone on it. Believing himself to be the only survivor, he is shocked to come face to face with his boyhood friend, Matiu, ten years later.

Matiu is military and the military needs shifters for a crucial mission, but Jax refuses. Having spent ten long years burying his bizarre shifter past, he isn't about to resurrect it. But Matiu rouses other feelings too that Jax finds harder to ignore.

As the military ramps up pressure to force Jax's cooperation, he shifts to bird-form and flees to the last remaining island, where he crashes in the middle of Anahera's vision-quest.

She searches for her skin-spirit animal to transform her into Ikaika, a protector of her people. She dreams of finding the white-wolf but finds Jax instead and to save him, she must abandon her quest.

Her kindness only adds to Jax's turmoil. To decide who he truly is and where he really belongs, he must first confront his painful past but that isn't the worst of his problems. The forces that blew Jax's island out of existence threaten Anahera's as well, and he might be the only shifter who can save it. But time is running out.

Fantasy Short Stories

The Gift – A Deep Fantasy Short Story #1 – free on my website at www.ksnikakis.com

Excerpt:

Thariel sat for a long time, surveying all around her, as if she ate the world that would soon be memory. Then she took the harness from the mare, and with soft words, thanked her and bade her farewell. Her own feet she turned towards the forest, tossing her face-plate aside as she went, so that her hair fell loose to her waist, then she discarded her chest-armour, the sword and dagger, her bow and quiver.

The trees closed in and she came at last to the lake Men call Menios and stood for a while on its shore. An owl cried and a mouse shrieked, and all around her the souls of the newly dead jostled in their journey to the void.

She stepped into the water and the new life inside her quivered. 'Fear not, little one,' she whispered, in her own tongue. 'We are going home.'

The Tale of Prince Anura – A Deep Fantasy Short Story #2 –
free on my website at www.ksnikakis.com

Excerpt:

I should have been happy, for she was beautiful. Dark rivers of
curls, skin as white as moonlight on water, breasts softer than
spawn, and she loved me well. But her chamber was small, no
matter the comfort of her bed, and the old feelings of entrapment
rose, as persistent as gas that bubbles from rot below still waters.

I sat at the casement and listened, as I had once loitered
near the watery skin of the second world and waited. The moon
grew large and small many times, but it came at last, as I knew
it would.

The soft lament on the night-time air, the song of a soul as
confined as mine. It took me a journey of many days through the
depths of a massive forest to find her tower.

Stone it was and sheer, and as remote as the third world's
glimmer had once been. I sang to her and she answered with
sweet melodies of her own and we made love as frogs do, with
our voices. And when trust had built, she let down her shining
ladder of golden hair.

Glass-Heart – A Deep Fantasy Short Story #3

Finalist Best YA Short Story – 2019 Aurealis Awards

Excerpt:

Geth moved amongst his band, exchanging quiet words while they waited. Some he had fought with since the Tallon's foul ships had first found their shores while others had come later, when the burn of cot and kin had sent them from their valleys.

Hate drove them but hate was no shield against arrow and knife. It was fighting skills that kept them hale, and Geth ensured they had them aplenty. He needed them living, not just for their own sakes and his, but for what would come later. When the Tallon's stain had been scoured away, the destroyed must be rebuilt.

Kyth sat alone and he went to her and gazed about. 'The glass-heart's fled, has it?'

'I sent her to a place of safety. She will come to me when it is over.'

'Safety was what I wanted for you!'

'And what I wanted for Nyar.' Her eyes caught the star-sheen as she looked up at him. 'But you cannot always have what you want, can you, Ceannasai?'

Dragon Sprite – A Deep Fantasy Short Story #4

Excerpt:

Genn rocketed straight upwards, not just because she enjoyed seeing the limitless blue sky before her, but because a Waiwin's wing shape made vertical flight harder for them. Orin didn't try to catch her but swept in circles around her, gaining height in an ever-narrowing spiral. It was a clever tactic and one Genn didn't believe he had thought of in the instant she had cleared the trees. He had obviously studied her strategies and developed a plan to counter them *or so he thought*.

Genn waited until the spiral narrowed to *axeel*, the minimum distance a Waiwin must keep from a Velven unless she *accepted* him, then swerved towards him, narrowing the distance between them. Orin's eyes flashed to black, shocked she *had* accepted him, but before he could act, she folded her wings and dropped.

The strength that had driven Orin's pursuit had surged to his wing-tendrils in anticipation of locking them with hers and he would struggle even to stay airborne until it flowed back.